For Chris, Lyla and Rory, with all my love. Always.
(And a wee bit for Casey even though she's just a dog.)

1

Juliet

There should be a disclaimer at the beginning of teen movies:

CONTENT WARNING:
REAL LIFE IS NOTHING LIKE THIS. WE
ACCEPT NO LIABILITY WHATSOEVER FOR
THE UNREALISTIC EXPECTATIONS THAT
WILL ARISE FROM WATCHING THIS FILM.
VIEWER DISCRETION IS ADVISED.

Seems fair. People *should* be warned that the whole 'guy meets girl, they hate each other (or pretend to), they get forced together, and – BAM – they fall in love' thing is total bullshit.

And yeah, I know it's fiction. That none of this stuff is *real*. But I still get sucked in. Every. Single. Time. I even get *butterflies* when they stare at each other the way I stare at my hot-water bottle and painkillers after a day of too much standing up.

And you know which movies are the worst? The ones set at Christmas. Teenagers with above-average good looks, festive jumpers and mistletoe, Tiffany boxes and fake snow, wrapped up with perfect smug smiles.

Don't even get me started on Disney movies. Targeting five-year-olds with their happy-ever-afters? It's sickening.

Here's a spoiler. Real life doesn't work like that. Real life is a first kiss with *way* too much saliva, with someone you barely know, behind the sports hall at breaktime. Your best friend is keeping lookout and whispering that you're taking too long, when you're only trying to figure out a polite way of stopping the slushy horror show. Real life is your other best friend doing *way* more than kissing, with someone else, at the same time, a few metres away.

Real life is the doctor handing you disgusting grey crutches and telling you that you'll need to use a walking aid for the foreseeable future.

Real life is staring at yourself in the mirror and trying not to despise your new reflection.

In real life, all your problems aren't solved over the course of ninety minutes. There is no witty voice-over, no strategically placed plot points, and *definitely* no over-emotional soundtrack telling you exactly how to feel.

Because real life is *nothing* like a stupid movie.

Michael was already outside. I could hear music blasting from his car. I threw off my crutches, letting them slide down the stairs, almost taking out Jeffrey, our Chihuahua-Chewbacca cross.

Mum was in the hall beside the front door, watching me come down: one step, two feet.

'Maybe we should keep the other pair downstairs, so Jeffrey doesn't have to fear for his life every morning?' Jeffrey hid behind Mum's legs as she joked, gauging my mood with a smile that didn't quite reach her eyes.

'Yeah. Would probably be easier.'

Why don't we just get it over with and put some in every room?

'How are you feeling this morning?' Mum asked.

I didn't look up. I didn't need to. I could practically see the crease of concern in her forehead deepen.

'Fine, Mum. Completely, one hundred per cent fine.' Fake smile.

'Jules.'

'Mum.' I met her gaze and smiled, properly this time. And when I did that, the forehead crease disappeared for a second.

'It's the first day of your final year, love. It's going to be great. And nobody's going to notice the crutches.'

'Yeah, I know.' *Of course* everyone was going to notice the crutches. That wasn't the issue. The issue was what they were going to say about it.

She leaned over and kissed my head.

'Ready to take on the world, kid?' Dad came out of the kitchen holding a coffee.

'Something like that.' I looked down at my new trainers. Black Nike Air Force 1s. Not exactly Birch High regulation uniform. As if I needed another reason to stick out. But shoving my feet into leather school shoes hurt too much nowadays.

Dad kissed my head too. 'Promise me a game later? I've got a new move up my sleeve.'

'Sure.'

Mum opened the door. *And there endeth the leaving ceremony.* Thank God for that.

'Hey, Mrs C, Mr C!' Michael walked into the hall and headed straight towards the kitchen. He appeared two minutes later, his mouth full of one of Mum's home-made back-to-school blueberry muffins and another one in his hand.

'Juliet is the sun. Arise, fair sun, and kill the envious moon,' he intoned, bursting into overdramatic life. *Way* too much energy for this time in the morning.

He took my school bag from me, and we walked down the driveway. 'Your hair is on point today.' He kissed his fingers, then nodded at my crutches. 'And I *love* the new accessories.'

'I'll cut you.'

'What? I'm serious. They totally give you something extra. And are those new kicks? Watch that Princess Peach doesn't try and rob them off your feet.'

He nodded towards Tara, sitting in the back of his car. Michael picked her up at the crossroads every morning. He offered to pick her up from her house, but she always said she liked a little walk in the morning, something to do with the air making her skin glow. She was smiling at her phone as we approached.

'Bye, Jules,' Mum called.

God. Why have they followed us outside?

'All will be well, my friend. I promise.'

Easy to say if you're Michael. I'd never met anyone so comfortable in their own skin. Then suddenly his smile disappeared and he looked serious. It amazed me how

4

expressive Michael's face was, like it was impossible to hide the thoughts in his head. 'Actually, though, how are you? The new look can't be easy.'

'Seriously, I'm *fine*. We don't need to talk about it. Wait – is that a top knot?' Michael's dark hair had been pulled back off his face into this tiny bun on top of his head.

'Yeah, it is. Do you like it? My dad was watching Italian football last night, and what can I say? Something he watched finally appealed to me. Don't you think it makes me look like an Italian stallion?' His movie-star smile almost blinded me.

It was impossible not to smile back at Michael.

He squeezed my bag into the back seat with Tara and helped me into the passenger seat of the car. His parents had bought him a new black Audi over the summer.

Some of us got crutches, some of us got an Audi . . .

'Is that a muffin, Michael? I'm starving – did you bring me one?' Tara asked.

'No, sorry. You should've come in instead of sitting on your phone.' He shrugged.

'Ugh, whatever. Oh wow, you're actually bringing them to school?' Tara eyed my crutches like they were carrying some infectious disease. Michael slid them into the back seat beside her, next to my bag. 'Ouch, Michael! Watch where you're sticking those things.'

'Yeah. Remember what I said? Dr Patel –'

But she wasn't listening. She was on Insta. 'Oh my God, Hana got a *lob*. What do you think?' She pushed her phone through the space between me and Michael, and there was

Hana, head cocked, lips parted, peace sign in the camera and her black hair cut into a long bob with a blunt fringe. Gorgeous. It was pretty much the reason Tara decided to be friends with her in Year Ten. 'Hot people have hot friends,' she'd said.

She used to say that about me.

'She looks amazing,' I said.

Michael sighed. 'Yeah, looks fine.'

'Well, *your* hair looks ridiculous, Michael,' Tara said. 'Love your shoes, though, Jules – are they new?'

'Yeah, Dad bought me them yesterday.'

'Ugh, lucky bitch,' she said as Michael started the car.

'Just get yourself a disease.' I smiled.

'Do you think I could pull off crutches?'

To be fair, she probably could.

'Oh, you know that *thing* we were talking about last night, Jules? Hey, Michael, turn down the music, will you?'

I noticed Michael grip the steering wheel more tightly before reaching for the volume control.

Tara and I had spent an hour on WhatsApp last night. She'd decided she wanted to go for it. To lose her virginity this year, and we were basically going through all the guys at school, trying to find the perfect candidate. We hadn't found one.

'Yeah?' I said.

'Well, there's this party next Friday. You know, Daniel from St Anne's?'

No.

'Yeah?'

'Well, I figured that might be the perfect opportunity –'

6

'Am I missing something?' Michael asked, looking at me.

I shrugged and looked at Tara. I wished she'd just tell him. I hated the weird tension.

'It's kind of a "best friend only" thing.' She smiled at the back of Michael's head, and I tried to soften his side-eye by pulling a stupid face.

Michael had never liked Tara. Well, that's not true. We all used to hang out in this big group: Tara, me, Michael, Hana, Luke and Charlie.

Michael and I had met on our first day. We sat beside each other in English, and he passed me a note saying, 'Please, sir, can I be your friend?' I laughed, then we both got told off, and he's been making me laugh ever since.

Michael and Tara actually used to get on, for a few years at least. Until she told him that her second favourite ex-One Direction band member was Louis and not Zayn (first was Harry, obviously). He said that made him suspicious of her as a person. Michael took his stanning of One Direction really seriously and never trusted her after that. That's what he said anyway when I asked why he didn't like her. There are loads of other reasons now, but that triggered it. *Apparently*. He just never went into details.

'Oh, Jules, I forgot to tell you – I totally went up a cup size this summer.' Tara grabbed her boobs. My neck hurt from turning round.

'Riveting,' said Michael, rolling his eyes so hard I was surprised we didn't run the red light.

I thought about my barely-there chest, hidden underneath my school jumper.

As if she'd read my mind, Tara piped up: 'You know, Jules, you really need to get smaller jumpers – that one looks like a sack. You'd look really hot in a tight jumper.'

But I liked my big clothes. The baggier they were, the better I was doing at hiding how skinny I was. I pulled my sleeves over my fingers. Michael called my style 'hobo chic'.

'I don't know,' I said. 'I don't think Mum would buy me them just for that.'

I noticed Michael raise an eyebrow, and he was right not to believe me; there wasn't much Mum wouldn't buy me. Mum was never done buying me stuff, mostly clothes. She'd got to the point now that she'd make excuses for it, saying things like, 'Oh, I was in town and saw this!' or whatever. And it wasn't like I didn't appreciate it; I just knew why she was doing it – so the new clothes were kind of tainted by the fact that their existence had been triggered by my disability.

'Boo. Your mum is such a bore,' Tara said, rolling her eyes, and Michael turned up the music again.

Luke was waiting for us (well, for Tara) when we got to school. He'd not-so-subtly fancied her for ages, but until last year had barely talked to her. I don't know what happened over the summer after Year Twelve, but he came back to school with new confidence. He started showing up everywhere. Every breaktime, every lunchtime, trying to get her attention. I think the first time Tara actually spoke to him was the day he came to school with two tickets to see Taylor Swift and asked her if she wanted to go. She said yes, then took Hana instead.

'Hey, gorgeous,' said Luke, directed at Tara.

She ignored him.

I tried to get out of the car too quickly and my ankle twisted as I stepped out. When I tried to steady myself with the door, it swung open further and I landed on my side, my right knee hitting the ground.

'Jesus,' said Michael, jumping out of the driver's seat.

'Help Jules!' Tara snapped at Luke. I wouldn't have been surprised if she'd clicked her fingers too.

'I'm fine. I don't need help – I'm fine,' I spluttered.

But Luke was already there, at Tara's request.

Pain.

I'd learned to do this thing where I'd bite my tongue as hard as I could instead of screaming. But it didn't get rid of the shame. My face was burning, and I squeezed my eyes shut, wishing to God I was back at home in front of my laptop.

I felt Luke's hands under my arms. I kept my eyes closed, as if he wouldn't see the humiliation all over my red face. For a minute I enjoyed the feeling of his hands on me, and for a second I pretended I was in one of those teen movies. And that Luke was some hot guy touching me because he couldn't keep his hands off me, not because he was helping the disabled friend of the girl he was obsessed with off the floor.

'You OK?' he asked. But by the time I'd made some witty joke and balanced myself on the crutches that Michael handed me, he was already five steps ahead, carrying Tara's school bag.

2

Ronan

Chess is about control. From the very first move, the player has the opportunity to gain control of the centre, strengthening their position from the outset. Some people say the opening is the most important move. But it doesn't end there. To maintain control, you have to plan your moves as you go, so you always know (to some degree of accuracy), what's coming next. So I made sure I always knew my next move, and sometimes even my second, third and fourth.

Of course by doing that, you're assuming your opponent will go for the most obvious moves. And if it's someone you've played before, it's *usually* safe to assume that they'll follow a pattern. The same pattern that they've always followed.

But if your opponent becomes unpredictable, or loses control, you may as well not have planned anything. An unpredictable opponent is dangerous. They can screw with your head. Leave you wondering whether or not there was something you could have done to change the way the game played out, convincing you that the whole outcome was something you could have avoided altogether. But like everything, chess makes more sense with hindsight.

When I walked out of St Anne's that day, it had felt like a good idea. More than that. It had felt like the only option. When you have a lunch hall full of people staring at you, waiting for answers that you don't want to give, it makes a hell of a lot more sense just to get out of the situation before you say something you'll regret.

In chess they call it retreating.

Ciaran taught me how to play chess. He was really good at it too. But it helped that he had brains to burn and a photographic memory. Thing is, I was never jealous or anything. People acted like I should have been, like sibling rivalry was just a given. They'd talk in hushed voices when Ciaran got another prize for coming top of the county, or country, in whatever exam it was. But they didn't have to – I thought it was awesome. *He* was awesome. And it wasn't like I was stupid or anything. But it's weird, because it's him who seems like the stupid one now.

Even though things fell apart long before, it's the phone call that sticks in my head. It still makes me feel sick. It wasn't so much the words she used, but the realization that I was in this alone.

She was sitting at the kitchen table, with one hand playing with her newly dyed blonde hair. She was wearing full-on make-up too. And it's not something I'd usually notice because she always wore make-up, but there wasn't even a smudge. Her nails were red. The perfection disturbing. Like the opening to my own personal horror movie.

'Is that Principal Heath?' I didn't know how Mum did it, making her voice normal when . . . everything.

'I just wanted to talk about Ronan Cole . . . yes . . . he won't be back this term . . . we've had some . . . issues with his brother . . . Yes, Ciaran. I sent a letter, I'm not sure if you got it? . . . Good.'

Issues? That's what she was calling it?

In the silence Mum held out her hand and examined her nails, like she was talking to one of her friends. I didn't know what she was saying then. I couldn't hear anything now; my heartbeat was thudding in my ears. All I heard through the haze was 'a shame', 'disappointing', 'sorry'.

'Disappointing? Sorry?' I had to shout the words, force them out because they were catching in my throat. Her expression didn't even change. Her face was still; there was nothing there.

'Ronan, please. I'm on the phone.'

'Is that what you think? That he's a disappointment?'

She scraped her chair back and walked right past me, closing the living-room door, leaving me in the hall with my stomach twisted in my throat.

That was six months ago.

Six months of ignoring my friends, of not playing chess, six months of trying to remember everything about the Ciaran I grew up with, while at the same time trying not to think about him at all. Six months of sleeping no more than three hours a night because my stupid brain wouldn't shut off.

And now I was starting a new school. Birch High. At least nobody knew me there, and nobody knew Ciaran. I just hoped that it'd be better than St Anne's, where everyone thought who slept with who was the most important thing in the world.

I stared at myself in the mirror. The uniform looked so weird after a summer of hoodies and jeans, although the navy woollen blazer was better than the ridiculous purple of St Anne's. You don't stand out as much in navy.

A year. It was all I had to do, get through this year then I could get away from this town, this life, this everything.

I pushed an earbud in and went downstairs. Mum was dressed for work and making breakfast. Her high heels clicked on the kitchen tiles, and she gave me a red-lipped smile as she put pancakes down on the table like it was some kind of sitcom. I almost expected canned laughter.

But nothing was funny any more.

'Ronan, eat something. I've made pancakes – you and Ciaran used to love pancakes,' she said. 'Do you remember that time Ciaran made them and stuck one to the ceiling when he tried to flip it?' She laughed at the memory, like it had happened only the other day.

I didn't answer, just walked past her, opened the fridge and took out a can of Coke.

'Ronan, please. You look thin – you need to eat something before school,' she pleaded. I was almost out of the door when she added, 'I'm passing the school on my way to work if you want a lift?'

Mum was an estate agent. She showed people round perfect houses, selling perfect lives, day after day. I wondered how people could believe the stuff that came out of her mouth when she talked about a place being a 'perfect family home' or that 'you'll be so happy here'. Maybe they didn't really believe it, deep down. Maybe they just liked pretending their lives could be better than they already were.

I acted like I hadn't heard her when she offered me a lift. Just walked out of the front door, slamming it behind me. I was five minutes down the road when I remembered. 'Shit,' I muttered. I don't know how I'd forgotten it. I'd carried it about with me for months, in my pocket, in my bag, even in my sock. I didn't want to go back in and see Mum again, but I had no choice.

I turned back, went into the house, then ran upstairs two steps at a time, and picked up the pawn I'd left on my desk. Black and carved, still pristine after so many games. I slid the chess piece deep inside my blazer pocket. With it, I felt lighter. Mum was standing at the bottom of the stairs when I came down, looking at me like she was going to say something. I turned up my music, with my earbuds in, and kept my eyes locked on the door until I got outside.

Birch High was about two miles away from my house, a walk through Belfast suburbia: four-bedroomed, loft-converted, double-garaged perfect lives. I crushed the can I'd just finished and dropped it over someone's little picket fence, where it sat, out of place, on just-cut grass.

My phone buzzed in my pocket.

AUNT SARAH: Good luck today, Ronan. Let me know how it goes x

Aunt Sarah had been sending me messages all summer. None of which I'd replied to. She'd turn up at the house sometimes, though, and then I couldn't avoid her. But I did make sure that she never got me alone. I knew that if she did I might slip. And if I slipped, so would everything.

Slowing down as I reached the big iron gates of the school, I could hear the calls from the schoolyard over my music and watched a football fly towards a group of screaming girls. Just like St Anne's. Full of morons. I thought I'd at least make it through the schoolyard without anyone talking to me, but as soon as someone yelled that I was new, they swarmed around me like flies on shit. Someone slapped me on the back and asked who I was, someone else asked if I was any good at football and a voice from too far away called me a dick. Nice. I mumbled responses, hoping they'd get the hint. I noticed a couple of girls staring at me, doing that thing where they look up just long enough for you to notice before turning to each other and laughing. They were pretty hot. But the brown-haired one (total Queen Bee vibes) was looking around like she was only interested in who was looking at her. We had one of those in St Anne's too: Casey Molloy. I didn't have time for people who thought they were better than everyone else. And even though her friend had a bright pink backpack with badges and shit all over it, she looked way less try-hard. She caught my attention. Black hair, nice smile.

I looked at my timetable for the first time. Apart from maths, they'd put me in the middle-of-the-road sets so I could catch up. I was going to be bored to tears.

It made me think of Ciaran and the time I played f6. Which *I* didn't think was a bad move. I had a plan. But Ciaran clearly thought differently.

'You've just weakened your king position, Ro. You're better than that. It achieves nothing in terms of central control or piece development. It also takes up a square that you might want for a knight. Think. Make your moves count. Push yourself, it's the only way you'll improve.'

He laughed then, but not in a bad way. I knew he just wanted me to get better. But he took no prisoners. I'd only just learned the set-up of the board: eight horizontal rows called ranks, eight vertical columns called files. Ranks were numbered, files were lettered. The moves were coordinates, and coordinates made sense to me. Ciaran used to make sense to me too.

And there he was, in my head again, filling up space.

I stood in the hall and felt for the pawn in my pocket.

Still there. Still weak.

3

Juliet

Being Tara's friend meant that it was hard to stay under the radar. Everyone wanted to talk to Tara, to be seen with Tara, to go out with Tara. I wondered if she ever got bored of it.

It didn't used to be like this.

At primary school, Tara and I did everything together – 'BFFs for life' with little half-heart necklaces to prove it. We were inseparable. We'd spend every weekend at either my house or at Tara's, camping out in her bedroom or in my living room under tents that Mum would make for us. Sometimes Tara's little sister, Annie, would join us and we'd all watch Disney movies together, before I hated them. Mum would paint our nails and buy us takeaway pizzas.

I remembered thinking that Tara and Annie felt like my sisters.

When Tara's dad left, they moved house and after that Tara always asked if we could just go to my house instead because it was bigger. I haven't even seen her new house. After a while I stopped asking to go there and she just spent more and more time at mine.

I never felt less-than, back in primary school.

Then came the diagnosis.

Sometimes when I tell people I have arthritis, they laugh. In fact, some people even tell me I don't have it, that I'm too young and arthritis is for old people. I totally get it. When I was twelve and Dr Patel told me I had it, I laughed too.

Then I cried. A lot.

And changed my name.

Michael was the only person who was still *allowed* to call me Juliet. And only because he refused to call me anything else. I think he would stop if I asked him to, but I remember telling him how much I used to love my name, and I think it's just his way of keeping it alive. Either that or he was too busy thinking about Harry Styles to listen to anything I had to say. 'Juliet' was fine when I was a kid. In fact, I *loved* it when I was a kid because Mum would tell me the story of how she named me. She was watching some olden-days version of *Romeo and Juliet* when she was pregnant and apparently I kicked when Juliet said, 'What's in a name?' Mum was a sucker for love stories. But when you're at school and can barely walk, the last thing you want is any kind of name that makes you stand out. 'Jules' slipped under the radar. 'Jules' just made more sense.

Tara had disappeared with Luke to find Hana and Charlie. Michael waited for me.

He must have heard my slow exhale as I stared at the school because he nudged me. 'Let's do this.'

'Or we could, you know, go home or something? Maggie's? I hear they do excellent breakfast shakes,' I said.

'Don't try and tempt me with my milkshake weakness. Anyway, you'd never cut class, you're too scared. And besides,

I have my new hairstyle to flaunt, so you're all out of luck, J. Boo hoo.' Mock sad.

'These could double up as weapons, you know!' I poked him with a crutch.

'Yeah.' Michael considered my threat for a second. 'You'd never cut it in prison. Sorry, you're stuck with me.' He looked at his phone. 'Hey, found this gorgeous picture of you online.'

Michael and I had this game. We'd find the most ridiculous pictures and send them to each other, editing over them with 'that's you'.

I looked at the screen and burst out laughing. There was a picture of the bird lady from *Mary Poppins* sitting on some stone steps covered in pigeons.

'You're such a dick.'

'What? I thought you could get some style tips. Look how happy she is being hobo-chic like you.'

'Actually, on second thought,' I said looking at the picture again, 'I think she's pretty hot.' I shrugged.

He shuddered. 'You disturb me.'

The bell had already rung, and the halls had emptied as we walked to registration. Now that Michael was staring at his phone, there was nothing to distract me from the fact I was about to crutch-walk into a class full of people who thought wearing a *coat* to school was social suicide.

I hated being late. Even before, without the crutches, I hated their eyes on me, my eyes in their heads, like I could see what they were thinking.

Why is she walking like that?
What's wrong with her knees?

Can't she move any faster?

And now it was worse. The *tap-tap* of plastic on lino was all I could hear, filling my head.

'J, we have to go.'

'What?'

'Haven't you been listening to anything I've said? To the party, that one Tara was talking about. This is our year.'

'Ugh, really? I don't know. I was thinking of sitting this one out.'

The last time I went to a house party I had a couple of drinks and kissed Caleb Harrison, who then tried to do more than kiss me in a room full of people, as if access to my mouth was an open invitation to everywhere else! At least he had the decency to look ashamed when I asked what the hell he thought he was doing. Then I got drunk to try and forget what happened and didn't sit down all night. When I woke up the next day it was like someone had tightened all my joints with a spanner. It took hot-water bottles and massages to get me out of bed. And I had to take Monday off school.

'Yeah, that's not an option. Sorry. And Caleb will be there, waiting with his tongue for your mouth. And his handsy little fingers.'

'Another reason to sit this one out.'

'Poor boy. He loves you. Not sure why.' Michael smirked at me.

'He loves everybody. I saw him kissing Emily in the music room last week. She looked weirdly into it.' I screwed up my face at the unwelcome memory of his tongue in my mouth.

'It was probably a rebound kiss to mend his broken heart.'

After our drunken kiss, Caleb went through this weird phase of sending me a message saying 'Good morning, sexy' *every day*. What are you even supposed to say to that? Hi? I gave full responsibility to Michael who replied in memes until he stopped.

Michael pushed the classroom door open to join registration, and twenty-five pairs of eyes looked up at us. At me. Heat from my face bled down my neck and over my chest, making my hands sweat on the crutches.

'Good morning, Juliet. Michael, please take a seat.' Mr Dawson barely looked up. But I heard whispering.

I'd thought I was ready for this. I'd told myself I was going to ignore everyone; pretend I didn't care. But the hushed voices stung like shampoo in my eye, a background itch before the slow, stinging burn took over.

Michael pulled out a seat for me and made as much noise as possible. I sat down and slid the crutches under my desk, massaging the insides of my elbows where they'd dug into the skin.

I eventually looked up again. And when I did, I realized that nobody was looking at me at all. Michael raised an eyebrow towards the door.

'What is it?' I whispered.

'Oh my God, J, you have to see this.'

'See what?'

'My future husband.'

I shuffled round so I could see. Some guy walked in, earbuds in, shirt hanging out. Black-rimmed glasses, with dark hair that fell over his face. He had light eyes, blue or green, from what I could see, and the kind of cheekbones you only see on TV.

'Earphones, Mr Cole.' Mr Dawson sighed, pointing at his ears. 'And for future reference, registration is at nine, not nine fifteen.'

The boy just shrugged and sat down on a spare chair at Luke's table, took out a notebook and started drawing in it. His other hand stayed in his pocket. He didn't look up once.

Great. Because that's just what we needed in this school – someone else who looked like they'd stepped straight out of some American movie.

Someone else who thought they were better than everyone.

Fan-bloody-tastic.

4

Ronan

I sat down on the first free seat I could find, and reluctantly pulled out my earbud. The teacher was some guy in a too-big suit with a ridiculous moustache and it actually pained me to do what he said. But it was my first day. The less attention I could get away with the better.

I clicked my pen and started doodling in a notebook, drawing 3D shapes. Hexagons, octagons, dodecagons. And as much as I didn't care what people were saying, I couldn't help but listen in on the conversations around me. They weren't exactly whispering.

Some girl was asking the girl next to her if she thought she looked hotter from the right or the left. And she actually answered. In fact, she paused and gave *actual* thought to her question. Someone else was talking about how hot 'Tara' looked at 'the party' last week.

'You're new, right?' A guy moved up a seat to sit beside me. The one who'd just been talking about the party. He had a big dopey grin on his face, like something you'd see on a cartoon Labrador, eyes shining like he'd just been told a dirty secret. Just then I wished it was a real class, instead of the stupid waste-of-time half hour where the teachers read out a list of names and made announcements about things nobody cared about. Then people wouldn't be switching seats.

'Yeah,' I said, and went back to my doodling, hoping he'd take the please-fuck-off hint.

'Well, there are a few things you need to know if you want to survive here. First, Tara Williams is the hottest girl in the year, brunette with great tits, and next is probably Hana Mori – her parents are from Japan. She has that totally hot Asian thing going on. Kelly Raddison, if you're into redheads. Chloe Piwko is up there too; she definitely jumped a few rankings in the last year.' He mimed a pair of tits on his chest. 'I've been trying to get into Tara for years, but she pretends she's not interested. I mean, come on.' I looked up and he was just nodding his head like I should agree. He slapped my shoulder. 'But yeah, fair play if you get anywhere with her. You'd be a hero,' he said, laughing. He was way too close to my face, and I could smell his coffee breath.

I didn't know if I was supposed to laugh too. It wasn't funny and I had no idea who Tara or any of the others were.

He must have seen the hesitation on my face because he continued, 'Or wait, maybe you're not into girls. I mean, that would kind of suit me, to be honest. Michael Crawley, Corey Lee, Evan Armour, Leon Jackson are your resident gay guys. There are some bi guys too – Marc Myers. He was actually going out with Kelly last year then dumped her for some dude. Mental.' He took a break from his monologue and looked at me. 'I'm Luke, by the way,' he said and offered his hand. I put down my pen and shook it.

24

'Ronan,' I said. 'And yeah, I'm not exactly looking at the minute.'

He burst out laughing, like it was the funniest thing he'd ever heard.

Christ.

'You may not be looking, but they'll be looking for you. I already heard Hana talking about the "new hot guy" so good luck with that.' And he laughed again, then handed me his phone. 'Here, stick your number in this. I'll keep you in the loop.' I hesitated before I took it. But giving my number didn't mean I had to respond if he got in touch. And not giving my number meant making an enemy on my first day.

I tapped it in and handed the phone back.

When I was fifteen, Ciaran gave me the book *Inside the Mind of a Grandmaster* by Sergei Fedorov and I read it from cover to cover. But it was Alexander Kotov who first came up with the idea of a 'Candidate Move'. A Candidate Move is the strongest move you can possibly make after analysing all the options, which is the exact opposite of what I did six months ago. I wasn't going to make that mistake again.

I looked around the classroom. Then my eyes settled on someone. A girl with crutches. She was cute. She saw me looking, then her eyes flickered away. I wondered if she'd heard the rumours. She had a nice face, huge eyes, browny-blonde hair and cheeks that had just turned pink. Why the hell was I even thinking about her? Adding that kind of complication to my life was exactly the kind of thing I absolutely didn't need right now.

'That's Jules. Used to be a nine before the crutches. Solid

seven now,' Luke whispered when he saw me looking. 'The crutches are new, dunno what happened. Turned into Crutch Girl over the summer, I guess.' He laughed again. I didn't. 'There was this one time she even came into school in a wheelchair, like just for a couple of days and then never again. Not really sure what that was about. Attention maybe.'

What an asshole.

I managed to avoid him for the rest of the morning. In fact, I managed to avoid talking to anyone except the maths teacher when he asked me stupidly easy questions. It was like he was trying to catch me out. Nice try. I ignored the looks from other kids. I suppose I expected them, and I probably would have done the same, stared at some new St Anne's kid, not because I was a dick or anything, just interested, I guess. So, I didn't blame them. I just wasn't about to engage.

Lunchtime. The canteen was exactly like at St Anne's. Except here, I didn't fit in.

I didn't have to think about it before. I knew where I sat, with Alex and Sasha. After that fell apart, I sat with whoever was free. I liked that about St Anne's. No real cliques.

I kept my head down and stood in the queue, eventually grabbing some chips that they served with a depressing little side salad on a plastic plate. I wanted anything I could eat quickly to get out of there.

'Hey, man, over here.' I knew even before I turned round it was that guy Luke again. I was hoping he'd taken the hint earlier but clearly not. He was standing up, waving me over, and when I scanned the table, I saw the little group just staring at me. The two girls from earlier were there, the black-haired one chatting to some guy beside her and Queen Bee staring right at me with a half-smile. I looked down at my tray.

Luke must have thought I hadn't heard him because he didn't stop calling me. Then everyone was looking again, and the memories of that last day at St Anne's flashed in my head. I couldn't leave, not again. I walked over.

The lunch hall had rows and rows of tables pushed together, so by the time I made it to where they were sitting, I realized there'd be no quick exit. I felt my heartbeat quicken. I ignored the kids who stared at me as I walked behind their chairs, whispering to their friends. On the joined-up table next to Luke's, I noticed that girl from registration, the one with crutches, sitting beside some huge dude, though only he was looking at me. I walked round them and sat down beside Luke. The room closed in.

Luke talked and talked. The other guy, who I learned was Charlie, only joined in once to tell me that there was no space left on the football team so if I wanted to play, I'd have to be a sub. Then there was Tara, Queen Bee. She was staring at me so intensely it made me squirm. The other one was Hana. Less stary, cute, but no less intimidating.

'Great,' was all I could say to whatever Luke had just said.

'So, I'm Tara, and this is Hana,' Tara said. 'You're Ronan, right? You used to go to St Anne's?'

'Yeah, that's right,' I said and stuffed some chips in my mouth.

She did have a great smile. One of those smiles that showed just the right number of teeth, dark brown eyes and hair to match. I chewed slowly and tried to ignore the heartbeat in my ears, hoping by the time I'd finished eating they'd have moved on to someone else.

Then it was too much, the silence, the eyes. I got up.

'Sorry, I have to go.'

'What? Where you going?' Luke called. But I was already walking round chairs and trying not to drop my tray on the way out. Then my foot caught something, and the plate of salad fell everywhere, bits of lettuce, tomato and cucumber, all over the floor. No, not the floor, on to someone. I looked down and saw the crutches I'd just kicked over. Jules. She glanced at me once, then turned back to the table.

'Shit,' I said.

'Watch where you're going, man,' said the huge guy with a top knot, standing up and scooping her crutches off the floor.

That's when I looked at her. 'You have a . . .' I pointed at her head. There was a piece of lettuce in her hair.

The guy brushed it off for her, but she didn't move an inch, just stared down at the table.

'Sorry,' I said. Then I remembered the eyes, that everyone was still staring at me. I dumped my tray on the table and just kept walking until I got outside. I didn't stop until I got to the back of the sports hall where I could have a smoke.

5

Juliet

'Shit, J. He's even hotter up close,' Michael said, nudging me. 'Those cheekbones, those glasses. Be still my heart.' I was still looking down at the salad sandwich Mum had made me, barely touched, waiting for the burning in my face to fade.

'Yeah, I guess,' I said, and shrugged. Hot, yeah, but he couldn't get away fast enough when he kicked my crutches, like he was scared he was going to catch something. Maybe that's what happens when you're born like that, all cheekbones, blue eyes and floppy hair. You don't *have* to care about anyone else. I looked up to see him climbing the stairs out of the lunch hall. Definitely hot though.

'What do you think his deal is?' I heard from down the table. It was Hana.

'I don't know, but the mysterious thing is so sexy,' said Tara, staring after him too.

'Sexy is right,' said Michael, throwing a Malteser up in the air and catching it in his mouth.

'I think I just found my new conquest,' said Tara, loud enough for the whole table to hear. Michael snorted.

'Here we go,' he whispered. 'How does she even know he's straight?'

'I don't think she cares,' I whispered back.

'Hey, Michael.' I looked up to see Tara staring at us from down the table. 'I'm going to go into town with Hana after school, so I don't need a lift home.'

Michael shrugged. 'OK, Your Highness,' he whispered.

I didn't need a lift either. Mum was picking me up early to go to physio.

The joy.

After his lunchtime exit, Ronan was back in my English class. He sat at the back by himself, earbuds in. If the teacher asked him a question, he'd just shrug and she'd move on. Part of me wanted to tell her that he was listening to music. Then he wouldn't look so smug. I couldn't believe Miss Black hadn't noticed. She was pretty old, though, and probably didn't know what earbuds were. Then my thoughts were interrupted.

'Juliet, do you know the answer?' I winced at Miss Black's use of my full name and could feel my face start to burn. I'd been too busy looking at Ronan and hadn't heard a word she'd said. 'Honestly, it feels like I'm talking to myself sometimes. *Parting is such sweet sorrow.* Which of Shakespeare's plays does it come from? It's the play we're going to be studying this term.'

Some Year Nine kid came into the classroom and handed Miss Black a note, giving me a few moments' grace. She looked up. 'Juliet, your mother is at reception. Do you have the answer before you go?'

I could feel a thousand eyes on me, and I was convinced they could all hear my heart. Of course I knew what it was. I had watched the Leonardo DiCaprio movie a million times with Mum. But saying it would just mean somebody making a joke about my name.

'*Hamlet?*' I said, before putting my things away and reaching for my crutches. When I turned to get my coat from the back of the chair, I noticed Ronan run his eyes over me, from head to toe. I could feel my face get hotter.

'No, Juliet,' Miss Black said. 'It was, of course . . . Eva?'

'*Romeo and Juliet.*' Eva emphasized the Juliet. Just in case I hadn't got the stupid-answer memo.

'Yes, well done.'

The rest of the class was pretending to listen again, so I took my chance and started to walk towards the door. And when I was closing it, I saw him, eyes on me again. I thought about how nice it was to have someone with that face look at me without laughing. Then I thought about my red cheeks, my wrong answer, the hair-lettuce, the *tap-tap* of my crutches and saw his look for what it really was. Pity. I wished the ground would just swallow me up completely.

Mum was waiting in reception.

'I can get myself to hospital, you know. I don't mind getting the bus,' I told her, not for the first time.

I hated that she had to take time off work for me. Not only did it make me look like a massive baby, but she had to make up the work during evenings and weekends.

'It's fine, Jules. I had a half day anyway.'

Yeah. Because you'd booked it off in advance for this appointment.

'Thanks.'

'Don't be silly. Jeffrey's in the car – I was going to take him for a walk when you're in with Sean. Unless you want me to come with you?'

'No, it's fine. I'll be OK by myself,' I said.

Jeffrey was in the front seat. We got him from the rescue centre the same year I was diagnosed. I think everybody needed a distraction. He's some kind of weird little mongrel. His fur is insane. He barked and jumped up, trying to lick my face.

'Are you ready for your own personal concert?' Mum turned up her Celine Dion playlist.

Mum's rendition of 'My Heart Will Go On,' always made me laugh. She is a terrible singer. Jeffrey sounded better when I trapped his tail in the door. Thank God the drive to the hospital wasn't long.

'I'll just come to reception with you, then I'll take Jeffrey for a walk, OK?' Mum parked in our usual disabled spot, the huge white wheelchair in the space telling the world what I was. For a while I'd made her park in the 'normal' spots. But that was before. When my arthritis was controlled, and I wasn't too sore to make a point.

Over the summer it had flared. I hoped it would go away in a couple of days, that the huge swellings on my knees and elbows would just disappear. But it didn't. It got worse. Constant burning joints, falling asleep at dinner. It got so bad that Mum ended up doing everything for me again. Like she had at the beginning. When her life was ruined as much as mine. But I'd promised myself I wouldn't let it happen again. So I agreed to start the new medication, one that I injected into my thigh once a week, despite my needle phobia. One I insisted on doing in my room so Mum and Dad wouldn't hear me scream. And I didn't complain about parking in the disabled space again. Because I was *fine*. I had to be fine.

'Fine.'

'Just take a seat. Sean will be with you soon,' the receptionist said. Mum stuffed some leaflets into her bag. I stared at my phone. Michael had sent me some memes and Tara had sent me some message about how hot the new guy was, or something.

'Tara's welcome to sleep over this weekend if you want. She hasn't been over in ages,' Mum said, looking over my shoulder at my phone screen. I locked it.

'Yeah, thanks. I'll ask.' I already knew what she'd say. And anyway, we weren't twelve any more.

'Juliet Clarke?' The receptionist called my name and I looked down the corridor to see Sean poking his head out and smiling.

'See you soon, Jules,' said Mum. 'Have fun.' I think it came out of her mouth before she realized. Or maybe she only realized when she saw my face twist. Which probably wasn't fair. I didn't mind physio when I was there. And Sean was great.

'Hello, my favourite patient. How are you today? Ready to start our training for the Belfast marathon?' He smiled and closed the door behind me.

'Ha, ha,' I said. 'Marathon runners are mental.'

'I agree completely,' said Sean.

'Haven't you done like ten or something?'

'Yep. Awful things. How are you, anyway?'

'I'm fine.' I gave him a thumbs up.

'You're not with your mum now, Jules. How are you really? Worse? Better? So bad you have to beg to listen to your mum's Celine Dion music to numb the pain?'

'Celine doesn't even touch the edges.'

He sucked air in through his teeth. 'That *is* bad. Where hurts?'

I almost laughed when he asked that. 'My left wrist doesn't hurt,' I said.

He put his hand on his chin and studied me for a minute. 'Bollocks,' he said.

And that caught me off guard. I laughed. 'It's not very professional to swear, you know.'

'Yeah, but I made you laugh. Would I be right in saying it's something you don't do much of any more?'

I couldn't answer straight away.

'See? I'm a physio and a therapist all in one,' he continued.

'Don't quit the day job.' I smiled. But he was right – I couldn't really remember the last time I had laughed.

6

Ronan

The girl I dropped the salad on was in my English class. Jules. When she left halfway through, she caught me looking at her. It wasn't like I was drooling or anything but at the same time I'm not *not* going to stare when there's someone blatantly hot right in front of me. She was probably thinking about how much of a clumsy idiot I was. I shook the scene from my mind.

The rest of English dragged. I just about made it to the end of class before I had to get out of school completely.

I thought I'd kept a low-profile when I left, but I heard Luke shouting after me as I was walking out of the school gates. If it'd been someone else, I might have turned round, but I couldn't face any more of him. I shoved my hands into my pockets and turned up my music until it was screaming in my ears. I went the long way home, through Sycamore Close, just in case there were any teachers about.

The first thing I noticed when I turned the corner on to our street was our empty driveway. Relief followed. Mum wasn't home. The last thing I needed right now was to listen to her.

Ciaran listened to Mum, to every word she said. To the constant talk about going to Cambridge, about winning the Silver Pawn Chess Invitational. The tournament that was happening here next month. That's what happens when you listen to her. Your life falls apart.

I closed my bedroom door, turned up my music one the Bluetooth speaker and opened my laptop. I scrolled through Reddit, not really reading anything. But something caught my attention and made me stop. An ad.

CHESS LIFE – chat while you play.
Completely anonymous. Bringing chess to YOUR life.

Chess was my life. *Was*. Past tense. I kept scrolling. Not really looking at the screen at all. I missed it. The chess. Ciaran and I used to play for hours, holed up in his room listening to death metal. He'd always win, but he always said it just took practice and I'd easily be as good as him one day. Since he's gone, it hurts too much. I put everything away: chessboards, books, awards. I even hid Ciaran's playbook under his mattress. The leather-bound 'secret' notebook was where he wrote down all his moves and studied them as if his life depended on it. If it all disappeared, I wouldn't have to think about it.

But I slipped. I couldn't remember how Bobby Fischer had won the game against Donald Byrne in New York in 1956. Ciaran was obsessed with Bobby Fischer. The Grünfeld Defence. That's how he'd won. I meant to delete my search history, to get rid of all the evidence. I guess I forgot. But the algorithms didn't. Then the ads started again. The ones for expensive boards and chess retreats, and now, Chess Life.

I let the cursor hover over the little pawn icon for the Chess Life website. It was anonymous. It would be like playing a computer, wouldn't it?

My heartbeat was in my ears again.

'Free trial' for one month.

Wise the fuck up, Ronan. Don't be a pussy.

I clicked on it.

A month wasn't long. And I could unsubscribe at any time. I probably wouldn't even like it – it was hardly the same as playing a real person.

After I filled in my email address, a box popped up. Screen name? Well, it was anonymous so obviously I couldn't use my real name. I let myself focus on the music. 'Angel of Death' was playing. I typed it in. Taken? Seriously? I twisted round to look at the posters on my walls for inspiration and felt the pawn in my pocket, digging into my thigh. The pawn. A lonely pawn.

The screen burst to life. You could send people invitations, or you could be randomly assigned someone to play. There was a little chat box on the side so you could – what? Talk and laugh at them for their terrible moves?

All this chess shit was bringing him back into my head.

I closed my laptop. What a stupid idea.

I thought about going into his room. The room that Mum constantly tidied. Instead, I turned my music up, so high it hurt my ears.

It was better than listening to the screaming in my own head.

7

Juliet

'Knock, knock,' Dad said, from outside my bedroom door. He'd just got home from work and always came up to say hello.

'Yeah?' I called.

'I got us some pizza from that place you love. Are you coming down?' He poked his head into my room.

'Yeah, I'll be down in a minute.'

'Heard you were skiving again?' Dad said.

'You know me,' I smiled. 'Mad for missing class.'

'Everything go OK?'

'Fine, Dad. Same old.'

'You're the bravest girl I know.'

'It was just physio.' I pulled myself off the bed and laughed at Jeffrey chasing his own tail, to mask the shooting pains in my legs.

There it was again. That word, *brave*. I never liked it. People threw it around like it meant something, like having joints that didn't do what they were supposed to do somehow made me brave. It didn't. I didn't *ask* for all this pain and I was just doing what anyone would do in my position, trying to pretend it didn't exist.

'After dinner, do you fancy a game of chess?' he asked. 'Oh, and there's post for you. That magazine that you love, I think.'

'Sure, to the chess,' I said. 'And great, thanks.'

The magazine was a subscription to *Teen Queen*, this fashion magazine that Mum thought she'd discovered. I don't think she knew I read the whole thing online anyway.

More than that. I'd save the pictures of celebrities into this file on my laptop in a folder named 'English Revision'. It was pathetic really. Mostly shots of famous women and teens in skirts, dresses, cut-off jeans, chosen so I could study their perfect knees and dream for ten minutes. I daydreamed about what it must be like to have knees like that. The whole joint outlined, the dents at the bottom of their tanned thighs where lean muscles protruded. I'd pore over the clothes I could never wear. Would it hurt to get on? Anything without buttons was hard to take off. Would it show my knees? Skirts and dresses were out. Was the material stiff? It would bunch up in my crutches. I got the same feeling when I looked at the pictures every night before bed, an aching in my chest and a lump in my throat that had nothing to do with arthritis. But it was like I was compelled to do it. A punishment for having this stupid broken body.

Mum was so excited when I opened my first subscription after my seventeenth birthday that I pretended I loved it and spent an hour once a month with her, looking at pictures of beautiful women with perfect joints and perfect lives, even though it hurt more this way. In the open. Mum acted like I looked just like them, the perfect people. I'd just nod along, smiling when she said how lovely the clothes would look on me, like I believed it too.

In my head, it was one small payback to a mum whose life I'd already ruined a million times over. To a mum who'd put her dreams on hold because of me.

So when she treated me like I was twelve years old, I gritted my teeth and didn't say anything. When we looked at the magazine, I listened to the 'that would look amazing on you'. And I didn't complain when she came home from work with bags of new clothes for me, hanging them up in my wardrobe when I was at school and surprising me when I got home. My surprised face was almost as believable as my 'I'm fine' face.

I went downstairs, the smell of pizza making me realize how hungry I was. We hardly ever ate pizza.

'Your seat, *madam*,' said Dad, pulling out a chair and waving me to it. I rolled my eyes and smiled. Mum had set the huge bowl of salad she'd made beside my placemat. She didn't say anything, but over the last few years our diets had changed drastically. At first it was no meat, then no dairy, then no carbs. Now it was no sugar. I'd seen her watching programmes on how diet can affect inflammation and then she'd just pass it off as something she wanted to try herself. I just went with it.

'So, what did Sean say today then?' Dad asked.

'Just said to keep doing my exercises, keep the joints mobile, same old.'

But it wasn't the 'same old'. I was hoping he wouldn't, but Sean had noticed the muscle wastage. The way my thigh muscles had faded to nothing in the last few months. He told me how quickly you lose muscle mass and how it was so easy to do with my 'condition'. He told me I needed to really work on my quads, how more muscle would take pressure off the knee joints. He gave me extra exercises. More, on top of the leg lifts and stretches I did every day. But the pain made me not want to exercise at all, the vicious cycle making me feel even more of a failure than I already did.

'Jules is finally doing Shakespeare in school,' said Mum, cutting in.

'Oh really? *Romeo, Romeo, wherefore art thou, Romeo?*' Dad said.

'Maybe it's time to break out Claire and Leo again,' Mum said.

'No, thanks.' I regretted the edge to my tone as soon as the words left my mouth. Mum looked a bit hurt so I tried to save it. 'I think I still remember it line for line, you know.'

'Suit yourself.' She put some salad on my plate.

'Might help, you know. Save you reading the book,' Dad said, pulling a face.

'Brian!' Mum gave him a look.

Dad put his hands up in surrender. 'Sorry, sorry. I just always thought it was a bit boring, that's all.'

Mum changed the subject and spent most of dinner telling me about some new study. They'd found by eating turmeric, people could reduce their levels of inflammation by fifty per cent. I half listened. I didn't have a clue who *they* were. But I nodded anyway.

'Yeah, Mum, we can give it a go,' I said.

'Did you ask Tara round this weekend?'

'Not yet.'

Mum loved Tara. She was the daughter she never had. I mean, she never actually said that but it's what she was thinking.

Every time she asked about my day she'd ask about Tara, like a chaser. It didn't really bother me. It was just there.

After we'd finished the pizza, I looked at Dad. 'Are you ready for me to beat you at chess?' I asked.

'In your dreams,' he said.

Dad bought a fancy chess set last year. All the pieces were this really heavy, carved marble. My favourite was the queen. Beautiful, elegant, understated next to the king. But so much more powerful.

It was a huge set that now lived in the living room, to Mum's disgust. She thought it was ugly. I thought it was beautiful. To play, I sat on the sofa with my back right up against cushions and Dad would push the chess set towards me so I wouldn't hurt my back reaching over. He sat on a footstool, which must have made his back ache, but he never said anything. I set up all the pieces and Dad made cups of tea.

'OK, she's in the kitchen. Give me the low-down,' Dad whispered over the chessboard, straightening his black pieces.

'What low-down?'

'The drama. The fights, the who-said-what-about-who?'

'Oh my God, you're such a gossip queen.'

'I know. Your mum hates gossip, but I love it.' Dad winked and I laughed. 'Come on, you have to have something for me.'

'Nope, sorry, fresh out of juicy gossip.'

'Hm, that's a shame.' Dad rubbed his hand over his stubble and looked at me. More seriously this time. 'How did you get on at school? I mean, with the crutches. Is everyone being nice to you?'

'Yeah, fine,' I said and smiled, trying to ignore the pressure behind my eyes that had come out of nowhere. I looked at the board.

'Really, Jules?'

'Yeah, nobody's said anything at all. It's been great.' At least part of it was true. Sometimes it felt even worse lying to Dad than it did to Mum. It was easier to get angry at her, or at least think angry thoughts, which I knew wasn't fair either. But she gave me ammo, treating me like I was ten years younger. But Dad, he always said the right thing and it cut straight to the bone.

'OK, I believe you when thousands wouldn't.' He held up his hands and smiled. 'Seriously, though, if anyone says anything I'll sort them out for you.'

'Dad, you'd make a useless hitman. You ugly-cried when Darth Vader died in *Return of the Jedi*!'

'And you didn't! Which makes *you* a monster. He saw the error of his ways; he regretted going to the dark side. It was *very* emotional!' Dad looked away, pretending he was going to cry again, then turned back to me. 'Who said anything about killing anyone anyway? I was just offering to make a scene.' He moved his footstool away from me, pretending to be scared.

'What kind of scene?' I gave him the laugh he was angling for.

'The biggest scene.' His eyes lit up with a grin.

Mum came in from the kitchen, her eyes narrowed in mock suspicion. 'Who's causing a scene?'

'Nobody,' I said.

When Mum disappeared Dad whispered, 'Except Michael. If he's ever mean to you, you're on your own – he's way taller than me.'

'I'm good, Dad. I promise. Everyone can remain safe from your causing-of-scenes, for now.'

'Just as well. Wouldn't be good for my blood pressure anyway. Seriously, though, things are OK?'

'Yeah, they're good. I promise.'

Dad squeezed my hand, holding it to the side of the board while taking a pawn with his other hand.

'Was that all just a distraction tactic to try and beat me?' I asked.

'Maybe.'

The doorbell rang.

Mum opened the door and Tara burst in.

'Hi, Tara, everything OK?' Mum looked genuinely worried.

'Hi, Tara!' Dad called.

Tara appeared beside the chessboard. 'I need you, Jules. It's an emergency,' she said. She'd just come from hockey practice and was still wearing her skirt and socks – the skirt that was just that little bit too short and the T-shirt so tight it looked like it was cutting off her circulation.

'I'm just . . .' I looked at Dad.

'It's fine, love, you go. It seems important. I'll finish beating you later.'

Dad lifted the chess set away and I pulled myself up. By the time Mum handed me my crutches Tara was already halfway up the stairs. And by the time I'd caught up she was in my room standing in front of the mirror.

'So, spill then. What's wrong?' I asked. I already knew that the emergency wasn't going to be an actual emergency as soon as she got to my bedroom. She was in my wardrobe flicking through clothes while I sat on the bed, waiting for her to tell me what the big drama was.

'Remember I told you about Daniel from St Anne's having the party next week?'

'Em, yeah.'

'*Everyone* is going.'

'So, what's the problem?' I asked.

'The problem is, Jules . . . well, it's not exactly a problem. More like a revelation that needs some seriously immediate action.' She raised her eyebrows, looking at me like I should automatically know what she was talking about.

I drew a blank.

'Tell me! The suspense is too much,' I cried, playing along.

'Oh, Jules, you're so funny.' She bounced down on the bed beside me and the movement made my neck jerk. I winced. She lowered her voice to a whisper. 'I've figured out who I'm going to have sex with.'

I pulled a shocked face. 'What? Who? Luke?'

'Ugh. Gross. No way. Can you imagine?' She pulled a disgusted face at me before getting up to look at herself in the mirror again.

'So, who is it?' I asked the back of her head.

'Well . . . You know the new guy? Ronan something?' She posed in the mirror. 'The really hot one with glasses.'

'Yeah?' His face flashed in my mind and my stomach did a completely unwelcome roller-coaster flip.

'Well, him. He's totally gorgeous. And I *desperately* need something to wear.'

'Sure, borrow anything you like.' Autopilot.

Yeah, he was good-looking, but she didn't even know anything about him unless she was counting that better-than-everyone attitude that exuded from his every pore. But whatever. I watched her from the bed, pulling out all my clothes. Then she stopped looking in the mirror for a second and turned to me.

'Are you coming to the party? I think everyone is invited.'

I looked at myself in the mirror. Lank hair, pale skin, forehead creased with pain. Crutches. No way.

'Maybe,' I said, playing with my hair and pretending to check for split ends.

'Yeah, I didn't think you'd be interested, but just thought I'd check.' She pulled on my black cashmere jumper and discarded it just as quickly. 'Remember that last time you came to one, and you kissed Caleb?'

I squirmed at the memory. 'Unfortunately.'

'And you took like two days off school to get over the trauma?' Tara posed in the mirror again.

'Well, I wouldn't give Caleb that credit. It was pretty unmemorable actually.'

'I think you should totally go out with him.' Sometimes I didn't think Tara heard a word I said. 'He totally loves you.'

'Yeah, no, thanks. Not really my type.' I shuddered at the thought of him touching me again.

'Not even as a starter boyfriend?'

'I think I'll save myself for someone a bit less . . . Caleb.'

'Next you'll tell me you're getting a purity ring or something.' Tara laughed at her terrible joke.

I didn't think it was ridiculous to want to actually like your first boyfriend. Yeah, I didn't care about the odd kiss with the Calebs of the world, but more than that? I wanted that all-consuming sexual tension, lust-for-days feeling, and I wanted my first time to be with someone, I don't know, special to me. See? Hard evidence of the dangers of watching teen movies.

'Oh, can I borrow some make-up too? Your mum always gets you the good stuff.' She was already rifling through the huge box on my dressing table.

Mum had bought me loads of expensive sets when I'd mentioned it one day – foundations, highlighters, eyeshadows and things I had no idea how to use. She even watched YouTube videos with me to help figure it out, but I always chickened out and wiped it off at the last minute. I couldn't go into school one day with a face full of make-up after spending years wearing none.

I could see the headline: *Girl tries to distract world from her disabled body by wearing make-up*.

No, thanks.

'OK, sure. Wow, Tara, that looks amazing on you,' I said. And it did. Tara had put on the dress Mum bought me for my birthday last year. It was a black, skin-tight minidress and I'd never worn it. I wouldn't even try it on when I opened it. But it looked so good on Tara, even shorter than it would be on me and it showed off her amazing hour-glass figure.

'I think this is the one,' she sang.

'I think it is.' I wished this could have been me. Dressing up in something sexy in the hope that some guy would tell me how good I looked, and actually mean it.

'Right, I'd better go. Hana and all the others are at the park. Charlie has vodka,' she added with a smile. She pulled off the dress and got changed again. It was so easy for her, hanging out all night, no pain the next day, with parents who didn't treat her like she was still a kid. Sometimes I wished she'd just pretend to know how I felt. I couldn't expect her to 'know' because how could she? But it hurt when she wrote me off so quickly.

It was like she'd picked up on my pissed-off vibes, because just before she left she stopped, barely looking up from her phone and asked, 'Oh, do you want to come? To the park?'

'Oh, no, thanks, it's OK. I'm going to get an early night.' I smiled. My stock response. I'd learned to pace myself. By about nine p.m. I was exhausted, and going out made the whole next day so much harder. So 'no thanks' was something I said way more often now.

After she'd gone, I pulled myself up from the bed, picked up each piece of clothing, folded them and put them away.

An emergency . . . I sat down, trying to ease the throbbing in my knees.

I set my laptop on top of me in bed and it burst into life. There was something flashing. The little red pawn on Chess Life.

Someone was inviting me to play. I looked at my profile picture. A Japanese cartoon of a girl who looked a bit like me, blonde hair, big eyes, smiling.

```
Screen name: PRETTYBASIC
ALONELYPAWN has invited you to play a
  game.
```

Accept?
It wasn't like I was doing anything else.

8

Ronan

Nobody had their real face as their profile picture on Chess Life, so I used a picture of Kotov. I was left to my imagination as I scrolled through the candidates to play with before picking someone. I chose 'PRETTYBASIC' because her bio made me laugh.

Awesome at chess. Bored of winning all the time. Probably beautiful, definitely funny. Maybe just Pretty Basic.

I sent her an invitation to play, then closed the lid of my laptop. She probably wouldn't even accept. If 'she' even was a 'she'. For all I knew, they could be 'seventy-five-year-old Colin from Indiana'. Not that it mattered, really.

My phone pinged. It was Luke. I'd forgotten I'd given him my number earlier.

> **LUKE:** Hey, man, we're all heading to Westing Park tonight. Charlie's bringing vodka. Wanna come?

I didn't want to go, not really. But what was the alternative? Sit in my room until it was safe to come out without Mum trying to talk to me again? It could be next week before that happened. As much as I hated the idea, making an effort with these people was really my only option. A year of acting like I was the same as everyone else and then I could leave. I planned to apply to uni courses as far away as possible. Or have a gap year, or just get a job, whatever – it didn't matter, as long as it was away from here.

ME: Sure

I changed out of my uniform, shoved the pawn and a packet of cigarettes into my pocket and pulled my hood up. I paused outside Ciaran's door. It was open. I stared at his bed, perfectly made, imperfectly empty.

I used to sit in there with him all night, playing on the Xbox, or chess, talking shite. I never went in, not any more. But today I did.

His room was still warm. Mum kept the heat on, like he was going to walk through the door at any minute. If she'd wanted to pretend he was still around she should have thrown some clothes on the floor and left the bed unmade. I sat on his bed and scanned the room.

'Are you ever going to beat me, little brother?' he said, with a stupid half-smile.

He was always playing on the Xbox at the same time as playing chess with me. Pissed me off.

'Maybe I've been letting you win this whole time,' I said. He didn't take his eyes off the Xbox when I made my move, taking his knight. Fucking right.

'Shouldn't have gone e3,' Ciaran said, with that stupid smile again.

'What the fuck? How'd you know that?'

'You always go for the easy way out. Now do my job for me, I need both hands for this level. My rook to a4; I'm taking your bishop.'

And he'd beaten me in two moves. Again. Without even looking at the board.

'Fuck you,' I said, chucking a pawn at him. He laughed and caught it. 'Hey, that's my favourite piece you're throwing. Have some respect.' He set it on the bed beside him. 'Here, grab a controller – I need some help with this mission.'

'Can't, I'm heading out with Alex,' I said.

'The stoner?'

'Wise up, man. He's sound.'

'They all start that way,' he said.

I reached under the mattress. Still there, where I hid it. Ciaran's playbook. His bible. I sat on his bed and flicked through the scrawled pages, notes to himself that made no sense to me at all. It was almost full, except for a few blank pages at the end.

I ripped out the blank pages and slid the book back under his mattress.

Westing Park was where the Birch kids hung out. It was on the edge of Ferndale, just down the road from the school.

Everyone at St Anne's used the football pitches at the other end of town. I felt like a traitor walking into Westing.

'Hey, Ro. You came,' said Luke, stating the obvious.

Ro?

I pulled my earbuds out and lit a cigarette. Charlie took a slug of vodka before handing it to Luke. 'Who invited you?' he said.

'*I* did,' Luke said. 'Chill out, man. He's new.' Charlie just shrugged at Luke and started talking to that girl Hana.

'How'd you get round your parents this time?' he asked her.

She rolled her eyes. 'Mum's doing some mental health diploma, so she goes to the library after work and Dad's on nights. I just told them I'd be studying all night too so not to phone and disturb me.'

'Nice work.' It was the first time I'd seen Charlie smile.

Luke's voice barged into the conversation and unfortunately, it was directed at me. 'Where'd you go this afternoon?'

'Just went home, couldn't be arsed with any more school,' I replied.

'Hear that, guys? He's a fucking rebel. Not just a good-looking bastard but doesn't give a fuck either, nice.' He put his hand up to high-five me.

When I didn't put up my hand, Hana laughed.

'OK, I get it. Too cool for high-fives,' he said.

'Yeah, Luke, maybe you could learn something,' Hana said before taking the vodka from him and passing it to Charlie without taking any herself.

I was starting to get the feeling that nobody really liked Luke that much.

'Happy to learn, if it helps me get Tara's attention,' Luke said.

'Seriously, man, give over with Tara. She's not interested. What do they call it again when dudes keep annoying girls for attention?' Charlie asked. 'Oh yeah, *harassment*.'

Luke pretended not to hear him and looked at his phone.

Hana just laughed again. I could feel her staring at me as I took a deep drag of my cigarette. I blew the smoke the opposite way. When I looked back, she was scrolling through her phone and asking Luke where Tara was. I felt in my pocket and found the pawn. I squeezed it into my palm until the grooves dug into my skin. I didn't belong here, with these people I barely knew. But leaving would be weak; it's what the old Ronan did. The only problem was, I didn't really know who the new Ronan was supposed to be.

By the time Tara got to the park it was dark and most of the vodka was gone. We'd got tired of standing and had moved to the kids' playground. Hana and Luke were on the swings and Charlie and I stood awkwardly beside each other in front of them.

'So, what's your deal anyway?' Luke asked in my direction.

Hana looked up at me, and I could feel Charlie's eyes on me too.

'What do you mean?' I asked.

'Like, why'd you leave St Anne's? You get kicked out or something?'

I took a drag of my cigarette and looked at the ground, buying some time. 'Just fancied doing Year Fourteen somewhere else.' I shrugged. It wasn't a lie.

'Yeah, but *why?* Who leaves their school for the last year? Unless you murdered someone or something.' He burst out laughing.

'Leave him alone,' Hana said, saving me. 'You don't have to tell us anything if you don't want to, Ronan. Especially him.' She nodded at Luke, who already looked bored with the conversation.

'There she is,' Luke said. He jumped off the swing and walked in Tara's direction.

'Better have saved me some vodka,' she said, and took the almost-empty bottle from Luke. 'Hey, Ronan.' She stood so close I could smell her sickly sweet perfume.

'I take it you're all going to Daniel's party? *Everyone* is going.'

'Course we'll be there. Not a fucking party without us, is it, Charlie?' Luke said, looking at him as if for approval.

'Nothing better to do,' he replied.

'Well, obviously me and Hana are going,' Tara said.

'Well, as long as I can think of a good excuse to get out of the house,' Hana said with a shrug. She let the swing rock back and forth. 'My parents literally think I should be studying *all* the time or practising the piano.'

'You'll think of something, Han, you always do. So that just leaves you, Ronan. Are you coming?' Tara leaned on my shoulder and flicked her glittery eyes up at me. 'You have to come, to get to know some more people.'

And they were staring at me again, waiting for me to answer.

'Yeah, whatever.' I shrugged.

Luke was going on to Charlie about who was bringing the vodka and beers, and Tara started asking Hana what she was going to wear. I wasn't listening to the conversation at first, just thinking about how I could get out of there without looking like an asshole. I kept hearing the name 'Jules'.

'Seriously, she has the most amazing wardrobe ever,' said Tara. 'Her mum buys her everything. She even has a Chanel bag; I'm going to see if I can borrow it for the party.'

'Is she coming?' Hana asked. 'Is Michael?' She looked hopeful.

'Michael Crawley. Creepy Crawley.' Tara laughed. 'Nah, she never comes to parties any more and he's like her permanent tag-along now so I guess he won't either.'

'Why not?' I asked.

Everyone looked at me. Eyes on me again. I squeezed the pawn.

'She's got some weird disease. Crutch Girl, remember?' Luke cut in. 'Why are you friends with her again, T?' He sat back down on the swing.

It was only a split second, but I noticed Tara wince at Luke's words. I thought she'd say something. Call him out or whatever. But the concern on her face disappeared almost as quickly as it appeared.

'*Luke!*' Hana looked offended on Jules's behalf.

'Because she was my best friend in primary school and it's not like I'm going to stop being friends with her *now*, am I?' Tara said. She said it like she expected everyone to agree with what she was saying. Like it was a completely obvious explanation.

'She's not bad, you know. And she's pretty hot,' said Charlie.

'You think?' Tara looked at him. So did Hana.

'Yeah. That's why I said it.'

'Why don't you fuck her, then? Take one for the team,' Luke said, and Tara snorted.

Something snapped in me. 'What the fuck is wrong with you?' I stared at Luke.

'Calm down, man, I was only joking,' he said.

'Well, it wasn't funny,' I said, louder than I meant to. I don't know what happened. Something just burned inside me when he'd said it.

'Everyone, calm down.' Tara moved into the middle of the group like she was the dictator of what we could or couldn't say. 'Luke, just chill out about Jules, 'kay?'

'Fine, whatever, it was just a joke,' he said.

'See?' Tara said. 'It's fine, so everyone chill the fuck out.'

'I'm out of here,' I said. I was only a few metres away when I heard footsteps behind me, and felt a cold hand slip itself into mine.

I should have done something then. Dropped her hand or told her I wanted to be alone. But I didn't. So I guess everything that came next was my fault too.

9

Juliet

ME: Want to come over?

MICHAEL: Sorry, can't. Mum's making me visit
Gran. Even though she knows how much old
people creep me out ugh! #Prayformichael.
Monday and Wednesday night hell. 😈

ME: Sorry, I forgot. Your gran is so nice
though. You're horrible. I'd make a much
better grandson.

MICHAEL: Probably.

MICHAEL: Oh, and we're going to Daniel's
party, no excuses . . . 😁

I stared at the mirror from my bed. Lank, anaemic hair, joints twice the size they should be and getting harder to hide. But maybe, if I talked to Tara, she'd help me get ready. Maybe she'd be excited too. Maybe . . .

MICHAEL: We're GOING ☺

ME: I dunno . . .

MICHAEL: Holy shit, she didn't say no for once. Can't back out

ME: MAYBE, not yes. And MAYBE it's just to get you off my back. Anyway, say hi to your gran for me and all the other people at the home

MICHAEL: *shudders*

I put my phone down and looked at my laptop. The Chess Life page was still open.

I pressed accept on ALONELYPAWN's invitation, then checked out the bio.

ALONELYPAWN
'Chess doesn't drive people mad. It keeps mad people sane' –
Bill Hartston

Hmm. Not giving anything away, I liked that. I hoped they were good; it had been ages since I'd had any decent competition on this thing.

I made my first move. Trusty e4. Just like Bobby Fischer. He opened all his games with e4. Dad had told me about him a few years ago. Grandmaster at fifteen. Insane.

No counter moves. I closed my laptop. My phone vibrated. Again.

> **MICHAEL:** Have you decided on an outfit? OMG, what am I going to wear? What are YOU going to wear?

> **ME:** Stop it.

> **MICHAEL:** Stop what? This is HUGE. You haven't been to a party in how long?

> **ME:** Crutches, Michael

> **MICHAEL:** Crutches Smutches, you're hot, J-dog, you just need to own it

> **ME:** Sure, maybe I'll get some fairy lights

I pulled myself up in bed and hugged the blanket round me. I was cold. I didn't use that many blankets because if I weighed down the bedcovers it hurt too much to turn over. I was too wide awake to even try and sleep now. And that was the worst – trying to find a comfortable position, finding it, then just lying there until some other part of me got sore and I had to start the process all over again.

I opened my laptop again. 'English Revision' was open behind the minimized Safari screen, perfect people framing the chess game. The little pawn was flashing again. There was a note in the side bar.

ALONELYPAWN: Hi

10

Ronan

Tara had tried to convince me to go back to the park, but when I said no, she said she was tired and wanted to leave anyway, so could I walk her home?

So I did. Like I said, despite what had just happened, I wasn't into making enemies on my first day and I wasn't about to let her walk home in the dark by herself. She lived about a fifteen-minute walk away from the park, in the opposite direction to my house, I think. She was pretty vague about where exactly her house was.

'So, you're coming to the party, right? Unless you want to, you know, do something else, just us?' She tugged on my hoody and made me stop, looking up at me with eyes that seemed to grow in front of me.

'Nah, I don't know, parties aren't really my thing.' I shrugged in the dark.

She burst out laughing. 'What? Are you kidding?'

'No. Why is that so funny?' I nudged her in case she thought I was having a go at her.

It was true though. At St Anne's, me, Alex and Sasha spent most of our time hanging out in Sasha's attic, playing video games and taking the piss out of the people who actually did go to those parties.

'There's nothing else to do in this town; it's literally the only thing that's any fun around here. And anyway, not going would be actual social suicide.'

'So you're telling me that if I *don't* go to this party, my life at school won't be worth living?'

'Won't be worth living at all,' she said, nudging me back.

It felt like I wasn't going to win this one. New school, new start?

'Fine then, I'll come. Wouldn't want to die by social suicide. And I should probably try and make up for getting pissed at Luke back there.' I started walking again.

'Who cares? It's only Luke. I yell at him all the time,' she said.

'Yeah, but it's not your first day at a new school,' I said.

'Suppose not ... It's freezing, isn't it?' Tara hugged herself and leaned into me.

'I don't think it's too bad actually.' I knew what she was doing, and I wasn't in the mood. I pulled my hoody over my head and gave it to her. 'Here, wear this.'

'Ro, you're so sweet.' She put on my jumper. 'It's so big on me,' she said, laughing. It *was* huge on her, my sleeves hung down over her hands and the hood drooped over half her face. She pulled the hood down and pushed her dark hair away from her eyes.

'Thanks.'

'No sweat,' I said.

'I'm OK from here,' she said and pulled my hand to stop me.

'It's fine, I'll walk you home.' I started walking again.

'No, seriously, here's OK. You live in the opposite direction, don't you?'

And before I could say anything else, she stood on her toes and kissed me. Hard, warm, hungry. I didn't hate it. How could I? She was a good kisser. So was I. And I didn't pull away until Ciaran flashed in my head, reminding me why I should just keep everything in my life simple.

'Seriously, let me walk you to your door, it's late.'

'You're such a gentleman.' She twisted the sleeves of my hoody while she said it, like she was thinking about whether or not to say yes.

'Let's go,' I said and started walking again. She didn't object this time.

She was quieter now. No banter, staring at her phone every few seconds.

We turned the corner on to her street. Rows of terraced houses. The street a bit more run-down than most of the other areas in Ferndale.

Tara filled the silence. 'We used to live in this really big house. It was totally amazing, but then my dad left and we had to move here. It's not as bad as it looks.' Her tone had changed. Her confidence replaced by self-doubt.

'I don't think it looks bad at all.' I didn't give her a chance to have to think of something to say to that. 'My dad left too.'

'Oh, really?' She sounded genuinely interested. Who knew I'd spend my first night at a new school bonding with some girl over absent parents?

'Yeah, he pissed off when I was six.' I tried not to sound too angry, but it was hard.

'I was nine. My sister was only one.' She sounded sad when she said it. I probably used to sound sad too, but when he didn't even come back for Ciaran, I felt nothing but disgust.

'Shit.' Tara stopped dead and looked down the street. There was a woman standing in the middle of the road in what looked like a nightdress. She started singing. An out-of-tune, happy warble.

'Ronan, I have to go . . . my mum . . . She's not well.'

She ran down the road towards her mum and I didn't follow her. I didn't know what to do.

'Can I help?' I called down the street.

But she didn't hear me. She was beside her mum now and I just stood there like an idiot, being absolutely no help at all.

'Mum, go back inside, it's after midnight,' Tara said loudly but gently. 'You promised you'd stay inside tonight. Remember you were to phone me if you needed to?'

'I'm sorry. So sorry, Tara.'

'It's OK, Mum. Let's just go back inside. It's so cold.'

Tara led her mum back inside, turning at the doorway to call 'sorry', before giving me a small, sad wave.

I waited until Tara had closed the door before turning and walking back in the direction of my own house.

When I got home, I made a cheese sandwich and went straight to my bedroom. I couldn't get the scene with Tara's mum out of my head. I sent her a message.

ME: Hey, hope your mum is OK. See you tomorrow

TARA: OMG so embarrassing. Sorry you had to see that. See you tomorrow. xxx

ME: You don't have anything to be embarrassed about

TARA: Would you mind not saying anything to anyone. Please? xxx

ME: Won't say a word

TARA: Night, Ronan xxx

I opened my laptop to a notification. PRETTY BASIC had accepted my invitation.

Did I really want to do this? Was I just about to open a Ciaran-shaped floodgate? My heart thudded.

Don't be a pussy.

She'd moved e4. Bobby Fischer. Everyone who didn't know anything about chess moved e4. This was going to be easy.

```
PRETTYBASIC: Hi
```

11

Juliet

ALONELYPAWN: Hey.

PRETTYBASIC: You already said that. My hi was a reply to your hi. But anyway, are you going to make a move or are we just here for conversation?

ALONELYPAWN: Give me a chance! And anyway, it's best to put some thought into your moves you know, Bobby Fischer.

PRETTYBASIC: It's the best opening.

ALONELYPAWN: Says who?

PRETTYBASIC: Says everyone. Maybe you just don't know enough about chess yet. Are you just starting out?

ALONELYPAWN: Something like that.

PRETTYBASIC: Oh dear. How will you feel when you're beaten by a girl?

ALONELYPAWN: I believe in equality so no worse than if I was beaten by Bobby Fischer himself. And how do you know I'm not a girl?

```
PRETTYBASIC: I don't, I guess. But your
    profile pic is of a guy.
ALONELYPAWN: A GUY?? That's Alexander
    Kotov.
PRETTYBASIC: . . .
ALONELYPAWN: Oh dear, this is
    embarrassing. Soviet Chess Grandmaster?
PRETTYBASIC: Obviously I knew that . . .
```

I liked learning new moves, but I wasn't obsessed. I had no interest in learning about all the Grandmasters, or chess history or any of that stuff.

```
ALONELYPAWN: And not that it's any of
    your business, but no, I'm not a girl.
    I'm a boy. A real boy.
PRETTYBASIC: Well, now we've got our
    identifications out of the way, are you
    going to make a move?
ALONELYPAWN: Telling me to make a move?
    How forward of you.
```

Well, this was different. No stilted conversation that just fizzled out into the ether. I didn't have to think about what to say; it was just coming out. It was easy. And I was surprised by how comfortable I was.

```
PRETTYBASIC: Ha. Ha. Well, it might
    be if it was Tinder. But no, it's
```

strictly chess. So don't send me any
dick pics.
ALONELYPAWN: On a chess website?
PRETTYBASIC: It's happened before.

And it *had*! Some random guy who invited me to play a game just sent a dick pic out of nowhere. Mum's always on at me to tell her if something like that happens but it was the middle of the night, and *as if*! I reported him and stopped playing for a while. But the lure of the chessboard was just too strong. So I came back.

ALONELYPAWN: You should be so lucky.
PRETTYBASIC: Move.
ALONELYPAWN: Read it and weep.
PRETTYBASIC: Sicilian defence. You know
your stuff.
ALONELYPAWN: Took me for a fool. Your
first mistake.
PRETTYBASIC: Where are you from?
ALONELYPAWN: A galaxy far, far away.
PRETTYBASIC: How old are you? Please tell
me you're not eighty or something.
ALONELYPAWN: Why? Are you ageist?
PRETTYBASIC: No, just prefer to have
something in common with my chess victims.
ALONELYPAWN: 17, but victim I am not.
PRETTYBASIC: Same. Nice move. Lucky
probably.

    ALONELYPAWN: Luck has nothing to do
    with it.

We played until I could hardly keep my eyes open any more; the codeine had taken hold of me. *That* was the reason I lost. Not because he was any good. It was a total fluke. I'd beat him next time though, for sure. Whoever he was.

Sometimes Michael messaged me in the morning asking my permission to *not* pick up Tara.

MICHAEL: Why are we still giving her lifts to school?

ME: Because we've always gone to school together. Before you it was Mum who gave us lifts, remember?

MICHAEL: OF COURSE I remember, I still bear the shame of being driven to school in the mum-wagon. ☹ ☹

ME: I'll tell her you said that

MICHAEL: She wouldn't believe you. She loves me

Tara barely looked up when I got into Michael's car. She was staring at her phone.

'Hey, good night at the park?' I asked.

'Yeah.' She sighed like she wasn't really listening at all.

'I think we're going to come to this party,' I said. Even I had started to feel a *tiny* bit excited.

Michael almost ran a red light because of the noise that came out of her mouth.

'What? Really?' she said. She was listening now. A look of complete and utter shock took over her face.

'Yeah, I mean, I probably won't stay late or anything. But I think I'm ready to try again after the last disaster.' I kept my eyes on the road as I spoke.

'*Yeah*, you are!' said Michael.

'Maybe you could give Caleb another shot,' Tara said, drawing out his name and reaching in to stroke my hair while she did it.

I batted her off. 'Ugh, no way. Don't be gross. Why do you keep talking about Caleb anyway? Maybe you're the one who fancies him.' I turned to give her a grin, but she didn't return it. She made a face into her phone.

Michael snorted.

'Oh, please, as if. I just want you to be happy, Jules. But if you don't want Caleb then maybe *you* can have him, Michael,' Tara said with an edge to her tone.

'Firstly, Caleb isn't gay. Secondly, ugh. And thirdly, I do not and will not ever take Juliet's dirty cast-offs. I have my eye on someone, anyway.' Michael looked at me with a smirk on his face.

'Oh my God, who?' I couldn't believe he hadn't told me.

'Well, I was doing some Insta research. And do you remember Francis Nowak from that ridiculously boring science trip in Year Twelve?'

'The one where you made me follow that dude from St Anne's about like a weird stalker?' I laughed at the memory. He was obsessed!

'That's the one. And anyway, it wasn't stalking. It was getting close enough for beauty appreciation. *Also* not the point. The point is that he's going to that party. And I have to talk to him.'

I'd almost forgotten Tara was there until she leaned through the middle of our seats and said, 'Oh my God, I forgot to tell you.'

'What?'

'Ronan kissed me last night.' She smiled when she said his name.

'Ronan, as in the guy who started our school *yesterday* Ronan?' Michael looked in the rear-view mirror and then at me for some telepathic moral support. I knew how much he fancied him.

'Yep, that one. And Jules, it was so hot. *He's* so hot. He's definitely the one *and* he said he's coming to Daniel's party,' she said.

'Wow. You don't waste any time.' I laughed but it came out weird.

'What can I say? I just have that effect on guys.'

Michael snorted again.

'What was it like? The kiss? Was it good?'

'It was amazing. You know when the coordination is just right, like your tongues meet at the perfect time and there's no extra saliva?'

No. I told you about the first-kiss saliva-fest and Caleb wasn't bad, but he wasn't great either.

'Yeah,' I said. 'Sounds amazing.'

'It was. I wouldn't be surprised if he asked me to be his girlfriend, and if he did, I'd totally say yes.'

'He'd be lucky to have you,' I said, ignoring Michael's side-eye. But I'd said the right thing; she was practically glowing.

'Thanks, Jules.'

I closed my eyes and let the codeine haze take over the rest of the drive, only waking up when Michael started yelling at other cars.

Michael was extra attentive as we walked to registration. Opening doors and asking me how I was feeling.

There was Ronan. Earbuds in like yesterday, shirt hanging out, clearly thinking he was too cool for the rest of us. He looked up and saw us staring. I looked away. Michael kept looking.

'Will you quit it?' I nudged him.

'How do you stop staring at a face like that?'

He had a point.

'I have some bad news,' I said, sitting down.

'What?' Michael's eyes widened when he looked at me. 'You're dying of the arthritis?'

'Not yet!' I narrowed my eyes at him. 'I'm not even sure if you *can* die from arthritis. But thanks for planting the seed.'

'You've decided not to go to the party? Oh God, please tell me it isn't that.'

'Trying to ignore the fact you sound way more concerned about missing a party than me dying . . .' I rolled my eyes.

'Sorry. I'm just *very* excited about the party.'

'It's actually about Ronan.'

'Do tell,' Michael leaned in, keeping his eyes on Ronan who was doodling on a piece of paper, earbuds still in.

'You know that *thing* Tara was talking about yesterday? And you can't tell her I told you, but she's decided she wants to lose her virginity. To him.'

He gasped and everyone turned to look at us. I willed my face not to turn red, but it didn't work.

'That bitch,' Michael said.

'Sorry, you know what she's like when she wants something. And I'm also pretty sure he's straight, anyway.'

'He could be bi,' said Michael.

'Clutching at straws?'

'Maybe. Time shall tell. I won't give up that easily,' he joked.

At lunch I tucked my crutches under the table to avoid a repeat of yesterday. Michael was facing the door and I could see his eyes following someone.

'Who is it?'

'The most beautiful person to ever grace the planet,' Michael said, sighing.

'Tara's boyfriend?' I smiled.

'Don't you dare!'

I watched Tara stand up and call him over.

'Ronan, over here!' She told Luke to move up so he could sit down. When he got there Tara kissed him on the cheek and glanced around the table. But Ronan's face didn't change. Still pensive, serious, like he was keeping something in.

Takes one to know one, I guess.

12

Ronan

Tara followed me around all day, laughing at things I said when they weren't even funny and talking incessantly about this stupid party. I didn't even know who Daniel was, but if I didn't go it seemed like it would be making a statement. Statements meant attention. And that was the last thing I needed.

I wanted to ask Tara about her mum after last night. But she seemed so OK that it almost made me think that I'd made the whole thing up. Almost.

It could have been since Ciaran that I'd become more perceptive or something. Always looking out for his mood, his body language, the look in his eye, gauging whether or not he was about to snap. It was like it made me more aware of everything.

I downloaded the Chess Life app on my phone. The stuff we were learning in class was just shit I already knew. So, during double maths I signed in.

ALONELYPAWN: Hey, BASIC, you there?

Nothing. In between too-easy algebra equations, I checked my phone. I'd finished the work but kept drawing on the page to make it look like I was still at it. That was the problem with finishing early: they were always dying to give you more.

```
PRETTYBASIC: I'm here.
```

Shit, no way. I wasn't actually expecting her to be online.

```
ALONELYPAWN: What time is it where you are?
PRETTYBASIC: School time. You?
ALONELYPAWN: Same.
```

I'd taken her knight at three a.m. last night. Another night of no sleep. But I was almost used to it now.

```
PRETTYBASIC: On your phone in class? A
  bit of a rebel then?
ALONELYPAWN: Could say the same about you.
PRETTYBASIC: Maybe it's lunchtime where
  I am.
ALONELYPAWN: Is it?
PRETTYBASIC: No. You took my knight. That
  wasn't very nice.
ALONELYPAWN: Who said I was nice?
PRETTYBASIC: Don't you want to be nice?
ALONELYPAWN: Nice doesn't always get you
  places.
PRETTYBASIC: Where do you live again?
ALONELYPAWN: HA! Nice try. First rule of
  chess, never give away pieces for free.
```

PRETTYBASIC: I'm taking your pawn for
  that.
ALONELYPAWN: Tell me something about you
  and I'll tell you something about me.
  Something real, not your favourite
  colour or some basic bullshit.
PRETTYBASIC: You first.
ALONELYPAWN: I used to play chess all the
  time, any spare time I had I'd be
  playing chess, reading about chess,
  dreaming about chess. This is the first
  time I've played since last year.
PRETTYBASIC: Why?
ALONELYPAWN: This is trading pieces, not
  the LONELYPAWN show. Your turn.
PRETTYBASIC: I'm not like other girls.
ALONELYPAWN: Why?
PRETTYBASIC: This is trading pieces, not
  the PRETTYBASIC show 😜
ALONELYPAWN: Touché. Say goodbye to your
  pawn.
PRETTYBASIC: HEY!
ALONELYPAWN: Oh, come on, that was an
  easy steal. Don't you plan your moves?
PRETTYBASIC: I don't plan anything.
  Planning is a waste of time.

She signed out.

*

78

I was halfway out of the school gates at the end of school when Tara came running after me. 'Hey, Ro, you walking home? Wait for me.'

And what was I supposed to say? No? Because it was the first thing that came into my head. I didn't sleep last night, or the night before. In fact, I couldn't really remember the last time I slept properly at all. I could imagine what Ciaran would think of it all. She was just his type – dark hair, perfect teeth, a bit full on. He'd ask me what I was waiting for, to ask her out. But I just didn't fancy her. And I didn't want to lead her on, but after everything with her mum last night something had changed. I don't know, I knew what it felt like to hide your home shit from everyone.

'Yeah, O K.'

'So, are you looking forward to the party?' She couldn't keep her excitement from her face. Her eyes had lit up and she looked desperate for me to say yes.

'Yeah, sure, though I still don't really know anyone.' I shrugged.

'You know me.' She leaned into my shoulder.

'True, it's nice to have at least one friend.'

'Friend?' She stopped and looked up at me.

I'd used the word deliberately. I knew what she wanted, and I was half-hoping only her subconscious would pick up on it and we wouldn't have to have this conversation.

'Yeah. What's wrong with that?' I played dumb.

'I thought maybe you wanted to be more than friends, seeing you kissed me yesterday.'

She had kissed *me* yesterday; I just didn't pull away. Maybe

I should have. But bringing that up would sound terrible. So I didn't.

'I know, I'm sorry. My head was all over the place after the park. I just want to keep things simple, starting a new school and everything. Does that make sense?' I gave her a half-smile, trying to bring some light to what I'd just said. I could see her thinking about it.

'OK, sure, friends it is.' She smiled back but there was a look in her eye, making it obvious she was humouring me.

'Where is the party anyway?' I changed the subject and noticed that we were nearly at her street. Thank God.

'Carron Avenue. I'll get the actual address and message you this week.'

We loitered at the top of her road.

'OK, thanks. See you tomorrow?' I said.

'Yeah, see you tomorrow. Thanks for walking me home, Ronan.' She walked away, turning back after a few steps to give a little wave. Then a few steps more and she turned again.

'Hey, wait a minute, didn't you go to St Anne's? It's a St Anne's party. You'll probably know everyone there.

My stomach lurched. 'Whose party is it again?'

'Daniel – Daniel Evans, do you know him?'

'Yeah. Yeah, I do.'

Shit.

13

Juliet

The end of another day. Michael took my bag for me, and we walked towards his car. I told him about Chess Life. After he'd stopped laughing, he asked about ALONELYPAWN. 'You dark horse. Let me see his profile pic. Is he hot?'

I showed him the picture of Alexander Kotov.

'Oh Jesus, Juliet, that's him? He's about sixty.'

I elbowed his arm. 'No, that's not him. That's some Soviet Chess Grandmaster.' I didn't let on I'd just found that out myself.

'Whatever. If it makes you happy then who am I to judge? Just don't come asking me to accompany you on your trip to Russia to meet the love of your life.'

'He doesn't live in Russia.'

'How do you know?'

'That's not him. Alexander Kotov died in 1981.'

'Well, it could be anyone. You do know he's probably lying about *everything*, you naive little buttercup. But we do have more important things to talk about anyway: the party.'

'Michael, I've got nothing to wear,' I said. He opened the passenger door of his car and slid my crutches into the back seat, holding my elbow as I climbed in.

'*Juliet*. You have more clothes than anyone I've ever met. Ever. You can't use two pieces of plastic as an excuse not to do stuff all your life, you know. And anyway, I think you should be kinder to those guys, taking the pressure off your knees and all. I don't think you give them enough credit.'

'How have you made me feel sorry for my own crutches?' I looked down at them and felt like apologizing.

'Because I'm a master manipulator. Like how I've managed to *still* not tell my mum and dad I'm gay. I mean, Gran is harder to get around, even with her dodgy memory. She keeps putting on *Queer Eye* when I'm there, claiming to fancy Jonathan. A likely story. It would be Karamo if anyone. But yeah, Gran's pretty sneaky, always asking about my love life.'

I loved Michael's gran. She was this tiny little woman with this massive personality. She used to pick us up from school sometimes, drive us *way* too fast into town and give us money for milkshakes while she went into the bookies.

'How is she doing?'

'Old Evelyn? She's OK. Well, not really, I end up telling her the same hilarious stories about five times every visit and even though they're *my* hilarious stories, they don't seem that funny by the fifth time.'

Michael's shoulders dropped a bit when he said it and the usual piss-take tone was gone from his voice. He was so close to his gran. Mainly because his parents worked so much, which is par for the course when your mum's a judge and your dad's a barrister. I could tell he was done talking about his gran when he started playing with his topknot. It used to be his emo fringe but now when he felt uncomfortable his hands went on top of his head.

'Isn't it weird for you that you've come out at school but not at home?'

Michael snorted. 'Coming out at school was a piece of cake. Can you imagine? "Hi there, Gloria, can I make an appointment with Judge Crawley please? Make sure she has a glass of water and somewhere to lie down." One does not simply out oneself to Judge Crawley without *serious* planning.'

'Well, I'll be here for moral support whenever you need me.'

'Damn right, you will. Ten years suit you?' He winked at me.

'I'll pencil you in.'

'Anyway. More pressing matters. The party: we're going, we're going to look hot AF, you're going to pull some random from St Anne's and I'm on Mission Francis Nowak.' Michael sighed like saying the name brought him peace.

'Oh, look, it's Tara.' Michael's voice darkened. I looked out of the window to see Tara hanging off Ronan's arm. She was talking and he was looking at the pavement.

'Christ, she really doesn't waste any time, does she? But her taste is impeccable, I'll give her that.' Michael gazed at them in his rear-view mirror.

'Don't slow down. They'll see us staring.' I tried to slide out of sight, but it hurt too much with my school bag tangled round my feet.

'Oh, please. Tara wouldn't notice me doing the moonwalk naked right now. Look at her with her claws out. It's kind of cute, if you like that predatory, overbearing thing.'

'Michael,' I pleaded. I didn't want to tell him that it wasn't

83

anything to do with them seeing us, but the stupid feeling I got when I saw them together. Was I jealous? No. It wasn't like I fancied him. He was ridiculous, walking about with his earbuds in all the time and his shirt hanging out, like he was better than everyone else.

'*Juliet*. You know I'm right. I'm always right.'

'It's not like she isn't ridiculously pretty,' I said. Now I was looking in the mirror, too; how easy it was for her and how good they looked together.

'A lot of people are pretty. For example, you're pretty and you're not an asshole.'

'Firstly, thanks, but shut up, and she's not an asshole.'

'You'll defend that girl until the day you die.' He rolled his eyes, turned up the music and drove far too fast to my house.

It was like an automatic reaction to anyone saying anything negative about Tara. Even I thought it was strange when it came out of my mouth before I'd even realised what I was saying. But we'd been friends for years. Friends at nursery, friends at primary school, friends at grammar school. I couldn't just throw her under the bus now. And it was weird – ever since the diagnosis it was like I needed her friendship even more. Like her being friends with me was some kind of validation that I wasn't a loser.

I could hear Jeffrey barking before Mum had even come to the door. When it opened, she was holding him so he wouldn't charge towards me.

'Hi, love, good day?'

'Was OK,' I said. I went straight to the kitchen to take some painkillers while Mum tidied round me.

'I got you something today,' she said.

'Oh yeah?'

'It's on your bed.'

Mum kept Jeffrey in the kitchen while I walked upstairs. She always did this now after an unfortunate incident when I was walking upstairs and he crashed right into me, making me fall. I was lucky I didn't break anything, but I'd never felt pain like it.

And there on my bed was a paper bag filled with white tissue paper. I pulled out a dress. Navy with a white Peter Pan collar and tiny diamanté details.

Mum had followed me to my room. 'I just thought it was nice. I know you don't wear dresses that often, but I thought it would look lovely on you. It's the one we saw in the magazine. Remember? You could wear it with tights.'

'Mum, I love it,' I said, holding the delicate fabric to my chest. But she was right. I didn't wear dresses. My knees. My stupid knees.

'And there are shoes too – flats. It's what the model in the shop had on and I just had to buy them as well.'

I laughed. 'Thanks, Mum. There's this party next Friday that I might go to, so maybe I'll wear it then.' It felt like I was trying the words out for size. And I didn't hate them.

'Oh, really? Whose party? Where is it? Will there be boys?' Mum sat down on my bed like she was waiting for gossip.

'Some guy from St Anne's and yes, Mum, there will be boys, real-life boys.'

'Jules, you will be careful, won't you? No alcohol – it doesn't mix well with painkillers. And you know I'll pick you up whenever you want, if you're too tired or too sore or anything.'

'I will, Mum,' I said, quietly. Suddenly any excitement about the party had been swallowed by Mum's words. *Painkillers, too tired, too sore.* Like an ice-cold shower bringing me back to reality.

'Oh, maybe you could wear it to your birthday dinner too?' Mum said with a smile, probably noticing the look on my face. If she was trying to make me feel better, it didn't work.

'Yeah, maybe. I think I'm going to play chess for a while now.'

That did the job. Our code for 'I want to be alone now please'.

Chess was something that was suggested when I refused therapy after I was diagnosed. Well, not chess exactly, but something 'just for me' and 'a hobby'. I didn't *need* therapy; even then I felt the need to pretend I was fine, hoping that one day I'd believe it too.

I clicked open my 'English Revision' file and started scanning through the photographs, imagining looking like those people, thinking about how easy life must be if you looked like that.

```
PRETTYBASIC: Can we make a deal?
ALONELYPAWN: What?
PRETTYBASIC: No lies.
```

I needed something in my life to be real. And I knew how ridiculous that sounded, when the person I was talking to was only as real as messages on a laptop. I needed someone I could spill my guts to. It should be Michael, or even Mum, but neither of them felt right. They had their own versions of me, the ones I'd created, the ones that made me less of a burden. On Chess Life, I was ready to be me. I think.

```
ALONELYPAWN: Deal.
PRETTYBASIC: Do you live in Russia?
ALONELYPAWN: Definitely not.
PRETTYBASIC: Good.
```

14

Ronan

No lies. OK. I liked that, but it was risky. How deep did she want to go? Would the truth scare her away? Of course it would. She'd hate me. But I wanted to know more about her. I needed to. And maybe she'd want to know more about me too. The not-so-shit stuff.

```
ALONELYPAWN: Personal fact-swap again?
PRETTYBASIC: Sure. But how will I know
  you're telling the truth?
ALONELYPAWN: Because we said no lies.
  Remember? And I, for one, tend to keep
  my promises.
PRETTYBASIC: That makes two of us. OK,
  go for it.
ALONELYPAWN: Once I had to go to hospital
  because I stuck Lego up my nose.
```

I was testing to see how serious she was, how deep she wanted to go.

PRETTYBASIC: Unless it was last year then it doesn't count. I want something else, something real.

ALONELYPAWN: You drive a hard bargain. OK. When I was fifteen, I ate so much on Christmas Day that I threw up everywhere.

PRETTYBASIC: That's disgusting. And amazing. I didn't even know you could do that past the age of like five. I'm impressed.

ALONELYPAWN: Thank you, one of my greatest achievements. Now you.

PRETTYBASIC: I have over twenty pairs of trainers.

ALONELYPAWN: That's mental! Why does anyone need more than two pairs of shoes?

PRETTYBASIC: Just into clothes, I guess. And chess. Obv.

ALONELYPAWN: Me too. Obv. One thing we have in common. What are your thoughts on draughts?

PRETTYBASIC: Chess for people who aren't cool enough to play chess.

ALONELYPAWN: Agreed.

ALONELYPAWN: What do you want to be when you grow up?

PRETTYBASIC: What, like I'm five?

ALONELYPAWN: Why not? What did you want to be when you were five?

PRETTYBASIC: A flight attendant. You?

ALONELYPAWN: Nice one. I hate flying though, no control, so high in the air, it's not right.

PRETTYBASIC: You know you're more likely to die in a car crash than in a plane crash?

ALONELYPAWN: Well, statistically yes, I suppose. BUT if you have a car crash there's still this chance that you're going to be OK. A plane crash? No way, you're a goner.

PRETTYBASIC: Well, that's morbid. I like to think of plane journeys as teleporting me somewhere better.

ALONELYPAWN: That's all well and good, if you reach your destination.

PRETTYBASIC: Which I would.

ALONELYPAWN: Maybe. Batman.

PRETTYBASIC: What?

ALONELYPAWN: It's what I wanted to be when I was five.

PRETTYBASIC: Haha, love it. In a class of future doctors and astronauts, you wanted to be part of the Justice League. That's fair though, he IS the best superhero.

ALONELYPAWN: Exactly. Thank you. No real
    superpowers, just this overwhelming
    need for justice to be done.
PRETTYBASIC: So you don't want to get on
    a plane, but you think you could scale
    buildings and take on the Joker?
ALONELYPAWN: Batman isn't real, BASIC.
PRETTYBASIC: Just sayin'.
ALONELYPAWN: Well, now you've destroyed
    my childhood dream, dream crusher, I'd
    like to destroy one of yours. What do
    you want to be now?
PRETTYBASIC: As if I'd tell you so you
    can stomp on it.
ALONELYPAWN: I was joking. I'm
    interested.
PRETTYBASIC: Chess master obv.
ALONELYPAWN: Grandmaster you mean?
PRETTYBASIC: That's the one.
ALONELYPAWN: What happened to the flight
    attendant thing?
PRETTYBASIC: Things change, I guess.

Daniel Evans? Yeah, I knew him. He was one of the better
ones. Not like Alex and Sasha. But they didn't go to those
parties. It used to be because we all thought they were lame
but then they didn't want to go because nobody else wanted to
smoke. Alex and Sasha were my best friends. Until they
discovered weed. I remember when Alex brought it to my

house that night and tried to light up in my bedroom. I told him to get out.

He was pissed at me for that. But I didn't care; it wasn't my thing, never would be. But clearly it was theirs, because they started doing it all the time. Hanging out together, smoking joints, without me. So I started playing more chess with Ciaran, staying in at weekends or hanging out with whoever wanted to do something that didn't involve drugs.

But one night I came back, after hanging out with Daniel and his mates at the park and they were there. In my house.

But they weren't there to see me. Mum had gone away for the weekend with Aunt Sarah, so the house was free. I'd expected Ciaran to have a party or something. I never saw this coming.

They were sitting outside, huddled together round the patio heater, the smell of weed bleeding into the night sky.

'What the fuck are you doing? You can't do that here,' I said.

I don't know if I was more pissed off that they were smoking at my house, or that more often than not those days, Alex wanted to hang out with Ciaran instead of me. They were both really into football and I couldn't give a crap who won the Champions League. All those lifts Ciaran gave us, into town, to and from school, ended up being me and Sasha sitting in the back and Alex and Ciaran upfront commentating on whatever match had been played the night before. It wasn't long before the conversation moved on to other things. Like weed.

'Chill out, Ronan,' Ciaran said. Alex and Sasha laughed.

'You seriously smoking?' I ignored their laughter and looked at Ciaran, joint in his hand. He used to take the piss out of people who smoked weed. 'Wasters,' he said.

'Yeah, why? Going to tell Mum?' And they laughed again.

Mum had told us about Dad. How he was an alcoholic, how he got into drugs. That's why she left him. I swore that day that I'd never touch them. I would never be like him. I just assumed Ciaran thought the same.

I'd gone into Ciaran's room again. I'd found myself doing that a lot recently, just sitting on his bed and thinking, remembering. About him, about school, about how if I'd never been friends with them in the first place then Ciaran wouldn't have met them. Then none of this might ever have happened.

One good thing was that they wouldn't be at the party. Good, because the thought of seeing them and their stupid faces made the rage come back. I didn't realize how hard I was squeezing the can of Coke in my hand. I dropped it on the floor and droplets of Coke leaked on to Ciaran's carpet. I remembered standing outside his door while Mum was on her hands and knees scrubbing vomit from the exact same spot.

'Ciaran, you need to get some help for this, you're drinking too much.'

'I'm not. I'm not even drinking,' he slurred, half on his bed with one leg on the ground, his hand over his face.

'And was that weed I found in your coat pocket?' Mum scrubbed at the carpet angrily, trying to clean the whole thing *away. 'You've got a brilliant future ahead of you; you can't throw it away now.'*

'Fuck off.'

It even made me wince. I saw her stop scrubbing and look at him. She closed her eyes, took a deep breath and started scrubbing again, mumbling something about Ciaran being just like Dad.

He had always been like Dad. Short temper, perfectionist. That's what Mum used to say anyway. And it made sense. That addictive personality. The one that made him start smoking weed before school, the same fucking genetic flaw that made him try something bigger than weed, that made him say yes to Alex and Sasha, that made him go so far that he couldn't find his way back.

I made a list.

Pros
Might make me seem normal
Might see some of the decent people from St Anne's
Alex and Sasha won't be there.

Cons
Seeing all the St Anne's kids will make me think of that
day again. The one where they'd all showed up (except Alex
and Sasha). The day they were all so fucking nice it
lessened some of the pain for a second.

I pulled the pawn out of my blazer and turned it over in my fingers. Ciaran's favourite piece. Controversial. Weakest piece on the chessboard: can't go backwards. But a pawn is also the only piece that can promote to something else. A queen, a rook, a bishop, a knight, anything it wants to be. The possibility to better itself. I think that's why he liked it. He used to tell me that I was a pawn, the weakest piece of the two of us, that maybe one day I'd be promoted to something better. And I knew he was joking, but he was right. Maybe, if I wasn't such a stupid fucking pawn, I could have done something to change what had happened. But I held on to the fact that it was his favourite, that maybe he had some faith, behind the jokes and the impossibly high IQ, that maybe I could be something better.

15

Juliet

I hadn't thought about my future plans for a long time.

Until my diagnosis, being a flight attendant was the big dream. When other kids dreamed about being singers or YouTubers, I dreamed about being thousands of miles off the ground, perfect face, perfect hair, perfect smile, showing people to their seats and serving them drinks from tiny bottles. Mum and Dad took me to Disney World in Florida when I was five, and we got on a huge plane. I was wearing my Minnie Mouse ears and this flight attendant told me how much she loved them. I was fascinated by her. She was so beautiful. The kind of beautiful I'd only ever seen in Disney movies. I asked her had she been to Disney World before and she told me yes, lots of times. Then she told me about all the places in the world she'd been. This long list of countries I'd never heard of. I remember I cried when she had to leave to help other customers and Mum spent the whole flight promising me that we'd go to all those places one day. But it wasn't the places so much. I wanted to be like her, do what she did. But all the standing up, the constant bending, it would just be too much. That's when the dream died. And now, because of PAWN

I thought about it all night. Not in the worst way, but just thinking about what I wanted to be now. The truth was, I'd stopped coming up with things. There'd always be something I couldn't do, something too awkward or difficult. So I just didn't think about it at all. But maybe I should.

'Jules, can I come to your house after school this week to try on clothes for the party?' Tara asked, leaning between the seats of Michael's car on our way to school. Her sweet perfume was extra strong this morning.

'It's weird. The amount of clothes you borrow from Juliet, some people might think you don't have any clothes of your own,' Michael said.

'I don't. Well, none I want to wear anyway.'

'Sure, Tara, that's fine,' I said.

'I'm meeting Ronan after school today so maybe tomorrow or something?' She said his name slowly, like she wanted to taste it. 'Michael, can I have a lift home tomorrow then? To Jules's?'

'Fine. Maybe I'll bring my outfit too, seeing it's turned into some kind of fashion show.'

'Have you decided yet?' I asked him.

'Yes. Well, I have a choice of three outfits, I'll let you cast the final vote. As long as it's the one I like the best.'

'Jules, what are you wearing?' Tara could never stand the attention being on Michael for too long. Or on anyone else actually . . .

'Mum bought me something yesterday. I think I might wear it.'

'Oh, do tell,' Michael said.

'You can see it later,' I told him. I don't think Tara even listened to my answer.

'Oh my God, Jules,' Tara said quickly. 'I walked home with Ronan yesterday and I think he likes me. Like, *really* likes me.'

'Oh yeah?'

'Yeah. I mean, he doesn't say that much . . .'

'Probably can't get a word in edgeways,' Michael said.

'Ha, ha, Michael. No, he's more the strong, silent type: totally broody. Sometimes less is more, did anyone ever tell you that?'

'Pot . . . kettle . . .' Michael sang.

'What?' Tara said.

'And he's going to the party?' I asked. 'Ronan?'

'Yep, we're going together, so I guess it's pretty much a date.'

'Yeah, pretty much,' Michael said.

Tara made a face at him.

Michael pulled into the school car park, driving dangerously close to Luke who was there, on cue, waiting for Tara. I massaged the ache in my neck from all the turning round in the car. Sometimes I thought it would be easier if I sat in the back, but I'm not sure Michael wanted Tara any closer to him than necessary.

'Hey, beautiful,' Luke called to Tara as soon as I opened my door. I tried to get out as fast as I could so I wouldn't have to listen to too much of Luke. But I was still slow.

'What's this I hear about you and Ronan, then?' Luke asked, slinging his arm round Tara's neck. She giggled.

'Do you think Luke knows that Tara just likes the attention and thinks he's as much of a creep as we all do?' Michael said, staring after them and waiting for me to put my school bag on my back.

'Maybe she just doesn't want to be rude and tell him to piss off.'

'It wouldn't be rude. It would be doing the world a favour, and Tara's never had any trouble telling anyone what she thinks.'

'True,' I said. My school bag was heavy today, making my crutches cut into my arms. 'She's a good friend though.' It sounded like I was trying to convince myself.

'I don't know – not sure I've seen any evidence of her being a good friend.'

'Except that time . . .'

'That time she made you a "get well soon" card when you got diagnosed – even though everybody knows that arthritis isn't exactly something you "get well soon" from – and sat with you and watched Disney movies for the afternoon? Even though *you* despise Disney movies? While at the same time your *better* friend scoured the internet for info, had a little weep on your behalf and stole fifty quid from his mum's purse so he could buy you a shitload of sweets to try and make you feel better?' He breathed in, out of breath from his rant.

He was right though. Disney was Tara's thing.

'You know I can't eat those fizzy strawberry laces any more after we made ourselves sick?' I laughed. 'It was worth it though. It did make me feel better. Until the vomit.' I thought about what he'd said about Tara. 'I think she just doesn't know how to react in those kinds of situations – some people are just like that! And do I *despise* Disney movies?'

'You do.'

'OK, I'll give you that one,' I agreed. 'But she was trying. She definitely gets some points for effort.' I shrugged.

Michael sighed. 'I'm going to beat some sense into you with one of those crutches one day, arthritis or not,' he said, opening the door for me and pointing the keys at his car to lock it. 'She's ridiculously lucky to have you as a friend.'

On the way to English I listened to Michael talk about the party, about his game-plan to seduce that guy Francis and all the other thoughts that randomly crossed his mind, of which there were many. I didn't say anything; I just let him talk. Sometimes, when I took painkillers it was hard to think of things to say, like they clouded my brain as well as detaching me from the pain, and it was easier to just listen.

I had double English first and my plan was to switch off completely and give my head a break altogether. I sat at the front, as I do for most classes, so I can get out easily if I need to. I pulled out my chair with my foot and pulled off my crutches, sliding them under my desk. I checked my phone: no notifications.

The door swung open, and Ronan came in. He looked as pissed off as he always did. You'd think if you'd just started a new school, you'd make a bit of an effort to be nice to people. There was just something about him. Like this vibe that he thought he was some kind of king and the rest of us were pawns. He walked straight past my desk, and as he was about to go right past, he looked down at me. Straight into my eyes. And I just stared back because I didn't know what else to do. Looking away would have made a point, or made him think that he made me nervous or something. Which he didn't. So I stared into his glasses and into those stupid blue eyes until he looked away first.

'What was that?' Michael's elbow dug into me as he whispered.

'What was what?'

'Oh, please. The look you just shared with the most beautiful man on earth!'

'I was staring him out. Making him realize that I wasn't just going to fall at his feet because he deigned to look at me.' The colour of my face was probably telling a different story.

Michael didn't say anything else for a second, then burst out laughing.

'Mr Crawley!' Miss Black's voice was shrill. But it still didn't stop Michael from laughing. 'You've had enough chances. If you can't manage to keep your mouth shut for five minutes, I'll have to move you somewhere you can't talk.'

'No, miss, I'm sorry. I was talking about the play.' Still laughing.

I looked at Miss Black, who wasn't looking at Michael any more; she was scanning the classroom.

'Mr Crawley, please switch with Mr Cole. I've given you far too many chances. This way you'll have a whole desk to yourself and won't be able to bother anyone else.'

No. No. No!

'You can thank me later,' Michael whispered and took his bag off his chair.

I glared back at him.

If murder was the same as thank, then yes, I would.

16

Ronan

I was about to look at my phone, to see if there was a notification from PRETTYBASIC, when the teacher made me move seats. As I got to my new desk, Jules gave me this weird angry stare. I'd absolutely no idea what I'd done to piss her off so much. I hadn't even spoken to her, and she couldn't still be pissed of about a bit of lettuce in her hair, could she?

'We're going to spend this period reading through Act One; just see how far you can get, then we'll have a short quiz to see how much of it you retained. OK? Good.' Miss Black sat down at her desk and took out her own phone.

Jules looked away from me as I sat down. Not that I cared. I couldn't be bothered interacting with someone who just looked like she was annoyed at me constantly.

'Please open your books at Act One,' the teacher said with a sigh, as if she couldn't be bothered to be here as much as I couldn't.

I looked in my bag. Maths textbook, chemistry textbook. No English books.

'Jules?'

'Yeah?'

This time she looked at me. And when she did, her eyes narrowed slightly.

'Can I share your book?' I asked.

'Yeah, fine if you *have* to.'

'Well, yeah, I do. I forgot mine.'

Her sleeves were too long and hung down over her pink-nailed fingers. When she shifted towards me, I smelled flowers. Could have been her shampoo. Nice, whatever it was. I'd expected her to smell spicy or something. An angry smell to match her personality.

'Fine,' she conceded, pushing the book closer to my side.

'Thanks,' I said, overenthusiastically. Her brow furrowed at the page.

'Why aren't you reading?' she asked. She was talking to me but staring at the book. I watched her eyes roll at the page, but not-so-secretly at me.

'I know the play. We did it in my last school,' I replied.

I don't think she could have looked more disinterested if she'd tried. Which was pretty unfair when you think about it. There I was, new boy, starting a new school and there she was with her blonde hair and eyes the colour of winter sea – and she makes *me* make all the effort?

'You know the *whole* play?' she whispered, looking right into my eyes this time. Challenging me.

'Yep, pretty much.'

Her eyebrow cocked. 'Good. Then you can answer all the quiz questions. I hate this play.' She let the book go and the pages fanned shut.

'Don't all girls love *Romeo and Juliet*? Isn't it like the greatest love story of all time or something?'

'So just because I'm a girl, I automatically like love stories?' Challenge face was back.

'That *and* your name. Obv.'

Her eyes narrowed again.

'Aren't we both friends with Tara? Does that not mean you should be at least a little bit nice to me?' I asked innocently.

'Because we have a mutual friend?' She looked at me, waiting for me to explain myself.

'Exactly. In case we all end up hanging out sometime. I'd hate to have this awkward tension between us.' I knew I was winding her up. She was clicking the top of her pen now.

'I don't trust you.' She said it like she meant it. And even though it was completely unfair, I kind of liked how upfront she was. I hated all the fake crap, nice to people's faces then a dick behind their backs. At least I knew where I stood with her.

'Why not?' I asked.

I watched as a deep red bled across her face. We both pretended to read the book. 'It's none of your business.'

'None of *my* business why you don't trust me? For *no* apparent reason?'

'Just call it a sixth sense.' She shrugged.

'I won't. I'll call it prejudice.' She wasn't getting away with it that easily.

I got a shocked face this time. 'Are you kidding me?'

'Not at all. You can't just hate someone for no reason. I'm guessing you have a reason, and you just don't want to tell me.' I tried to look offended.

'I never said I hated you.' She was backing down. But she was still red. And flustered. Flicking through the pages. 'You just walk around like you're better than everyone else, dropping salad on people, acting like you don't care about anything or anyone.' She squeezed her eyes shut as if it would take back what she'd just said.

But there it was again. Judging. Without knowing anything about anything. I squeezed the pawn in my pocket.

'For the record, the salad situation was clearly an accident, and as far as I remember, I said sorry for that. And maybe I *don't* care? Have you ever thought about the fact that not *everybody* cares about the next stupid party?'

I pushed the book towards her, and she just stared at me open-mouthed.

'Question time!' Miss Black called. She put down her phone. I stared at the desk, but I could feel Jules looking at me.

Miss Black stood up, holding the play in one hand. 'Which character claims to hate peace?'

Tybalt.

'Anyone? Come on – that's easy. Rebecca?'

'Tybalt.'

'Yes, correct. Good start. Come on, people, a bit more enthusiasm, please.' She clapped her hands and stood up.

'Who stops the street battle? Juliet?'

Prince Escalus.

'I don't know,' Jules said, staring at the desk and clicking her pen again.

'If you'd been reading at all, Juliet, which I suspect you weren't, you'd know the answer is . . . Anyone?'

Jules visibly shrivelled in her seat, moving her feet and nudging the crutches beneath her.

'Kanye West,' I said, loud enough for everyone to hear. And then they were laughing at me.

'Kanye West? I don't know what play you've been reading but it certainly isn't this one. You know I despair of you lot sometimes,' Miss Black said.

I turned to see Jules staring at me with an almost-smile. I tried not to smile back – and failed. Miss Black moved on. But now everyone else had started taking the piss and she was getting more and more frustrated. When the bell rang, I grabbed my bag and stood up. I noticed Jules's crutches poking out from under her desk again. I bent down and picked them up for her, leaning them against her desk before walking out of the door.

17

Juliet

'Tell me *everything*.'

Michael appeared behind me, making me jump.

'About what?'

He held my crutches and waited for me to put my bag over my shoulders.

'About *what*? Maybe about the fact that for the whole of English you were talking to the hottest guy at school. About *what* indeed.'

I shrugged and took my crutches. 'He's a jackass. Just like I thought he'd be. I don't know why you and Tara like him so much; she deserves much better.'

Michael snorted and held open the door. 'I know exactly why we like him so much. What did he say anyway? What's got you all hot under the collar?'

'I'm not hot under anything, I just don't like him. I'm allowed not to like people.'

'OK, OK, I get it. You fancy him too, that's fine. I'm prepared to fight to the death. Hunger Games style.'

Usually, Michael could make me laugh in any situation.

But not today. I don't know what it was about Ronan that made me *so* angry. Maybe it wasn't him, just everything he stood for. Poster-boy for the elite.

'I *don't* fancy him. He's an arrogant tease who just walked into our school with his perfect life and perfect face, and is probably going to go out with the perfect girl. Walking around rubbing it all in. Not everyone can be so damn lucky.'

Michael put his hands on my shoulders and stopped me stabbing my crutches furiously on the ground.

'There it is,' he said gently.

'There *what* is?'

'The truth. Well, *your* truth anyway, which I totally get. And that small person rage that turns you into this mad little fireball.'

'Shut up.'

'Maybe you need to bang someone to get rid of all these angry vibes.'

'I haven't even done more than kiss anyone yet!'

'Who says you need to do things in order? I saw Harry checking you out earlier too.'

'What? No way; he was probably checking out my crutches, like everyone else.'

'Definitely not. He was practically drooling. It wasn't the crutches that gave him a boner.'

'Michael!' A laugh caught me off guard.

'What? He *probably* had one.'

Michael shrugged and smiled to himself, then snapped out of it as another thought crossed his unfiltered mind. 'Are you going to tell Brian and Melanie about your conversations with your online pervert?'

I bumped him with my shoulder. 'How dare you! And no, my parents don't need to know anything about my new friend, thanks.'

Michael snorted. 'Friend.'

They really didn't need to know how excited I get when he's online, how he makes me laugh more than anyone. How I'd never felt like this about anyone before. And it sounded insane, given he could be on the other side of the world or a total catfish, but I couldn't help it. He made me feel like more than a pair of crutches.

'Oh, well, that's no big deal. In fact, you're right not to tell them. I'm sure they'd discourage you from talking to an online pervert as much as I do.'

'But you don't really.'

'Only because I love you and it makes you weirdly happy.' Michael grinned. 'Oh, and tell Melanie I would love to come to your birthday dinner tomorrow. Sorry I didn't RSVP yet. So rude. Especially because she asked me weeks ago. But you should take me as a cert anyway.'

'Oh my God, she gets so excited about birthdays. I've told her I don't want a party a million times.'

'I don't think dinner with me and Tara is exactly a "party",' Michael noted.

'Ugh.'

'Ugh nothing. Your mum is fabulous, even if she does seem to think you're turning twelve. I'll see you tomorrow, birthday girl. Don't think just because *you* don't seem to care about the fact you're turning *eighteen* that nobody else does.'

'You're all insane.'

As soon as I got home that day I went straight upstairs to my laptop.

```
ALONELYPAWN: Want to know something
  really awesome?
PRETTYBASIC: Always.
ALONELYPAWN: I was Grandmaster at seven.
PRETTYBASIC: Oh yeah? Then how come your
  name isn't listed?
ALONELYPAWN: It is.
```

Five minutes later he sent a document. A list of chronological Chess Grandmasters, his username, ALONELYPAWN, at the top.

```
PRETTYBASIC: Ha, very funny. You could
  have at least put your real name to try
  and make it look more convincing.
ALONELYPAWN: And give away my secrets?
  Maybe it is my real name. Maybe you've
  just insulted my name by doubting its
  authenticity.
PRETTYBASIC: You're right. I'm sorry.
  I shouldn't be so narrow-minded.
ALONELYPAWN: Agreed.
```

```
PRETTYBASIC: Are you ready to lose?
ALONELYPAWN: Try me ;)
```

I was glad I was alone. And that I couldn't see my mirror from where I was sitting. Because there was a ridiculous smile on my face.

18

Ronan

Maggie's Milkshake Bar. That's where Tara wanted to meet. She said she needed to get out of the house. I didn't ask her why, but I guessed it was something to do with her mum. I'd asked her if anyone else was going but she said Hana and Charlie were busy and that it would be nice for us to have a chat.

I couldn't argue with wanting to get out of the house. Before Chess Life it was something I wanted to do a lot too.

I told her I had some homework to finish and that I'd come after. I was actually playing Chess Life. Beating BASIC obviously.

She was close this time. Well, not *close* exactly. But I liked the way she gave me an actual challenge.

I walked into town, wondering where this place was. But you couldn't miss it. A huge neon pink 'Maggie's' sign lit up the street and there were fairy lights round the doorway.

I found myself checking my phone. Just to see if BASIC had sent me any more messages. But there was nothing. Just one from Tara telling me she was running late. Something to do with her hair. And one from Aunt Sarah.

The 'offer' she was talking about was packing up my shit and moving in with her across town. Then what? Mum was alone? No, thanks. I think I'd hold on to whatever scraps of family I had left, even if those scraps were Mum.

The choice of milkshakes here was insane. So many ridiculous flavours. What was wrong with the classics? I ordered strawberry and sat down in a booth. Then, I took out my phone and invited BASIC to another game.

19

Juliet

> **MICHAEL:** Apparently Maggie's have released an anniversary flavour . . .

Over the last year Michael had challenged himself to try every single flavour of milkshake in Maggie's. He'd tried all one hundred and seventy-two. He was a strange boy.

> **ME:** Yeah . . . And?

> **MICHAEL:** You KNOW what that means

> **ME:** But I'm in sweatpants and a hoody!

> **MICHAEL:** Sweatpants are hot

> **ME:** I know what you're doing

MICHAEL: Pick you up in fifteen. I'm buying.
Birthday-eve present

ME: Fine

I thought about getting changed, but it felt like way too much effort, so I just pulled my hair into a ponytail and made my way downstairs.

'Going to Maggie's, Mum,' I called.

'Have fun, love.'

Michael was already at my house. It had not been fifteen minutes.

'What speed were you driving?' I said when I opened the door. I stepped outside and Michael closed the door behind me.

'Not fast enough. My mouth has been watering since I heard about it. Let's go!'

Michael threw my crutches into his car, and we drove way too fast to Maggie's despite me half-heartedly begging him to slow down.

Autumn was my favourite season. Especially in Ferndale. Most of the streets were tree-lined and when you were going at a *normal* speed, or got stopped by the train line and could actually look at it properly, there was something almost magical about it. But when Michael wanted a milkshake, I barely had time to look out of the window before we were in the village one-way street, and he was yelling at someone to hurry up and move so he could park.

'Oh my God, I know it's kind of hard for you and all, but can you please hurry up?' Michael waved me over to the door of Maggie's that he was holding open.

'I hope the anniversary flavour is mushroom.' I tried to go a bit faster but by this time of night my arms were always tired from holding myself up all day.

'You're a monster,' he said.

He waited until I got through the door then practically ran to the counter.

'*Autumn nights*: pumpkin, cinnamon, ginger, double cream. Oh my God, J, I think I'm in love.' Michael ordered the special and my usual – triple chocolate brownie with salted caramel sauce – and we looked around for a seat.

Then I saw him. Ronan Cole. And all of a sudden, I wished I'd made more effort with my clothes. Not that I cared, but something in me had definitely softened towards him since the 'Kanye' comment. I mean, he still totally loved himself obviously, but maybe there was a tiny bit of OK-ness there too.

He was just sitting there, sipping a milkshake. Alone. It's weird how cheekbones get way more pronounced when you're sucking through a straw. Maybe it wasn't weird. And oh God, Jules, stop staring!

20

Ronan

I heard my name and looked up. That guy Michael was standing beside me and downing a milkshake. No straw, just full-on drinking it from the glass. And beside him, Jules.

'Hey.' I glanced up at them before looking back at my phone.

'Hey,' Michael said and sat down across from me. For a second, I wondered if Jules had brought Michael over to have a go at me. He was at least twice my size, height and weight. I'd have no chance if he wanted to crush me. But I wasn't getting those vibes.

I looked up to see Jules standing awkwardly beside the table, giving Michael some serious side-eye.

'You sitting down?' I slid over into the corner so she could get in. And I guess she didn't know what else to do, because she did.

'Waiting for someone?' Michael managed to detach himself from the milkshake just long enough to ask before drinking the last few drops.

'Tara's on her way,' I said and looked at my phone. I could feel Jules's eyes on me.

'Well, we can keep you company until she gets here, can't we, J?' Michael looked at Jules and the angry look from earlier was back. At least it wasn't directed at me this time.

'So, how are you enjoying Birch so far?' Michael was looking at me like I was an interview candidate. He waited enthusiastically for an answer.

'Yeah, it's fine,' I said and didn't elaborate.

'How come you left St Anne's?'

'Michael!' Jules cut in. 'You can't just ask that.'

'Why? In case it's something shady?' He smiled at her and looked back at me. 'Is it? Are you a criminal?'

'I don't think going to a school ten miles away would be the best hiding place for a criminal. Do you?' This time I turned to Jules, who shrugged.

'Sounds like something a criminal would say,' Michael said. He studied me then stood up. 'I'll continue this investigation shortly.' He disappeared in the direction of the bathroom.

And then it was just me and Jules.

I stopped looking at my phone. BASIC hadn't accepted my game yet anyway.

'Kanye West?' she said, trying not to smile.

'You're welcome. You come here often?' I asked, wondering how someone managed to look so cute in sweatpants and a hoody.

'Yeah. Michael's obsessed. He's tried every single flavour.' She rolled her eyes. 'I think milkshakes are overrated, but they do great waffles here,' she whispered, her cold breath making the hairs on my neck stand up. 'Don't tell Michael.'

'I'm good at keeping secrets,' I said and turned my phone

face down. Why? In case she saw Chess Life and thought I was a loser? In case Tara sent a message and she saw? Why would that matter?

'Sorry about him, by the way.' She nodded her head in the direction of the bathroom. Then said 'Michael' to clarify.

'What? Why?' Had I looked pissed off at him or something? I hadn't meant to, if I did.

'Asking you about St Anne's. He can be pretty blunt sometimes.' She searched my face for my reaction.

'No, it's grand!' I probably said it too enthusiastically. I would just hate anyone to think I was pissed off at him. He seemed really nice.

She smiled at my over-the-top reply.

'I guess I just find it hard to be open with people I've just met.' I shrugged and took a sip of my milkshake, recovering my nonchalance.

I watched her pull her sleeves over her hands and wrap them around her milkshake glass. 'Yeah, I get that. I'm kind of like that too, except my lack of openness even extends to people I know pretty well.' She rolled her eyes and gave a little laugh.

'Did you just trump my character flaw?' I raised my eyebrows at her.

'Ha! Who said it was a flaw?' She stuck out her tongue and when she did, her nose scrunched up.

'Are you going to this party everyone's been talking about?' I asked.

'I think so. Michael's dying to go so, yeah, I think I'll be there. You?'

'Yeah, Tara won't stop talking about it.' I hadn't meant the sigh to come out when I said it.

'Well, there she is.' Jules nodded towards the door and sure enough, Tara was there, wearing a miniskirt and trainers.

I hadn't even noticed the bell go.

21

Juliet

'Oh, hey, Jules.' Tara stood beside our table, twisting her hair in her fingers and half-laughing when she said it. But her eyes weren't smiling. 'What are you doing here?'

'Michael wanted to try the anniversary flavour.' I pulled my crutches out and stood up just as Michael approached, begging him with my eyes to hurry up. I hated that I felt like I had to explain myself to her. It was that thing again. Less-than.

'Is he still doing that?'

'What?'

'That weird challenge thing, where he drinks like a million milkshakes?' She laughed and looked at Ronan, expecting him to laugh too, but he didn't. He took a sip of his own milkshake instead.

'No, they just brought out an anniversary flavour and he wanted to try it. So did I, actually.' A pathetic attempt at sticking up for Michael.

'Cute.' Tara slid into my space beside Ronan and Michael appeared behind me.

'You ready, J?'

'Yeah. See you both later,' I said.

Ronan looked up at me then, holding up his hand in a half-wave with a half-smile to match.

'Yeah, bye,' I said *again* because I hadn't left quickly enough and it felt like I needed to say something else. *So awkward.* I felt heat rise in my face.

I turned to say something to Michael, but he wasn't there. He was already at the door, holding it open for me with a knowing smile on his face.

'I thought you didn't like him,' Michael whispered as I walked under his arm and out of the door.

'What? Who?' I enjoyed the feeling of the autumn air cooling my still-hot face.

'*Who?* Ronan, obviously.' Michael looked at me like I was insane. 'You two looked *very* cosy.'

'I don't like him. What are you talking about? You ditched me with him. What else was I going to do? Sit in silence? Move seats?' It came out more frustrated-sounding than I'd meant. And only because I was trying to work out the thoughts in my own head.

'Oh, looks like I've hit a nerve . . .' Michael laughed as he opened the passenger door to his car and I got in.

'You have not!' I folded my arms, ignoring the twinge in my elbow.

I side-eyed Michael when he got in.

'One more thing.'

'Michael!'

He held up his hand to silence me. '*The lady doth protest too much, methinks.*' Then he turned up the music so loud he couldn't hear me protesting even more.

22

Ronan

It was weird. I didn't get any of those angry vibes from Jules at all just then. When she first came over it looked like she was trying to act pissed off, but then that completely disappeared. I realized I wanted her to stay. But I chickened out of saying anything when Tara got there. I'd known girls like Tara before: unpredictable, dangerous if you were on the wrong side. I kept my mouth shut, like a coward.

I wanted to know more about Jules, why she had to use crutches, what she liked to do in her spare time. There was just something about her that got me intrigued. Maybe it was the colour of her eyes, that blue-grey that you could drown in, or the fact she just admitted that she found it hard to open up to people like I did. I don't know what it was, but what I did know was that even when she was acting all pissed at me, I didn't feel on edge when I was around her like I did with Tara or Mum or any of the other people at Birch. And it felt good.

23

Juliet

I woke up to my phone buzzing with a thousand messages from my aunts and cousins, wishing me happy birthday. I read them through in my half-asleep blur, looked around my room and only then did I notice something different. There was a sea of pink, gold and rose-gold balloons all over the floor. The same way this day had begun every year since I was five. This year, eight huge helium gold balloons spelled out EIGHTEEN. Mum usually goes with a colour theme. Last year was pastels. Mum loved birthdays and made so much effort. But for me, it just made me think of how happy Mum and Dad must have been when I was born. How happy they were for the first eleven years when they thought I was just a normal kid. Until I wasn't.

When the pains started, nobody knew what they were and we ignored them for ages, until they got so bad that going to see the doctor was the only option. Months of tests, needles and scans. And finally, the diagnosis that made the colour drain from Mum's face like I'd just been handed a death sentence. She'd held my hand so hard and then let go almost immediately, like she thought holding my hand was hurting me too much. That was the day I ruined her life.

And I'm not saying this as some kind of martyr. I know it's not my fault that I got sick, but Mum was – *is* – this amazing artist. She doesn't paint any more, but back then Mum talked all the time about going to art college. It was a huge deal. Her parents had always wanted her to get a 'proper job' and put her off going to art college after school, so she said when I was out of primary school and a bit more independent, she would go. The plan was that she would quit her job and Dad would support us both. She was so excited. But then I got my diagnosis and it was all hospitals and research and me, me, me. That was the end of art college, the end of something she'd dreamed about all her life. All because of me.

A reminder flashed on my phone: HOSPITAL. Mum had wanted to reschedule, but I knew she'd taken the day off work for my birthday already and if I changed it, she'd have to take another day off. So, the hospital on my birthday it was.

Mum burst into my room holding two cups of tea. She set one down beside my bed and looked like she was going to cry.

'Happy birthday! I can't believe you're eighteen. Where did the time go?'

I pulled myself up in bed, tongue in teeth. I smiled. 'Thanks, Mum.'

'Brian! She's awake! Bring in the presents,' she called excitedly towards my door.

I could barely see Dad's face behind all the boxes, wrapped up in pink and gold paper, every single one tied up with a bow.

I swallowed the painkillers that had appeared beside my bed.

'Do you like the theme this year?' Mum asked.

'I love it.'

'Happy birthday, love,' Dad said, putting the presents at the bottom of my bed. 'You know, when I was eighteen, I got so drunk I threw up all over Nan's living room. Ah, the memories.' He smiled.

'Your father is an idiot,' Mum said. 'Now open.'

Mum helped me unwrap the presents. Boxes and boxes of amazing clothes and shoes and perfume. All the clothes were ones I could actually wear: trainers, sweatpants, hoodies, T-shirts. No skirts or dresses, jeans, or jackets that were stiff around my elbows. It meant so much, I had to take a deep breath, forcing the tears that were threatening to escape to go back where they came from.

'Mum, Dad, I love them, thank you,' I said quietly so my voice wouldn't crack.

Mum kissed the top of my head. 'I still have the receipts if you want to take anything back.' She walked towards the door, followed by Dad. 'I've made pancakes, by the way, so I'll see you downstairs when you're ready. Are you sure you don't want to take the whole day off school?'

'No, Mum, it's fine. Michael's probably on his way already.'

As soon as they'd left my room, I opened my laptop. My stomach fizzed when I saw it. The little pawn notification. I had messages. From him. At three a.m.

PRETTYBASIC: Why were you up so late?
ALONELYPAWN: I don't really sleep any
  more.
PRETTYBASIC: That sucks. My sleep isn't
  great either.

ALONELYPAWN: Maybe we should start a
    middle-of-the-night club.
PRETTYBASIC: And have midnight feasts?
ALONELYPAWN: Are you 12?
PRETTYBASIC: Actually, no. I'm 18.
ALONELYPAWN: You said you were 17. Are
    you like one of those ageing celebrities
    who like to knock years off their age?
    Except in reverse?
PRETTYBASIC: Ha, no, it's my birthday.
ALONELYPAWN: HAPPY BIRTHDAY, BASIC!! ☺
PRETTYBASIC: Thank you. Because it's my
    birthday, does that mean you have to do
    what I say?
ALONELYPAWN: Maybe. For today, your
    wishes are my command.
PRETTYBASIC: Can you play/chat around one
    o'clock?
ALONELYPAWN: Sure. Why?
PRETTYBASIC: I have somewhere I need to
    be. But I'd rather my mind was here.
ALONELYPAWN: Done. And as much as I wish
    I could stick around and chat to you
    all day, I better go, school calls.
    Happy birthday again, BASIC.
PRETTYBASIC: Thanks, PAWN.

Half an hour later I made my way downstairs to Michael in
the hall wearing a party hat. 'Happy birthday!'

'You came for breakfast!' I said, smiling.

He pulled me into one of his hugs at the bottom of the stairs, crutches and all. He released me.

'Of course I did; I love Melanie's pancakes. And your little birthday-denial game doesn't work on me, J. I love birthdays as much as your mum. Oh, I tried to pick up Tara super early, like we'd arranged, but she didn't answer her phone. Good thing, if you ask me.'

'Michael!' I tried and failed to sound angry.

'OK, OK, I'll try and be nice because it's your birthday and you've agreed to go to the party with me next Friday.'

'*Did* I agree?' I loved to wind up Michael.

'Yep. Can't change your mind now. I smell pancakes – let's go!' He walked towards the kitchen. I checked my phone – no message from Tara. I followed Michael and watched him hoover three pancakes, drowned in maple syrup, with a side of chocolate-chip muffin. The spread was amazing. Mum had really gone all out. But I'd lost my appetite, my mind distracted by the lack of a message from Tara.

When Michael had finished, he grabbed a croissant to take with him and we walked to his car. He opened the passenger door and took my crutches from me, sliding them into the back. There was a little wrapped box on my seat.

'Michael.' Sometimes the little things Michael did made my breath catch in my throat.

'What? It's not like I'm *not* going to get my best friend a birthday present.' I picked it up and sat down. I pulled off the ribbon and tissue paper and looked at the box. Swarovski.

'Michael, this is too much.'

'Will you shut up, J? Cassandra and David are loaded.'

That was true. Michael lived in one of the biggest houses in Ferndale. You couldn't even see it from the road. It had huge gates surrounding the whole estate and CCTV cameras everywhere.

I opened the box. Inside was a sparkling cuff bracelet with the Wonder Woman symbol on it.

'Do you like it? I was going to get you this really awesome ring, but I remember you'd said that your fingers get sore sometimes, so I went with the bracelet ...' Michael was speaking so fast. I cut in to stop him.

'I love it! But Wonder Woman?'

'Seriously, J, you don't get it?'

'What do you mean?'

'You have to go to school on crutches. It's hard enough being a teenager at Birch without something like *that* to deal with. Getting up every day and coming to school makes you *my* Wonder Woman. And besides, I thought it would be the perfect accessory for the party.'

I slid it on to my wrist, leaned over and gave him a hug, inhaling deeply to stop the lump in my throat growing.

24

Ronan

When I saw the empty wine glass in the kitchen the next morning, a Sunday flashed in my mind. I don't remember which one. There were so many like that.

'Is that wine?' I watched as he took a slug from a bottle.

'Yeah. Want some?'

'No, thanks. It's two o'clock. Isn't it a bit early? We've got school tomorrow.'

'Who cares? School is a piece of piss, not like they're going to take away an unconditional offer anyway.'

'So you're going to practise becoming an alco, so you fit in when you go to uni?'

'Maybe. Or maybe it's a cry for attention because I miss our long-lost father.'

'Mum will love that.'

'Bet I can still beat you when I'm wasted,' he said. 'Play me.'

It was the first and probably only time I didn't want to. He must have had something else to drink before the wine; I could tell by the slur of his voice and the edge to his tone.

'Fine.'

And I'd like to say I wasn't trying when he beat me in five minutes, but I always tried.

'Fucking right. Hey, you seeing Alex tonight?' he asked.

'No, why?'

'No reason. Can I have his number?'

'Sure.'

I gave it to him.

I'll regret it until the day I die.

25

Juliet

I met Mum outside straight after lunch, before she could come into reception.

'Hey, birthday girl, you ready?' She smiled and looked at her buzzing phone.

'Is that work?' I asked.

'I'll phone them back later,' Mum said and took my bag from me. 'Anything exciting happen at school?'

'Not a thing.'

'Well, once we get this over with, you can relax and enjoy your birthday.'

Once *we* get this over with. She was right, it was a 'we'. Since the diagnosis it went from being a 'me', to a 'we'. My pain meant people (Mum and Dad) doing more for me. Appointments meant time off work, new bathrooms and broken dreams. I would give anything for it just to be 'me'.

'Yeah.' I smiled. My heart raced as we took the familiar route, through town, on to the motorway, off at the first junction. I wished it was further away. I knew what was coming. All the attention on me, my disease, needles that slid under my skin into veins that wouldn't take any more, squeezing my eyes shut so hard they hurt and wishing so bad that I could have someone with me. So it could be 'we' without everything that came with it.

'Want me to come in?'

'No, Mum, I'm fine. It won't be long, just a chat and then some blood tests. Easy.' Just part of my long, boring routine: physio every two weeks, sometimes more, blood tests at the GP every four weeks, an appointment at the hospital every three months to discuss my medication with the rheumatologist and have an examination (today). Every six months or so I'd have steroid injections. Needles that slid under inflamed kneecaps, making me scream, and two days off school for bed rest. I told Mum those injections didn't hurt any more. I did my best smile. The one that made her smile back and nod. She looked at my wrist, where the light caught the diamanté cuff that had escaped from under my sleeve.

'What's that?' She nodded at it excitedly.

'Oh, just something Michael got me for my birthday.'

I opened the door and got out of the car before she could ask to see it.

Right then I didn't feel like Wonder Woman at all.

26

Ronan

I tried to keep my head down all morning. Wishing the time would hurry the hell up. The way it used to with Ciaran. How we'd lose hours, and it would feel like minutes. I didn't want to talk to anyone, couldn't be bothered with the mundane shit they were talking about, like any of it actually mattered. BASIC was the only person I wanted to talk to. One o'clock – she needed me. And I was going to be there.

When I got to class, there was an empty seat where Jules was supposed to be. And I surprised myself when I felt mildly disappointed. When I saw her at Maggie's, it was like I saw a different side to her. A side that didn't *totally* hate me.

'Please take out your books and read Act Two.' Miss Black barely looked up. She sat down and opened a book at her desk. I took out my phone. One o'clock.

```
ALONELYPAWN: Hey, I'm here.
PRETTYBASIC: :)
ALONELYPAWN: I'll take that to mean
  you're happy to 'see' me.
```

PRETTYBASIC: How'd you crack the code?

ALONELYPAWN: I'm very smart. Why am I here?

PRETTYBASIC: I just wanted some company.

ALONELYPAWN: Where are you?

PRETTYBASIC: An appointment. Hate waiting. Thought we could play a game?

ALONELYPAWN: Your wish is my command, birthday girl. An appointment on your birthday? A fun appointment? I see you've gone e4 again, Bobby Fischer.

PRETTYBASIC: A fun appointment? What IS a fun appointment? Going to a brothel?

ALONELYPAWN: I wouldn't know. Would you? Are you at a brothel?

PRETTYBASIC: No, and not a fun appointment sadly.

ALONELYPAWN: Shall I keep guessing?

PRETTYBASIC: I'm at the dentist. I hate the dentist. Even the smell of the place makes me feel sick with nerves.

ALONELYPAWN: Shall I distract you?

PRETTYBASIC: Yes, please. Tell me more about you. How'd you get into chess?

I scanned the room. Miss Black still hadn't looked up. I could be watching shit on YouTube right now and she wouldn't even notice. I hadn't told anyone at Birch about Ciaran. As far as anyone knew I didn't have any brothers or sisters at all. And here I was, about to tell some stranger on the internet. But I guess it made sense. It was easier than real life.

ALONELYPAWN: My brother taught me.
PRETTYBASIC: Ah, so you have a brother.
  Older or younger?
ALONELYPAWN: Older.
PRETTYBASIC: Is he better at chess?
ALONELYPAWN: It might be hard to believe
  that ANYONE could be better than me,
  but last time I checked, yes.
PRETTYBASIC: Do you get on with him? I
  don't have any siblings (boohoo).
ALONELYPAWN: Better than anyone.

I could see where this was going. A conversation that I wasn't ready for.

ALONELYPAWN: Not watching the game,
  BASIC. Say goodbye to your bishop.
PRETTYBASIC: HEY!
ALONELYPAWN: Not my fault you're a
  Woodpusher.
PRETTYBASIC: WEAK CHESS PLAYER?
ALONELYPAWN: You googled, didn't you?
PRETTYBASIC: Obv.
PRETTYBASIC: What about your parents? Do
  you get on with them?

ALONELYPAWN: It's just my mum. And no,
not really. I mean, I used to, she used
to be different. But this year
she's . . . I don't know. I don't really
know who she is any more. Do you get on
with your parents?

PRETTYBASIC: Yeah. They're really great.
Kind of treat me like I'm still a kid.
But I let it slide cos I'm not exactly
who they want me to be . . .

ALONELYPAWN: Who do they want you
to be?

PRETTYBASIC: Someone better, I guess.

ALONELYPAWN: I don't know, you seem
pretty great to me.

PRETTYBASIC: :) Thanks, but it's easy to
say that over a screen.

ALONELYPAWN: This is the part of the
conversation that you tell me I'm great
too :D

PRETTYBASIC: You're great, PAWN.

ALONELYPAWN: Why do I sense sarcasm?

PRETTYBASIC: I'm only joking. But I
have to go. Thank you for this, I'm
much less scared than I was twenty
minutes ago.

ALONELYPAWN: Glad to be of use. I'll just
take your knight before you go.

PRETTYBASIC: Dick.

```
ALONELYPAWN: Why are you talking about my
    dick?
PRETTYBASIC: :P
```

'Something funny, Mr Cole? I don't remember *Romeo and Juliet* being a comedy? Unless you find death amusing.' Miss Black raised her eyebrows at me.

'No, Miss Black, I don't. I was just thinking about something else.'

It felt like I was on autopilot for the rest of the day. I was just going over the conversation with BASIC. And that feeling, at the end, how she made me feel high. Like that thing where you're flirting with some girl you really fancy, and you know they're into you too.

After school, Tara smashed that bubble.

'Hey, babe.'

Babe . . .

'I forgot my spare key today and my mum isn't there. Can I hang out at yours?'

I hadn't planned to do anything, but I was hoping to go home and play chess with BASIC.

'Yeah sure, fine.'

She hung on to my arm the whole way back to my house, talking about this party next week. The party I wished was fucking over so I wouldn't have to hear about it again. But I guess after this there'd be another party, and another. And maybe that's what high school was supposed to be, an endless stream of pathetic distractions from the real world. It was probably OK for them – they never had anything in their perfect lives to make them realize that all this shit was fucking pointless.

27

Juliet

It wasn't a *proper* lie. The dentist. I just wasn't ready to tell this person I'd just met and seemed to be getting on with, that no, actually, it was a hospital appointment for my arthritis.

Arthritis wasn't sexy. In fact, it was probably one of the least sexy diseases a person can have. Not that any disease is 'sexy' but if there was a disease sexiness scale, arthritis would definitely be at the bottom.

I couldn't tell him. Not yet.

The needle didn't sting as much as usual. I think it was because I was scrolling through our conversation while the nurse did her job. The conversation with the doctor felt shorter, better, less soul-destroying than usual. They all wished me happy birthday, but that wasn't it. Only one thing had changed: PAWN. *He* was in my life, and I don't know, even though I hadn't told him everything, or anything much at all, it was like a release.

I'd almost forgotten that they'd booked me in for physio straight after.

'How's my favourite patient?' Sean asked.

'Good.'

'What? That sounded almost genuine.' Sean smiled. He had one of those smiles that made his eyes shine.

I pulled my phone from my pocket to check my messages. Just in case.

'Someone interesting?' Sean eyed my phone.

'Nope, just … no one.' I shook my head but couldn't stop smiling.

'I know love-sick when I see it. But if you're not going to spill, then so be it. Hop up on the bed there and let me take a look at these legs.'

'Hop?'

'You know what I mean – shuffle.' He helped me on to the bed. 'Let's start with leg lifts.'

Sean liked to talk to me about completely random things when I was doing my exercises. He said distractions always made things easier once you have the technique down. Which I did after years of this.

'So, what's the great career plan for next year? Are you university-bound?'

'I haven't thought about it.'

'What do you mean, you haven't thought about it? Let's think about it now! What do you want to be?'

'I dunno,' I said with a shrug and avoided Sean's eyeline. I knew I'd have to give in at some point and actually think about it. And soon. UCAS forms were the teachers' favourite topic of conversation at the moment.

'What? You're what, seventeen, and you don't know what you want to be? Shocking. I've wanted to be a physiotherapist since I was two.'

I laughed. 'We can't all be as focused as you, Sean. And I'm eighteen. Today, actually.'

He put my leg down gently.

'What?' He checked his notes. 'So you are. What on earth are you doing here? On your birthday? You should be out making an eejit of yourself, getting drunk, or whatever you kids do these days. Don't tell your parents I said that.'

'It's just a normal day. I just happened to be born on it eighteen years ago.'

'A normal day, my ass. Another year of improvement, another year of getting through school despite all the classes you miss. You're a superstar, Jules, and it should be celebrated.'

'Thanks, it's just, it feels worse this year. Trying to think about what I want to do. Trying to think what I *can* do.'

Sean had this habit of making me speak the truth. I don't know how he did it. This room just felt safe.

'Jules. Look at me.'

I looked up and his face was serious.

'There is *nothing* you can't do with your life if you want to. *Nothing* that can't be adapted to your needs. I mean, unless you're going to tell me you want to be an Olympic sprinter or something.'

'Definitely not.' I smiled through the heat in my face.

'I'm serious, Jules. Don't write yourself off at eighteen. You have such an amazing life ahead of you. Promise me.'

'I promise.'

I tried to make it sound like I meant it.

'And don't forget about that Facebook group I told you about. I think you could really get a lot from it, you know.'

Sean had told me about this group. For young people with arthritis. 'Joint Adventure.' I hadn't even looked at it. I knew what it would be: people talking all day about their pain and medication. I had to live it, so why would I want to talk about it too?

'I'll check it out.'

Mum looked cold when I got back in the car. She never put the heat on any more. One time she sat outside for five hours during one of my particularly long appointments, radio on, heat blasting, and the car battery died. We made it home two hours later, in foul moods. She decided never again. I hated it. I've asked her to go home in between, go to a cafe even, but she refused. Said she wanted me to be able to find her if I needed her. So I made sure that I never needed her. That I dried my tears before coming back out to the car.

'How'd it go?'

'It was all fine, Mum. Let's get home.'

Tara had still not said anything to me, so I'd sent her a message before I'd left school asking her if she was coming for dinner. It felt lame and I was embarrassed. An eighteenth birthday dinner with my parents. It was even worse when Tara didn't reply.

I could see the table had already been decorated as soon as I walked into the house. Gold tablecloth, pink and white flowered centrepiece, more balloons. The good cutlery. I ran my hands over the wooden place mats. Everyone had one: me, Michael, Tara, Mum and Dad. All carved out and painted by Mum with our names on them, intricate pink and gold flowers around the edges. They were so beautiful.

'Looks great, Mum. These are so amazing,' I said, picking up my placemat and running my fingers over the design.

'Thanks, do you like them? They're nothing really.'

'Took her three days,' Dad whispered loudly and then kissed my head.

'Mum.'

'He's exaggerating. Anyway, what time are Tara and Michael coming?'

'I said six?'

I got a message from Michael at five thirty.

MICHAEL: I'm so sorry, J. I can't come. Gran's had some kind of old person turn and I have to go and see her

ME: OMG, Michael, is she OK?

MICHAEL: I think she's fine; she's telling us not to come but you know what Mum is like. I'm so sorry. At least Princess Peach will be there

ME: You know I don't care about birthdays, don't worry about it. Hope your gran is OK

MICHAEL: Thanks, J, I'll message you later. I really am so sorry

'Jules, this is nearly ready. Are you coming down?' Mum called.

When Mum had asked me what I wanted for my birthday dinner a few weeks ago I'd said lasagne. Mostly because Michael loved it. I didn't really like lasagne. But it was like, if he had to come to this 'party', then I might as well try and sweeten the deal. I stared at my phone as if doing that would make Tara send a message. But there was nothing. I hated how it made me feel. Ashamed. How could I even ask her to come to something like this? Of course she wasn't going to come. There was a lump in my throat.

Mum and Dad were sitting at the table downstairs with party hats. Mum had even decorated Jeffrey's bowl. It was the most pathetic sight I'd ever seen.

They were both smiling at me.

'Michael can't come. His gran's not well.'

'Oh no, I hope she's OK. At least there's more for us then.' Dad smiled and held up a bottle of champagne. 'I thought we could share this. A glass each to celebrate.'

'We should wait for Tara,' I said.

I sat opposite Mum, the lasagne turning cold between us as the minutes ticked by, while Dad filled the time making terrible jokes.

'Maybe we should start and when she comes, we can always heat it up again.'

'Yeah, maybe,' I said quietly and stared at my phone again. Nothing.

ME: Hey, are you coming tonight?

TARA: Oh shit, sorry, Jules, I completely forgot. I'm with Ronan at the minute 😊 Can we celebrate another time? I hope you have a nice birthday! X

ME: Yeah, of course, have fun! See you tomorrow x

I looked up to see Mum and Dad staring at me. I inhaled.

'It's fine, let's go ahead. Tara can't make it.'

'Oh no, Jules, why not? Is everything OK?'

'Does it matter? She just said she can't come.'

'OK, OK,' Dad held up his hands. 'I, for one, have been dying to eat this all day.' He dug a spoon into the lasagne.

'Brian.' Mum hissed at him. 'Champagne.'

'Oh, of course. A toast. To our favourite daughter,' he held up a glass.

I couldn't look up at them. At the faces that were trying so hard to make me smile when all I wanted to do was cry.

'To Jules, whose bravery impresses me every day,' Dad said.

'To Jules,' Mum said, and they clinked glasses with each other.

And here it was again, another day where Mum and Dad do everything for me. Take time off work, spend all day doing something entirely for me. I ate some lasagne, but I had to force it down. I took a long sip of champagne to help.

'Not hungry, Jules?' Mum's crease was back.

'No, I am. I just can't believe how much effort you've both gone to. Thank you so much.' I ate a tiny bit more lasagne to make a point. 'I'm just saving room for cake.'

Mum smiled at that. 'Why don't we skip right to the cake instead?' She didn't wait for me to answer, just got up and went into the kitchen, turning off the lights on the way.

She came back a few minutes later carrying a two-tiered pink and gold cake. *Happy Birthday, Jules!* was written in swirly white icing on the top and tiny little roses fell in a waterfall down one side. It was incredible.

They sang 'Happy Birthday' and I wished they'd stop. But instead, I smiled and covered my face like I was embarrassed. Mum put some cake on my plate, and I took a few bites even though eating was the last thing I wanted to do.

'I'm just going to take this to my room,' I said when Mum and Dad had finished eating theirs.

I stood up and slid my crutches on my arm, holding the paper plate between a few fingers.

'Jules, I'll get it. You can't take it upstairs with those.'

'I'm fine, Mum.'

And it must have come out more harshly than I'd meant because she just said OK, then sat down again. They both watched as I struggled towards the stairs.

Before I reached the top, I stopped and looked back down at the effort Dad and especially Mum had put into today. I took a deep breath.

'Mum, Dad, thanks so much for today. Seriously, I really appreciate it.' And I smiled. So did they, the sadness in their eyes mirroring mine.

I made it – all the way to my bedroom with my piece of cake.

I just about made it to my bin to dump the cake before my fingers seized up. I dropped the crutches and hobbled to my bed where the tears that I'd learned to keep silent streamed down my face.

I was angry at Sean for making me feel for a second that I could be something different. Angry at Tara for not coming and for having an easy, perfect life. Angry at myself for feeling like this. But I couldn't help it, and part of me didn't want to. I sat on my bed and didn't even wipe away the tears that wouldn't stop coming. Right then I hated my life. I was *eighteen* and this was it? Was I going to be twenty-five and still having a birthday party with my parents because nobody else wants to hang out with me? I knew it wasn't fair to put Michael in that category; it wasn't his fault. But it didn't change the fact he wasn't there. Sean always said that things would get better, that I'd learn to adapt, and my life would be like every other young person with a few small differences. But right then, that seemed impossible.

I massaged my fingers and opened my laptop, scrolling through my 'English Revision', making myself look at every picture, scanning every single beautiful joint on the beautiful people before opening Chess Life in the corner.

PRETTYBASIC: Hey, you there?

28

Ronan

When I started at Birch, I spent my time thinking about the day I could leave this stupid school. One year, that was it. But already I found myself thinking about BASIC and it was like she distracted me from everything else. I'd wake up thinking about what moves I wanted to use on her, what I'd say to try and make her laugh. It was like she'd carved out this little safe space in my head where I could go when I wanted to get away from everything. Which was a lot of the time.

I hadn't wanted to talk to anyone in ages. After Alex and Sasha, I never got that close to anybody. So, I shut down. I couldn't face talking to the counsellor that the teachers at St Anne's suggested I 'chat' to. They made it sound like I'd just be stopping in for five minutes to tell them about my day, as if that wouldn't create even more whispering than there already was. But I knew what they wanted. To dissect me like a rat in biology, everything on display, pulling back my layers until I was just organs and flesh with nowhere to hide. BASIC was different. She made me feel so much less alone than I had for the past six months, and maybe, one day, I would tell her what happened. About all the things that were constantly swirling around in my head.

But talking hadn't helped Ciaran. Or maybe he just didn't talk to the right person.

My mind flashed back to an evening in the kitchen. Mum was folding washing and watching some crime drama. Ciaran and I had just come down for something to eat after he'd beaten me in our longest game yet. His head wasn't in it. He was quiet. I should have asked him if he was OK instead of enjoying the fact that he didn't wipe the board with me. Maybe if he'd talked to me instead . . .

'Mum, I don't really know if I want to go. I might take a year out.'

Telling her. Plain as fucking day.

'Don't be silly, Ciaran. It's just nerves.'

Putting washing away, acting like he'd just told her he didn't want to go to football practice.

'But what if I can't?'

And he'd said it quietly, as if he didn't want her to hear. She stopped folding the laundry. But just for a second.

'Ciaran. Of course you can – you'll be grand.'

Then she turned round and smiled at him like that would fix everything. Like it would just dissolve all the doubts that were mangling his already fucking complicated brain. She made his thoughts trivial. Like he didn't know his own mind. And that was just before he lost it altogether.

Chess Life flashed on my phone.

29

Juliet

```
ALONELYPAWN: Hey! What's up?
PRETTYBASIC: My best friend didn't show
  up to my birthday.
ALONELYPAWN: Aw, man, that sucks. Why not?
PRETTYBASIC: Seeing some guy.
ALONELYPAWN: FFS. Sorry.
PRETTYBASIC: Thanks.
```

He actually seemed to care. The pain diluted. It wasn't like it went away or anything, but it was like I'd been numbed. Like the injection before the injection. The one that's filled with anaesthetic to stop the next one hurting so much. But you can still feel it.

```
ALONELYPAWN: Watch the board, BASIC.
  Your knight is entirely open. But I'll
  let you away with this one because your
  birthday was shit.
PRETTYBASIC: Thanks for the tips,
  Mr Grandmaster, but I left it open
```

deliberately. You were supposed to take
it, then I was going to take your
bishop. But now you've ruined that.
THANKS.

ALONELYPAWN: Hm, Mr Grandmaster has a
nice ring to it, but I prefer Lord
Grandmaster actually. Anyway. Chess
lesson number . . . too many to count?
ALWAYS PAY ATTENTION!!!

PRETTYBASIC: Oh, but I have been paying
attention. To the fact that you seem to
have the exact same time zone as me.
You might have tried to confuse me with
your middle-of-the-night messages, but
now I know you just never sleep, I
think we're the same.

ALONELYPAWN: And?

PRETTYBASIC: And nothing, it's just
an observation. But I HAVE been
paying attention. What country do you
live in?

ALONELYPAWN: Next chess lesson. Don't
give away pieces for free.

PRETTYBASIC: What do you want in return?

ALONELYPAWN: The same answer from you.
Two ply.

PRETTYBASIC: Huh?

ALONELYPAWN: Keep up, BASIC. Someone
hasn't been learning their chess speak.

```
It means when both players move. Let's
go at the same time. 1, 2, 3.
```
PRETTYBASIC: Wait!!!
ALONELYPAWN: What?
PRETTYBASIC: Isn't it better this way?
    That we don't know?
ALONELYPAWN: Why? Are you catfishing me?
PRETTYBASIC: No, but I could be. Think
    about it, I could be anyone.

I pulled the blanket up over my head, as if hiding would help me figure out what I was supposed to say next. He couldn't see me. He didn't know anything about me, but it felt too close. I took a deep breath. I didn't give anything away.

ALONELYPAWN: I know how the internet
    works.
PRETTYBASIC: You probably live MILES
    away anyway.
ALONELYPAWN: I wasn't going to tell you
    my address, stalker.
PRETTYBASIC: I don't want to know your
    address.
ALONELYPAWN: You totally do.

I did. Obviously. My heart was going a million times an hour. But if I found out where he lived, he'd want to know where I lived and ... no, I wasn't playing this game. Not yet. Even though the chance of us being in the same country was small.

PRETTYBASIC: I don't. I like this. The way it is, chatting on here, beating you at chess.

ALONELYPAWN: *SNORT*

PRETTYBASIC: Taking your rook for that. It's true, tho, if I knew where you lived, it would ruin the whole illusion of you.

ALONELYPAWN: You have illusions of me? Are they good-looking illusions?

PRETTYBASIC: Those would be called delusions.

ALONELYPAWN: Ouch!

PRETTYBASIC: It's not an insult cos I've never met you.

ALONELYPAWN: *Sigh* Maybe ONE day you'll want to fill that MASSIVE hole in your life and be begging to meet me.

PRETTYBASIC: Ha! Who says I have a hole in my life?

ALONELYPAWN: Crater, imperfection . . . Call it what you will. What if I was the thing that made your life better?

PRETTYBASIC: You definitely think a lot of yourself.

ALONELYPAWN: Just putting it out there. I would never ditch you on your birthday . . . In fact, what if I was the missing piece that made your life perfect?

```
PRETTYBASIC: What makes you think meeting
    you would make my life perfect? Is
    there even such a thing as a perfect
    life?
```

Of course there was. And those lives belonged to people like Tara and Hana.

As if knowing where this random stranger on the internet lived was going to make my life perfect. For a start, there'd be no hiding the fact that I couldn't walk without stabilizers.

I was enjoying this online version of me.

In a movie, this is where the two anonymous messengers fall hopelessly in love and there's no other option BUT to meet up and have this ridiculously romantic kiss, then live happily ever after. Blah, blah, blah. But this is *my* life. And in the pathetic life of Juliet Clarke, things like that don't happen.

```
ALONELYPAWN: If you grew up not knowing
    what an Xbox was you might think your
    life was OK. But you wouldn't know how
    much better your life would be with an
    Xbox in it.
PRETTYBASIC: So you're an Xbox?
ALONELYPAWN: Exactly. I don't know,
    BASIC, there's something about you.
    I feel like there's more to you than
    you're telling me. It's like I can feel
    it through the screen, and I need to
    know more.
```

PRETTYBASIC: Let's keep chatting on here.
ALONELYPAWN: I suppose we could. It's
  weird, I feel like I can finally breathe
  when I talk to you.
PRETTYBASIC: I feel exactly the same.
ALONELYPAWN: God, you're so cheesy ;)
PRETTYBASIC: You started it.
ALONELYPAWN: Well, I meant it.

He didn't even wait for me to reply again before he signed
off. And for the first time that night I wasn't thinking about
my disastrous birthday at all.

30

Ronan

PRETTYBASIC: You took my bishop at 3 a.m.
Wasn't even there to defend myself. No
sleep again?

ALONELYPAWN: Maybe like an hour or
something?

PRETTYBASIC: ☹

PRETTYBASIC: Want me to set my alarm
tonight? We could have a middle-of-the-
night game. I might be pretty tired
though and that would be the only reason
I'd lose.

ALONELYPAWN: Is that why you lost
yesterday?

PRETTYBASIC: No, I let you win.

ALONELYPAWN: Ah, I see . . . Makes sense.

PRETTYBASIC: So, what do you say?
Midnight meet?

ALONELYPAWN: You make it sound so naughty.

PRETTYBASIC: That's because it is. I might
even have snacks.

```
ALONELYPAWN: I'm not sure I'm comfortable
  partaking in such risky behaviour.
PRETTYBASIC: I knew you were a loser.
ALONELYPAWN: Peer pressure. NICE. FINE.
  I'll 'see' you at twelve. Bring your A
  game.
PRETTYBASIC: Oh, I will.
ALONELYPAWN: It's a date.
PRETTYBASIC: ;)
ALONELYPAWN: And BASIC?
PRETTYBASIC: Yeah?
ALONELYPAWN: Thanks.
```

I had English next. I sat down in my new seat at the front and stared at my phone.

Just in case.

But there was nothing.

Then Jules was there, sliding her crutches in under the desk between us, sighing as she sat down and put her head on the desk, her blonde hair in a ponytail today, so I could see the studs in her ear.

'Rough night?' I asked.

'Something like that,' a muffled voice said from behind her school jumper.

'Out drinking at that park you all seem to love?'

'No, actually.' She turned her face towards me but didn't take her head off the desk. 'Why'd you want to know what I was doing anyway?'

'Dunno. Nosy, I guess.' I shrugged. I couldn't gauge her

mood at all. She was hiding her eyes, leaning her head on her arms now. I needed her eyes to tell if she was actually pissed off or just pretending. So I pushed it some more. 'Or maybe I'm trying to be friendly, in an attempt to thaw your icy exterior.'

She looked up then. Eyes narrowed, red marks on her cheek from leaning on her jumper. 'Oh, I'm sorry, just because I don't fall at your feet, jump to answer all your questions, and christen you the hottest guy in school, that makes me icy? That's sexist, you know, bringing up the "ice queen" thing when you don't get the answer you want.'

It was the angriest whisper I'd ever heard.

'The hottest guy in school?' I gave her a half-smile.

'Ugh!' If she hadn't had her arms on the desk, she would have smashed her head against the wood. Instead, it was a muffled thud. Then she turned to look the other way and I noticed her take out her phone.

I wasn't about to poke the bear any more, so I took my phone out too.

ALONELYPAWN: Did you know that from the
    starting position there are eight
    different ways to Mate in two moves and
    355 different ways to Mate in three
    moves?
PRETTYBASIC: Of course I know that.
    Everybody knows that.
ALONELYPAWN: You're a liar. Be impressed
    with my facts.

PRETTYBASIC: Sorry. WOW, REALLY? THAT
IS SO INTERESTING.

ALONELYPAWN: I knew you weren't a serious
player. Not like me.

PRETTYBASIC: Just because I didn't
swallow some boring history of chess
book doesn't mean I'm not serious. And
anyway, you probably just wanted to
talk to me about mating.

ALONELYPAWN: CHECKMATING. Get your mind
out of the gutter, BASIC.

PRETTYBASIC: I'll keep my mind on the
game, thanks.

ALONELYPAWN: Hey! That was my favourite
knight!

PRETTYBASIC: Should pay more attention
then.

'Mr Cole. Would you please pay attention?'

I looked up. So did Jules, probably as shocked as I was by
the fact Miss Black was actually paying attention herself.

'Sorry,' I said.

I slid my phone away and leaned over to share Jules's
book with her because I'd forgotten mine again. Our arms
were close. Really close. And when she turned the page, her
sleeve swept over my hand. Then it stayed there. Neither of
us moved. Maybe she just hadn't noticed. I kept my hand
still.

A buzz in my pocket.

PRETTYBASIC: Looks like checkmate to me.
  See you later. Loser x

An X. I didn't hate it.
I really didn't hate it.

31

Juliet

I don't know why I asked PAWN to meet me in the middle of the night. It was a terrible time for me. In the middle of the night I'd be groggy from painkillers, and my joints would all have seized up. But it felt like a good idea at the time. And I felt bad for him. About the insomnia. There's nothing worse than lying there in the pitch black, dealing with all the thoughts that come into your head. Although maybe he didn't have those kinds of thoughts. The ones like spiderwebs that get bigger and more complicated, sticking all over your brain until you can't think of anything else.

When it happened to me it was usually because of the pain. Sometimes Mum and Dad would wake up and I'd be in the shower. An attempt to loosen my joints, and clear my head, before crawling back into bed with wet hair and saying no to Mum when she offered to dry it.

And I guess I hated the thought of PAWN like this. I doubt he was having showers at two a.m., but not sleeping? It sucked.

At least tonight he'd have some company. And it was the closest I'd come to having a real date.

32

Ronan

```
ALONELYPAWN: You awake?
ALONELYPAWN: Wake uuupppppppp.
ALONELYPAWN: That wasn't checkmate
    earlier btw. Got a bit ahead of
    yourself. So your winning streak is
    still . . . zero
ALONELYPAWN: BUT if you move your knight
    you can save that sad little pawn.
ALONELYPAWN: See, I'm even giving you
    tips!!
ALONELYPAWN: BASIC?
PRETTYBASIC: Hi
ALONELYPAWN: About time. I was about to
    call Search and Rescue.
PRETTYBASIC: I'm here! :)
```

I'd been waiting for this all day. I just sat at my desk playing chess with randoms and studying Ciaran's playbook until twelve a.m. It wasn't late for me. This was just my night getting started. And it was nice to have company.

ALONELYPAWN: I'm excited for our first date.

PRETTYBASIC: Me too.

ALONELYPAWN: Did you bring snacks?

PRETTYBASIC: No, but I do have a delicious, lukewarm glass of water.

ALONELYPAWN: You're making me jealous. I wish I could trade you for my PIZZA.

PRETTYBASIC: Ugh, not fair.

ALONELYPAWN: You still haven't moved your knight.

PRETTYBASIC: Done. Sorry, my head isn't thinking straight.

ALONELYPAWN: Maybe I should take advantage then. Storm the board.

PRETTYBASIC: I couldn't stop you.

ALONELYPAWN: I don't want to.

PRETTYBASIC: Why not?

ALONELYPAWN: I don't want you to go away ☺

PRETTYBASIC: I'm not going anywhere.

ALONELYPAWN: Good. Favourite singer?

PRETTYBASIC: Taylor Swift.

ALONELYPAWN: Of course it is.

PRETTYBASIC: What's that supposed to mean? ☺ Who's YOUR favourite singer?

ALONELYPAWN: Well, it's more a band. Slayer.

PRETTYBASIC: *opens Spotify*

PRETTYBASIC: . . .

PRETTYBASIC: WHAT THE HELL IS THAT?

ALONELYPAWN: HAHAHAHA Did you just play death metal out loud?

PRETTYBASIC: You could have warned me. That's not even music, it's just noise!

ALONELYPAWN: OK, Grandma ;)

PRETTYBASIC: Favourite food?

ALONELYPAWN: Pizza? You?

PRETTYBASIC: Chocolate. Not just any chocolate, the Lindt stuff, in bunny shape. Tastes much better as a bunny.

ALONELYPAWN: Monster. Favourite movie?

PRETTYBASIC: Any movie that doesn't end up the way you think it's going to end up.

ALONELYPAWN: You've lost me.

PRETTYBASIC: Like a love story, except at the end they don't end up happily ever after, they just never get together, or they break up or something.

ALONELYPAWN: So you like happy movies then? :D

PRETTYBASIC: I like realistic movies.

ALONELYPAWN: Ah, a cynic.

PRETTYBASIC: A realist. You?

ALONELYPAWN: I'm cool with happy endings actually. In fact, I like most movies

```
        with happy endings, even those horrible
        romcoms. Life is depressing enough
        without watching it on television too.
PRETTYBASIC: So we can never watch a
        movie together then?
ALONELYPAWN: We could stop it before the
        end? Make up our own endings.
PRETTYBASIC: Not that we're going to do
        that - meet, I mean.
ALONELYPAWN: We could . . .
PRETTYBASIC: We couldn't.
ALONELYPAWN: Two ply?
PRETTYBASIC: Huh?
ALONELYPAWN: I told you this one the
        other day! Don't you listen to ANYTHING
        I say? It means when both players move.
        Let's go at the same time, what country
        do you live in? 1, 2, 3.
```

Come on, BASIC. I knew she was scared. I could practically feel it through the screen, but feeling like *this*, through a screen, is not a normal thing. There was something there. And we both knew it.

```
PRETTYBASIC: OK.
ALONELYPAWN: 1,2,3.
PRETTYBASIC: Northern Ireland.
ALONELYPAWN: Northern Ireland.
ALONELYPAWN: Holy shit.
```

PRETTYBASIC: 😲😲😲😲😲😲😲😲😲

ALONELYPAWN: That's insane. I mean, no
matter where you live in NI, I could be
at your house within two hours.

PRETTYBASIC: Technically.

ALONELYPAWN: This is incredible.

BASIC lived in the same country? I was so distracted and
happy; I hadn't even touched the pizza beside me.
Happy.
It was a weird feeling.

PRETTYBASIC: I mean, it doesn't mean we
have to meet.

ALONELYPAWN: I know, but we could?

PRETTYBASIC: I don't think my boyfriend
would like it.

ALONELYPAWN: You have a boyfriend?

PRETTYBASIC: Kind of.

ALONELYPAWN: You have a kind-of
boyfriend? You have a girlfriend?

PRETTYBASIC: No, I do, I have a
boyfriend, but it's not serious or
anything yet. We've just started going
out. It's actually a sort of secret
relationship.

ALONELYPAWN: Oh really? Why's it a
secret? What's he like? Can he play
chess?

```
PRETTYBASIC: Secrets make it more
    exciting. And no, he's not really into
    chess.
ALONELYPAWN: Loser. Anyway, I got to go,
    pretty tired, talk later.
```

And it's strange how you can go from feeling so fucking happy and excited to sick with disappointment in the space of a few seconds.

33

Juliet

Blunder, blunder, blunder. Why the hell did I say that? I panicked. Online it was safe. Online he didn't have to see the real me. I had to do something. He wouldn't want to meet me if I had a boyfriend. My crutches, my zero experience with guys. These were the things that convinced me I'd done the right thing. But if I'd done the right thing, why did I feel like I'd ruined everything?

We both lived in Northern Ireland? What were the actual chances?

I slammed my laptop shut after he'd said 'talk later'.

Embarrassed. Frustrated I couldn't just be 'cool' for once in my life. Everything inside my head was telling me to look at myself. He's getting too close; he'll want to see you next. Then what? He'd see your crutches. He'd see you for who you really are. Someone not worth his time.

Tears leaked on to my pillow.

The aches in my knees and elbows reminded me what I was, over and over and over again.

34

Ronan

ALONELYPAWN: Wanna play?

ALONELYPAWN: I have some new moves I want
  to try out.

ALONELYPAWN: I'm sorry for not chatting
  for a while. When you said you had a
  boyfriend it kind of shocked me. But it
  doesn't matter, does it? We can still
  be friends.

ALONELYPAWN: Can't we?

ALONELYPAWN: Maybe not.

ALONELYPAWN: I miss you, BASIC.

*

ALONELYPAWN: Can you come back now? I
  don't even care if you're a catfish and
  it turns out you're my biology teacher
  or something (that's a lie, I really,
  really don't want you to be my biology
  teacher).

```
ALONELYPAWN: I invited you to another
  game.
ALONELYPAWN: It's rude to ignore people,
  you know.
ALONELYPAWN: I can't be myself with
  anyone else.
```

It had been three days of not talking to BASIC. Tara wasn't talking to me either because I told her I wasn't going to the stupid party. I couldn't be bothered pretending it was going to be fun, when really everyone was going to get off their faces on cheap vodka, screw someone they didn't like, and then spend the next few weeks saying, 'oh my God!' about everything.

On top of that, I hadn't seen anyone from St Anne's in six months. They might ask me questions, which would just make people from Birch ask me questions. And yeah, most of the kids from St Anne's were nice, but I wasn't ready.

All I could think about was BASIC.

So what if she had a boyfriend. I still liked talking to her. And that was OK, wasn't it? We could still be friends.

But there were no messages. And she hadn't been online for three days, though it felt like twenty.

Maybe she was just a catfish after all.

```
ALONELYPAWN: This is your last chance
  (it's not).
ALONELYPAWN: You must talk to me in ten
  seconds or I'm leaving. Forever.
```

```
ALONELYPAWN: 10
ALONELYPAWN: 9
ALONELYPAWN: 8
ALONELYPAWN: 7
ALONELYPAWN: 6
ALONELYPAWN: 5
ALONELYPAWN: 4
ALONELYPAWN: 3
ALONELYPAWN: 2
PRETTYBASIC: Jeez. Desperate much?
ALONELYPAWN: I missed you.
PRETTYBASIC: I missed you too.
ALONELYPAWN: Can we play again?
PRETTYBASIC: That depends . . .
PRETTYBASIC: Are you ready to lose?
```

35

Juliet

On Friday, everyone was talking about the party. Who was wearing what, who was going out with who, bets on who would throw up first. It was all I heard all day. Michael could not have been more excited. At the end of French, he practically threw my crutches at me and rushed me out of the door. As fast as someone can go on crutches.

'Hurry up, J, I need to see this dress of yours. You're going to look so hot; *we're* going to look so hot,' he said.

'*Hot* is not exactly the word I'd use.' I thought about the thick black tights I'd wear to hide my swollen knees, the cardigan I'd use to give me some padding for the crutches and the amount of time I'd spend sitting down.

'Well, it's lucky I'm here to use it for you then, isn't it?' He winked at me. I'd created a monster. 'Where *is* she?' Michael was leaning on his car looking back towards school for Tara. 'If she doesn't get here in five minutes we're going,' he said.

'She'll be here, just wait.' I was convinced she wouldn't flake on us again. Not after my birthday. She'd apologized again about missing dinner last week, and said she'd make it up to me. I wasn't sure what that meant but I just went with it. I didn't even like birthdays anyway.

'Why don't you get in, it's cold. I'll look out for Princess Peach.' Michael opened my door and I sat on the edge of the seat.

She was taking so long that I *had* started to get cold. When I got cold, all my muscles tensed, making my joints a million times more sore.

'Hey, Michael, can we turn on the heat?'

He looked up from his phone. He didn't say anything, but just came round and turned on the engine, twisting the fan towards me.

'Thanks.'

'And there she is, Princess Peach herself, like a limpet on that poor, hot boy.' He sighed.

I pushed myself up and looked in the same direction. Yep, there she was, hanging on Ronan's arm and looking at him like they were the only people in the schoolyard.

'Oi, Tara, hurry up!' Michael called, his hands cupped around his mouth. She didn't even look up, just waved her hand in our direction like she was swatting a fly.

'You know hyenas eat their prey alive?' Michael said.

'Put your claws away,' I said, laughing.

Tara finally let go of Ronan and came over to Michael's car with a face like thunder.

'Hey, what's wrong?' I asked.

'Ronan's not going to the party.' She sighed dramatically and then threw her bag on to the back seat and climbed in after it.

'It did look like you were trying to convince him though. Didn't your wounded puppy look work?' Michael got into the car after Tara, pulling my crutches with him and setting them as awkwardly as possible beside her.

'No! And neither did the flirting. I don't get him at all.' She sighed, and it was the first time I'd noticed her doubt her abilities to have whatever she wanted.

'Maybe he *is* gay,' Michael said hopefully.

'He's *not* gay!' Tara practically shouted. Then she paused. 'Although, that *would* clear up a few things.'

'Maybe he's just not that into you,' Michael said and shrugged.

'Michael!' I gave him side-eye.

'No, it's fine, Jules. Maybe he's right for once. I just need to up my game.'

'Want some tips?' Michael looked in his rear-view mirror at her.

'Oh, please. From you? The only tips you could give me is how to kiss your Harry Styles poster without your mum seeing.'

Michael was mock shocked. 'Please! Screenshots. Posters are a product of the nineties.'

'It doesn't matter. Ronan will change his mind. About the party, *and* about me.' Tara said it like she was trying hard to convince herself.

'Well, we're here. Get out of my car and let's go see how hot Juliet looks in this new dress,' Michael said.

I'd sent Mum a message to tell her we were coming so she'd tidied the whole house, again, and there were little bowls of crisps sitting on the table.

'Jules, is that you?' Mum called.

'Yeah, it's us,' I said before I reached down to stroke Jeffrey who was jumping up my leg. 'We're just heading upstairs.'

'OK, love. Hi, Michael. Hi, Tara.'

'Hey, Mrs C,' they said together.

'So sorry for missing the birthday dinner. Did Jules tell you about Gran?' Michael asked.

'She did, Michael, and don't worry, I'm glad she's feeling better,' Mum called.

'Oh yeah, I'm sorry too, I wasn't feeling well either.' Tara hovered halfway up the stairs.

'Hope you're feeling better now, love,' Mum called as she disappeared kitchen-wards as we went upstairs.

'It's beautiful,' Michael whispered when he opened the door to my room and gazed around. 'Does your mum seriously tidy your room every day?' He walked over to my bed and flopped on to his back like a starfish before propping himself up on his elbows. Tara planted herself in front of the mirror, as usual.

'I'm so jealous. It's amazing,' said Michael. 'I *want* a tidy room, but I just can't be bothered tidying up and Mum is too busy. So she says. I think she secretly goes shopping instead of work. She's always coming back with new clothes. Except they're for her, not me.'

'Yeah, my mum likes tidying,' I said. I leaned my crutches against my desk and sat down on the swivel chair.

'Mine too,' Tara said. 'Total neat-freak – won't leave the house until everything is in the right place. It's ridiculous.' She rolled her eyes. That definitely wasn't how Tara's mum had been when she was younger. She must have changed. One of the things I remembered about going to Tara's house was all the stuff everywhere. Not like normal clutter and lived-in mess but like rubbish and empty bottles and stuff in random places, like the bathroom. Except in Tara's bedroom. It was pristine! And if I moved something out of place she'd always move it back before I left.

'So, let me see this dress then,' Michael said. 'You point, I'll get.'

I pointed to my wardrobe, and when he opened it he gasped. Tara ran her hands along the hung-up clothes at the other end.

'It's glorious.' He pretended to cry, looking at the rows of colour-coded clothes. 'Is this it?' He pulled out the dress, the one with the tags still on, guessing, correctly, that it was the one I was talking about.

I noticed Tara look up for a second, her eyes on the dress, then she looked back into the wardrobe, like she was lost in thought.

'That's the one,' I replied to Michael.

'Oh my God, try it on. This will look amazing on you.' His enthusiasm was contagious. And it made me smile.

I'm not sure why I looked at Tara. For agreement? Validation? Whatever it was, I didn't get it; she was still looking in the wardrobe. Half-heartedly now.

'OK.' I took the dress from Michael and went into Mum's room to change, bringing my tights with me.

When I came back, they both just stared at me. Michael with a huge smile and Tara looking like she didn't know what to say.

'I mean, I *will* have shoes – they're flats, obviously, but they kind of go. I don't know – does it look stupid?' I was starting to feel ridiculous.

'Have you even looked in the mirror?' Michael asked.

I turned and faced the mirror. I didn't hate it. I didn't hate me. The navy dress sat half-way up my thighs. It was fitted, but not uncomfortably tight. The long sleeves clung to my arms and wrists and the diamante collar sparkled in the afternoon sun that sneaked through spaces in my blinds. Michael came up behind me, sweeping my hair from my shoulders and playing with a pretend 'up-do'.

'No, down, definitely down. I mean, you look great with your hair up, but wear it down, it's way more you. Hairband, have you got a hairband?' he asked.

'Yeah, that second drawer,' I pointed.

Michael put one on my head.

'A smoky eye, nude lip and you're set, J. Hey, Tara, what do you think?' Michael asked and we both looked at her reflection staring back at us. She didn't say anything.

'Oh God, you don't like it, do you? Do I look stupid?' I felt like an idiot.

'Do my words mean nothing?' Michael said.

Tara looked at me. 'No, it looks great, but I thought you usually wear trousers . . . you know, because of what you said about your knees?'

And you know that feeling? The one when you've just remembered you forgot to do something, or you can't find your purse and your stomach sinks to the floor and you feel like you want to throw up? That.

'For fuck's sake, Tara.' Michael looked really pissed.

'What? I'm just saying. I don't want her to feel uncomfortable at the party.' She shrugged.

'No, she's right, I do usually wear trousers and these tights, they don't really hide much anyway,' I said. I was getting hot. 'I'll try something else,' I said, grabbing my crutches and walking back to Mum's room, desperate to take off the stupid dress.

'Hey, Jules, can I try it on?' Tara asked me when I was halfway out of the door.

'Sure,' I said and I was glad of the distance because it meant she couldn't hear the shake in my voice.

36

Ronan

'Ronan, are you ready?' Mum was at my door. She was properly dressed up for dinner. Floaty black dress, blazer, hair pulled back from her face and fastened with some kind of silver clip. Her perfume crept into my room.

'Yeah, I guess.'

'Is that what you're wearing?' She looked me up and down: black hoody, black jeans, trainers. 'At least change your shoes.'

'Fine, I'll wear the black trainers.' She must have booked that snobby place. The one we went to when Ciaran got his acceptance to Cambridge.

I brought earbuds for the car, turning up the metal until my ears hurt.

I'd message BASIC.

Then, maybe, I could get through this dinner.

ALONELYPAWN: So yeah, I was thinking. I figured, seeing we both know that we both live in Northern Ireland, we should probably tell each other WHERE in Northern Ireland.

PRETTYBASIC: That's some pretty big
    thinking you did.
ALONELYPAWN: BIG THINKER - *Adds to
    (long) list of qualities.*
PRETTYBASIC: The answer's . . . NO.
ALONELYPAWN: COME ON! WHY NOT?
PRETTYBASIC: I want to keep some element
    of mystery.
ALONELYPAWN: I'll play you for an answer?
PRETTYBASIC: Why do you want to know so
    badly?
ALONELYPAWN: So I can travel the country
    looking for you, like in one of those
    cheesy romantic movies.
PRETTYBASIC: You know it would never work
    out like that, don't you?
ALONELYPAWN: Way to rain on my parade!
PRETTYBASIC: HAHA! Sorry. True tho.
ALONELYPAWN: MAYBE SO, but I still want
    to know, out of curiosity, if nothing
    else.
PRETTYBASIC: Fine. Next person to take
    a piece gets to ask a question. And
    if it's you, then I'll answer. IN MY
    OWN WAY.
ALONELYPAWN: JESUS, BASIC, WOULD YOU
    WATCH THE BOARD! Say goodbye to your
    knight ♘
PRETTYBASIC: GOD DAMN IT!!!

```
ALONELYPAWN: You owe me an answer.
PRETTYBASIC: FINE. I live about ten
   minutes from Belfast. YOU?
ALONELYPAWN: HOLY SHIT.
PRETTYBASIC: What? Don't do that to me.
   What is it?
ALONELYPAWN: We could actually be
   neighbours.
PRETTYBASIC: Shut up!
```

'Ronan, will you please put your phone away?' The smile disappeared from my face as Mum spoke.

'Two minutes.'

```
ALONELYPAWN: I'll be back to discuss this
   development later. But in the meantime,
   you do realize we have to meet now,
   don't you?
PRETTYBASIC: That seems presumptuous . . .
ALONELYPAWN: You have a boyfriend,
   BASIC, I wasn't PRESUMING anything!
   But I have to go now, talk later?
PRETTYBASIC: I have to go to a thing later.
ALONELYPAWN: So don't go. That's what I
   did. I was supposed to be going to a
   party, but I just said no. Try it, it's
   liberating.
PRETTYBASIC: I can't. I don't want to let
   anyone down.
```

ALONELYPAWN: Admirable.

PRETTYBASIC: Will you be online while I'm
    there? So we can talk?

ALONELYPAWN: The least I can do, I
    suppose, after I outwitted you again ;)

PRETTYBASIC: Talk later then xx

ALONELYPAWN: xx

The restaurant wasn't busy. I noticed that the waiter scanned my clothes before asking Mum to follow him to our table.

Mum waved at me to take out my earbuds.

I did. Reluctantly.

'Do you know why we're here?'

'No,' I said. I set my phone face up on the table beside me.

'To celebrate.' Mum was serious. Her eyes were shining, and she was smiling like she'd just won the lottery.

'Celebrate what?'

'Ciaran, of course.'

'What?' I said sharply.

The waiter came to take our order. I don't even know what I chose, whatever was first on the list.

'Well, today when I got home from work, it was just sitting there in the letterbox.' She pulled a tiny mirror out of her bag and started putting on more make-up.

'What was?'

I was trying to keep my voice down. I was also trying to stop the twisting in my stomach and the pain that filled my chest.

'His acceptance. To the Silver Pawn. He got in.'

I just stared at her. I didn't know what to say.

'Ronan. Are you listening? Ciaran got in. To the tournament – the Silver Pawn.' Perfect teeth, red-lipped smile, nodding like one of those dogs in a car window, showing me what I should be doing.

'That's great,' I said. I didn't know what I was supposed to say. I couldn't say what I wanted. Not here.

'I know. It's in six weeks. I can't wait to tell him; he'll be so excited. I'm going to buy him some new clothes. He'll have to look smart for something like that.'

My ears were ringing. Which was a good thing. Blocking out the words Mum was saying, words I couldn't reply to.

I ate my extortionate food in silence while Mum talked and talked about Ciaran, barely stopping for breath.

'Let's have dessert. Do you want dessert, Ronan? It is a celebration after all.'

'No.'

And at that point I'd had enough. I couldn't take any more talking about Ciaran.

So, I got up and walked out of the restaurant.

```
ALONELYPAWN: I've changed my mind. I'm
    going to go to my party. Let's keep
    each other company?
PRETTYBASIC: Sure ☺
```

37

Juliet

When Michael and Tara left to go and get ready, I sat down on my bed. I felt drained, like all the excitement had been sucked right out of me. Tara was right – I never wore skirts or dresses. I don't know why Mum bought it for me in the first place. She was probably thinking about Tara when she handed over her credit card.

Tara's very pretty, isn't she? Those old Hollywood looks; she's very lucky. Mum said I was pretty too, but it was never like that, never off the cuff. It was because she had to.

Obviously the dress had looked amazing on Tara, of course it did, but I hated that she was going to wear it. It was *my* dress and for a second I'd actually felt like I didn't look terrible. Michael still thought I should wear a dress. Well, he thought I should wear *that* dress, but even he gave up trying to convince me after a while. I still hadn't chosen anything to wear and the party was in an hour.

I opened my wardrobe and stared at the reams of clothes. I was drawn to the black section: black blouses, tops, dresses that I hadn't worn. Black was good. Black blended in. I ran my hand over the soft fabrics and left the dresses and skirts hanging up. I paused at a pair of black trousers. Mum had bought me them for a funeral once. They were nice. Not tight, comfortable. I lifted them out and held them up to the mirror. They'd look all right. And they'd go with the shoes Mum bought me. I lifted out a black silk blouse, dotted with tiny pink flowers, and put them on my bed. This would have to be it; I couldn't face trying on any more clothes. I was saving my painkillers so I could take them just before I left.

But most of me wasn't thinking about clothes; most of me was thinking about the fact that PAWN lived in Northern Ireland, and not only that – he lived as close to Belfast as I did.

And just like he was reading my mind, my phone buzzed.

ALONELYPAWN: Will your boyfriend be at
    the thing you are going to?
PRETTYBASIC: No.

It wasn't a lie. He wouldn't be there because he didn't exist. I still felt guilty about it, but it was safer this way. An excuse not to meet him. Less chance of having to show him who I really was.

38

Ronan

> **ME:** Hey, I've changed my mind, think I'm going to come tonight

> **TARA:** OMG RO YES!!! 🎉 ♡♡♡♡♡♡
> K, meet me at the usual place. You're going to love what I'm wearing xxx

> **ME:** See you soon

I couldn't face talking to Mum any more. It was worse than anything that could happen at this party. I thought about what that might be. Someone from St Anne's might ask me a question? I could handle a question. I think.

I was meeting Tara at the crossroads where we usually split up after school. I leaned against a lamppost and turned up my music while I waited.

She looked hot. This little navy dress that came no more

than a quarter of the way down her thighs. Black boots. Over her knees, sexy. Her dark hair fell like a shiny curtain and she had this little plait at the front. Like something from the seventies. I turned my music down.

'Hey, Ro,' she said, twisting on one of her boots. 'You look nice. Very mysterious all in black.'

'Thanks. Yeah, you look nice too.'

'Nice? Is that it?' She traced her finger over my hoody and pulled the zip down. She was biting her lip.

'Really nice. You look really nice, Tara,' I said. I'd just about started to calm down; the music had helped. Nothing better than someone else screaming in your ear to scare away the screams in your own head.

'Thanks, babe,' she said. 'I brought some vodka. Want some before we go?' She handed me the bottle, wrapped in a bag.

'Yes,' I said. I took it from her, twisting off the lid and enjoying the burn of the liquid down my throat.

'Wow, thirsty?' She laughed.

'Sure,' I said and gave it back.

I just kept drinking the whole way to Daniel's house so I wouldn't have to think of things to say to Tara, and I sure as hell wouldn't have to think so much about what I was going to say to people at this party. But somewhere beyond that – further than the vodka haze, the regrets, further than Tara and even Ciaran – somewhere, I was thinking about talking to BASIC. And for a second I could breathe, until I remembered the fact that she wasn't single. Then I needed more vodka.

39

Juliet

Sitting there, in front of my mirror, I couldn't get away from the guilt that had been building, and that I'd been trying to ignore. If PAWN had told me he had a girlfriend I'd be absolutely gutted. So I took a deep breath, took out my phone, and hoped he'd understand.

PRETTYBASIC: I have a confession . . .

ALONELYPAWN: Oh shit, should I be scared?

PRETTYBASIC: No . . .

ALONELYPAWN: Ominous ellipsis.

PRETTYBASIC: I don't have a boyfriend.
   I'm sorry, I totally freaked out when
   you told me where you lived.

ALONELYPAWN: This is a shocking (and
   welcome) development. Here's a piece
   for free. When you told me you had a
   boyfriend . . . it sucked.

PRETTYBASIC: Really?

ALONELYPAWN: Yeah, really. I think this
   is the part in the movie where you won't

    stop talking about something and you
    look so cute that I have to kiss you.
PRETTYBASIC: How would you kiss me?
ALONELYPAWN: Mid-speech, catch you off
    guard, pull you close to me so I can
    feel your heartbeat and thank fuck you
    don't have a boyfriend.
PRETTYBASIC: I like this movie.
ALONELYPAWN: God, I wish you went to
    Birch.
PRETTYBASIC: Birch?

As in Birch High?

ALONELYPAWN: Shit. Yeah. My school. I
    guess the secret's out now . . .
PRETTYBASIC: I actually better go and get
    ready now . . .
ALONELYPAWN: Hey! Wait a minute. You need
    to match my blunder, tell me what school
    you go to!
PRETTYBASIC: Sorry, no can do.
ALONELYPAWN: I dislike you having the
    upper hand.
PRETTYBASIC: Better get used to it ;)
YOU HAVE SIGNED OUT

Shit, shit, shit, what the hell? Birch High? I googled it.
There had to be more than one Birch High in Northern Ireland.

There was only one. And it was in Ferndale.

He went to *my* school?

> **ME:** Michael, I need you. Can you come over?

> **MICHAEL:** I'm in the middle of getting ready

> **ME:** I have news. It's pretty big

> **MICHAEL:** Well, why didn't you say that? You know I can't resist gossip. See you in ten

Michael showed up wearing bright purple trousers and a black-and-white patterned shirt with a tailored blazer. On anyone else it would look ridiculous, but Michael made it retro-chic.

'How hot do I look, J? Hotter than a swollen knee?' He posed in the mirror.

'You're definitely as attractive as a swollen knee.' I laughed, and he threw a pillow at me. He came to sit beside me on the bed. 'Joking, you look awesome. Francis won't be able to resist you.'

'That's what I thought. Go on then. Tell me.' Michael's eyes were shining.

I covered my face with my hands. 'He goes to Birch.' Muffled.

'What? Who goes to Birch? You're going to have to give me more, J. I'm freaking out here.'

'The chess guy. The one I've been talking to.'

'What?' Michael grabbed my shoulders. 'Your online pervert is a Birch High pervert?'

I nodded.

'Are you sure?'

'He said it out of nowhere. He has no idea what school I go to. And Michael, we kissed. Well, not really. A virtual thing, but it was amazing, and now . . . Everything is ruined.' I pushed my pillow over my face and lay back on my bed, slowly.

'Ruined? Are you kidding? This is literally the most romantic thing I've ever heard in my life! Your weird mystery crush goes to our school!'

'Michael, what do I do?' I pulled the pillow from my face and looked at him.

'Oh, sweet little virgin. You find out who he is, and you ride him into the sunset.'

I hit Michael with my pillow. 'You mean ride off into the sunset?'

'I said what I meant. Or you know, you find out who he is and kiss him in real life.'

The feeling I got when he said that was a million nerve endings doing a Mexican wave from my head all the way down to my toes.

'Oh my God, look at that smile. You love him. Why are you still wearing sweats? You do realize he's going to be at this party, don't you? You're not going looking like . . . whatever

192

this look is. And seeing as that bitch stole your dress we'll have to find something even hotter,' Michael continued.

He then threw open my wardrobe doors and stared for a second before going to the black section. I decided not to mention the outfit I'd already chosen.

'What if he doesn't fancy me? What if he thinks crutches are weird?'

'Well, then he's not worth your time, is he? And anyway, what if *you* don't fancy him? What if you think *he's* weird? Oh my God, do you think it's one of the Dungeons & Dragons guys? Board-game fanatics.'

'Please, no.'

'I've got it – it's Luke.' Michael snorted when he said this.

'You think Luke plays chess?'

'Not in a million years. Oh my God, what about Charlie? It could easily be Charlie – he's super smart, got like ninety per cent in the last French exam.'

I thought about Charlie – serious, quiet, sandy hair and pretty hot. We'd barely said more than two sentences to each other. But the thought of it being him wasn't completely awful.

'Try this on.' Michael threw me my ripped high-waisted jeans and a black cropped jumper. If it was anyone else, I'd say the choice of jeans was a coincidence, but these were the only ones I could wear without pain, the rips giving my knees extra room.

I winced as I picked up my crutches to go into my mum's room.

'No, don't leave. I'll just turn round. Promise I won't look.'

I shuffled out of my sweatpants and avoided looking at myself in the mirror, sitting down to pull on the jeans. I liked the jumper. The sleeves were long enough to pull over my fingers. Mum had bought me it last year after I'd seen a model wearing it in *Teen Queen*.

'OK, I'm ready.'

Michael stopped scrolling through his phone and turned round. He let his mouth fall open.

'You look amazing.'

I didn't hate my reflection.

'Do your make-up and I'll do your hair. I haven't been this excited since Cassandra gave us those tickets to *Hairspray*.'

I sat at my dressing table, a YouTube tutorial open on my phone, using all the make-up Mum had bought me. I did big smoky eyes and finished them with glitter. Michael blow-dried my hair for me until it was straight but with loads of body.

'Mirror time,' he said.

He stood behind me, playing with pieces of my hair while I stared at myself. I still looked like me. Just, better.

Then I felt sick. 'I can't do this.' The reality came back like a brick to the face, and I felt ridiculous.

'Of course you can do this. *We* can do this.' Michael was always good at pep talks. 'And anyway, he still doesn't know who you are. Only *you* know what school *he* goes to. We totally have the upper hand. All we need to do is figure out who he is and then you can decide whether or not you want to tell him who you are. See?'

'Well, when you say it like that . . .' I gave him a half-smile in the mirror.

'Oh wait, finishing touch.' Michael appeared beside me with the new Marc Jacobs perfume Mum had bought me. He sprayed it in a cloud in my direction. 'Walk.'

I shut my eyes and walked into the floral mist. Then we went downstairs, into the kitchen where I swallowed some painkillers.

'Didn't know it was *that* kind of party. Come on, share the wealth,' said Michael, holding out his hand for some codeine.

'You wouldn't want it; it just makes you tired.'

'True, I'll need all my energy tonight if I'm going to make Francis fall in love with me. I plan to show him all my sick moves too.' He did a moonwalk on the tiles and the water I was drinking almost shot out of my nose.

'He's definitely going to be there?' Michael was so excited, I was worried he might actually die of disappointment if Francis didn't show.

'*Definitely.* I've been stalking his Instagram and he replied to some girl's comment on his photo saying he would see her on Friday, with a little dance emoji.' Michael grinned and nodded at me as if this was actual confirmation.

Mum walked into the kitchen and looked at us. 'Well, don't you two look fancy!'

Michael burst out laughing.

'Fancy, Mum?' Mortified.

'Or whatever you say nowadays. I don't know, cool?'

'Please stop talking,' I begged.

She ignored me. 'Oh, Jules, I got you this to bring.' Mum opened the fridge and handed me a bottle of Coke.

'I know it's not exactly . . .'

'Alcohol,' Michael cut in.

'Not that you should be drinking anyway, *Michael*, because you're underage, but it's something to bring anyway.'

'Thanks, Mum,' I said. 'And FYI, I'm not underage any more.'

'I keep forgetting. Eighteen, how did that happen?' Mum put her hand on her heart. 'Still, no alcohol is better with your medication anyway.'

'Right, let's get out of here. The party needs us. Got your bag, J? Your crutches? Your crack?' Michael smiled at Mum who pretended to look angry. 'Joking, Mrs C.'

'And Jules, just give me a call if you want me to pick you up. I'll be on the end of the phone. Be careful!'

'Not cool, Mrs C,' Michael whispered.

'Thanks,' I said. I gave Michael the bottle of Coke and followed him out of the door to his car, a kaleidoscope of butterflies dancing in my stomach.

40

Ronan

ALONELYPAWN: I'm at the party and it sucks so much. Hate parties.

PRETTYBASIC: Me too! Well, I'm not at mine yet, almost. I want to turn round and go home.

ALONELYPAWN: What if it was the same party? What would we do?

PRETTYBASIC: It's not the same party.

ALONELYPAWN: I know that (although it could be), I'm talking fantasy here, BASIC.

PRETTYBASIC: You want to know my fantasies?

ALONELYPAWN: Of course I do, the dirtier the better.

PRETTYBASIC: Well, there'd be lots of kissing, of course. I enjoyed our last kiss.

ALONELYPAWN: I'm an excellent kisser.

PRETTYBASIC: Could do better. But that's OK, I'm willing to help you practise.

ALONELYPAWN: Would we do anything else?

PRETTYBASIC: What, like play chess ;)?

ALONELYPAWN: Wasn't exactly what I was thinking . . .

PRETTYBASIC: I'm not sure what kind of girl you think I am . . .

ALONELYPAWN: An awesome one.

I can't remember the last time I felt like this. Happy, excited. Maybe that time Ciaran came back after days of no contact. I woke up and there he was, fully dressed and passed out on top of his bed. And even though it was totally different, it was the same feeling then. Like someone had taken their fist out of my chest.

'What are you smiling at? Who are you texting?' Tara nudged me.

'Nobody you know,' I said.

'You can tell me later,' she said and yanked my hand to follow her. 'Come on.'

I hit the lock on my phone and despised her for intruding into my virtual life.

About five different people stopped me on our way outside. Their hands on my shoulder, asking, 'Are you all right, man?'

I just nodded back at them. And none of them felt the need to say any more. And I was so bloody grateful. Tara didn't even seem to notice. She was in her own world and probably thought they were just saying 'hi' anyway. BASIC didn't have a boyfriend and nobody was asking too many questions. Maybe this party wasn't going to be so bad after all.

We walked outside, where some girl was already throwing up. It wasn't even nine o'clock. There were little groups of people all over the garden, smoking mostly. I pulled my hand away from Tara and pulled out the cigarettes from my back pocket, while Tara found another group to talk to.

'Anyone got a light?' I asked.

'I do,' said a voice behind me.

I turned round and there she was. Sasha. Shit. What the fuck was she doing here? My stomach dropped. What happened to 'those parties are lame' and 'nobody smokes at them'?

'Ronan!' she said, surprised.

'Thought you hated these parties.' I could feel the anger twisting in my gut.

'Yeah, I did . . . I do. But Alex wanted to come, so . . .' She shrugged.

'Still doing whatever he says then?' I couldn't help myself. There was so much more I wanted to say.

'Leave it, Ronan.' She wouldn't look straight at me.

I forced myself to calm down. It wasn't worth it. She wasn't worth it.

'Whatever,' I said.

Then an arm slung itself round Sasha's neck. Lips on her cheek. Her eye contact disappeared. I looked up to see who it was.

'Alex,' I said.

'Fucking hell, Ronan Cole.'

The anger that I'd managed to push away was back. Front and centre. There he was, smiling at me, drunk, and probably stoned too, acting like he wasn't the fucking catalyst that shattered my life. What the hell was I even doing here?

'Decided to come out of your drug den for a party then?' I spat. I couldn't help myself.

'Wow. First time we see you in months and *this* is the reunion?' He was slurring.

'Alex. Let's just go.' Sasha tugged on his arm.

'No, not yet. Because the last time we saw Ronan, do you remember what he said?' Alex looked straight at me, then at Sasha.

'Alex, don't.' She pulled his arm again and he wrenched it away.

'He said it was our fault. All of it.' And he gave a little laugh that pissed me off even more.

'Wasn't it?' I asked through gritted teeth. I didn't want everyone to hear our conversation.

'Ronan, that's not fair.' Sasha looked at me.

'Not fair?!' I couldn't believe the words coming out of her mouth. 'Not fair is what happened to me and my family. Not fair is nobody taking the blame for it. Not fair is that Alex is walking around like nothing ever fucking happened.' I moved closer to him, and he stumbled backwards, making it obvious how drunk he was.

'Ronan, is everything OK?' I turned to see Tara at my side. 'You coming?'

'Yeah, good idea, go with your girlfriend.' Alex nodded at Tara.

'She's not my girlfriend,' I said.

It wasn't that I didn't want to punch him. I've never wanted to punch someone so much in my life. But I watched him stumble again and decided against it.

Sasha looked like she was going to say something to me. Sorry, maybe? But before she said anything, Alex threw his arm round her, and she almost fell over. I squeezed the pawn in my pocket, turned and walked off with Tara.

It didn't matter. Even if she was going to apologize it wouldn't change anything.

It was too fucking late for any of it.

41

Juliet

There were cars parked halfway up the street, loads of them. And I could hear the music as soon as we turned into the cul-de-sac.

He went to my school. I still couldn't get my head round it. Of all the schools in the world, it felt like fate.

'Oh my God, it's packed, J. This is going to be amazing,' Michael said, looking for a space. 'I'll try and get as close as I can.'

'Mmm,' I mumbled.

'You know it's rude to ignore your chauffeur while you send dirty messages to a mystery chess player, don't you?'

'Sorry.'

'Oh my God, you can't stop smiling. Shit, J, you've got it bad. I'm just taking the piss. Text away.'

We parked in front of Daniel's neighbour's house in a space that wasn't really a space.

'Close enough for you?' Michael beamed at me.

'Couldn't you get a wee bit closer?' I said. 'My legs are pretty sore today.'

Michael's face dropped and he looked for another space that didn't exist. I started to laugh.

'You're such a dick,' he said. 'You ready?'

Was I ready to 'walk' into this party and maybe meet PAWN for the first time? *No.*

Was I going to suck it up and do it anyway because it's the most exciting thing that has ever happened in my life? *Yes.*

Michael got out, taking the bottle of Coke with him. He opened my door and offered his hand.

I took it and stood on the pavement, watching him bend over the front seat to reach for my crutches in the back.

'Leave them, Michael.'

'No, it's fine. I've got them. Here you go.' He turned round and handed them to me, his hair all messed up.

'I don't want them tonight.'

'Oh. Are you sure?'

'I'm sure,' I said.

'What if I bring them and keep them for you, just in case?'

'No, I don't want them,' I repeated. I knew it was stupid. I needed them, but I just couldn't. Not tonight.

'OK, well, they'll be in the car if you change your mind.' He leaned back into the car and pulled out a half-empty bottle of whiskey. 'Arm?' He held out his elbow for me.

I hooked my arm through his and inhaled. I could hear shouting and screaming and singing blasting through the walls of the house.

'What's our plan of attack?' Michael said.

'Attack? Who are we attacking?'

'You know what I mean – we can't just go in without a plan. We'll have to be vigilant. Keep watch for anyone using their phone for longer than usual. And you need to make sure you send him a constant stream of messages. So exciting.' Michael looked down at the cobbled path before he asked, 'You OK?' He'd remembered. Walking on cobbles was the worst. The distribution of pressure was all wrong, making it ten times more likely that I'd fall on my face.

'Fine.' I smiled, closed-mouthed, and concentrated. Knee over foot. Balance.

I let out a breath and walked inside.

I looked around. There were groups of people everywhere, as if the party had started hours ago. Music blaring; people shouting. And he could be here. He could *actually* be here. My stomach lurched in excitement. And I felt brave. I leaned against the wall and took my phone out.

```
PRETTYBASIC: What are you wearing?
ALONELYPAWN: Why do you want to know?
PRETTYBASIC: So I can imagine what you
    look like when you're talking to me.
ALONELYPAWN: OK, just imagine someone
    wearing all black.
PRETTYBASIC: Like the Grim Reaper?
ALONELYPAWN: I was thinking more like
    Johnny Cash, but the Reaper will do, yeah.
PRETTYBASIC: So you came in fancy dress?
ALONELYPAWN: Do you like fancy dress?
PRETTYBASIC: I LOVE fancy dress.
ALONELYPAWN: Is your party fancy dress?
PRETTYBASIC: Sadly not, I've gone for a
    pretty basic jeans and jumper combo.
```

```
ALONELYPAWN: I see what you did there. I
    bet you don't look basic at all.
PRETTYBASIC: ♡
```

'Oh, it's all heating up now, heart emojis and jokes about Johnny Cash. Who is that by the way?' Michael was looking over my shoulder at the messages.

Then someone crashed into us, standing on my toe and falling against Michael. My arm jerked.

I bit my tongue.

'Watch where you're going.' Michael pushed him out of the way. Then he turned round and I watched his face soften in slow motion.

'Sorry,' the guy said. 'I didn't see you and your girlfriend there.'

'She's not my girlfriend,' Michael said, now with the dopiest grin on his face.

Francis Nowak. Michael had showed me his pictures on Instagram so many times I felt like I knew him. He was better looking in real life. Almost a foot shorter than Michael, fine features, blonde hair and the smoothest looking skin I'd ever seen.

'Birch?' Francis asked Michael. It was like I wasn't there; they were just staring at each other.

I'd seen this look from Michael before. It's the one he gets when anyone talks about Harry Styles, like he's in a completely different world. Well, there goes my spy partner for the night.

'Hey, Michael, I'm going to go and look for Tara.' I pulled away from his arm. I'm not sure he even noticed me leave.

I scanned the living room. There were *so* many people. But no Tara. I kept my head down and headed towards the kitchen, hoping nobody else would crash into me.

The kitchen was even busier than the living room, people against every counter, but still nobody I knew. I felt my phone vibrate in my pocket. I stopped, leaned against the counter and pulled it out.

It was just Mum.

MUM: Have fun tonight. Don't forget to call for a lift if you need one.

I slid my phone back into my pocket and walked through the patio doors into the garden. It was cold. The air made my muscles tense. I let myself think about PAWN and scanned the garden. It was too dark to see. And anyway, what was I looking for? Someone wearing all black? If that was even the truth.

I wished I had my crutches now. I'd forgotten how unstable I felt without them. One wrong step, one bump from the side and I'd be on the ground in a heap of pain.

I saw Tara, leaning into Ronan as he talked to some girl from St Anne's. Tara was safe. Familiar. I walked towards her, careful in the darkness. Not careful enough apparently. My toe caught on a paving stone, and I lurched forward. My stomach dropped, the way it does when you know you're about to feel all kinds of pain.

But then there was an arm round me, pulling me back up.

'Jesus, you were about to go on your face, Jules.'

I turned round and he let go of me. It was Charlie. He smiled. Which wasn't usual for Charlie. I was glad of the darkness, hiding the pink of my cheeks. Dark clothes, all black? I couldn't tell. It was a nice thought, that it might be Charlie, and for a second I imagined what it would be like to kiss him, then remembered he was still right in front of me.

'Thanks, it's just so dark out here and I've had a couple of drinks. You know how it is.' I laughed, wishing that was the reason.

'Just be careful; people act like dickheads when they're drunk.' He rolled his eyes and smiled when he said it.

'Yeah, I will. Thanks, Charlie.'

I was doing OK. By myself, looking for Tara. I was fine without Michael, and kind of fine without my crutches. I could do this! I smiled back at Charlie, who, before turning away, made sure I was properly back on my feet before disappearing again. And instead of allowing my nerves to take over again, I decided to let myself be excited for whatever might happen tonight.

42

Ronan

I walked to the fire pit with Tara.

'Oh my God, who was that? What happened?' she asked as we joined Hana, Charlie and Luke.

'Nobody. They're nobody,' I said. I tried to think of something else to get rid of the anger that was burning in my chest. I took a drink of the vodka Tara handed me, while she exaggerated what had just happened to the group.

Then I checked my phone.

```
PRETTYBASIC: OMG, I almost tripped and
    fell on my actual face in front of
    everyone.
ALONELYPAWN: Are you OK?
PRETTYBASIC: Aw yeah, I'm fine ☺ How's
    your party going?
ALONELYPAWN: I just ran into people I did
    not want to run into . . .
PRETTYBASIC: OH NO! HATE THAT! Quick,
    have a drink.
```

```
ALONELYPAWN: Good idea. Keep checking
    your phone ;)
```

'Oh my God, Ronan, I thought you were going to punch him for a minute!' Tara looked at me, her eyes shining.

'I thought about it,' I said.

'Why? What did he do?'

'I don't want to talk about it.'

Tara stepped in front of me, blocking my path, her hands on my waist again and looking up at me. 'You know you can talk to me about anything.'

No, I can't.

'Yeah. Sure.' I let more vodka burn my throat and started walking, nudging her into moving too.

'Oh my God, Han, who are you texting? Have you got a secret crush?' Tara said.

Relief. They started whispering about Hana's crush and I took out my phone again.

```
ALONELYPAWN: What are you doing now?
PRETTYBASIC: What, since five minutes ago?
ALONELYPAWN: A lot can change in five
    minutes.
PRETTYBASIC: I'm looking for my friends.
ALONELYPAWN: I wish you were looking for
    me. For real.
PRETTYBASIC: Pretend I am. Pretend I've
    found you and we're talking. What would
    we be saying?
```

```
ALONELYPAWN: I'd tell you how much I
  wanted to take you somewhere else, so
  it was just us.
PRETTYBASIC: Somewhere like where?
ALONELYPAWN: And give away all my dating
  secrets? No chance. You'll have to meet
  me to find those out.
PRETTYBASIC: Would you kiss me again? If
  I was here, right now.
ALONELYPAWN: I don't think I'd be able to
  stop myself.
PRETTYBASIC: ☺ x
```

'Ronan, am I going to have to confiscate your phone?' Tara had finished her conversation with Hana and was now at my side again.

I just ignored her. It wasn't worth saying anything. I didn't know why I was still here, knowing they were here too, acting like they hadn't done anything. It made me feel sick. But why should I let them be the reason I leave? I wouldn't give them the satisfaction.

'They're starting the game soon, you know,' Luke said to everyone, but his eyes were on Tara.

'What game?' Hana said.

'Seven minutes.' Luke actually licked his lips.

'Mm, you ready, Ro?' Tara said, leaning against me and finding my eyes.

'Ready for what? What is it?'

'It's like spin the bottle. Well, it *is* spin the bottle but then each couple gets seven minutes in a room alone, total privacy, to do whatever they want.' Tara winked at me.

'Who else is playing?' Tara looked at Luke, the oracle of useless information.

'Some people from St Anne's, I think, you, me, Ronan?'

He looked at me and I pretended not to hear, just drank some more vodka.

'Han? Wouldn't mind the bottle landing on you.' Luke grinned and made her recoil.

'Gross, no thanks, thirty seconds in public with you is too much, never mind seven minutes alone. Sorry, pass.'

'Luke, do you ever listen to the words coming out of your mouth? At any point do you think, "no, I probably shouldn't say that?"' Charlie had moved beside Hana.

'Nah, not really,' Luke said and shrugged.

'You probably should. Some guy, or girl, is going to knock you out one day.'

'Leave it, Charlie,' said Hana. He took a drag of his cigarette. Luke looked like he'd already forgotten what Charlie had said.

Michael walked past us, deep in conversation with some other guy. Minding his own business until Luke shouted, 'Bet Michael will want to play if there's a chance of getting his tongue down some guy's throat.' Luke laughed and I looked at Michael, who hadn't even looked up, just fired Luke his middle finger.

That made me laugh.

'Oh, so he *can* laugh,' Luke said in my direction.

'Yeah, *at* you, Luke,' said Tara.

Then I saw her. Jules. Walking down the garden path towards us delicately. She didn't have her crutches with her. She was staring at the ground, watching her feet. She half looked up and smiled towards us, but then she looked quickly back down to the ground.

'Oh my God, she actually came.' Tara's voice was dripping with pity.

'What? Who?'

'Crutch Girl,' Tara said. 'Sorry, I mean Jules.' She looked at me and in that moment I hated her. I really fucking hated her. Who said that about their friend?

I watched Jules stop. Squeeze her eyes shut. Just for a second. And I knew she'd heard.

43

Juliet

I felt sick. The kind of sick I felt when the reality of my diagnosis sank in. Like there was literally nothing in the whole world that could make that moment better. Being by myself made everything worse. No Michael to shout back some witty reply, or hide behind, no group to get lost in and pretend I hadn't heard.

It wasn't like I hadn't heard the words before. From Luke, mostly. But others too. They always thought they were out of earshot, but they never were.

'Crutch Girl.' Tara's mouth was moving like it was in slow motion. Her red lips and perfect teeth opened in a huge grin, like the words she'd said hadn't felt like a punch in the throat. I swallowed, froze, closed my eyes and turned on my heel, stumbling on the path. I found my balance. My heart was in my ears. I wiped my sleeve across my eyes, hard. And looked for Michael. I couldn't see him. Anywhere. PAWN flashed in my brain, and I thought about checking my phone, but something stopped me. What was the point of trying to figure out who he was when I was like this? Fucking Crutch Girl.

I walked back towards the house, through crowds of people I barely knew, struggling to stay on my feet and desperately trying not to cry. The words she'd said were on repeat in my head. Over and over and over. I walked into the kitchen, using the counter for balance.

'Jules, isn't it?'

Harry from the football team threw his arm round my shoulders. He smelled like sweat and aftershave. His eyes were glazed, pupils dilated, a sloppy, friendly grin on his face.

'Yeah,' I said. Concentrating on not falling, I squeezed the tears back from where they came.

'We need another player.'

'For what? Have you seen Michael?'

'Who's Michael? Michael? Where are you?' he called out and laughed. 'Michael is not here. But anyway, we're playing Suicide Sourz. In teams. I need someone else for my team. Need to drink as many Apple Sourz shots as we can in five minutes.'

'No, I . . .' I tried to pull away. I wanted to look at my phone, message PAWN. Message Michael, even message Mum to pick me up.

'Too late, Jules, you're in. And we're going to win. Say it. I don't want any slackers on my team. We're in it to win it. You with me?' He had his hands on my shoulders and was looking into my eyes like this was the last game of the season and I was the star striker.

Tonight, I didn't want to be like me. Not after what she'd said. I didn't want to be the 'sick girl' who had to be sensible all the time. The one who falls asleep at nine p.m. every night and sometimes needs her mum to help her get dressed. Tonight, I didn't want to be 'Crutch Girl'. 'I'm in,' I said.

They'd lined them up – Harry, Aaron, Josh, Liam and Rebecca – tiny green shots in lines at either end of a little coffee table.

Harry led me over. 'OK, I got one. Everybody say hi to Jules, she'll be joining me and Aaron on our way to victory.' Aaron high-fived him.

'Yeah, nice try,' Liam said. 'She looks like she weighs about one hundred pounds. You'll never win.'

'What are you trying to say about *me* then?' Rebecca elbowed him in the stomach, and he doubled over.

'Nothing. I just know you can hold your drink. Jesus.'

'Right,' Harry said. And everyone just shut up and looked at him. 'Rules are simple. Aaron will start the timer on his phone. Five minutes. Whichever team has drunk the most shots when the alarm goes off wins.'

'Wins what?' I asked.

'Glory,' he said, like that was obvious. 'Everyone ready?'

No, I wasn't ready. But looking at the little green plastic cups of alcohol had made me stop thinking about what Tara had just said.

Harry bent down to whisper in my ear. 'Look, Jules, if you don't want to do too many shots just pour them in here.' He nodded to a sad little fern to his left. 'Just be sneaky about it, OK?' He smiled. He had one of those easy smiles that made you automatically smile too.

'I'll do my best.' I inhaled, thinking of Tara's words. I had no intention of using the flowerpot.

'Let's do this!' Harry squeezed my shoulder one last time before Aaron turned on the timer. 'Go.'

And they'd downed at least two before I'd even picked one up. It smelled like those fizzy apple laces Tara and I used to eat after school.

I swallowed one and squeezed my eyes shut as the bitterness coated my throat.

'Gotta drink through it.' Harry nudged me before he downed another one.

I used one hand to steady myself on the table and took another one. He was right – this one tasted better. And the third was even better than that. I'd managed four before the alarm went off. I looked at the table. Harry and Aaron had drunk about twenty shots between them. The other team – I couldn't focus properly, but I knew not as many.

'Yes, fucking right!' Harry exclaimed. He turned to me and pulled me into a hug. He squeezed me and lifted me off my feet. It hurt, but not as much as usual. Perhaps alcohol wasn't such a bad thing after all.

'Maybe you should start coming to some of the matches, Jules. You're a lucky charm.'

'Ha! Don't think anyone's ever called me lucky before.' I smiled at him.

'Thanks, though. Are you away now?'

'Where?' I turned and followed his gaze behind me towards the far side of the living room where a crowd had gathered on the sofas and some girl was clearing the coffee table by chucking things on to the floor.

'Over there. Seven minutes is starting. The pretty girls always play that.'

'I'm not . . .'

Before I could finish, Aaron had pulled Harry into a hug, and I had to move out of the way before I got crushed.

'Why didn't you ask me if *I* was playing seven minutes?' I heard Rebecca ask Liam.

I leaned against the wall and enjoyed the rush of alcohol to my head. My knees didn't hurt as much, I didn't care about being by myself, and even about what Tara had said. Yeah, it still stung, but even the edges of that were blurred. I walked over to where the game was starting. There were a few people from St Anne's, but they were mostly from Birch. They sat on the sofa I was leaning on. Some guy I didn't know reached up and grabbed my arm.

'You playing?'

'OK,' I said. I walked round the side of the sofa and sat down in between two people I didn't know. I looked up to see Michael and Francis staring at me in horror from the other side of the room.

'What are you doing?' he mouthed and waved me over.

But I shook my head. I wasn't budging. The drinks had made me feel better and this was what 'normal' people did.

Maybe, for once, I could just be one of them.

44

Ronan

'Seriously? Crutch Girl?' I looked at Tara and hoped my disgust showed through the drunken haze.

'Chill out, Ronan. I was kidding. Where'd she go, anyway?'

'You know she heard you, don't you? What the fuck is wrong with you?'

'What's wrong with *me*? Nothing, Ronan. But still not good enough for you apparently.'

'This isn't about *you*. Well, no, sorry, it is. It's about why you're such an asshole to your supposed friend for no reason. She can't help using crutches any more than you can help being a dick apparently. And she didn't even *have* crutches tonight.'

Everyone around us was staring.

'What's got into you? People said you came with baggage – is that what this is?'

'Tara, just leave it.' Luke stepped in between us. 'We don't know what he's capable of.'

'Oh, fuck off, Luke,' I said.

'Can everyone just chill out? Seven minutes is starting,' Hana said, looking like a rabbit in headlights.

218

'Ronan.' Tara was right beside me again, trying to hold my hand, though I didn't let her. 'I'm sorry, I don't want us to fight.' She was talking to me like we were a couple.

I ignored her and walked back inside. Had I led her on? I hadn't meant to. I didn't even realize I'd done it. I just didn't want to deal with the confrontation and now look where it'd got me! I went straight towards the seven minutes people because I needed a distraction.

I sat down in a random chair and scanned the room. A few girls I remembered from St Anne's, a few from Birch that I'd seen before but didn't really know. And one I didn't expect to be there at all. Jules. She was sitting between two people, like a graphic novel on a shelf of textbooks, ripped jeans, black top. Looking around, not talking. She caught my eye and smiled, raised her hand slightly, then put it down like she was embarrassed. Either that or she forgot she hated me. I smiled back and meant it.

Tara and Luke barged through the middle of the room to sit to the right of me. Tara threw me a dirty look while Luke didn't let her out of his sight.

Some girl with huge tits and red hair stood up and grabbed the bottle.

'OK, whoever it lands on has seven minutes alone together in the downstairs bathroom, OK?'

'Just spin it, Fiona,' Luke said.

'Let the game begin!' Fiona called and some girls beside me cheered. She put the bottle in the centre of the table and I watched as it spun. Quickly at first, making its way to the far edge of the mahogany coffee table before slowing down.

I thought it was going to fall off, but it didn't, it kept spinning. Slower and slower until . . .

It landed on Tara. And she made sure to look at me when it did.

'OK, our first contestant is the lovely Tara Williams.' Fiona pointed at Tara who responded by standing up and taking a bow. 'Isn't she lovely, ladies and gentlemen?'

She was taking her job of seven-minute host really seriously.

'And who will she be spending seven glorious minutes with, I wonder?' She picked up the bottle again. I looked away for a second and caught Tara's eyes on me.

Please not me, please not me.

Fiona spun the bottle again. I didn't watch it this time, instead I raised my gaze and caught Jules's eye. She was sitting opposite me with her hands twisted in her lap. She gave me a little smile. I returned it.

'Yes!' Luke's voice went through me when it landed on him.

Thank God.

He jumped to his feet and grabbed Tara's hand. 'Don't want to waste any time.'

She got up slowly, eyes locked on mine. She smiled as she went with him towards the bathroom, while the rest of us just waited. I took a drink. Everyone was drinking something. If this game took too long, everyone would be completely wasted, and Christ knows what that bathroom would see. I pulled out my phone. Nothing from BASIC.

I looked across the table at Jules, who must have been looking at me. She looked down right away and I watched as a flush of pink crept over her whole face.

'We're back,' Tara sang.

Her lipstick was smudged. She made sure to go the long way round back to her seat, brushing against my legs on the way past. She sat down and leaned into Luke, shooting me more looks than I could ignore.

Fiona stood up again and took the bottle. I should've left ages ago. This wasn't me. But Tara had pissed me off so much I wanted to piss her off too.

And it was like my anger was some kind of magnet, because the bottle slowly pointed to me. I watched Tara's face drop, and her eyes glued themselves to the bottle again. Fiona spun it. The bottle was a blur until again it slowed and slowed, glass on wood. Then stopped. I followed its neck to see Jules looking back at me. I couldn't work out the expression on her face. Unsure? Nervous? After a moment's hesitation as I tried to work it out, she gave me that little smile again. It felt like she was telling me to go for it. So I stood up and walked round the table, holding out my hand towards her.

Jules looked at Tara before putting her hand in mine. I pulled her hand and she stood up slowly.

'You coming?' I asked.

She hesitated, looked at Tara again, and then let me lead her towards the bathroom.

The bathroom was tiny. Just a sink and a toilet and barely enough room for two people. That's probably what made it so great for this game, two bodies forced together.

She looked up at me. 'It's you.' Then she diverted her gaze away from me, pretending to be interested in a little framed painting on the wall.

'You didn't have to come with me, you know,' I said, trying to tease out what she was thinking.

'I did, actually.' She was looking at me again now with her big eyes.

'And why's that? Does seven minutes come with some sort of rule book at Birch?' I smirked.

'Well, yeah, actually, I think it probably does, but that's not why.' She started tracing the wall with her finger, following it with her eyes.

'Why then? Is it because of what Tara said?'

She looked straight at me then and I swear her eyes glistened with tears. She blinked them back.

'You heard that? It's fine, it doesn't matter. And I guess I just know she fancies you, so I wanted to annoy her by coming in here, and now I just sound totally pathetic . . .'

I interrupted her. 'It's not fine. It was such a dick move and if it's any consolation, that's not what I see when I look at you.'

It was like she didn't know what to say. She leaned against the wall and studied my face, biting her bottom lip like she was concentrating.

'What do you see?' she asked quietly.

'I see someone who's funny and pretty and doesn't take any bullshit from the hottest guy in school.'

That got a laugh. A laugh on the verge of tears.

'You said it, not me!' I laughed too and moved closer to her so there were only inches between us.

'I did not! I said that's what *you* think about yourself.' She pushed my chest gently, but instead of taking her hand away, she kept it there, leaning on me.

'Same difference.' I whispered it because we were so close.

'Well, maybe you're not as much of a dick as I first thought.' She was properly smiling now and the tears in her eyes were sparkling, like the sea on a sunny day.

'That could be the nicest thing anyone has ever said to me,' I said. I let my fingers find her other hand, the one that wasn't pressed to my chest. I twisted my fingers through hers and I didn't have time to wonder if she felt my heart beat faster because she leaned into me even more and looked right up at me. I let my head tilt, just a bit, just to see if she did it too.

I hadn't planned this. What was I doing? In a chess game this was the point I'd stop myself. Think about what I was doing and plan the best way forward. But there wasn't any time for thinking.

So I kissed her.

And it was like time stopped.

Sometimes the most unexpected moves turn out to be the most beautiful.

45

Juliet

He kissed me. And it wasn't that I didn't want him to, but I definitely didn't expect him to. Someone who looked like that kissing someone who looked like me. He knew what he was doing. Even the way he kissed felt confident. Like a dance he was leading, and I was struggling to keep up.

I don't know if it was just the alcohol swimming through my bloodstream, but it felt like my whole body had pins and needles. Every time he touched me, it was like an electric current bursting into life. His hand on my waist, one on my cheek and then in my hair, every touch gentle. Perfect. And just in that second, I felt almost normal. The way I felt when I talked to PAWN. Like it was the real me, not the version of myself the rest of the world saw.

I let myself lean into him, closer. My leg leaning against his. Then I felt something and pulled away.

'Have you got something in your pocket?' I asked, laughing. He was so close to me that he was breathing into my mouth. Then he put his hand in his pocket and pulled something out.

'I mean, I'm not saying that you don't do that to me, but this is what it is. Just something stupid.' He twirled a black pawn in his fingers and then shoved it back into his pocket and came in for another kiss. But I moved out of the way and leaned back against the wall.

'A chess piece? Why do you have that?' Had someone told him I play chess? Was he taking the piss?

'It's stupid. Lucky charm, I guess.' He gave a little laugh. Was he embarrassed? I stared at him for longer than was normal without saying anything. The alcohol was making it take longer to get my thoughts straight. He wasn't taking the piss. He liked chess too?

'You play chess?' I asked.

He hesitated, like he was trying to think of the right answer.

'Yeah, I do. Just something me and my brother used to do,' he said, looking down at his hand. He'd taken the pawn out again and was twisting it between his fingers.

'I play chess too,' I said. It couldn't be him. Could it? Right then I couldn't hear anything outside the door; no music, no shouting. It was like my mind had focused on this moment only and everything else faded away.

He stopped moving the pawn. Trapping it in his palm, he folded his fingers over it before looking at me.

'Do you play online?' he asked, finally.

I looked at his clothes: black jeans, black hoody. Black, black, black. Grim Reaper. Ronan was PAWN? My head was spinning from the alcohol and the realization that I'd just kissed my mystery crush.

I nodded. 'Chess Life?'

'Yeah.' He said it like a breath he'd been holding. He ran his hand through his hair and looked at me with that smile.

'You're ALONELYPAWN, aren't you?' I said.

'PRETTYBASIC?' he replied.

And it wasn't me. It was the alcohol that made me brave enough to step away from the wall and put my arms round his neck. It must have been the alcohol that made me kiss him the way I did. Like this time I knew what I was doing and I never wanted to stop. Because the regular me would have been too scared. I only pulled away when I heard someone knocking on the door.

'Time's up.' Someone from outside was getting pissed off.

'Piss off!' I shouted and then put my hand over my mouth in shock.

Ronan laughed. 'Didn't expect that.'

'Yeah, I don't normally swear, but . . .'

He didn't say anything, just pulled me into him again, harder this time. His mouth was on mine.

We ignored the banging on the door, which soon turned to cheering and then to silence.

Ronan Cole was PAWN. And I couldn't have been happier.

46

Ronan

Jules was BASIC? I looked at her as the knocks on the door got louder. I couldn't take my eyes off her, leaning against the wall, her make-up smudged, and her face flushed. So beautiful.

'What now?' I asked.

'What do you mean?'

'I mean, like, are we official now? Seeing that we've been flirting online for so long and all.'

'Flirting? Is that what that was?' She grinned.

'Maybe from you. Not me, of course.'

'Well, I guess I'm happy to make it official then,' she said.

She looked at me with a half-smile, holding on to the wall so she wouldn't fall over.

I leaned in and kissed her as if to seal the deal.

She pulled away. 'Shit, what about Tara?' She squeezed her eyes shut.

'What?'

'She totally fancies you.'

'And what? It doesn't mean that she can control who I can go out with.'

'It doesn't matter. There are rules about this,' Jules said, sounding stressed.

'Rules?'

'Yeah, like, don't go out with your best friend's boyfriend, ex-boyfriend, crush.'

'Even if she called you Crutch Girl?'

She winced and I wished I hadn't said it.

'Sorry. But she did. She's a dick, Jules. She only cares about herself. And you have no idea how happy I am that you are BASIC.' I moved closer and took her hand, bringing it to my mouth and kissing her knuckles.

'You're right. I can't believe she said that.' She looked so sad and I hated Tara all over again. 'I'm pretty happy it's you, too.'

'Pretty happy?'

'Really happy.'

I kissed her again.

They'd left us alone for a while. Whoever was banging. But now they were back, and it sounded like they were going to break down the fucking door.

'We'd better go. Are you ready?' I asked.

She shook her head, her eyes wide with fear.

'Fuck it, let's do it.' I held out my hand and she took it. I unlocked the door and pushed it open to a crowd of people standing outside.

'Yeoooo,' they shouted. Jules stood behind me, like she was using me as some kind of shield. I didn't mind.

I guided her through the crowd, trying to stop people banging into her.

'What the fuck?' Tara was standing right in front of us, and clearly pissed.

'What?'

'You're together now?' She wasn't looking at me, she was looking at Jules.

'No,' Jules said. I hated that Tara made Jules sound even smaller than she was.

'So what if we are?' I asked.

Tara stared at me for a second before stomping off into the crowd.

Michael appeared as if from nowhere, towering above everyone.

'J, what's going on?'

'Michael, hey, where's Francis?' she asked.

'Getting drinks. Shit, are you drunk?' Michael asked. I hadn't even noticed. Jules gave my hand one last squeeze, let go, and followed Michael through the crowd. I followed them to the corner of the room.

'Are you OK?' I asked. But even though she nodded, her eyes were red. I pushed some hair out of her face, behind her ears.

'You've angered the beast,' said Michael, nodding in Tara's direction. I looked at her ranting to Hana and throwing dirty looks in our direction.

'I don't give a shit,' I said.

'Well, you might. The last time she was pissed, when Aimee Choo took her place on the hockey team, she made her life hell for like a year. And I'm not saying that was the reason she left the school, but it was definitely the reason she left the school.' Michael pulled a face.

'I'm not scared of her.'

'Literal knight in shining armour, J.' Michael nudged Jules and I thought I saw a hint of a smile.

'Anyway, I'm away to find my own knight in shining armour. He went to get us drinks about twenty minutes ago. You OK?'

Jules nodded. 'Thanks, Michael, I'll text you.'

'You better,' he said before disappearing.

'Want to get out of here?' I looked down at her.

'Yeah. I'll just message my mum for a lift.'

'Wish I had someone to phone for a lift.' I shrugged. She looked at me like she wanted me to elaborate. But I wasn't ready for that. Would I ever be ready for that conversation?

Then she stared at her phone screen and typed a message. She put her phone away and looked up at me. 'Will you wait outside with me?' she asked.

'Let's go.'

I opened the front door. The night was quite warm, or maybe that was the vodka. There was someone throwing up in the bushes. Jules sat down on the little garden wall, and I sat beside her, our legs touching.

I put my hand on hers, threading our fingers together.

'I still can't believe it's you,' I said. Because it's what I was thinking. And it just came out when I was with her. What I was thinking.

'I know, I mean, of all the schools in the world. It's like it's fate or something.' She leaned her head on my shoulder.

'I don't believe in fate. But I do believe in luck.' I turned and tilted her chin towards mine, kissing her again, wishing I could just forget everything and kiss her forever.

A car pulled up on the kerb in front of us, lights shining.

Jules pulled away and stood up, slowly. Unsteady. I didn't know whether it was the alcohol or the fact she didn't have her crutches. I still didn't even know why she needed them, but it didn't feel like something I could ask. Not yet.

'That's my mum,' she said. 'How are you going to get home? Do you want a lift?'

'No, thanks, I need the walk.'

'See you on Chess Life?' There was that smile again.

'If you want to lose again,' I said.

'In your dreams.' She walked towards the car.

You're my dream, I thought, which kind of shocked me. I hoped that this time, though, my thoughts wouldn't come out of my mouth. I waited until they drove away before walking in the opposite direction, back into the shadows.

47

Juliet

'Who was that?' I could practically see Mum's eyes shining in the dark.

'Nobody.' God, I couldn't stop smiling.

'Doesn't seem like nobody.' She pulled away from the kerb. 'Very dark and mysterious though. Did you have a good night?'

'The best.' My head was spinning and I couldn't tell if it was from the shots or what had just happened.

I turned on the radio and leaned my head against the window, hoping Mum wouldn't ask me any more questions. I wanted to go over that kiss. Those kisses. The things he said, the way he touched me. I wanted to feel everything I felt for every second until I died.

It was like I was floating and nothing else came close. Not Tara, not the arthritis. Not anything.

When we got home Mum made me tea and toast that she brought up to my room. She sat on the bed beside me. And I knew it was horrible, but I wished she'd go away. I couldn't wait to get into bed, turn on Chess Life and go to sleep dreaming of Ronan Cole.

'I'm so glad you had fun,' she said.

'Thanks, Mum.'

'Oh, where are your crutches?' Mum looked around my room.

'I didn't use them tonight, I left them in Michael's car.' I avoided Mum's gaze and scrolled through my phone instead. I heard her sigh.

'Well, at least we have a spare pair that you can use tomorrow. Give me a shout in the morning if you need any help.'

'Sure. Thanks.'

When she left, I got changed. I ran my hands over my stomach, where Ronan had touched me, pretending it was him again. I touched my face, and I was back in that bathroom, his hand on my cheek and his tongue in my mouth. I put my hand on my chest and I could feel his heartbeat thudding against mine.

I turned on Chess Life. He was online.

```
ALONELYPAWN: I was hoping I'd see you
  here.
PRETTYBASIC: Why?
ALONELYPAWN: Because I miss talking
  to you.
PRETTYBASIC: Already?
ALONELYPAWN: You have a strange effect
  on me.
PRETTYBASIC: You have a strange effect on
  me too.
ALONELYPAWN: I wish I was there with you
  right now.
```

```
PRETTYBASIC: I wish you were too.
ALONELYPAWN: What would we be doing?
PRETTYBASIC: You'd be lying beside me,
    your arm round me, so close I could
    feel your heartbeat and you could feel
    mine.
ALONELYPAWN: And what about my other arm,
    what would it be doing?
PRETTYBASIC: You'd be tracing your fingers
    gently over my stomach.
```

Oh my God, I couldn't believe I was doing this. But the way it made me feel, like I was going to explode inside, I couldn't stop.

```
ALONELYPAWN: And would you like it?
PRETTYBASIC: I would love it. So much
    that I'd do the same to you.
ALONELYPAWN: It's very frustrating that
    you're not here.
PRETTYBASIC: I know. But you haven't even
    taken me on a date yet. Maybe we should
    do that before I lose my virtual
    virginity.
ALONELYPAWN: That can be arranged. Leave
    it with me ;)
PRETTYBASIC: As much as I want to
    stay, I'm really tired, I better go
    to sleep.
```

```
ALONELYPAWN: Have sweet dreams of me
  BASIC xx
PRETTYBASIC: As long as you dream about
  me too xx
ALONELYPAWN: I already am xx
```

The next morning when I woke up, I knew two things. One, that I'd had the best night of my life, despite it being tainted by Tara, and two, I was in a world of pain. The pain shot through my knees, up my thighs and towards my ankles and my elbow had swollen to twice its normal size.

'Mum,' I called out, my voice hoarse, my head throbbing. My mouth was hot and dry. I reached out for a glass of water that wasn't there.

She must have been awake because she came in almost immediately, the crease of concern on her forehead.

'How bad?' She bent down and pulled the blankets away from my legs.

'Nine,' I said. Tears I didn't even know were there spilled down my face.

I hated that I couldn't pretend. That I couldn't even get the words 'I'm fine' out of my mouth. And that even if I did, they would be completely unbelievable.

'Oh, Jules,' said Mum. 'I'll run you a bath.'

First, she brought up water and painkillers. Then a hot-water bottle and an ice pack. She sat on the chair beside my bed, and I swallowed the pills like they were sweets. She held the ice pack on my knees until it was too cold to take, then switched it for a hot-water bottle. The smell of hot lavender filled the room from the bath next door.

'You know, you really shouldn't drink when you're on your medication. It makes you forget to sit down.'

'I know.'

And she inhaled like she was going to say something else. But instead, she held out her hand for me to take.

'Shall we try?' Mum said.

I nodded.

She helped me swing my legs over the side of the bed, slid her arms underneath mine and lifted me. She moved to my right and let me lean on her. I saw the crease deepen when a noise came from the back of my throat. She helped me the whole way to the bathroom, to the bath that had a grab rail on one side. What kind of teenager needed a granny bath?

Mum helped me get undressed. I didn't care.

I didn't care that I was eighteen and my own mother had to see me naked.

Even when, according to every single movie I'd ever watched, it should be some hot guy in that scene.

I didn't care that she helped me get into the bath and waited until the suds covered my toes.

I didn't care that she brought me my phone and a glass of water and waited until my jaw unclenched. What other choice did I have?

The water was almost too hot. But it helped, giving my body something else to think about. Loosening the joints that had stuck overnight.

I shouldn't have left my crutches in Michael's car. I shouldn't have had anything to drink. I shouldn't have been outside so I could hear what Tara said about me. I wiped tears from my face, leaving suds in their place. I dried my hands on a face cloth and picked up my phone that was balancing on the edge of the bath. I was about to flick through our Chess Life messages from last night, fill my head with everything I felt again, but there were about a million WhatsApps from Michael. So I looked at those first.

MICHAEL: Miss you, J. And I'm so fucking happy for you. I can't believe it's Ronan, you lucky bitch! Don't worry about Tara. She'll move on to someone else in no time.

MICHAEL: I think Francis is totally into me, you know. He said his parents are away tonight.

MICHAEL: Shall I?

MICHAEL: Seeing you're not here to say no, I'll just have to make my own decisions.

MICHAEL: Ah, I'm going home with Francis. I'll tell you everything in the morning. Bit drunk. God, he's so hot.

MICHAEL: Oh, and Tara seems to have got over Ronan pretty quickly. Her and Luke are making me want to vomit. Or that might be the vodka. Or both. They're equally vomit-inducing.

MICHAEL: Love you, J. As much as my gran loves Fry's Peppermint Creams. Maybe more . . .

MICHAEL: Wish you were here now. Can't wait to find out all the explicit details about you and Ronan on Monday, you dark horse.

MICHAEL: But for now, I must go. I bid you adieu. Wish me luck.

MICHAEL: Thanks for the luck, I know you send it in spirit.

I smiled but didn't write back. I was in too much pain for the energy I'd need to hear all about Michael's night. Then I saw the Chess Life notifications. The little red pawn that flashed and my stomach made its way to my throat. I tried to push myself up with one hand so I could concentrate on what the messages said. But Mum had put oil in the bath, and it was slippy. I stayed lying down instead. I opened the messages, holding my breath and feeling the ache in my ribs. The tiny muscles that felt bruised every time I inhaled, exhaled.

ALONELYPAWN: Good morning xx

I held my phone above the water, closed my eyes, let my head sink, thanking God it wasn't all a dream.

48

Ronan

I woke up the next morning thinking about Jules. I relaxed into thoughts of her, thinking about that kiss, and the fact that she was BASIC. It was completely unexpected. And completely amazing. It didn't take long for the rest of the night to creep into my mind. I got out of bed so I could do something and distract myself. Seeing Alex and Sasha again . . . I wasn't ready. I would *never* be ready. As far as I was concerned, they were dead to me.

I avoided Mum the whole day. She'd spent all day cooking stupid dinner and talking about the Silver Pawn Tournament. As if food and delusions were going to make things better. I went for a run, pushing myself until my lungs screamed for air and my legs felt like they belonged to somebody else. I came back to roast chicken going cold on a plate in the kitchen. I took it up to my room and ate it alone. I sent messages to BASIC, to Jules. All day. Everything about her was effortless and I couldn't fucking wait to see her at school. I immediately hated anyone who sent me a message when I was waiting for one from Jules. Especially from Aunt Sarah, who never did anything but shove everything back into my head.

ALONELYPAWN: You know, last night was the best night I've had in a really long time.

PRETTYBASIC: Me too ☺

ALONELYPAWN: Were you surprised it was me?

PRETTYBASIC: Yeah.

ALONELYPAWN: I was surprised too. But good surprised. Really good surprised.

PRETTYBASIC: ♡

ALONELYPAWN: You OK? You don't seem like your usual annoyingly chatty self.

PRETTYBASIC: Yeah, sorry. I don't feel very well today.

ALONELYPAWN: Hungover?

PRETTYBASIC: I wish that was it. I mean, it's no secret that I have a 'thing' so I should probably just tell you what's wrong with me.

ALONELYPAWN: I wanted to ask, I just wasn't sure how.

PRETTYBASIC: It's OK. You can ask me anything. I have arthritis.

ALONELYPAWN: Jules ☹ That's shit.

PRETTYBASIC: Yeah, that's exactly what it is!

ALONELYPAWN: Since when?

PRETTYBASIC: Since I was twelve.

ALONELYPAWN: ☹ Jesus. Will it get worse or is it one of those things that stays the same? Sorry, I'm probably saying the wrong thing.

PRETTYBASIC: No, it's fine. Actually, it's kind of nice to talk. And it's weird because I don't really talk about it to anyone except for the doctors and my physio. Yeah, it can get worse. It's progressive, but it's controlled at the minute. I inject myself once a week and take a heap of other tablets.

ALONELYPAWN: Does it hurt? Injecting yourself?

PRETTYBASIC: Yeah, a bit, I guess but it's worth it. I don't think I'd be able to walk at all without them.

ALONELYPAWN: Do you hurt all the time?

PRETTYBASIC: Yeah. I mean, I do get used to the pain and I've adapted to it so it's not like I'm inwardly screaming in agony at all times.

ALONELYPAWN: ☹

PRETTYBASIC: NO! STOP IT! NO SYMPATHY, THAT'S THE WORST!

```
ALONELYPAWN: Fine. Just took your rook.
PRETTYBASIC: How dare you. Here I am,
    spilling my guts to you about my POOR
    SORE JOINTS and you take advantage?
ALONELYPAWN: HEY!!! You said no
    sympathy!!
PRETTYBASIC: ♘ 🖐
ALONELYPAWN: That was my favourite
    knight.
PRETTYBASIC: Thanks, though, for asking.
    I better go now, going to sleep off
    these painkillers.
ALONELYPAWN: Have nice dreams. Of me xxx
```

I hadn't expected that at all. For her to have arthritis, although I don't really know what I thought. I just hated that she was in pain most of the time.

Chess practice could wait. I turned on my laptop and typed 'Arthritis' into google. I wasn't a doctor. I couldn't help her pain, but I could learn about it.

Studying chess made me understand the game.

Studying arthritis might make me understand Jules.

And maybe if I understood, I could find a way to help.

On Sunday, Jules and I played chess non-stop. I didn't care about the games though. I was just so happy to be talking to her.

```
ALONELYPAWN: Are you feeling any better
    today?
```

PRETTYBASIC: A bit, yeah, thanks.

ALONELYPAWN: I didn't realize there were so many types of arthritis . . .

PRETTYBASIC: You googled?

ALONELYPAWN: Yeah. I don't like not understanding things.

PRETTYBASIC: That's really sweet.

ALONELYPAWN: It's not sweet. It's cool and sexy. What type do you have?

PRETTYBASIC: Juvenile Idiopathic Arthritis.

ALONELYPAWN: And there are even more types of that?

PRETTYBASIC: Yeah, I have psoriatic. Like psoriasis, the skin condition. USUALLY people with psoriatic arthritis have that too, but I don't. Just the dodgy joints. Lucky me?

ALONELYPAWN: I read that bit. I read a lot about all the pain too . . .

PRETTYBASIC: Sounds like a fun read.

ALONELYPAWN: Jules, I didn't realize how bad it can get. I hate that you have to deal with it.

PRETTYBASIC: Thanks, but yeah, it's not ALWAYS bad, just sometimes.

ALONELYPAWN: Thanks for telling me ☺

```
PRETTYBASIC: No worries. But you owe me
    something in return . . .
ALONELYPAWN: What do you want to
    know?
PRETTYBASIC: Anything. Something
    personal. I want to know everything
    about you.
```

Here it was. The moment I tell her what happened. With Ciaran, about Mum, about how my life is such a goddamn mess.

```
ALONELYPAWN: My brother was kind of into
    drugs.
PRETTYBASIC: Kind of?
ALONELYPAWN: Yeah, not kind of . . .
    Really into drugs.
PRETTYBASIC: ☹ That sucks. But you
    said 'was' so past tense? That's good,
    isn't it?
```

I couldn't. I just couldn't.

```
ALONELYPAWN: Yeah ☺
PRETTYBASIC: Have you ever taken drugs?
ALONELYPAWN: Never.
PRETTYBASIC: Me either. Except
    prescription ones.
```

ALONELYPAWN: Drugs just don't seem worth
    the chaos.
PRETTYBASIC: I agree, there are so many
    better things to do.
ALONELYPAWN: Like taking your pawns.
PRETTYBASIC: And being with you x
ALONELYPAWN: x

49

Juliet

I couldn't believe that he'd googled my arthritis. Or that I didn't want to slam my laptop shut when I was talking about it. He made it easy to talk. His brother being into drugs, that must have been so hard. But it sounded like things were better now. Thank God.

I spent the rest of Sunday in a painful, dreamy haze. Some of it because of the painkillers but mostly because of Ronan. It was like, for once, things were actually working out the way I wanted.

I didn't look at English Revision once on Sunday. I let myself enjoy the fact that the hottest guy in school actually liked me, and it wasn't just one of my fantasies.

It was weird driving to school without Tara. Screw her though. I'd had the weekend to think about it and it was the pain that helped me see things more clearly in the end. That Michael had been right. Everything he'd said about her. That she only cared about herself, that she treated me like crap.

And Ronan. I'd told him everything. And he didn't run a mile. He was sweet and interested and his reaction was everything I'd ever wanted, even though I'd never even dared thinking about that scenario before.

'Do you reckon she'll even bother coming in today, seeing as she has to get the bus?' Michael asked.

'She'll probably have made Hana give her a lift.' I shrugged. I'd gone from being brave over the weekend, to having my head taken over by thoughts of Tara.

How dare she say that about me?

She's the one who should feel shit.

There's no way I would talk to her until she apologized.

'And ... you're right.' Michael sounded like a gameshow host. He pulled into the school car park, and I followed his eyeline to Tara standing with Hana, Luke and Charlie, staring towards us.

'Oh God, she saw us.' I looked away, shimmying myself down in my seat so I was blocked from her view by Michael.

'So what! She's the dick here, not you! You have *nothing* to be embarrassed about.'

I nodded. 'I know, but let's just stay here for a wee minute, OK? Tell me about Francis. I was too full of painkillers this weekend to take it all in.'

And I relaxed as Michael talked about Francis, letting his joy seep into my pores.

'We're going to see a movie tonight. *Ida*, it's called. It's Polish and we're going to that place, what's it called ... Queen's Film Theatre! Because that's where they show all the fancy, sophisticated movies. Did I tell you he speaks fluent Polish? He's so metropolitan. He's going to teach me how to speak Polish too.'

'Did he teach you any on Friday?' I tried to raise my eyebrow.

'What's wrong with your eye? No, we didn't have much time for language lessons, unless you want to count tongue exercises.' He winked. 'Oh, J, he's just perfect. I can't wait for you to meet him properly, you're going to love him. And you'll never guess what.'

'What?'

'He likes chess! I was making fun of you to him yesterday and he was like, "I play chess."'

'Hey!' I dug my elbow into Michael's side.

'Sorry. Needs must, it was a whole joke ... *hilarious*. But anyway, yeah, he's a chess nerd like you. But *he* makes it kind of hot.' Michael sighed. I dreaded to think of the image in his head.

'Well, Ronan Cole also plays chess, and he's also hot. So it seems like you're the uncool one now. Sorry.'

'Don't worry, Francis is going to teach me chess too. Strip chess.' Michael opened his car door. 'We're safe.' He walked round to my side and opened my door.

Miss Black appeared from a black Mini Cooper beside us. 'Mr Crawley and Miss Clarke, unless you've got some reason to be congregating in the car park at ten past nine, I suggest you hurry up and get to class.'

'Sorry, Miss Black. We were having a crisis.'

'Well, unless it's some kind of medical crisis, get a move on!'

I leaned even harder on my crutches than usual on the way into school. Making it look even more painful than it was. Figured that I might as well take whatever benefits I could from this shitty disease.

'It's OK, Juliet, take your time,' Miss Black said gently as I hobbled past.

'Thanks, Miss Black.'

I wondered when I'd see Ronan. Part of me wished I'd just got out of the car earlier, walked right past Tara and into the schoolyard where Ronan might have been. Maybe he would have kissed me again and I could have sat through history with the taste of him on my lips. But the other part was glad I hid; forcing Tara out of my head was the only way I felt I could deal with the situation at all.

When Mr Tsang had given us some insanely boring pages to read about the Tudors, he sat down and started marking work. I took out my phone and hid it under the desk.

I logged into Chess Life. No messages. None since the ones he sent yesterday.

'Miss Clarke, a message from reception.'

I looked up to see Mr Tsang staring at me. 'Your brother is at reception. Said your parents forgot about one of your appointments and you're to go immediately? He's waiting outside for you.'

My brother? I didn't have a brother.

'I don't ...' Then the penny dropped. 'Thank you, sir.' I smiled at him, unhooked my bag from the chair and crutch-walked my way out of the door.

I smiled at Mrs Harrison on reception as I walked past.

'Hi, love,' she said. She was so used to me coming and going that she barely batted an eyelid.

My phone buzzed in my pocket. I waited until I was safely outside to take it out.

Chess Life.

ALONELYPAWN: Round the corner. Where the
    bad kids smoke.

When I appeared around the corner there he was, smoking a cigarette.

'Hey,' he said, stubbing his cigarette out on the ground.

'Hi.'

'Want to get out of here?'

'Out of school? What? Illegally?' I tried to make my face look less shocked than I felt.

Ronan snorted. 'I don't think you're going to get arrested for skipping school.'

'You don't know that.'

'I do. I do know that. But anyway, isn't it lucky that you're not actually skipping school, but going to an appointment with your brother?'

'But what if Mr Tsang says something to Mrs Harrison about me leaving with my brother and she'll be like, "Jules doesn't have a brother" and he'll be like, "We've been swindled!"'

Ronan watched the anxiety take over before laughing. He sat down on the concrete steps.

'Swindled?' He tried not to laugh again. 'Want to sit down for a bit first? I mean, we don't *have* to leave if it's going to stress you out too much.'

I inhaled and slowly lowered myself on to the step beside him. 'No, I think I'll be OK. It'll be OK, won't it?' I mean, obviously *he* was going to say yes.

'Of course it will. I did it all the time at St Anne's. As long as you're sneaky, nobody notices.' He was looking right into my eyes when he said it and I swear I felt sick. In that good way, like when you eat too much chocolate, and the sweetness gets stuck at the back of your throat. 'Do you trust me?'

I narrowed my eyes, pretending to think it over, when really, I was just thinking about kissing him again.

'I trust you . . . I think,' I added.

Then he leaned in and kissed me; his mouth was warm and tasted like smoke. So this was what it was like. To have a proper boyfriend. Sneaking round, stealing kisses with my heart working overtime. I could get used to this. He had one hand on my face, the other on my knee. I surprised myself by not jerking my knee away. The thought of him feeling the swelling beneath the skin horrified me. But right now, it felt OK. Almost like his hand was meant to be there.

And there I was. My head spinning in circles, my stomach in knots, and feeling like the luckiest person in the world.

50

Ronan

I'd come to school early, hoping she would too, but she was in Michael's car so long that I had to think of something else. And then my amazing plan was born.

That smile of hers when she walked round the corner made it impossible not to smile back. Impossible not to think about kissing her. That's why I stubbed out my cigarette when it had just been lit.

Just after we'd kissed, she leaned her head on my shoulder and I breathed her in. Flowers. I didn't want to move and risk her taking her head away. She threaded her fingers through mine and squeezed.

'Can I ask you something?' she said, like it was something she was scared to ask.

'Anything.'

'Why did you have that pawn with you at the party? I know you said it's a lucky charm, but why the pawn?'

'This one?' I pulled the pawn from my pocket, and we looked at it together.

'Yeah.'

'The pawn is the only piece than can be promoted to something better. It can become anything it wants to be. And it makes me think, I dunno, maybe I could too.'

'What do you want to be?'

'Nothing special. Just happy, I guess.' Christ, I wish I hadn't come out with that. I wish she'd stop disabling my filter.

'And you aren't?' Concern flashed across her face.

'I am. Now.'

I kissed her again. It was so hard not to when she was looking at me with that face.

'But yeah, enough delaying. I know what you're doing. Trying to seduce me into going back to school. Let's go somewhere. Have a date.'

'Where? I can't exactly walk very far.' She looked at her crutches.

'We'll get the bus.'

'You're serious, aren't you?' There was her half-smile again.

'Never been more serious in my life.' I stood up and held out my hand for her. She took it and I picked up her bag while she slid her crutches on to her arms. 'Can you make it to the bus stop? We'll have to go out of the side gate.' I checked my phone. 'Yeah, we should be OK, we have twenty minutes to get out unnoticed before next period starts.'

'How many times have you done this?'

'Enough to know that there's a bus in five minutes that stops right outside that milkshake place you Birch people seem to love.'

'They do waffles too. I could definitely eat some waffles right now. Let's go.'

Her eyes were shining when she said it. 'You know, nobody will ever suspect me either. You, on the other hand . . .'

'What's that supposed to mean?'

'I think they have you pegged as a bad boy.'

'Don't girls like bad boys? Do *you* like bad boys?'

'We'll see.' She walked towards the side gate, and I followed with our bags. I could see she was in pain by the time we got to the bus stop. At least there was a seat. I made sure I picked up her bag when the bus pulled up. I waited for her to get on in front of me, so she could choose whatever seat was easiest for her. She chose one at the front, with loads of leg room.

We got off at Maggie's. The last time I was there, Tara offered me a blow job in the bathroom. But I said no. I can just imagine what Ciaran would have said. He would have called me a fucking pussy. I didn't care. It didn't seem right, not when I wasn't into her. This time felt so different. Here I was, with a girl I couldn't get enough of, and we were about to have our first date.

'What do you want?' I held the door open, and she walked under my arm. 'You grab a seat and I'll order.'

'Triple chocolate brownie with salted caramel sauce, oh, and waffles with cream and chocolate sauce. Please.'

I stared at her in disgust. 'Complicated and ridiculously sweet. That fits, I guess.'

'How dare you. I am not sweet. What are you getting?'

'Strawberry.'

'Boring,' she sang.

'Reliable,' I corrected. I ordered and then slid into the booth opposite her and pushed my feet to her side, so we were touching.

255

'So, why *did* you come to Birch?' she asked.

I shrugged, because I was used to shrugging if anyone asked me personal questions. 'Because of the stuff going on at home, and I guess Mum thought it would give me a new start.'

Tell her.

We were as good as alone in the cafe. She'd understand. I knew she would. She'd told me about her arthritis. She trusted me and I could trust her.

'You mean the drugs?' she asked easily. No judgement.

'Yeah, exactly,' I said. And just as I was thinking about elaborating, the waitress slid our milkshakes on to the table and put the waffles in the middle, with two forks.

'Why'd she bring two forks?' Jules pretended to look confused. 'This isn't for sharing.'

I couldn't help it. I put my finger into the cream and flicked a bit at her face.

'I can't believe you just did that.' She looked shocked and grabbed a napkin.

I leaned over the table and took the napkin from her hand, kissing the cream from her nose and cheek.

'That was an elaborate scheme to get a kiss,' she said, after I'd kissed her on the mouth. It tasted of chocolate.

'I like elaborate. It's why I play chess. Speaking of chess, you now know that my favourite piece is the pawn. What's yours?'

She pushed a huge piece of waffle into her mouth, loaded with cream and chocolate.

'I see what you did there, buying yourself more time. Lucky that I think you look sexy when you eat.'

And it wasn't a lie. She did. Which is fucking ridiculous because who looks hot with a face full of waffles?

'The queen,' she said when she'd swallowed.

'Why?' I was genuinely interested.

'She can move anywhere she wants.' And the light disappeared from her eyes when she said it.

51

Juliet

My phone buzzed.

> **MICHAEL:** Em, where the hell are you? I waited for you outside history. Mr Tsang said you had an appointment? It is not the fourth Friday in the month, and you've just had physio. Please confirm that you're not dead

> **ME:** Am still alive . . .

> **MICHAEL:** Explain yourself

> **ME:** Ronan kidnapped me. I'm at Maggie's

> **MICHAEL:** WHAT? ARE YOU SERIOUS? YOU NEVER CUT SCHOOL!!!

ME: I know, he was really convincing

MICHAEL: You're just a sucker for a pretty face. Totally get that. Oh, Harry asked me for your number. It was so cute

ME: Harry? Really? Did you give it to him?

MICHAEL: Yeah. I didn't know what else to do, I didn't think you and Ronan were public yet. I got your back

ME: Thanks ☺

MICHAEL: Come back now, I'm bored, and we have English soon, even though the only entertainment I get is watching you flirt really awkwardly from the back of class

ME: HEY!!

MICHAEL: What? It's true. See you soon, SCHOOL CUTTER

I looked up to see Ronan staring at me.

'Sorry, that was just Michael. He wanted to know where I was.'

'You guys are really close, aren't you?' Ronan took a sip of his milkshake and it made me think of his lips on mine again. I rubbed my foot against his under the table.

'Yeah, since Year Eight. He's my best friend.'

'What about Tara?' Ronan looked genuinely curious, like there was no agenda to his question except for actual interest. His eyebrows were raised under the dark hair that fell across his forehead. As if he'd heard me thinking about it, he swept it away and pushed his glasses up his nose.

'Well, Tara has been my best friend since I was about five. When we started Birch, we became really different people but it's hard to just not be friends with someone you've been friends with since primary school. Maybe it's not the same with boys,' I suggested. I hated talking about Tara like this. It brought back all the good memories. Stuff we did as kids; promises to be best friends forever; when we told each other all our secrets. And now? It just made me sad.

'Kind of. Maybe not the same. I was friends with Alex and Sasha from my old school for a while, but we were never really that close, I guess.' He shrugged. 'Not like you are with Michael or anything.'

'You're not friends with them any more?'

'Nah, they didn't turn out to be all that great in the end,' Ronan said. His voice was quieter, sadder. I wasn't sure if he wanted me to ask more.

'Do you want to talk about it?' I asked and drained the last of my drink.

'Aw no, it's fine. It's boring. We just aren't friends any more. Good riddance.'

Something changed in Ronan's tone when he said it. Like whatever it was that lit him up dimmed when he mentioned his past. It was like there was something he wanted to say but he was holding it back.

I'd been there.

'Doesn't it make you sad? Sometimes I get sad about Tara, that things aren't the same.' I tried to say it easily, like it would give him an opening to tell me whatever he wanted.

'No. Life goes on. Things change, and the sooner people realize that the better.' It was like he wasn't really talking to me when he said it. He stared at the table as if he was deep in thought.

'Oh.' I ran my finger around my plate in the chocolate sauce, destroying the heart I'd just made.

'I didn't mean you. I just meant me, that's how I think. There's no point wishing things were the way they were, because that's never going to happen.'

I thought about the million times I'd dreamed about not having a stupid broken body. How I'd look at all those pictures saved on my laptop and wish so hard that I looked like them instead. I'd even think up scenarios in my head, where I wasn't disabled, and I was the most popular girl in school. That I had Tara's life.

'You're probably right,' I agreed.

'I hate that I'm right,' he said.

I hadn't noticed Ronan take the pawn from his pocket, but he was squeezing it in his palm, halfway across the table.

I reached out and put my hand over his fist, feeling his grip loosen under my fingers.

He looked right at me and said, 'If things were still the way things were, I never would have met you.' His eyes that were so intense looked even more so because they were magnified by his glasses. 'So sometimes, good things happen in spite of the shit.'

It was my turn to get up. Even though I couldn't do it as effortlessly as he did, I stood up and walked to his side of the table. He turned so his legs were facing me. I stood between them and this time it was me who pulled his chin towards mine. Taking the kiss that I had a feeling he needed. His hands were on my hips, holding me gently as if to keep me steady.

'What was that for?' He smiled.

'Just cause I could. In spite of the shit.' I smiled back. 'Shall we get back to school?'

His eyes lit up. 'Why? You panicking?'

'No ... definitely not. Maybe ...'

'Newbie.'

Ronan stood up while I grabbed my crutches. He picked up my school bag and we waited for the bus to school. When it arrived, we sat at the back, in seats usually reserved for bad kids and couples. Today, I was somewhere in between. We barely came up for air. His hands were on my leg, tracing lines above my knee, up my thigh and back down again, and I never wanted him to stop. I let my hands explore his chest, over his shirt under his blazer, the heat from his skin making me desperate to slip my hand underneath. We jolted to a stop.

'We're here.' I couldn't get rid of the disappointment from my voice.

'We should have stayed out all day. Or stayed in.' Ronan's hand squeezed my leg gently.

'That would not have been the right thing to do.' I grabbed his hand and took it off my leg, holding it in mine for a second before I let go.

'Sorry, was that too much?' He looked at me with a face so concerned it made me laugh.

'No, it's just I figured if you didn't stop then I wouldn't want to get off the bus at all.' I pushed away the hair that had fallen over his glasses, so I could see his eyes properly. They reminded me of when my family and I went to Thailand when I was thirteen. We stayed at this amazing hotel on the beach. It was the most relaxed I'd felt in a year, after the diagnosis. I'd lie in the lukewarm, crystal blue water, close my eyes and forget about the millions of doctor's appointments, the ones I'd already had, and the ones I had to go to when I got back. I felt the same when I looked into his eyes – that for a second it was just me, Juliet, he was looking at, and not my disease.

'Would that be a bad thing?'

I gasped. 'It would be a *terrible* thing.'

'You always do the right thing, don't you?' He handed me my crutches, smiling as he said it, like he found it cute.

'Of course. Unless I'm being led astray by some St Anne's blow-in.'

As we walked down the bus it took everything in me not to turn round and kiss him, go back to our seat and tell him I just wanted to ride the bus all day instead.

'Lunchtime in –' Ronan looked at his watch – 'two minutes. So it'll be easy to blend right back in. If you're going to cut class, remember to come back at break or lunch. Just for future reference.'

'Future reference?' We walked towards the side gate.

'Yeah, don't worry. I'll keep you right.'

The bell went just before we got to the gate. Swarms of kids came out of every door. And Ronan was right – nobody even noticed.

52

Ronan

I didn't go to the lunch hall. I just grabbed some crisps and chocolate from the vending machine and sat on one of the benches in the schoolyard. I couldn't face running into Tara and that lot. I sent Jules a message.

```
ALONELYPAWN: When can I see you again?
PRETTYBASIC: Are you asking me on a
   second date?
ALONELYPAWN: Yes. Do you accept?
PRETTYBASIC: Mmmmm, I'll have to think
   about it . . .
PRETTYBASIC: . . .
PRETTYBASIC: . . .
PRETTYBASIC: . . .
PRETTYBASIC: OK ☺
ALONELYPAWN: Don't do that to me,
   BASIC.
PRETTYBASIC: Don't do what? Take your
   pawn?
ALONELYPAWN: I'll get you back for that.
```

PRETTYBASIC: We'll see. Do you want to
    come round to my house later? Then I
    can beat you in person.
ALONELYPAWN: Those are big words.
ALONELYPAWN: So confident.
PRETTYBASIC: 😃
ALONELYPAWN: ♡
PRETTYBASIC: ♡

53

Juliet

At lunchtime Michael and I sat in our usual seats. I filled Michael in on our date, watching the door at the same time, waiting for Ronan to come in.

When Chess Life flashed, I knew he wasn't coming.

'OMG, could that smile be any bigger? You look like an absolute lunatic smiling into your phone like that. Let me guess, Ronan?' Michael tried to look at my screen and I turned it away.

'Maybe.' I was still smiling.

'Well, come on – spill!'

'He's coming round to my house tonight.' My stomach flipped when I said it.

'To do terrible, sordid things?' Michael's eyes lit up.

'To play chess.'

Michael's face dropped. 'Each to their own, I suppose. Wish I could bring Francis to my house and "play chess".'

'We're *actually* going to be playing chess, though, that's the difference. And also . . . What if you came out to your parents? Then you could bring him home.'

'Cassandra is way too busy this week. Can you imagine? She comes home from a day of locking up convicts to that news? Nobody needs a shock like that when all you want to do is take off your Jimmy Choos and have a glass of wine.'

'Are you sure it would be a shock though?' I asked gently.

'Of *course* it would; she has no idea.' Michael said it like he was one hundred per cent sure.

'Well, whenever you're ready to do it, the offer of my company still stands.'

Michael put his hand on his heart. 'You'd brave Judge Crawley for me?'

'Always.'

Michael's head tilted like Jeffrey's when he was confused. 'Will *you* tell her?'

I burst out laughing. 'Sorry, that's all you.'

'Bitch.'

'Oh, how was the movie?' I'd almost forgotten about Michael's big date.

'I don't know.' Michael grinned.

'What do you mean, you don't know? Did you not go?' I panicked then. Had I missed something? Had he told me, and I hadn't been listening?

'It's a bit hard to watch a movie when you have your tongue in someone else's mouth.'

I smiled. 'So it went well then?'

'Juliet, I think I'm in love.'

Tara's voice broke into our conversation. 'He's totally into me, he's just playing hard to get.'

I looked up to see Tara looking half at me as if she said it for my benefit.

'Don't rise,' Michael whispered in my ear.

I peeled back the foil from the Lindt chocolate bunny I was holding.

'What are you doing to that chocolate bunny?' Michael was staring at me with a disgusted look on his face.

'Giving him a slow and painful death.' I took tiny bites from his ears. Then went in for his nose.

'Imagining it's Tara?'

I shoved the rest of it in my mouth and looked at Michael. 'Maybe,' I said, through a chocolate-mouthed smile.

'Nah, she wouldn't taste as good. She'd be all bitter. Like those bits of lemon rind you get in mince pies.' Michael retched and it made me laugh, spluttering out chocolate on the table. And there it was, the heat in my face, again. I was glad Ronan wasn't there.

'I have an idea,' I said.

'Oh, do tell.' Michael leaned in closer.

'Why don't we go on a double date? You and Francis. Me and Ronan?'

'Juliet, I think that's probably the best idea you've *ever* had. Where will we go? Ludo's? I've wanted to break out that new suit Mum bought me for ages.'

Ludo's was this super expensive Italian restaurant in the village. One that people only ever went to for special occasions. Unless you were Michael's parents.

'Em, not sure I can afford Ludo's right now. My six-figure salary hasn't been paid this month,' I said. I pulled a sad face.

'Don't be silly, I'll pay. We can get all dressed up and it will be *amazing*.'

'I was thinking more like Maggie's?' I grinned, hoping I wouldn't disappoint him too much.

'Hm, I *could* show Francis my downing-a-milkshake-in-fifteen-seconds trick.' Michael contemplated my idea.

The first time Michael had tried that 'trick', half of the milkshake came out his nose. I told him he shouldn't have chosen the one laced with popping candy, but did he listen to me? No.

'OK, deal. So exciting!' Michael's voice came out like a squeak.

And even though *my* voice wasn't three pitches higher than normal, and my smile wasn't about to break my face (like Michael's), I thought so too.

54

Ronan

I'd meant to ask Jules to meet me after school but then I remembered that she always got a lift home with Michael, so I sent her a message instead.

```
ALONELYPAWN: Can't wait to see you
   later x
PRETTYBASIC: Me either x
```

I let myself daydream about Jules, conjuring up some image of her house, her bedroom; we'd be alone and I'd be kissing her. It was so nice to fill my head with her, instead of all the other stuff. The dark stuff that took over, repeating over and over in my head. The stuff that made my chest tighten and my palms sweat.

'Hey, Ro. Walk me home?'

I turned to my right and there was Tara. Slightly out of breath like she'd hurried to catch up with me. I resisted the urge to sigh.

'I'm going this way anyway,' I said and nodded down the street.

'Great!' She smiled.

She didn't talk that much on the way, but she still made sure to brush against me every few seconds, as if to remind me she was still there. As if I could forget. Tara was a lot of (mostly annoying) things, but she was impossible to ignore.

When we got to the crossroads I was about to turn the other way when she stumbled and dropped her file all over the pavement, pages flying everywhere.

I helped her pick them up and she shoved them back in, most of them upside down. The arch was broken.

'Thanks,' she said, struggling to hold it together.

I looked at her. Remembered about her mum. I held out my hand for the folder.

'Here, I'll carry it,' I offered.

She hesitated but then gave it to me. 'OK, thanks.'

We walked to her house in almost-silence. I didn't have much to say, not after the party and what she'd said to Jules. But the image of Jules's face when Tara said it kept coming back to me. I had to say something.

'That thing you called Jules the other night, it really hurt her, you know,' I said.

She didn't look at me then, just kept walking.

'I didn't mean it,' she said quietly.

'Maybe you didn't, but it still made her feel really shit. Why don't you just say sorry? I think she'd really appreciate it.'

'Yeah, maybe.' Tara shrugged as we turned the corner on to her street.

'Tara!'

A woman's voice screeched from the bottom of the road. Then I saw her. Stumbling out of the gate and on to the street towards us. She was wearing pyjamas, her top half open, no bra. I could see . . . everything.

'Oh my God. I thought . . . she's usually asleep at this time.' Tara looked horrified. 'Mum,' she said. Sort of to me, but mostly to the figure running towards us. And then she was in front of us, pulling Tara into a huge bare-breasted hug.

'Mum.' Tara's voice was gentle. 'Mum.'

'Sorry, Tara. I'm so sorry.'

Her mum pulled away and looked at me. 'You must be Ronan, I've heard so much about you.' She looked at me, the drunken haze of her eyes bringing me back to Ciaran. She was pretty. She looked like Tara, just older, with hair that was dyed blue at the ends.

'Mum, your top.' Tara tried to button it, but it was my turn for a hug. I could smell alcohol as she squeezed her arms round my neck.

'*Mum*,' Tara said more loudly, but gently still. 'Let's go inside.' I could feel Tara pulling her mum's arm off me. She finally released her grip. 'Come on.' Tara took her mum's hand and led her into the house. I followed because I didn't know what else to do.

We walked into the house. Dark, small, an empty wine bottle on the floor and more of them lined up behind the door, as if someone had tried to tidy up. The whole house smelled of smoke and booze.

'Annie?' Tara called up the stairs. 'Mum, is Annie home yet?'

'I don't know.'

Tara shook her head and walked into the kitchen, leaving me and her mum in the hall that was barely big enough for two people.

'She loves you, you know. Tara does. Says you're different from all the other boys,' her mum said.

'Please don't, Mum,' Tara called.

She reappeared with a glass of water, and I moved backwards to give her more space.

'Why don't you have a nap? You must be tired.' Tara took her mum's hand and guided her up the stairs. Halfway up she turned back to me.

'You don't have to stay. I'm OK from here.'

She didn't wait for a reply, just took her mum upstairs and I waited at the bottom. I tried to ignore the bangs and shouts, though it was harder to ignore when it sounded like Tara hurt herself. I was about to go up when she appeared at the top of the stairs again.

'You stayed,' she said.

'Yeah. Just in case you needed any help.'

When she got to the bottom of the stairs, she hugged me. And for the first time, it felt like she meant it. That she really needed it. I hugged her back.

'I thought she'd be asleep. She usually is at this time.' Tara looked up at me. 'Here, let's go into the kitchen.'

I followed her into a tiny kitchen, made smaller by all the dishes and bottles that cluttered the counters.

'It's not what you think,' she said.

'What do I think? Have you a bin bag?'

Tara hesitated then opened a drawer and handed me a roll of bags.

'That my mum's some mad alcoholic.' She gave a sad laugh.

We started filling up the bags with takeaway packages and bottles.

'People get addicted,' I said. 'It's no big deal. Well, it is, but I get it.'

'Thanks, but that's not it. Well, it's only part of it.'

I had already filled a bag of rubbish and had started on another one. Tara continued. And I didn't interrupt. I just let her talk.

'Mum's not well. She hasn't been well for years. That's why Dad left; cause things got too hard. Ha, too hard for him! It's a personality disorder. So sometimes she's fine and we get on so well and she tries so hard with me and Annie and then this happens. Or she brings people home or something. Then she ends up in hospital.'

'Hospital?'

'A psychiatric hospital.'

'But what about you? And your sister?'

'Well, I'm kind of like Mum's carer. Just not officially. God, sorry, this is so embarrassing. I haven't told anyone. Not even Jules. When we were kids, Dad was still around, and things weren't that bad. But now it's just easier to pretend I have this perfect life. Pathetic, right?'

'No. It's really not.' And I meant it. I thought about everything I was hiding. Mum, Ciaran, and how fucking brave it was to come out with it.

Tara stopped putting bottles into the bin bag and looked up at me. 'You have no idea how good it feels to finally tell someone about this . . . You won't tell anyone, will you?'

'Of course I won't.'

Before today, I didn't think Tara could cry. But right there in the kitchen she broke down, racked with sobs, sliding to the floor, surrounded by rubbish.

I put down my bin bag, sat beside her, and put my arm round her until the tears stopped.

55

Juliet

When we got to my house, Michael came in. We went straight up to my bedroom and sat on my bed beside each other so we could stare at our phones in peace.

'Regular people don't have bone structure like that, do they?' I showed the screen to Michael. I was on Ronan's Insta and scrolled way back to old photos of him. There weren't that many – mostly pictures of places, rather than people, but there were a few from a couple of years ago with some other guy. He looked a bit like Ronan but didn't wear glasses. His brother? The one who took drugs? They looked happy. There was a photo with a chessboard set up. Then the photos just stopped.

I told myself to remember to ask him more about his brother later. I hated that it made me feel uncomfortable, asking people about personal stuff. I think I'd just gone so long not wanting to talk about *my* personal stuff that I assumed nobody else wanted to talk about theirs. Maybe they did.

I looked at the post again.

'Getting ready to beat C.'

And a picture of a pint of beer straight after.

'Drowning my sorrows.'

My phone buzzed with a message, and I almost knocked over the popcorn. But it wasn't him. It was a message on Whatsapp from an unsaved number.

> Hey, Jules, I got your number from Michael. It's Harry, by the way. I know this is pretty random, but do you want to maybe go out sometime? It's OK if you don't, I was just checking

I showed Michael.

'Oh my God. Don't you just have all the men.'

'Hardly *all* the men.'

'More than me. What are you going to say?'

'I don't know. That I can't because I'm going out with Ronan?'

I looked at Michael so he would come up with some good wording for me.

'Ask him if he wants a threesome.'

'Michael!'

'What? Best of both worlds.' He shrugged and ate the popcorn Mum had left in a little bowl on my desk.

'Definitely not.'

I shifted myself on the bed, stretching my legs that had stiffened.

'I can't believe he even wants to go out with me after my pathetic shot-drinking display.'

'He's probably one of those guys who thinks your dainty drinking is all cute and feminine. Gross. But he does have excellent shoulders.' Michael looked as if he was contemplating whether or not the two things cancelled each other out.

'No, he actually seems really nice. Really sweet.'

I flicked my phone on to Harry's Insta. Mostly football stuff. There were hardly any pictures of him by himself; he was always in a group of three or four other guys. But he always looked ridiculously happy.

'Yeah, and nice shoulders.'

'You said that.'

'It's important.'

'Is it?'

'So much to learn.' Michael sighed as I typed a message back to Harry.

> **ME**: Hey Harry! Thanks for the message, it's really sweet. But I've just started going out with Ronan Cole, so I'll have to say no, sorry!

Typing it felt real. I had a *boyfriend*. And I could still hardly believe it.

56

Ronan

I'd stayed at Tara's all afternoon, helping her tidy her house. Her sister came home at some point. A mini-Tara, asking if I was Ronan and telling me that Tara wouldn't shut up about me. Then she was told to shut up. In a nice way. This Tara was different. Softer. Kinder. And didn't come on to me once.

Once we'd tidied the house, Annie watched TV and Tara brought us cans of Coke.

'We're OK, you know. I know it doesn't look like it, but it's not always like this.'

'Does the school know what's going on? You know, because you're off sometimes?' I asked. Curious about the situation. For her. For me.

'No. I've got really good at lying.' Tara shrugged and drank her Coke.

It was getting dark when I left. Tara's life was still in my head. How different it was from the image she showed the world. Was I the same? It wasn't like I pretended to have this perfect life, but I hadn't told anyone. I guess in my own way, I'd got pretty good at lying too.

Mum was in the kitchen when I got home, the television was on, and she was cleaning the counters. Still in her work clothes and heels.

'Hi, love, did you have a nice day?' She turned and smiled at me when I walked towards the fridge.

I thought about Jules and how I *had* had a nice day. It would have been nice if I could have talked to her, told her about Jules and how amazing she was, but I couldn't.

'It was fine.'

I took some leftover spaghetti bolognese out of the fridge and stuck it in the microwave, wishing the seconds would go faster.

'You know, I was thinking about Christmas. Do you think we should get a real tree this year? Ciaran always said he liked the smell of real trees.'

I squeezed my eyes shut.

'I don't know,' I replied.

Christmas, ten years ago. Ciaran and me climbing on the window sill to reach every single chocolate on the tree. We shared them out but there was an uneven number, so he gave the extra one to me. The next day Mum asked us where all the chocolate went and neither of us would tell her. We were always a team.

'It's something to think about anyway. I want this year to be our most special yet.'

She was acting like Christmas was in a few weeks. Try a few months. A few months of Christmas lights and cheesy music, television adverts showing happy families as if the sole purpose of them was to make you feel shit unless you had a perfect life.

I left Mum to clean and took the pasta to my room.

```
ALONELYPAWN: Can I come over yet?
PRETTYBASIC: Sure. Will you do my
  homework for me?
ALONELYPAWN: I knew it! You're only using
  me for my massive brain ☹
PRETTYBASIC: So modest. But yeah, maybe.
  You know anything about the Tudors?
ALONELYPAWN: No, but I bet Google does!
  I'll show you how to use it when I get
  there.
PRETTYBASIC: What would I do without you?
ALONELYPAWN: Be very, very sad ☹
PRETTYBASIC: A little bit sad maybe . . .
ALONELYPAWN: Send me your address?
PRETTYBASIC: 14 Oakville Avenue.
ALONELYPAWN: See you in twenty x
PRETTYBASIC: Can't wait xxx
```

I left the house quietly, not risking Mum coming at me with stupid questions again. I must have walked quickly, because by the time I'd got to Jules's street I was really hot. I pulled off my hoody and walked to her door. I hesitated. I hadn't thought this far ahead. I pulled the pawn from my pocket and looked at it, turning it over in my fingers.

'Be better,' I whispered to it, before shoving it back into my pocket.

I wasn't used to feeling nervous. It wasn't usually something I felt, but with Jules it was different. I wanted everything to be perfect. Because *she* was perfect.

I knocked at the door.

A woman answered. Brown hair, brown eyes, not like Jules at all, except for in height (or lack of it).

'Hi, I'm Melanie. You must be Ronan. Come in, come in. So lovely to meet you.' She waved me inside.

'Hi, thanks.' I pushed my hand through my hair and walked into the house. Heat surrounded me.

'Is Jules here?' I asked, scanning the huge hall. It was filled with photographs. Mostly of Jules from what I could see without being weird and going to look at them properly. There were plants in corners, flowers in vases, candles burning. A proper home.

'Jules!' Melanie called upstairs. 'Ronan's here.'

'Coming!' she called back.

'Hey,' Jules said, appearing at the top of the stairs. 'Watch out.' Before I knew what she was doing, she took off her crutches and slid them down the stairs. They landed at my feet. She followed them down, slowly.

I picked up her crutches and handed them to her at the bottom.

'That's dangerous, you know. You could have killed me,' I said, trying to sound serious.

'Killed by a crutch? You'd lose loads of respect points for that. Terrible way to die.'

'You wouldn't be a little bit sad?'

'Nope, just embarrassed for you.' There was that smile again. She nodded her head in the direction of another room.

I followed her into the living room where the chessboard was set up. The most beautiful chessboard I'd ever seen. A thick marble board with matching marble pieces. It must have cost a fortune.

'Oh wow, this is insane.' I picked up a knight, holding it up so I could see the detail.

'Dad bought it for me a few years ago.'

'It's so beautiful.'

'All right, calm down. I mean, I can leave if you want some time alone with the board.' She pretended to turn round.

'Wait. I hadn't finished . . .'

'So finish then.' She raised her eyebrows and walked towards me. She stared at me, challenging me to say something better.

'It's so beautiful, but not as beautiful as you.'

She made a retching noise then laughed.

'Yeah, sorry, made myself want to throw up a bit there too,' I said.

Then she kissed me without warning, and I swear to God my legs almost gave way.

57

Juliet

Mum and Dad were in the kitchen when I kissed him. The thought of them seeing me do that made me cringe so hard, but he was just standing there looking so hot it was like I didn't have any option. OK, I did, obviously. I could have *not* kissed the hottest guy I've ever seen in real life. But that wouldn't have been as much fun.

'Are you ready to lose? We're on my turf now.' I went towards the chessboard and sat down in my usual seat. I'd got Dad to bring over a proper chair earlier, instead of his little footstool.

'Oh, please. Have you actually beaten me yet? At all?' Ronan sat down opposite me, a half-smile on his face.

'Yeah, remember that time . . .'

'No.'

'With the knight.' I nodded to myself. 'Yeah, that was a good one. Checkmate in five moves.'

'That never happened.'

'Just because you don't remember, doesn't mean it never happened.' I shrugged and moved my pawn to e4.

'You can't distract me with your mind games, you know.' Ronan was studying the board.

It was weird playing him in real life. Nice-weird. This way I got to study his face, watch how he pushed his glasses up his nose when he was thinking and how he shook his leg up and down at the same time. I wondered if he knew he was doing it.

'Horsie to f6? What are you up to?' I squinted at him.

'Horsie?'

'Yes. The technical name for a knight.'

'Alekhine Defence. Nf6. First introduced in a Budapest tournament in 1921 by Alexander Alekhine.' He gave me a smug smile. I was about to make a joke about all the chess stuff he knew, but actually I found it really attractive that someone knew so much about something. I don't think I knew that much about *anything*, except maybe my own disease, which was the opposite of attractive.

Mum poked her head round the door from the kitchen, making me think she'd been listening to us the entire time. I could feel my face flush. 'Does anybody want anything? Coke? Cookies?'

'Mum!' Oh dear God, did she have to be so embarrassing. Coke? Cookies? I wasn't ten!

'I'd love some, Melanie, thank you.' Ronan smiled his easy smile at Mum.

'Lovely. Won't be a minute.'

'You didn't have to do that,' I whispered at Ronan across the board.

'What? I want Coke and cookies. Who *wouldn't* want Coke and cookies?'

'So embarrassing.' I shook my head.

'No, it's not. It's nice actually. Wish my mum was like that.'

There it was again. The same look he had when he talked about his friends from his old school.

I wanted to ask, to dig a little deeper, show him that I cared, that I could be there for him the way he was for me about my arthritis. But then Mum came in. And I hated that I felt a little bit relieved.

'Here we are.' Mum came in with a tray holding two glasses and a little plate of the fancy chocolate chip cookies she'd bought when she heard I'd invited Ronan over. We never had those in the house normally. Sugar content, blah, blah, blah, but when I had someone round Mum always made an exception.

She pulled over a side table and set the tray down.

'Jules said you're in her English class? And you're learning *Romeo and Juliet* this year? Maybe you two could watch the movie? Did Jules tell you how much she loves it?'

I wanted one of those sink holes that you see on the news to appear from nowhere and suck us all underground, just so I wouldn't have to deal with Ronan's questions about this.

'No, actually, she didn't.' Ronan was trying not to smile. 'Yeah, that's a great idea. Why don't we watch that?'

I remembered what I'd said to him in English. How I *hated* the story.

'Sure.' I managed a fake smile.

'Glad I can be some help. I'll be in the kitchen if you need me.'

I couldn't believe Mum was in the room for less than five minutes and had managed to embarrass me *twice*!

'Thought you hated *Romeo and Juliet*?' Ronan leaned back in his chair with his hands behind his head.

'I do.' I stared at the board and moved a pawn.

'I don't believe you. What's the deal?'

'The deal is it's S-T-U-P-I-D.' I made sure to sound out every letter of stupid, to make my point even clearer.

'I don't think you can call Shakespeare stupid.' Ronan moved a pawn too.

'I didn't call *him* stupid. I called the story stupid. Like how could two people fall in love in such a short space of time, and get so into each other that they're willing to *die* to be together? It's *ridiculous*.' I unleashed my knight.

'I think it's romantic.' Ronan shrugged and there was no hint of a joke in his voice.

'You think that can actually happen? Leaving out the death scenario. You think it's possible for two people to fall in love *that* quickly?' I could feel my heart thud against my chest like my body was answering my own question.

'Yeah, of course. Don't you?'

And those eyes, crystal blue, looking into mine, were asking me to agree.

I grabbed a cookie and took a bite, as Juliet's words played over in my mind.

'Although I joy in thee,
I have no joy of this contract tonight.
It is too rash, too unadvised, too sudden,
Too like the lightning, which doth cease to be
Ere one can say, "It lightens."'

Rash. Ill-advised. Sudden. Juliet had doubts. Maybe she should have listened to them. Because then she might not have got hurt.

58

Ronan

The next couple of weeks were a blur of chess moves, flirting online, flirting in real life, that smile, those eyes and God, the kissing! So much kissing. When I was with her, she consumed me, and the dark thoughts never stood a chance.

Michael would drop us both off at her house after school and we'd play a game of chess. Her mum always had snacks waiting in little bowls on the side table beside the chessboard. And Jules complained about it every single time. I didn't get why she hated it so much. To me it felt like a normal parent thing to do. I would give anything for a normal parent.

One day, after she'd put up a decent fight during one of our games (but still lost), she asked if I wanted to see her room.

Which made me think of sex. But not in that way. I'd done it before, a few times, with a girl from St Anne's. Me and Sasha ended up doing it once too. But it was different with Jules. I was enjoying getting to know her without sex getting in the way.

I think it meant a lot to her, inviting me upstairs. I watched her glare at her mum, like she was warning her not to say anything. Like they'd already had a conversation about this before I'd arrived. Which they probably had.

And then I was nervous.

I let her go upstairs first, even though she asked me to go ahead because she was slow. But I carried her crutches and let her lead the way.

Jules's room was huge. Huge bed with a million cushions on it, huge built-in wardrobe, huge window surrounded by fairy lights and patterned curtains. She had a dressing table with one of those mirrors that had lights around the edge too. It was like something you'd see in one of Mum's estate agent magazines.

'Well, this is it,' she said, before leaning her crutches against the bed then sitting down on it, looking at me. I didn't know where to go. Presume she wanted me to sit beside her on the bed and risk her asking what I was doing? Or sit at the dressing table and risk offending her?

'It's really nice,' I said, setting my hoody on her chair.

'Want to watch something?' She pulled herself into the corner on her bed, against the wall, and opened her laptop, making the decision for me.

'Sure, *Romeo and Juliet*?' I sat beside her, our legs touching, listening to the rhythmic sound of her breathing as she scanned Netflix.

'No chance.' She looked away from the screen this time, at me instead.

This time it was me who kissed her. I tilted her chin towards mine and moved my hand to the back of her head, holding it gently as our lips touched.

She pulled away.

'I'm not ready, for you know, *that*, or anything,' she said. Her eyes were wide. Worried.

'That's fine. We can just do this for as long as you want. I'd even be happy just holding hands with you.' I threaded my fingers through hers and squeezed. She leaned her head on my shoulder and I smelled her flowery shampoo again.

'You surprise me, Ronan Cole.'

'What do you mean?'

'I didn't expect you to be like this at all.'

'Like what?'

'So sweet. You make it so easy to be me. I don't feel like I'm a burden with you.'

I turned to her and looked into the huge eyes that now glistened with tears.

'How could you be a burden?' It hurt when she said that.

She closed the laptop and pushed it down the bed. 'It's just, I always feel like I'm holding people back – Mum, Dad, Michael. My stupid joints being the way they are just ruins everybody else's life too. And I don't know, being with you is the first time I haven't felt like that in a really long time.'

I wiped a tear that had escaped from her eyes.

'Sorry,' she said. 'I didn't mean to cry. It's so pathetic.' She tried to laugh.

'It's not pathetic. I know you won't believe me, but I don't think anybody else sees it like that. All those people love you.'

'I *can't* believe you.' She shook her head, and more tears came. 'Even if I tried, something would happen, like I'd get worse, or need another appointment and Mum would have to reschedule something or miss work, or Michael would have to cancel plans yet *again.*' She was properly crying now. 'I hate my stupid broken body so much.' Her hands were over her face and there was nothing else I could say. I pulled her close and held her until her chest had stopped heaving.

'You know there are things I hate about me too,' I said.

She looked genuinely surprised. 'What? What could you possibly hate about you? You're perfect.'

I laughed then, because she was so off the mark.

'I'm so far from perfect, Jules, I really am.' I didn't look at her then, because if I did, everything would come out. And how could I tell her after that? After she told me all those things about what she thought about me and then I told her what I really am? That I did nothing to stop the most horrific thing happening to Ciaran?

'At least your joints are perfect.' She smiled and that made me smile too.

'Show me where hurts.' I sat up and moved so I was sitting beside her feet. I clearly wasn't getting anywhere with what I was saying. I needed to show her.

'My knees are the worst.'

I leaned over and kissed both of her knees gently. That made her smile.

'What else?' I asked.

'My elbows, mostly my right one.'

I held each hand in turn and kissed her elbows, being careful not to straighten them. I set them down again.

'Anywhere else?' I asked. I hoped this would make her understand that she could never be a burden to me.

'Em, my finger joints.' She wriggled her fingers in front of her. I moved towards them, so I was kneeling in between her legs. I took her hand gently and kissed each beautiful knuckle one by one. I heard her inhale. A long, deep breath, like she was relaxing. She lifted her hand to her neck, squeezing the base of it gently and screwing up her face.

'Sorry, Ronan, my neck hurts. Do you think you could fix that too?' She gave me a mischievous grin. I pretended not to catch on.

I pushed her hair behind her ear before taking my own weight by leaning on the mattress over her. She tilted her head to the side and I planted little kisses from her ear to her shoulder. I could feel the tiny hairs standing up against my lips. She had her eyes closed, but she was still smiling.

'Have I done it? Have I cured you?' I grinned, still leaning on my arms, hovering over her, our faces inches apart.

She opened her eyes. 'Hmm. Not quite, sorry.' She pulled a sad face. 'My lips are the sorest part.' She whispered that bit.

'Well, I am a bit of a perfectionist,' I whispered back before leaning in to kiss her again.

So we did that for a while. Safe in the bubble, where I could make her feel better and she didn't have to know about what I'd done.

Until Mum sent me a message that ruined everything.

59

Juliet

The afternoon that Ronan came up to my room was perfect.

Until he left.

His phone buzzed and I watched his face drop as he read a message.

'Everything OK?' I asked.

He looked at me then back at his phone.

'Yeah, it's nothing. But I should probably go,' he said, without even looking at me.

I'd felt so safe with him. It was amazing how quickly that could change. How someone can go from feeling completely secure to so painfully vulnerable and exposed in a matter of seconds?

Was it Tara? Reminding him that she was a better catch? That he should be with her instead? Was it someone else, making fun of him for going out with me? Had he actually been disgusted when he kissed my swollen joints?

'Are you sure? I think Mum is making curry if you want to stay for dinner?' I tried to sound breezy. But it didn't change anything.

'Yeah, sorry, I really have to go.'

Then he just left.

I pulled my laptop on to my knee again and opened English Revision. I looked at them over and over, each beautiful girl and each of their beautiful joints. The tears came back. The ones that Ronan had helped make disappear. How could I have been so stupid to think that he actually wanted me? That this would actually work? How dare I even dream about those things?

His hoody was still hanging on the back of my chair. I stood up and walked over to it, without my crutches, just taking the pain instead. I picked it up and pulled it over my head, breathing in the smell of smoky aftershave.

Instead of going back to sit on my bed, or on a chair, I sat on the floor, letting myself drop the few inches that would have been cushioned for people with normal knees. I pulled my knees up towards my chin, as far as they could go.

It hurt.

I buried my head in the hands that were covered by his sleeves and cried until I couldn't cry any more.

60

Ronan

> **MUM:** He's coming home! He's on his way, Ronan.

That was the text message that made me leave. It took every bit of happiness I'd felt right then and smashed it into a million pieces, bringing me back to reality. I was glad I'd kept my mouth shut and not told Jules anything. How could I explain this? How could I drag her into my mess when she had so much to deal with herself?

I couldn't.

When I got home, something was different. There was music playing and the Hoover was on. The air smelled of cinnamon. Anywhere else it would make me think Christmas, but here, all I thought was, *what the fuck*? Mum came dancing towards me, dropped the Hoover on the floor and sang along to the music. She grabbed my hands and started to swing them in time with the beat, pupils dilated. Drinking?

'He's coming back, Ronan! He's on his way.'

'What?'

Please no.

'Ciaran – he's on his way home. Isn't it amazing? The three of us, together again.'

I closed my eyes, as if that would erase the words she'd just said.

'I'm making apple crumble, his favourite. We're going to have a proper family dinner tonight. Just like we used to.'

It was nine p.m. I twisted my hands out of hers.

'Mum.'

'What? What is it? Do I look OK? Should I wear something else?'

Panic in her eyes.

'No. It's nothing. I'll be there,' I said.

This was completely fucked up. Even I couldn't deal with this by myself.

> **ME:** She's invited him for dinner. She thinks he's coming

> **AUNT SARAH:** Oh Ronan, I'm coming over

> **ME:** No, it's OK. I promise I'll phone you this time, if anything happens. I just needed to tell someone

> **AUNT SARAH:** I'll be at the end of the phone. We need to talk Ronan, properly. Lots of love xx

'I knew you'd say yes, Ronan. We can ask him all about Cambridge, see how he's getting on. He hardly ever phones, you know. Does he phone you? I suppose that's what university is for though, ignoring your parents.'

I hated that she looked so happy. I hated it so much that I couldn't ruin it.

'No, Mum, he doesn't phone me either.'

Of course he didn't phone me. He didn't phone anybody. It was getting too hard to shove everything to the back of my head. Too hard to pretend any more.

'Well then, it'll just be great for us all to catch up, won't it?' She picked up the Hoover again and started on the living-room carpet pushing it along to the rhythm of the too-happy music.

I trailed upstairs and closed my bedroom door behind me, before letting my legs give out beneath me. I slid down the back of my door until I was sitting on the carpet. I took off my glasses and forced my eye sockets into my knees, squeezing my hands into fists at my sides.

CIARAN: *Can I borrow £50? I'll pay you back*

ME: *I don't have £50*

CIARAN: *Don't lie, man. Come on, I promise I'll pay you back*

ME: You didn't pay back the last £200

CIARAN: Add it on then. What kind of brother doesn't lend £50?

ME: Sorry, Ciaran, I don't have it

CIARAN: Fuck you then

Fuck you then. That was the last message I got from Ciaran. Maybe I should have lent him the money. Maybe I should have done more than that.

Maybe, maybe, maybe.

Mum called me downstairs.

She'd set the table like she used to do at Christmas. Tablecloth, gravy boat, napkins, the centrepiece Ciaran had made at primary school one Easter.

'What do you think? Do you think he'll like it?'

I nodded. Because it was the only movement I could make right then.

She rushed around me, brushing non-existent crumbs from the table, rearranging candles, looking at her watch.

'You look nice. It's nice that you made an effort. I think he'll really appreciate it. Ciaran's always so perceptive, isn't he? Sit down, sit down. We'll just wait until he gets here.'

I sat down. I hadn't made an effort. I'd left my hoody at Jules's house so I just pulled on whatever jumper was first in my drawer.

The smell from the kitchen made me feel sick. Not because it was bad. But because I didn't think I could stomach something made with so much false hope.

Mum sat down opposite me. Every time she looked at her watch, or the clock on the wall, she'd take a sip of wine. Like a tick.

Tick, like the time. The time that was almost ten o'clock. The bitter smell of burning.

'Mum, the chicken.'

'It's almost ready, Ronan. I timed it so it would be ready as soon as our Ciaran walks through that door.'

She stared at the door as if it would magically open.

Ten o'clock.

Mum drank wine, watched the clock, watched the door. Drank more wine.

I pushed back my chair and went into the kitchen. I turned off the oven and the pots that were boiling dry on the cooker.

'Ronan, what do you think you're doing?' Mum was at the doorway, disbelief in her eyes. She pushed past me and turned everything back on.

'Let's eat, Mum, before it burns.'

'We need to wait for Ciaran.'

He's not coming.

I sat down again at the table, waiting until she got up, to go to the toilet, to go anywhere. And she did eventually, excusing herself. Her smile was too perfect, stretched so wide, like a guitar string tuned so tightly it was about to snap. Something was starting to come undone. Maybe it already had, and I just hadn't noticed.

Tonight couldn't be the night she fell apart completely; it just couldn't. Not when I was just about holding it together myself.

I got up and turned everything off again, pulling the kitchen door closed so she might not notice.

'Ronan, is that him? Is he here?' Mum called from the hall.

'No, it's just me, Mum. I'll wait with you.'

And we sat there for another three hours. Waiting, in silence, for Ciaran to walk through that door.

61

Juliet

> **ME:** He just left. We were having a really nice time and then he got a message from someone and disappeared without saying why ☹

MICHAEL: Don't panic! There's probably a totally innocent explanation. Maybe he just wants to keep you on your toes

> **ME:** Or maybe he realized that he doesn't want to be with me at all

MICHAEL: Well, that would make him a fucking idiot. And I don't think he is. Also, I'm never wrong. Did he say yes to the double date?

ME: I forgot to ask

MICHAEL: Ask now!

ME: You don't think that looks desperate?

MICHAEL: NO! Do it! Then he'll say yes, and you'll feel better. Listen to Uncle Michael 😊

ME: OK

Maybe Michael was right. Maybe I'd jumped to the wrong conclusion. I opened Chess Life.

```
PRETTYBASIC: Hey, I had such a nice time
    tonight. Michael has invited us on a
    double date with him and his boyfriend
    Francis on Friday if you want to go? x
```

It was eleven p.m. He was usually online now. It was me who was normally asleep. But tonight I couldn't sleep. I sat up, watching trash TV on Netflix. Programmes I could watch without having to think, so I could have half my brain on what was happening with Ronan.

It was after two a.m. when he replied.

ALONELYPAWN: I'm not sure we're a good
    idea at the minute, I just have too
    much going on. Sorry.

I couldn't believe what I'd just read. He was breaking up with me? I turned my phone over on the bed so I couldn't see the message and held my sleeves to my face. The sleeves from his hoody that I was still wearing. I breathed him in, as the crying started again. But this time I felt numb. I stared around my room, looking at all the things he'd touched. I dropped my gaze to the crutches propped up against my bedside table. And then I wanted to throw up. I pushed them over, letting them fall to the ground so they were out of sight. They'd ruined my life. Again.

I don't know how I fell asleep in the end. Exhaustion maybe, from all the tears. But I did. And I woke up in the morning with a swollen face and the realization that everything I thought about myself was true.

'Are you OK, love?' Mum's voice sounded far away when I was eating breakfast. I'd put on some make-up. An attempt to hide the redness around my eyes.

'I'm just tired.'

Even I couldn't get the words 'I'm fine' out of my mouth. Like my brain wouldn't let me because it knew if I said it, I'd fall apart completely.

'Will you be home after school today? Or are you doing something with Ronan?' Mum tidied away the teapot as she asked me. I knew she was digging.

'I'll be home,' I said.

She didn't ask any more questions.

Then Michael was outside.

'What's wrong, J? What happened?'

I couldn't speak. If I did, my voice would crack and tears would stream down my face. So I handed Michael my phone, open on Chess Life.

'What the hell? Ask him why.'

I shook my head. I didn't understand. I felt so fucking stupid. I was twelve when I learned that everybody's life doesn't work out as perfectly as the melody in a Taylor Swift song. Twelve! I knew this! So why did I even think for a second that things could be different?

'You need to ask him about all this stuff he has going on!' Michael hadn't even pulled away from my house yet. He had his hand on my hand. I was staring at my knees.

'I can't.' I shook my head.

'Why not?'

'Because it's an excuse, Michael. Obviously, it's an excuse because of the way I am. And if it is just an excuse and I ask him about it, he might actually say it in real words and that would make everything a million times worse.'

'Juliet. You're gorgeous. You're smart, you're funny, you play chess like he does. I'm sorry, but no, Ronan Cole does not care one bit about your arthritis.' He squeezed my hand.

He didn't seem to care. Actually, he did. In a good way. He wanted to know things, even did his own research. And last night, when he'd kissed my joints, it was actual heaven.

'Yeah but . . . Why else?'

'I don't know, J, I'm sorry. It sucks.'

'It hurts, Michael. It really hurts.' And I turned in the car and leaned over into Michael for a hug. Even though leaning over the gear stick hurt, I needed it.

'What about Harry?' Michael pulled away from the hug and looked at me.

'Are you serious?' I attempted a laugh.

'Yeah, why not? He might take your mind off Ronan, and who knows, you might end up really liking him. He has really great shoulders, remember,' Michael said, grinning. 'And anyway, I need you to find someone for our double date on Friday. Francis is really looking forward to meeting you and it's far too embarrassing for me to bring you as a sad little gooseberry.'

I hadn't said yes. But I had stopped crying. And I *was* thinking about it. I didn't fancy Harry. Yeah, he was nice, but he wasn't Ronan. He wasn't the chess games and the conversations and the chance to just be myself without thinking about my stupid disease.

But Ronan wasn't an option any more. Ronan broke up with me. And every time it went through my mind, I wanted to cry all over again.

'No, I don't think so.' I shrugged.

'Aw, J, give it a go. You never know, you might actually hit it off and in the meantime, Ronan will get super jealous.'

I looked over at Michael's evil grin. 'Do you think?'

'Totally. It's a win-win situation.'

'He *does* have nice shoulders.' I managed a half-smile despite the emptiness in my chest.

'That's the spirit. Now text him.' Michael still had my phone and he flicked it back on to Harry's message.

'I don't know . . .'

'You do know. None of this waiting around crap to see if Ronan deigns to change his mind. You need to take matters into your own hands.'

Michael was right. Why would I wait around to see if somebody decided I was good enough when I had someone else who was perfectly nice willing to go out with me?

'You're right,' I said and took the phone from Michael.

'Obviously.'

> **ME:** Hey, Harry. If you're still interested, Michael's invited us to Maggie's on Friday with him and his boyfriend. Want to go?

> **HARRY:** Sure, sounds great. I can't wait 😊 x

'It's done.' I showed Michael his reply as he pulled away.

'Don't sound so excited.'

'Sorry, it's just . . .'

'I know. He's no Ro, but he really likes you and . . .'

Michael looked at me to fill in the blank.

'Shoulders.'

'Exactly. And yeah, I didn't want to bring it up because you're sad, but did you do the English homework? I think Miss Black might lose the plot if nobody does it.' Michael pulled a face.

'Yeah … no, I haven't, what was it?' I hadn't been paying attention in any of the English classes lately because of the stupid boy-shaped distraction.

'Write a modern take on a letter from either Romeo to Juliet or Juliet to Romeo?' His voice tailed off when he realized I didn't have a clue what he was on about. 'OK, it's easy. I did a gay take. Romeo, writing to Juliet, confessing that he's secretly in love with Tybalt. Miss Black is going to *love* it. Come on, get out your book, you can do it now.'

I pulled out my English folder and a pen.

'What are you going to say?' Michael leaned over.

'Eyes on the road.'

Dear Romeo,

This is called a letter. It's something people use to communicate with each other when they have something to say that takes up more than 140 characters. You might want to try it sometime.

You know what I'm talking about.

Breaking up with someone by text message? With no explanation?

If you think it adds to the 'cool' mysterious persona you've tried to create, then I'm sorry to say that you've FAILED. It just makes you look like a jackass.

You promised me the world and then took it away.

Who does that?

But anyway, I don't care.

I've come to my senses. I am no longer heartbroken by your abrupt departure from my life. Looking back, it's clear that your behaviour was a total red flag. I know that you and Tybalt were never friends so his view may be biased but when I let him read the messages you sent me, he was outraged. He explained (eloquently) that you have behaved terribly and could not possibly love me if you speak to me this way. I have to agree.

It is why I have had to take the fate of my happiness into my own hands. I have been secretly dating Mercutio. We have been having great ~~sex~~ fun and I'm about eighty per cent sure that he's the man for me.

Goodbye forever

(#Romeoiscancelled)

Juliet x

I didn't see Ronan when I got to school. Which was a relief. But I did see Harry, who jogged over to me and Michael when he saw us, like he'd been waiting. Michael decided to disappear.

'Hey, Jules. You OK?' Harry grinned at me. He was like the opposite of Ronan, muscly not thin, blonde not dark, soft, happy features instead of sculpted, serious ones. He had a nice smile. One of those smiles that lit up his entire face.

'Yeah, how are you?'

'I'm good. I'm so glad you changed your mind. I've been thinking about you since Daniel's party, you know.' His face turned red when he said it.

'Really? Did my drinking skills really make that much of an impression?' I laughed.

'No, but you did.'

Yeah, it was cheesy, but it was nice, and exactly the kind of thing I needed to hear right then.

I nudged him. 'That's sweet. Want to sit down?

'Sure.'

We sat on one of the benches that were dotted around the schoolyard.

'You're on the football team, aren't you?' I asked. Then I realized that was about the only thing I knew about Harry.

'Yeah, I am. I love football. I play for Westing Giants too, outside school.'

'That's a lot of football. What else do you like to do?'

'Hang out with friends, go to the cinema, that's about it really, with all the football and everything. What about you?' He was speaking quickly. Like he was nervous. Because of me?

'I play chess.'

As soon as I said it, I wished I could take it back. But then he looked impressed.

'Chess? Like the game?'

'Yeah. Online mostly.'

I tried to push the thought of my games with Ronan out of my head.

'Wow, that's cool. You must be really smart.' He looked like he really meant it. And it made me feel good. Even if it wasn't true.

'Not really, just loads of practice.' I shrugged. I wondered if he was going to ask about *why* I had so much practice. And whether he was going to ask what was wrong with me. But we were saved by the bell.

'Oh man, I'd better go. I have football after school, but I'll send you a message later?' He stood up and started backing away, like he couldn't bear to be late.

'Great, yeah!' I stretched my mouth into a smile.

Then he came back towards me, kissed me on the cheek, pushed a piece of hair behind my ear before turning and *running* towards the school entrance, leaving me on the bench in an almost empty schoolyard.

I wish I hadn't looked up then. But I did. Ronan and Tara were walking into school. Together. He didn't look broken or like he'd been crying all night. He didn't look like he'd just had his heart ripped from his chest and dissected right in front of him.

He looked fine.

And that hurt even more.

62

Ronan

Mum waited until one thirty a.m. for Ciaran that night. So I sat there too. She barely spoke. Sometimes she'd talk about Ciaran – things he did when he was little, like how he knew all the prime numbers off by heart by the time he was eight, or the time we all went on holiday to France and Ciaran split his head open when we were playfighting in the hotel. I remembered that. He didn't even cry. There was so much blood.

He had to get stitches. The real ones, not the paper ones that they glue together. Real ones with a needle.

That's when he cried.

Ciaran was terrified of needles. Back then.

When he hadn't shown up by one thirty a.m., Mum just got up from her seat and went upstairs without saying anything, leaving me sitting there, wishing so hard that things were different.

I couldn't sleep. I logged in to Chess Life and let myself imagine that I'd never sent the message to Jules calling everything off. We'd be chatting now, laughing about stupid stuff and I'd be counting the minutes until I could see her again. But it was better this way, better that she hated me instead of knowing what kind of screw-up I really was.

I even thought about ditching Chess Life altogether. What was the point of it when she wasn't there? But I stopped myself. It was still a connection to Jules, even if she despised me and was never online. So I paid the subscription instead, hoping she would too.

When Mum went to bed I went into Ciaran's room and pulled the playbook out from under his mattress.

I sat on his bed and ran my hand over the soft leather cover with C.C. engraved on it. I opened it at a random page.

*'Chess is life' – Bobby Fischer** was written in the middle of the page and starred. Underneath that he'd written *'The Silver Pawn Tournament – To play a match for the World Championship is the cherished dream of every chess player' – David Bronstein**

I stared at it for a while. Did it really mean that much to him? I flicked through some more pages. And found more quotes. All of them starred.

*'In chess, as in life, opportunity strikes but once' – David Bronstein**
   *'Chess is like bodybuilding. If you train every day, you stay in top shape. It is the same with your brain. Chess is a matter of daily training' – Vladimir Kramnik**
   *'Every chess master was once a beginner' – Irving Chernev**

I closed the book and pushed it underneath the mattress again. Then I went downstairs. Straight to the letter rack. There it was, the letter that Mum had brought to the restaurant. I took it up to my room.

Dear Mr Cole,

We are delighted to inform you that you have been offered an invitation to take part in the annual Silver Pawn Tournament. Several of these tournaments will take place across Ireland and the UK, as well as internationally. Two hundred of the best chess players from the United Kingdom and Ireland will compete in the tournament, which will take place on 22 October 2023. Please use the reply slip to accept your invitation by 20 October 2023.

Should you be successful on this date, you will be invited to the Golden Pawn Tournament which will take place in New York City in 2024.

We wish you every success.

Please refer to the enclosed documents for details about the day.

Yours sincerely,

Miss Klein

I didn't realize how much he wanted it. How much he needed to be great. I'd missed it, like I'd missed how bad everything got. Or maybe I just didn't want to know.

I filled out the form.

Mr Cole would love to accept the invitation to play.

I played chess all night, against the computer, forcing myself to think about moves when thoughts of Jules and the guilt about what I'd done came into my head.

I set the pawn on my desk as I practised.

I would do it for him.

63

Juliet

After Harry left, I was right back in my head, thinking about Ronan. Even when Harry was there it was hard to keep my mind on track. It felt like it did when Mum decided we were cutting out carbs or sugar or whatever. It was all I could think about. Except this time, Ronan cutting himself out of my life meant that *he* was all I could think about. Even when I was chatting to Harry, I was thinking about how different they were. How Ronan would have made me laugh when Harry just said something kind. And that wasn't fair. Harry was nice. I'd hate it if someone I liked was thinking about someone else the whole time. I tried to kick the thought that that was exactly what Ronan had been doing. But it was hard. I was so relieved when Michael came to find me and spent the whole walk to registration talking about Francis.

For once we were there early.

'Oh wow, I don't think I've ever seen nine a.m. in this room.' Michael gazed around, pretending to be fascinated. 'Nope, just as boring as usual.'

'Have you seen him today?' I asked from the same seat I sat

in every morning, the one in the corner, near the back but not right at the back.

'Juliet, do you think if I'd seen Ronan that I would have been able to contain myself and not tell you? I might even have attacked him.' Michael sat down beside me. I nudged him.

'What? It's true. He can't go around treating you like that. He'll have to face the consequences.' Michael held up his fist and a noise a bit like a laugh came out of my mouth.

'Thanks, Rocky, but I don't think that's necessary,' I said.

'Well, just say the word.'

The thought of Michael punching someone was a ridiculous one. I was grateful for the sentiment but Michael could never even bring himself to kill an insect, never mind inflict pain on another human being.

'Thanks, Michael.'

I could hear other kids come in, chatting easily like they had zero problems in their lives. Which they probably didn't. I leaned my chin on my hands and all the feelings rose in my chest like emotional vomit.

'It really hurts, Michael,' I said. And my voice shook.

'I know it does, J.'

Michael squeezed me and I let the sleeves of my school jumper soak up the tears that I couldn't hold back any more.

64

Ronan

The next morning the kitchen had been cleaned. Everything had been put away, and it was as if the dinner had never happened.

Mum was sitting at the kitchen table with a cup of coffee. She smiled at me.

'Can't believe your brother didn't show up last night.' She shook her head and gave a little laugh, as if it was no big deal.

'Yeah.'

I thought about Tara then. All that she did for her mum, and the guilt hit me like a brick in the face. But how could I help my mum when she acted the way she did? I suppose I could call Aunt Sarah, ask her to come over, but wasn't that cheating? She was *my* mum. I thought about the video on my phone. Almost took it out of my pocket. If I just pressed play and slid it across the table in front of her then maybe, just maybe it would fix things. Not *fix* them, because something like that can never be *fixed*, but she couldn't deny it then, if it was staring her in the face.

'I was thinking of having a party, for his birthday. Nothing big, just here in the house. I'm sure he'll show up for that.' Mum didn't look up from the news she was reading on her phone.

'I'm not sure Ciaran's into parties, Mum.'

She still didn't look up at me.

'Everybody loves parties, Ronan. Don't be silly. Invite some of your new friends and I'll phone the caterers – it will be brilliant.'

She smiled at me this time, this red-lipped, perfect smile that raised the hairs on my neck.

'Got to go,' I said, forgetting why I was in the kitchen in the first place.

Ever since Tara and Jules fell out, Tara had started walking to school sometimes. She'd sent me a message last night asking if I would meet her at the crossroads, that she didn't like walking by herself because she was scared. It felt like the old Tara was back, like she'd telepathically figured out that Jules and I weren't together.

I was going to say no. After everything she'd done and said. But then I thought about Mum last night, and Tara's mum.

I said yes.

I tried to ignore Tara's monologue the whole way to school. When I could see the school gates I thought about that time a few weeks ago when Jules and I had cut school. How scared she was that we would get caught, and how amazing it felt to be together, just us. It was the best day I'd had in such a long time.

I made my escape from Tara when we ran into Luke, who was all over her as usual. I got out of their way and walked towards school, wondering if Jules was even here yet.

Then I saw her, sitting on a bench with some guy. She was playing with her hair, the way she did when she was nervous. Why was she nervous?

The guy she was talking to was on the football team. Harry, maybe. Tall, pretty good-looking if you like that sort of thing, and he was making her laugh? He was so close to her. A few inches closer and he'd be able to touch her. Then he *was* touching her. His hand round her waist and he kissed her on the cheek. What the hell?

I never thought I'd be the jealous type. But nausea filled my stomach and words were stuck in my throat. I squeezed the pawn and thought about what Ciaran would do. Not make the fucking mess I was making. I knew that much.

I was still staring, but I couldn't help it. He pushed a bit of hair back behind her ear. What the fuck did he think he was doing?

'You OK, Ronan?'

I turned to see Hana looking at me with concern on her face.

'Yeah, fine, just couldn't remember where to go.'

'Registration. It's this way, come on. I'm going that way too. I'll show you.'

I followed Hana and her pink backpack. I had to force myself to look away from them.

'How are things with you and Jules?' Hana smiled at me, interested.

'It didn't work out actually.' I tried to sound like I didn't care but either I failed miserably, or Hana had some kind of sixth sense.

'Aw no, are you OK?' She stopped and put her hand on my arm like she really cared.

'Yeah, yeah, I'm fine. How are you, anyway?' I was desperate to change the subject.

'I'm pretty good. Me and Charlie are official now.' She couldn't help smiling when she said it. I half-wondered if she was talking about a different Charlie. The only one I knew never even cracked a smile.

'Oh, that's good. Maybe that'll make him a bit happier.' I wasn't sure how she'd take it, but I didn't have the energy to filter all my thoughts.

'Ronan!' She nudged me, pretending to be offended. 'He's just serious, that's all. Think he saw you as a bit of a threat. Don't know why,' she said, laughing. And I forced out a laugh too.

'Hey, we're all going to Maggie's this Friday. Me, Charlie, Tara, Luke.' She rolled her eyes when she said Luke's name. 'You should come too, maybe you and Tara can sort out whatever it was that happened between you.'

'Nothing happened really . . .'

She held up her hands. 'Not my business. Just saying, if you need some friends right now, that's where we'll be.'

'Maybe,' I said. I couldn't say straight-up 'no' to Hana, she was so nice.

'Here you are.' Hana stood beside the door to my registration class.

'Thanks, Hana.'

She walked off. I went inside and looked for a seat out of the way. There were hardly any spaces, but I found one at the back, beside the wall.

Then there she was. Sitting right in front of me with Michael. I noticed him first, it was hard not to. She was sort of leaning into him and he said something that made her laugh. She didn't see me. I wished I'd found another seat.

Then they started talking.

'So, Harry then,' said Michael, rubbing his hands together.

'What about him?' Jules asked.

'You could make a really cute couple.'

'You think? Really?

No! I mean, I know I didn't have the right to be pissed off, or jealous, but *that* fact clearly hadn't been communicated to my brain. I thought about how he kissed her on the cheek, how he touched her hair. How he wasn't, and never would be, good enough for her.

'Eh, yeah. Oh, and we can totally go to all the football matches now and not be one hundred per cent out of place. Yay.'

'You don't like football,' Jules said.

'I like watching people play football. It's very different.'

'I think I might be a bit excited now.'

'About Harry?'

'Yes.'

I didn't have to see her whole face to know she was smiling. Well, that didn't take long. I know it was me who ended it. *I* sent the stupid message. It was *my* fault. But I didn't expect her to just move on to someone else so quickly. I told myself I should be happy that she's happy. Because that's what I wanted, wasn't it? To make her happy? And if this was the only way to do it, then I'd just have to suck it up.

'Good. I'll make sure me and Francis leave you two alone

on our date at some point, so you can, you know, do whatever you want to do,' Michael said.

I almost choked, trying to stifle a cough. And scraped my chair in the process. So much for sucking it up. They both turned round.

Michael gasped and Jules's face turned bright red.

I made a point of fixing my earbuds, so they'd assume I hadn't heard what they'd said. I turned the music all the way up until it hurt.

65

Juliet

The colour of my face said otherwise, but I didn't care if he'd heard what I said. In fact, I *hoped* he'd heard what I said.

We'd turned back to face the front. I could hear Ronan's music even though he was wearing earbuds. I hoped he'd burst his eardrums.

I didn't really.

No. I did.

'Think he heard us?' Michael whispered and glanced back at Ronan.

'Don't care.' I shrugged.

'I think I like this new you,' Michael said, nodding. 'Think you can keep it up through English?'

'Shit.'

'You forgot we had English first period, didn't you?'

I put my head in my hands then took them away in case Ronan was looking and thought it was something to do with him.

'Can't you get your seat back beside me? I don't want to sit beside *him*. Did you see him walk in with Tara? They actually walked to school together, like nothing ever happened between us. I should have trusted my gut. People like him. Ugh.' I was finding it hard to whisper and Mr Dawson looked up.

'Are you quite all right, Miss Clarke?' He stroked his moustache.

'Sorry, sir, I'm fine. Just had something in my throat.'

He held my gaze for a few seconds then looked back down at the newspaper he was reading.

When the bell rang, I wished so much I could push back my chair and run out of the door. Away from him. But because it was me, I waited until everyone else had left before picking up my crutches.

'Has he gone?' I asked Michael to check behind us.

'The coast is clear. You don't need him, J. Don't waste any time thinking about him.'

'But how can I not? He sits right beside me in English, all dark and brooding and probably smelling of Tara's perfume today.'

'Why does she always smell like dessert?' Michael screwed up his face.

'She thinks boys like sweet smells.'

'What, so they want to eat her?' Michael thought about this then shook his head like he was trying to shake the idea from his brain.

'And there she goes, again. Getting everything she wants like she's queen fucking bee of the whole school!' Actual rage burned inside me now.

Michael put his hands together like he was praying. 'Finally. Finally you see!'

'It must have been her who sent him that message.'

'Ah, let it all out, little J.'

We were alone in the corridor; everyone else was already in class.

'She called me Crutch Girl, she *stole* Ronan and she *probably* sent him that message that made him leave my house.' I tried to slam my crutch on the lino, but it slipped. And so did I. Michael wasn't fast enough to catch me, and I landed in a heap on the floor, my knees screaming with pain.

'Jesus, are you OK?'

I wanted to say yes. But it's hard to say anything when tears are leaking down your face. So I just nodded.

'Oh, J. Come here.' Michael helped me up and then hugged me, squishing my face into his now-damp school jumper.

'You've got Harry. Don't worry. He's great. And we can forget about Ronan. I can ask Miss Black if I've paid my penance and can return to my regular seat, if you want?'

I nodded.

'I will. I'll move back to my seat, and we can pretend Ronan Cole doesn't exist. That he and Tara died a horrible death. Eaten by a Chihuahua. A *pack* of Chihuahuas. Jeffrey clones . . . Was that a laugh?'

I pulled away from Michael and wiped my nose on my sleeve. He handed me my crutches back.

'Jeffrey *is* pretty loyal.'

'That's the spirit! Are you ready?'

I must have looked disgusting. Hair everywhere, face red from pain and crying.

'No, but if we stay out here any longer, they'll send out a search party.'

'Let's do it.'

The whole class looked up when we walked through the door. Michael went straight to Miss Black to make his case about getting his old seat back. But she wasn't having any of it.

Ronan was already there. He looked right at us, then back down at the work he was pretending to do.

I sat down.

Ronan didn't look up. There was a buzz in my pocket.

I checked my phone under the desk.

Chess Life.

ALONELYPAWN: New boyfriend? You don't
  wait around.

PRETTYBASIC: Are you kidding me?

ALONELYPAWN: Not about this.

PRETTYBASIC: Are you forgetting the fact
  you said no when I asked you out? And
  you're with Tara now?

ALONELYPAWN: I'm not with Tara.

PRETTYBASIC: Looked pretty girlfriend-y
  to me. Walking to school together.

ALONELYPAWN: That was it. Walking
  together. You don't even know the
  context.

PRETTYBASIC: Tell me the CONTEXT then.

ALONELYPAWN: I can't.

PRETTYBASIC: So you and Tara have
  secrets now?

ALONELYPAWN: It's not for me to tell.

PRETTYBASIC: Keep your secrets. I don't
    care anyway.
ALONELYPAWN: You know, sometimes people
    have shit going on that you don't know
    about. In fact, my guess is that every
    single person in this room has something
    they're dealing with at home, at school,
    whatever. It's not always obvious.
PRETTYBASIC: So what's your point? That
    you have shit going on so that allows
    you to treat ME like shit?
ALONELYPAWN: I didn't say it was my shit.

I signed out.

I moved my pencil case as far away from Ronan as possible.
And my chair.

'Miss Clarke, will you please try and settle yourself.'

'Sorry.' I stared at the pages I'd just been handed, letting the
words bleed out of focus as I thought about what Ronan had
just said. *I didn't say it was my shit.*

Then whose?

66

Ronan

In chess it's called a *zugzwang*, where any move you make will be a bad one.

Tell Jules I want to be with her, *only* her, then let her find out what kind of person I am and destroy everything? Tell Tara I don't want to walk to school with her because it might make the girl I was dating get the wrong idea? She'd laugh in my face.

And yeah, I got why Jules was pissed. But at the same time, she didn't know *everything*. And she didn't seem to care that seeing her with Harry felt like a fucking punch in the throat.

'Please hand in your *Romeo and Juliet* letters. I will mark them and get them back to you with the many changes you'll no doubt have to make.'

There was a groan from the class.

'That's the kind of enthusiasm I like to hear,' Miss Black said.

I looked to my right and Jules was rubbing something out on her letter.

'Bit late for a rewrite isn't it?' I whispered.

'Shut up.' She shielded the letter from me.

'I forgot to do one.'

'Ugh. Typical. Probably too busy with Tara.' She rubbed furiously at her page.

'No, actually, too busy this morning on Insta, stalking that guy you were kissing. He has quite the collection of photos.'

She stopped rubbing. I knew I'd got to her.

'Why were you on his Insta?' She narrowed her eyes. 'I wasn't kissing him anyway.'

'His lips, your cheek, looked like a kiss to me.' I shrugged and tried to erase the image from my mind. 'And anyway, I wanted to see if he was good enough for you.' It wasn't hard to wind her up.

'And you think you know what's good enough for me?'

'OK, maybe "good enough" isn't what I meant. Checking to see whether he's like me or not. See if you have a certain type.'

'And what did you discover?' She gave me a pleased little smile.

'That he's the opposite of me in almost every way.'

'Well, that's exactly what I want.'

Miss Black cut through our conversation. 'Five minutes and I'll be collecting your letters, finished or not.'

I pulled out a piece of paper and started writing.

Dear Juliet,

'Well, then you've succeeded. He plays football. I do not. He listens to terrible music. I do not.'

'How do you even know what kind of music he listens to?'

I miss you.

'Because in one of his pictures he's wearing a Soulscape T-shirt and *either* he's one of those people who wears band T-shirts without *actually* listening to the band – and they're a whole other breed of awful – *or* he actually likes Soulscape, which is unforgivable.'

She snorted. 'According to you.'

I wish we could be together.

'Yes. Hm, what else? He has loads of friends.'

'What? Like that's a bad thing?' She'd stopped rubbing out completely now and was just staring at me.

'Can't trust people with too many friends.'

I'm sorry.

'Why not?'

'They can't be real with everyone. I mean, it's probably just this surface-level friendship or something. Meaningless.'

'Yeah, you're right, having *no* friends is much better.'

Seeing you and not being able to touch you is torture.

'Two minutes until collection,' Miss Black called.

'So, in conclusion, he's perfect for you. If you want someone at the opposite end of cool to me, you're sorted.'

'Yeah. I do. Oh, I thought of another difference.' She handed her letter to Miss Black as I finished mine.

I love you,
Romeo.

'He's not a complete and utter jackass.'

I put my pencil down and Miss Black took the piece of creased paper from my desk. 'A bit short, Mr Cole. But don't worry, this is just a first draft. Plenty of time to rework it over the coming week.'

The bell rang and Jules didn't move, waiting until everybody else had left. I thought about picking up her crutches but, scared she might throw them at me, I left them on the floor and walked into the corridor. I was barely out of the door before Tara was touching me. Hanging on to my arm.

'Thought I'd surprise you. We can walk this way together. You have maths, don't you? I have business studies.' She stood on tiptoes and kissed my cheek as people banged into us from all sides. I leaned against a locker to get out of their way. She stopped too.

'Tara . . . I . . .'

Just as I was about to finish, I looked up to see Jules and Michael staring at me. At us. And I realized she was right, that no matter what I did, even if I tried to do the right thing, it always came back to punch me in the face.

But she put it better.

I *was* a jackass.

67

Juliet

I couldn't stop thinking about him the whole way through history. And not in a good way. I'd almost rather listen to Mr Tsang talk about Henry the Eighth. But no. His stupid smug face was in my head. All that stuff he said about whether or not Harry was good enough for me. It made me so angry. Who did he think he was?

Right on cue, my phone buzzed. I checked it under the table.

> **HARRY:** Hey, can I see you at break time? X

He didn't have to ask, but I guess it was sweet.

> **ME:** Sure ☺

I tried to think of Harry instead, replacing Ronan's face in my mind. But it wouldn't work. And now I was thinking about kissing him again. I thought at this point in my life I'd be able to control my mind, put things away in some little box somewhere, but no, there Ronan was, front and centre. I hadn't listened to one word of history.

I was still thinking about him at the end of class. Even when everybody else had left and I walked out of the door straight into Harry.

'Oh, hey!' I smiled.

'Hey, can I carry your bag?'

'Sure, thanks.' I slipped the bag off my shoulders and handed it to him. We started walking down the corridor.

'You know, I've never actually been to Maggie's before,' Harry blurted it out like it was something he'd rehearsed.

'What? Really? How?' Anyone who lived in Ferndale had been to Maggie's. It was like a rite of passage. Mum used to take Tara and me every Friday after school when we were at primary school. I even used to have my birthday parties there.

'Yeah, I don't know, my mum and dad are vegan, and I guess I am too, mostly, so I suppose that's why.' He shrugged and I noticed he had gone bright red again.

'Well, I think they do vegan shakes now, so you're in luck.'

'I don't think the lack of a vegan milkshake would have put me off going on a date with you to be honest,' Harry said. He held the door open for me. A blast of cold air made me shiver.

'I think that's the most romantic thing anyone's ever said to me.' I gave a little laugh and he turned red again. We sat down on the closest bench to the school, overlooking the entire schoolyard.

'Are you OK? Are you cold? Do you want my blazer?' Harry dropped the school bags to the ground and took off his blazer.

'Thanks, Harry,' I said, and let him drape it round my shoulders.

'Suits you, the green.' He nodded at me.

Harry had a green blazer. The one you got if you were super good at sports. I noticed that he was twisting his hands together.

'Thanks. You must be freezing though.'

'I'm fine. Tell me more about you anyway. Did you hurt yourself? I didn't want to ask before, but now it feels like it would be rude if I *didn't* ask.' Harry eyed my crutches and had turned a new shade of red.

'I have arthritis actually, unfortunately not something that will get better any time soon.' I sighed and then smiled because he looked horrified. 'It's pretty annoying but I'm a bit used to it now. I'm excited for our date on Friday.' I forced out a smile and hoped he'd take the hint that I wanted to change the subject.

But he didn't.

'My granny has arthritis too. She said she eats dulse and takes cod liver oil and she's almost pain-free. Maybe that would help . . .'

I didn't want to jump in with, 'Yeah, it's probably a different kind of arthritis. Eating seaweed and fish oil isn't going to touch the edges of what I have. But thanks for the tip.' So instead I said, 'Yeah, I might try that. Thanks.'

There was too much silence then.

'I'm really looking forward to our date too.' Harry filled the silence and looked at me. 'Would you mind if I kissed you?'

I was not expecting that at all. Nobody had ever asked if they could kiss me before and now my hesitation made an already awkward situation even more awkward. I looked around, at all the kids hanging around the schoolyard who weren't even looking at me. Part of me thought I didn't want anyone to see, that it would have been much better if we were somewhere private. But the other part? I wanted everyone to see, just so it would get back to Ronan, just so he could see what he was missing.

'No, I wouldn't mind.'

So I let him kiss me. Right there in the schoolyard. He tasted like Coke and his tongue was cold. I tried to focus, tried to get the coordination right, but Ronan kept illegally entering my head. The way he kissed, the way he touched my face. I pulled away.

'Sorry, there are just so many people,' I said.

'Don't worry, that's fine. Different for me maybe. I've learned to block out crowds now. You have to when you're playing football, or you'd never be able to concentrate.' He smiled at me but not as widely as before.

My phone buzzed. I checked it.

```
ALONELYPAWN: Having fun with Brad Harvey?
PRETTYBASIC: I don't even know who
    that is.
ALONELYPAWN: The lead singer of your
    boyfriend's favourite band. Soulscape.
PRETTYBASIC: He's not my boyfriend.
ALONELYPAWN: He kissed you like he is.
PRETTYBASIC: Kissed me like he WISHES he
    was maybe.
ALONELYPAWN: Well, you're rather sure of
    yourself.
```

```
PRETTYBASIC: Someone has to be.
ALONELYPAWN: That hurt.
```

I turned round, almost jerking my neck, looking for Ronan. But I couldn't see him anywhere.

'You OK, Jules?' I looked up to see Harry staring at me, then he glanced at my phone.

'Yeah, sorry, just my mum sending me messages.'

```
ALONELYPAWN: I guess you paid the Chess
  Life subscription, seeing how you're
  still here.
PRETTYBASIC: So? You're not the only
  person I've played games with on here.
ALONELYPAWN: Doesn't your boyfriend mind
  that you're sending messages to some
  other guy?
PRETTYBASIC: GO AWAY!
```

'She's just reminding me about my appointment later,' I said and shoved my phone back into my pocket.

The bell rang and Harry stood up. He held out his hand to help me up.

'I'd better go. My Spanish teacher gets really mad when I'm late.'

I slid his blazer off my shoulders and handed it back to him. 'Thanks for this.'

'Any time.'

Harry kissed me on the cheek and then ran down the

schoolyard to the languages building. I wished he'd stop doing that. Or at least wait until most of the other people had gone back inside before leaving me standing by myself.

Michael appeared from a crowd of kids, walking towards me, tipping the remainder of his crisps into his mouth.

'Well, how'd that go?' Michael asked. Waiting for me to fill him in with details.

'He kissed me.'

'What? You dark horse. How was it?'

'Tainted with thoughts of Ronan.'

'That's not good.' Michael shook his head and picked up my school bag.

'Not good at all. But also, I think he was *nervous*? Which is fine, obviously, I just didn't expect anyone to be nervous around me. Ever.'

'Get used to it, J. The world has finally woken up to your hotness.'

'Well, I'm about to lose some hot points with this appointment. I should go and wait for Mum at reception.'

'GP?' Michael said.

'How did you remember?'

'It's been a while since your last GP appointment.' He shrugged. 'And please, no hot points lost there. Who said losing blood isn't sexy? Worked for Bella Swan and Sooki Stackhouse.' Michael gasped. 'What if the nurses are secretly vampires and your blood never gets tested at all, just made into smoothies and alcoholic jelly?'

'That would definitely be more interesting.'

Michael walked me to reception.

He set my bag down. 'See you later?'

I nodded.

Streams of pupils walked past me, some not even noticing I was there and half-tripping over my crutches. I bent down to pull them on to the chair beside me, but before I could, somebody sat down in it.

Then I saw who it was. My heart sank and my stomach flipped at the same time.

'What do you want?'

68

Ronan

It was hard to keep watching Jules and Harry when Tara was all over me, pulling my face towards hers and asking if I was listening to what she was saying. Spoiler: I wasn't. But I suppose it was OK. Staring too much would make me look like a massive creep.

At the end of break, I saw Harry run off in the other direction and decided that this was my chance. My chance to what? I didn't know. Make sure she wasn't forgetting about me, I guess. And then, perfect timing. There she was in reception. Alone.

And all I got from her was, 'What do you want?'

So rude. But I knew what she was doing. She didn't really mean it. I hoped.

'Hello to you too.'

'You'll be late to class if you don't leave,' she said without looking at me. She was gazing out of the door like she was looking for someone.

'I don't care if I'm late for class. In fact, I don't care if I miss class. I feel like you should know this about me by now.'

'It was a polite way of saying "go away".' She still refused to look at me.

'That's not very nice.'

'Nor is breaking up with someone by an online chat message . . .'

Jesus, that felt like a slap in the face.

'I didn't mean to,' I said, without thinking. Then she looked at me hopefully. Shit. That didn't come out right. 'I meant to talk to you in person about it, but I panicked.' I cringed.

'Well, you got your point across anyway.' She gave me a fake smile.

'It's just . . .' I didn't actually know how I was going to put it. *It's just that my mum texted me to say my brother is coming home, which is completely impossible, and by telling you, you'd find out how much of a mess my family was. Then you'd realize what a horrible person I am.*

'Really don't care,' she said, in a sing-song voice.

I took out my phone.

```
*YOU HAVE INVITED PRETTYBASIC TO A
 GAME*
*PRETTYBASIC HAS DECLINED THIS GAME*
*YOU HAVE INVITED PRETTYBASIC TO A GAME*
*PRETTYBASIC HAS DECLINED THIS GAME*
*YOU HAVE INVITED PRETTYBASIC TO A
 GAME*
```

'Ugh, will you stop?' she said, putting her phone face down on her knee.

'One game.'

'Why? Why do you still want to play this? Why do you still want to talk to me when you said we weren't a good idea? Those were your words, weren't they?'

'I like talking to you. And I need to practise.'

'Well, it's not all about *you*. You gave up the right to talk to me when you sent me that stupid message.'

She looked really pissed off. I needed to defuse the situation.

'You're right. I'm sorry.' I put my hands up. 'One game. That's all I'm asking. You win and I'll never talk to you again. And we don't even have to talk while we're playing.' I didn't mean that bit. I couldn't face just playing chess with her; I needed her chat – it kept me sane.

'Ugh, shut up. And if you win?'

'If I win? You come to watch me at the tournament.'

'What tournament?'

'The Silver Pawn Tournament at Ellis Hall on the twenty-second of October. So yeah, it's this weekend.'

'What makes you think I'd agree to that? I've moved on, Ronan.'

'With Soulscape?'

'If you mean Harry, then yes.'

'And how's that working out for you?'

'It's only just started.'

'Did I see him running away from you earlier after your kiss?'

'Shut up. He wasn't running away *from* me. He was just running.'

'If you say so.' I shrugged and smiled at her. 'One game. Please.'

She narrowed her eyes. 'One game.'

I didn't want to smile too hard because I'd look like I was insane, but I was so fucking happy.

'There's your mum,' I pointed at the door.

'Yeah. You should go.' She stood up and walked towards the door, not even looking back at me.

'Your wish is my command. Maths awaits.' I got up and walked to class, slowly.

'Where were you, Mr Cole?' Mr O'Neill *hated* lateness, *hated* mobile phones and I was pretty sure he hated kids too.

'I was helping a friend.'

'Care to elaborate on your flimsy excuse?'

'Not really. But if you want me to embarrass my friend in front of the whole class, then I'll go right ahead. She needed my help, and I gave it to her.'

Mr O'Neill stared at me. Unblinking.

'Well, seeing as you're so helpful, Mr Cole, I could use some help with this algebraic division.'

He lobbed the whiteboard marker at me. I caught it and walked to the front of the class.

I caught Hana's eye and she smiled at me.

It was too easy. He expected me to fail. And I loved that. Proving people wrong. I finished and lobbed the marker back on to his desk.

'Well done, Mr Cole,' Mr O'Neill conceded and started teaching the class again.

*PRETTYBASIC HAS ACCEPTED YOUR
  INVITATION*
ALONELYPAWN: You almost got me in
  trouble.
PRETTYBASIC: ME?
ALONELYPAWN: You made me late for class.
PRETTYBASIC: Good! I'm going first.
ALONELYPAWN: d4? Was that a mistake or
  are you going all Boor attack on me?
  What happened to your trusty e4?
PRETTYBASIC: None of your business.
ALONELYPAWN: Interesting. I'm going d5
  then.
PRETTYBASIC: I'm taking your pawn.
ALONELYPAWN: Well, I'm taking YOUR
  pawn too.
PRETTYBASIC: Got to go. I'll beat you
  later.
ALONELYPAWN: Good luck x

69

Juliet

The surgery was almost empty when I got there. Just an old lady and a woman with two kids who wouldn't stop crying. Mum had offered to come in, like she always did, but I wanted to be alone.

I was only thinking about one thing: Ronan. I tried to think about Harry. Our date on Friday. I even tried to think about what I'd wear, but it always came back to Ronan. His stupid sexy face, and the way he smiled, and the way he made me think about doing things that I'd never done before. Then the pain came back. The one that reminded me that Ronan had broken up with me, that he didn't want me any more and that *he* seemed completely fine about it.

As if he knew I was thinking about him, my phone buzzed.

```
ALONELYPAWN: I'm not copying your moves,
    by the way. I have a plan. Are you
    excited to come and watch me at this
    tournament?
```

I hadn't noticed, but his moves mirrored mine.

```
PRETTYBASIC: Will be pretty embarrassing
   if you don't win.
ALONELYPAWN: So you're coming?
PRETTYBASIC: Only if you win. And only
   because I like chess.
ALONELYPAWN: Knights are coming at ya
   from all directions.
PRETTYBASIC: So scared.
ALONELYPAWN: You should be. There goes
   another pawn. So sad for you.
```

Usually when I was here, I'd be getting nervous, every minute feeling like an hour. But today, time was flying.

```
PRETTYBASIC: Didn't like that pawn
   anyway.
ALONELYPAWN: Is that what you tell
   yourself about me?
PRETTYBASIC: I don't tell myself
   anything about you. I already know how
   I feel.
ALONELYPAWN: And how do you feel?
PRETTYBASIC: 👎
ALONELYPAWN: That hurt. It's a terrible
   emoji as well.
PRETTYBASIC: Gets the point across.
ALONELYPAWN: Want to know how I feel
   about you?
PRETTYBASIC: No.
```

Yes.

ALONELYPAWN: Fine.
PRETTYBASIC: You already made it clear
   how you feel about me.

A message flashed on my screen.

HARRY: I was wondering if you wanted to come
over to my house tonight? Hang out? X

ALONELYPAWN: Sometimes things aren't
   always as they seem.
PRETTYBASIC: We talk in riddles now?
ALONELYPAWN: Do you like riddles?
PRETTYBASIC: NO! Shouldn't you be
   hanging out with Tara right now anyway?
ALONELYPAWN: No. She doesn't do biology.
PRETTYBASIC: Shouldn't you be listening
   to your teacher?
ALONELYPAWN: Some people might think you
   don't want to talk to me any more.
PRETTYBASIC: Some people would be right.
ALONELYPAWN: I'm taking another pawn for
   that.
PRETTYBASIC: My name's just been called.
   I better go.
ALONELYPAWN: I miss you.
YOU HAVE SIGNED OUT

I wished he hadn't said that. But I was glad he did. The explosion in my stomach reading those words: 'I miss you.' And then the way it turned to dust when I remembered everything else. Tara. Harry.

Harry.

> **ME:** Why don't you come to mine instead?

> **HARRY:** Yeah, sure, great. Text me your address ☺ xx

The needle hurt more than usual. The nurse had to go in *three* times to find a decent vein. My head was all over the place. Harry coming over. What were we going to do? Watch a movie? Not sex. I hoped he wasn't expecting sex, because I definitely wasn't ready for that. And definitely not with him. Then I felt mean, even though I didn't say it to him, or even out loud; just having those thoughts felt cruel. He was nice. And I'm sure he'd be a great choice for someone's first time. Just not mine.

On the way home I prepped Mum.

'Mum, I have a friend coming over. You haven't met him before so try to be, I don't know, normal?'

'I'm always normal.' She did a fake shocked face. 'What about that other boy, Ronan? He seemed nice,' Mum said gently, not really looking at me.

'Things didn't work out. Anyway, we'll just go up to my room to watch a movie, OK?'

'Your room?'

'Yeah, just like I did with Ronan.' I had no idea why she was making a big deal of this.

I could see her going over this in her head. Searching for the right thing to say. Wondering whether to say no and be a complete hypocrite or just go with it.

'Just make sure you leave the door open.'

'Mum! We're just watching a movie.'

'Jules, I know what watching a movie can turn into. I've heard of "Netflix and chill".'

'Oh God.' I shrank in my seat, covering my face, which was obviously bright red.

'Or you could just watch a movie in the living room?'

'What, so you can be there? Mum, seriously. Nothing's going to happen. We've just started hanging out.'

'OK, OK, fine, you win,' Mum conceded.

We didn't speak the rest of the way home. And when we pulled into the driveway, there was a Jeep waiting outside.

'Who's that?' Mum turned off the engine and we watched the door of the Jeep open. Harry jumped out. He came to open my door.

'Hi, Jules, sorry I'm early. Need a hand?'

'That's very sweet, thank you . . .' Mum answered for me.

'Harry,' he said, because I still hadn't said anything.

I wished I could be more enthusiastic. But it just wasn't there.

Harry carried my bag inside and bent down to stroke Jeffrey, who was immediately all over him.

'He likes you,' Mum said. 'I'll be making dinner soon. You're more than welcome to stay, Harry.'

'Thank you, Mrs Clarke, but coach has us on a strict diet for football. I've already eaten.'

'A footballer.' Mum made a really embarrassing face at me. 'I'll leave you to it then. And Jules . . .'

'Yes, Mum.' I knew she meant the door and just thanked God she didn't say it again.

'Shall we go upstairs? You go ahead, I'm pretty slow.'

'Are you sure? I don't mind.'

'I'm sure.'

Harry bounded up the stairs two at a time leaving a trail of Lynx in his wake. He waited at the top, watching my one step, two feet.

'Which one's yours?'

'Second on the left.'

Harry opened my door and I walked through. The first thing I noticed was Ronan's hoody, folded and sitting on my desk.

I let him close the door behind me. Not because I was just about to get naked with some guy I hardly knew, but because I was eighteen and deserved some actual privacy.

'So, you want to watch a movie or something?' I sat down on my bed. Harry looked like he didn't know what to do. 'Come sit over here.' I smiled and realized that it was probably the first time since he'd got here.

He sat beside me and I opened Netflix. We put on *Stranger Things*. At least there was no chance of getting carried away with *that* in the background.

Our legs were touching. And by the end of the first episode, Harry's hand was on my leg. When Ronan had touched my leg, it felt like a million different nerves coming alive all at once, but now it felt like nothing. Just heavy. When the end credits rolled, and it flicked to another episode, he turned to me.

'You're really pretty,' Harry said.

I wanted to feel more. He deserved more than I was giving. And the way he kind of tilted his head as he said it made me think he wanted to kiss me.

'Aw, thanks, that's really nice.' I pressed the 'watch now' button as I said it. The second episode started to play, and I felt bad, like I'd been leading him on. The truth was, I liked his company, but I just couldn't shake Ronan from my mind.

I was just starting to relax when there was a knock on my bedroom door and Mum poked her head round, with a tray of juice and crisps.

70

Ronan

The Silver Pawn Tournament played the Swiss system. All players are ranked by their ratings (Ciaran's rating) and unrated players are ranked alphabetically. They split the list in half and a player from the first half plays someone from the second half. I remember Ciaran explaining how it worked. That at the beginning you'll probably be playing weak players, but as it moves on, you get to play people who are as strong as you. That was the idea anyway. He had been so fucking excited for this. I had less than a week. Less than one week to practise as hard as I could and win it, for him.

'Do you think I could win it? Really?'

I thought it was weird. The cracks that were starting to show. The lack of confidence. It wasn't him.

'Of course you can win it. You're a fucking genius, Ciaran.'

'I'm not. But thanks.'

'What are you talking about? You're going to Cambridge, for fuck's sake.'

'Ro, you don't get it. This is different. The way Mum goes on about it. She really fucking wants me to win. And what if I can't?'

'She won't care. Nobody would care if you didn't win. It's just a tournament. It doesn't matter.'

'You're right.'

But when he said it, I knew he didn't mean it. That there was something more. But I didn't push it. I didn't ask. I just helped him practise. Game after game after fucking game.

> **TARA:** Want to go to Maggie's on Friday with Hana and Charlie? Xx

> **TARA:** I can see you typing . . .

> **ME:** I dunno, maybe

I couldn't bring myself to just say no. Or yes. So I went for something in between. I needed to practise, and she was disturbing me.

I wondered what Jules was doing right now. I knew it was dangerous, wondering that. The way she made me feel was the kind of distraction I definitely didn't need. But maybe she'd be around for a game. Because she always talked more when she played games. I missed the flirty banter, even though it would just be banter now. But still, even that was better than any relationship I had with anyone else right now. I hated so much that I'd fucked everything up. But the alternative was telling her everything, and that would be so much worse. I couldn't bear the thought of her knowing. Hating me was different. I could deal with her hating me. Because to hate someone you really have to care.

ALONELYPAWN: I have less than a week to
    practise for the tournament you're
    coming to watch me in.
PRETTYBASIC: You mean if you win this game?
ALONELYPAWN: WHEN I win this game, yes.
PRETTYBASIC: I'm sure Tara wouldn't be
    happy if she found out you were
    messaging me.
ALONELYPAWN: That would only be a concern
    if she was my girlfriend. Which she isn't.
PRETTYBASIC: Are you sure about that?
ALONELYPAWN: Yep. Last time I checked,
    I'm single. More single than YOU
    anyway. How's Soulscape?
PRETTYBASIC: He was just here actually.
    He's great.
ALONELYPAWN: Oh, is that right?
PRETTYBASIC: DID YOUR HORSE JUST EAT MY
    HORSE?
ALONELYPAWN: YOUR QUEEN? YOU'RE
    BRINGING OUT YOUR QUEEN?
PRETTYBASIC: I liked that horse ☹

Harry was at her house? Doing what? I hoped he hadn't gone up to her room.

```
PRETTYBASIC: I'm taking your other
   knight.
ALONELYPAWN: FFS. Does Soulscape play
   chess?
PRETTYBASIC: No.
ALONELYPAWN: Probably doesn't understand
   it. Have you tried to teach him?
PRETTYBASIC: I'm sure he'd understand it
   perfectly well, but we've been too busy
   doing other things . . .
ALONELYPAWN: Oh really? What kind of
   other things?
PRETTYBASIC: X-rated things.
ALONELYPAWN: OK, now I'm getting
   jealous . . .
PRETTYBASIC: GOOD.
ALONELYPAWN: I better go. Tara's texting.
PRETTYBASIC: So is Harry.
ALONELYPAWN: GOODBYE, BASIC.
PRETTYBASIC: BYE.
```

The next couple of days were hard. She always seemed to be with *him*. Kissing on the steps where *I* went to smoke. Not that I was spying on her or anything. But those were *my* steps. The steps I'd introduced her to that day we cut class. The steps where *I'd* kissed her. Way better than *he* was kissing her, I bet. He probably didn't even notice the way she turned her whole body round instead of turning her neck. That her neck was sore just like everything else, so when he was pulling her head towards his big gob, he was probably hurting her, and she was too polite to say. He probably didn't notice that she rubbed the insides of her elbows where the crutches had dug in, or that one of her elbows didn't straighten all the way out. I bet the only thing he noticed was how fucking hot she was, and how nice she was, because she was nice to everyone.

I'd slept even less than usual too, staying up to practise. Game after game after game. I'd let myself think about Jules in between. Imagining we were together. Those were my favourite moments. When I could feel my whole body relax and she filled my head, begging my mind to dream of her and what could have been.

71

Juliet

After the horribly awkward moment when Mum came into my room with her tray of snacks, I totally blew up at her.

I told her that she couldn't treat me like a baby, I was eighteen (I might have sworn, I can't remember) and I needed some fucking privacy (yeah, I definitely swore at that bit).

Immediately after, I felt horrible because Harry saw it all and she just stood there with her sad tray of juice and crisps and looked like she was going to cry.

Then Harry left.

And I felt even worse. I had to make it up to him. Prove I wasn't a complete dick. So I acted like I was really into him at school and hoped, maybe, that I'd pretend so much that I'd start to believe it myself.

Michael was waiting for me after break.

I felt bad. We used to spend break together, people-watching, taking the piss, sharing Maltesers, but now I spent it with Harry's tongue down my throat while Michael FaceTimed Francis. It wasn't unpleasant. It just wasn't Ronan.

'Hey, J, how was today's tongue-fest?' Michael had saved me a Malteser that he put in my mouth to save me rearranging my crutches. By this point Harry had run to class again.

'Not bad.'

'Ouch,' Michael said and sucked air through his teeth.

'What?' I asked. 'I'd be lying if I said it was amazing and I'd also be lying if I said it was as bad as kissing Caleb. So, somewhere in between. Nothing wrong with that.' I shrugged.

'Nothing right with that either,' Michael said. 'Do you think you'll ever graduate past kissing with Harry?'

The face I gave Michael made it obvious the answer was no.

'Not any time soon. I'm just not ready. Are you ready? With Francis?'

'I think so. But I'm not sure. I'm going to hold off until I know for sure. He's definitely more experienced than me; he had a boyfriend for six months last year. Kris, with a K. About five foot ten, black hair, wears way too much Nike and clearly lives at the gym. I hate him.' Michael scrunched up his face.

'He told you all that about his ex?' That was mature. I'd *hate* to know about Ronan's ex. Or Harry's . . .

'No, I stalked his Insta.'

I nodded with approval.

'But yeah, not ready for *that*. But down for other stuff and who knows, maybe I'll be so ready that I'll want to come out to Cassandra and David, just so I can do those things in the comfort of my own home,' Michael said, then saw me looking at him. 'Maybe,' he added.

'You know that's the first time you've actually brought it up like it's an actual possibility . . .' I said.

'Yeah, it's strange, the time just feels right. You know?'

'I'm so happy for you, Michael.' I nudged him. And I was.

'I mean, not today or anything, but soon. Maybe.'

'You just had to add a caveat, didn't you?'

'Always.'

Instead of going back to my house like we usually did, we went to Michael's so he could choose a Maggie's-appropriate date outfit.

Michael's house had a huge stone wall around the whole property and coded gates, complete with CCTV cameras. I guess when your mum's a high court judge you need extra security. Cassandra Crawley was fabulous. She was so glamorous, with this long red hair, and always wore high heels. His dad was a barrister, tall and dark, and where Michael got his looks.

But they weren't there. They were hardly ever at home. Only Mary was there, Michael's parents' cleaner and cook – she was practically part of the family. She was icing a lemon drizzle cake when we came in.

'Hello, Jules. Lovely to see you,' she said and smiled. I hadn't been here in ages because Michael always came to my house.

'Hi, Mary.' I waved and breathed in the smell of the cake that had filled the whole (massive) kitchen.

'Give us a shout when it's ready, Mary, please. It smells incredible!'

'OK, Mikey,' she said.

Michael turned to me. 'Come on, let's go to my room.'

We eventually made it to Michael's bedroom, which was so big it had its own little living room attached.

'I brought you here with ulterior motives. I have a present for you. Well, presents actually.'

'There are multiple gifts?'

'Two. Over there.' He pointed to his bed.

I walked over and on his bed was a long black box with a red bow wrapped round it.

'Michael.'

'Just open it.'

I pulled off the ribbon and opened the box.

A lump grew in my throat.

Crutches. But not regular grey plastic, like the ones they gave me at the hospital. They were black and glittery and *padded.*

I pulled one out and tried it on.

'Michael, these are amazing. Thank you so much.'

'It's more for me. I don't like being seen with you when you have those horrible grey things. *So* embarrassing,' he joked.

I hugged him and wondered what I ever did to deserve such a great friend.

'You'll use them tonight, won't you? Ah, I'm so excited.'

'Yes, of course I will. And I'm excited too.'

At least that's what I told myself.

72

Ronan

The word 'Checkmate' comes from the Persian 'Shah Mat', meaning 'the king is dead'.

I think about it a lot, what this means, and how in life we're all just pieces on a chessboard, trying to win whatever game we think we're playing.

I knew I was the pawn. I've known it for a long time. Aspires to be better, willing to sacrifice. Weak. Knows the king sees me as easily replaced.

The knight, in your face, confrontational, sense of superiority. A piece that knows it has limited mobility and sometimes gallops out without thinking. Tara all over.

The rook. Dumb. Shouts 'I will rule the endgame' just before he's caught by a pawn or a knight. Luke, and probably Harry too.

Bishops. Cunning pieces that become more powerful when they work together. Hana and Charlie.

The queen. Most powerful piece on the board. Intelligent. Tries to socialize with the rooks but often gets no response. Protective. Beautiful.

Jules.

I watched the door as she came into Maggie's. Her crutches were different. Black, glitter. She was wearing trousers that looked like leather, white trainers, and this red flannel shirt. I looked away when I saw *him*, with his hand round her shoulder like he owned her.

Tara slid closer to me, blocking my view of the door. Hana and Charlie sat opposite us, and Luke was beside them like a spare part. Not like he cared. He hadn't shut up since we'd got there, mostly trying to make Tara laugh with unfunny jokes.

'Oh my God, what are *they* doing here?' Tara had noticed them come in, and stared at them until they sat down. They sat in a booth parallel to ours so if I looked past Tara, I was able to see her. She sat on the outside, her crutches balanced against the table. Michael was with someone I didn't recognize. I assumed it was his date. Confirmed when they started kissing at the table.

As if it had made him remember about his own date, I watched Harry push some hair behind Jules's ear. Such a cliché. As if she was going to fall for that one. *Oh, you pushed my hair behind my ear, now I have to turn round and kiss you.* She wasn't that stupid, and I could tell she didn't like him that much anyway.

Then she was kissing him.

Ugh.

'Ronan, what do you think?' An elbow in my side and Tara's voice in my ear.

'What?' I turned to her, dragging my eyes away from Jules's face being attacked by Harry's mouth.

'Want to play "Never have I ever"?' She put her hand on my leg, tracing her fingers up and down. I tried to ignore it.

'Aren't you supposed to drink when playing that?'

I was hoping that would put an end to it.

'Yeah. And look.' Tara nodded towards Luke, who'd pulled a blue hipflask from his pocket, and started pouring whatever was in it into each milkshake.

'Vodka,' Tara confirmed. 'Trust Luke,' she said and laughed. He returned her laugh with a smile.

I didn't complain. Actually, I hoped the vodka would take the edge off and make me forget about Jules and Harry on their stupid date. So I mixed the vodka into my strawberry milkshake with my straw and kept my eyes on my own table.

'OK, I'm going first.' Tara was in her element. She was grinning and I almost expected her to stand up, like she was chairing some meeting.

'Never have I ever ...' She looked around the table then found my eyes, before winking at me, 'had a dirty dream about someone in this room.'

Tara had barely finished speaking before taking a drink. I watched Luke take a drink too, his eyes on Tara. Hana and Charlie next, their hands twisted in each other's on the table.

'Ronan? What about you?' Tara brought her lips to my ear. 'I can tell you all about it later if you like?'

And I took a drink. Because it wasn't a lie. It just wasn't about her.

'So naughty.' Tara giggled. I caught Jules's eye and she looked away.

'Me next,' said Luke, putting more vodka into his milkshake.

'Never have I ever given a blow job.' He was looking straight at Tara when he said it, eyebrows raised and that stupid smirk again.

She took a drink and narrowed her eyes at him.

Charlie took a drink too. Then Hana.

'Charlie?' Luke looked at him in shock. Hana was unfazed.

'What? It was way before Han.' He squeezed her hand.

'You any good at it?' Luke laughed.

'You'll never know.'

'OK, Han, your turn.'

While Hana was thinking, I tried to catch another glimpse of Jules. She was holding Harry's hand on the table. And there was her milkshake. That ridiculously sweet chocolate thing. I wished she was at our table, playing our game. In fact, I wished we were alone. Somewhere. Anywhere.

'OK, never have I ever role-played during sex.' I watched her and Charlie both take a drink.

'What the hell, you guys?' Tara laughed and looked at them like she was expecting elaboration. She didn't get it.

I caught another glimpse of Jules and now she was kissing Harry at the table, and it made me so jealous I felt sick.

'My turn?'

'Yeah.' Hana nodded.

It was hard. There wasn't much I wanted to know about any of these people. I didn't care who they'd slept with or who they wanted to. Jules and Harry were still kissing; he had one hand in her hair and her hands were on his face. On his jaw, like they'd been on mine. Right here, in Maggie's.

'Never have I ever wanted to be somewhere else.' I downed the last of my vodka milkshake and stood up. Tara stood up too.

'Where are you going?'

'I need to clear my head.'

I took one last look at Jules kissing him, oblivious to everyone else around her. Because I guess that's what happens when you're kissing someone that you really like. When I kissed Jules, the whole world disappeared.

I walked past Tara and out of the door.

73

Juliet

Michael had picked us up, though this time I made sure to sit in the back so Francis could sit in the front. I knew it was a mistake as soon as Harry got in, sliding across into the middle seat to be closer to me. I had no room for my legs as it was, and it wasn't like I could ask him to move over. So instead of being able to stretch them out, they were crunched up into the corner, aching. At least the drive wasn't far.

Francis got into the car with a kiss for Michael.

'Everybody, this is Francis,' Michael said. He sounded so excited.

'Hey, Francis,' I said from the back. 'I think we met at Daniel's party, but I was a bit drunk. I'm Jules.'

'Oh, I know. I've heard loads about you. In fact, Michael barely shuts up about you. I was starting to think he was straight at one point.' Francis leaned over the gear stick and kissed Michael's cheek.

'Don't worry, babe, straight-up gay,' Michael said. 'Oh, and that's Harry. Jules's . . .' he hesitated.

'Friend,' I said. So glad it was too dark to see the look on Harry's face.

He took my hand. And it would have been rude to take it away. So I didn't.

When Michael opened the door to Maggie's, the heat and the smell of waffles blasted into our faces.

It was busy.

I looked around for a table and my breath caught in my throat when I saw them: Ronan and Tara, at a table with Hana, Charlie and Luke.

What the hell was *he* doing here? And with *her*!

She was sitting too close to him – any closer and she'd be sitting on top of him. I wished it was me. I felt Harry's arm on my shoulder, weighing me down. It's the kind of thing nobody else would think about. Obviously. Why would they? But when he put his arm on my shoulder, that was a whole load of extra weight for my knees to carry. And it hurt.

I let Harry slide into the inside seat so I could lean my crutches against the table. Also so I could see Ronan better.

Michael followed my eyeline.

'Is that?'

'Yep.'

'See that guy over there, the one with the glasses?' Michael whispered to Francis. I didn't know why he was whispering. The music was way too loud for them to be able to hear. 'He and Jules had a thing a while ago. Ended pretty badly. We don't like them.'

'Noted,' said Francis, pretending to write in a notebook.

Two seconds later Michael and Francis were kissing. Like full-on kissing with tongues at the table. I sipped some milkshake.

Harry tucked some hair behind my ear as if to remind me he was still there. When I turned to him, he kissed me. A surprise kiss. Like he didn't know what else to do.

It caught me off guard and messed up my coordination. It was *not* a good kiss. Teeth clashed and there was extra saliva from somewhere. I'd no idea whether it was his or mine.

I was so glad when it was over.

'I have a match tomorrow, if you were bored and maybe wanted to come watch? It's at home, so up at Westing, not too far away,' Harry said. His cheeks were flushed, and he sipped his milkshake.

I'd never thought I'd be the girl-on-the-sidelines kind of girlfriend. Girlfriend? Is that what I was? There hadn't been a proper conversation about it. And if there was, I really didn't know what I'd say. But I didn't hate the idea of going to watch Harry play football. I'd heard about how good he was.

'Will there be a burger van?' I asked.

'At the match?' Harry wasn't sure whether to laugh or not.

'Yeah, I used to go with my dad to football matches sometimes, and my favourite part was the smell of fried onions from the burger van.'

'If I say yes then you'll come?'

'Yes.'

'Amazing!' Harry coughed then, like he was trying to hide his excitement.

'So, Francis plays chess too, J,' Michael said from across the table.

Michael and Francis had stopped kissing and were now sharing a milkshake.

'Oh yeah?' I looked up at Francis and smiled. He was like the opposite of Michael. Small, fine-featured, blonde.

'Yeah. My dad was really into it. He used to take me to this weird chess club in town.'

'Poor baby,' Michael said and kissed his cheek.

'Yeah. I hated it at the start but then got pretty into it. We should play sometime, Michael.'

'Gross.'

'I've tried that one, Francis,' I said. 'But *you* might have better luck.' I laughed.

Then they were kissing again.

'I'd really like to learn,' Harry said. And it took me a second to realize what he was talking about.

'Oh, chess? Really?'

'Yeah, will you teach me?'

'Sure,' I said. I turned, pretending to fix my crutches so I could look across the room at Ronan. Tara was leaning on him now, like she was marking her territory.

I turned back to Harry.

'Maybe we should try that kiss again?' I asked.

'I'd like that.'

I leaned in and kissed him harder this time, acting like I really meant it, hoping Ronan was watching me.

'Wow, that was amazing,' Harry said after, pushing his hand through his hair. 'I can't wait to see you at the match tomorrow. I've never had a girl come watch before. I'll try not to mess up.'

Michael and Francis finally stopped kissing again. And Francis turned to me. 'Did you know the Silver Pawn

Tournament is coming up? I was thinking of going to watch,' he said, looking genuinely excited.

'Yeah, I did hear that actually.'

The tournament. The one I was, or wasn't, going to watch Ronan play in. I looked over at his table. Was Tara sucking his earlobe? Either that or whispering something to him. I couldn't see properly. One of her hands was in his hair and the other one was out of sight.

'Jules, Francis just asked you something.' Michael waved his hand across my face, and it brought me back to our table.

'Sorry. What?'

'I was just wondering if you have a Chess Life account?'

'Yeah, I do.' And my eyes found them again. He looked perfectly at home with her hands all over him. Enjoying it even.

I thought about the bullshit he'd told me about not being with Tara. About how he wanted me to come and watch him in this stupid tournament. As if I was going to go now. He'd probably have Tara there too, a couple of little cheerleaders, cheering him on. Waiting until the end so he could have his pick.

'Jules!' When I looked back at Michael he seemed really pissed off. 'Francis is trying to talk to you!'

'Sorry. Yeah, I have a Chess Life account. My username is Pretty Basic.'

And I ignored Michael's look and turned to Harry. I took his face in my hands and kissed him hard again. I pretended it was Ronan, closing my eyes and trying to imagine a strawberry milkshake tongue instead of the tropical vegan flavour that was filling my mouth.

I kissed Harry even harder, then he pulled away.

'Sorry, Jules, that just hurt a bit,' he said, his face pained.

'Oh, God. Sorry.'

And as the ding of the doorbell chimed, I turned to see Ronan disappearing out of the door, with Tara right behind him.

74

Ronan

'Oh my God, Ronan. Wait!' Tara's voice, and feet on the pavement, running to catch up with me.

I couldn't say anything. I was too pissed off. Pissed off at watching Jules and Harry with their PDA, pissed off at being such a fucking pussy that I couldn't just tell Tara what I wanted. Fed up of hiding everything, and pretending that my life was normal.

'Wait!' Tara shouted.

She grabbed my hand and pulled me to a stop.

'Ronan, what's wrong?'

'Everything is wrong!' I yelled, without thinking. A couple walking past us stared at me. I was about to let it all out, tell her exactly what was wrong, but I buried it. Shook my head and walked on, leaving her on the pavement looking confused.

I'd walked a few metres before I looked back. Thing was, when I did shit like that, it didn't take me long to realize I was being a complete dick and wanted to say sorry. But when I looked back, she wasn't standing there looking upset. About me anyway. She was on the phone. With her hand over her mouth.

I went back and stood next to her, the slope of her shoulders and the way she'd folded in on herself, telling me before she even said anything that something was very wrong. I leaned against the wall and tried to force the memory out of my head.

The phone call woke me up. 3.25 a.m. Intruding into my nightmare and masquerading as a police siren. Sweat pricked my forehead and my heartbeat was in my ears when my eyes burst open in the darkness. Though it wasn't completely dark, the hall light was on and a sliver of yellow light crept into my room. My door opened wider when the movement of Mum's desperate footsteps swept past, letting me hear the panicked breaths that matched mine.

'Hello? Yes, this is Mrs Cole.

'St Mary's Hospital? Yes, Ciaran is my son. What's wrong? What's happened? Is he OK?

'Heroin? No. My son doesn't take drugs. My son is at Cambridge. 'A birthmark? Yes, one on his left wrist, a heart shape.

'It must be a mistake. It must be someone else. Other people have birthmarks. It's not Ciaran. I'm telling you; it isn't my son.

'Identify the body?'

And that was all I heard before the bile stirred in my throat and I threw up in my bedroom bin.

But she didn't. Identify the body. Aunt Sarah had to do it. And I went too, even though she begged me not to. And it was him. Of course it was him. Mum knew as well as I did that he'd got himself into some deep shit and couldn't find the way out. Not even when I pleaded with him to stop. Not even when I hid every single thing he could possibly sell. Not even when I cried in front of him. I should have tried harder. I should've been better. Because what kind of brother stands by and watches someone like Ciaran disappear into the fucking abyss?

And I guess Mum was dealing with it as badly as I was. Worse even. She didn't even go to the funeral. Because if she didn't see it, it didn't happen.

'OK, thank you.' Tara's voice was small. She hung up the phone. Then she looked at me and burst into tears.

'What is it? What's wrong?' I forced my memories away and focused on this. I moved closer to her, to show her I was there. Because I wish I'd had someone to lean on when my life turned to shit.

'It's Mum. She's had a fall. She's at the hospital and social services are at the house.'

'Is she OK?'

Tara could barely speak through the tears. I followed her lead as she walked in the direction of her house, trying to stop the tears with her sleeves.

'She was drunk and hit her head on the kitchen table. Annie was there. I need to get home. They can't take her away.'

'But they might help.' I could hear the hypocritical words coming out of my mouth. Refusing to get any help myself.

'They won't. They'll take Annie away from us.'

'What about you?'

'I don't know. I don't care, I just, I just want things to go back to the way they were. I was dealing with it. I *was*.' Tara could barely get words out through her tears.

Everything Tara said hit home. Was *I* dealing with it? The way I'd act like everything was normal, how I'd let Mum do what she was doing, how I enabled it. This was what happened when people tried to deal with things too big for them.

'Maybe I can help.'

We slowed our walk as I told her about this charity Aunt Sarah knew about. She'd sent me the details, hoping I'd contact them after I made her promise not to do it on my behalf. 'Family First', helping young carers.

'No. No, they'll want to split us up. They'll take Annie away.'

'I don't know if it works like that. They want to help keep families together, and support you and stuff.' The truth was, I didn't know that much. All I knew was that Aunt Sarah had mentioned them again and again and again. She said it didn't matter when I told her that Mum wasn't sick, that she would go back to normal soon. That she didn't have any kind of diagnosis. And I'd been tempted to phone them, when Mum was outside his room pretending to talk to him, or when she rushed outside the house at the sound of an aeroplane, excited that he was coming home. Those moments, they were almost too much. Almost.

'How do you know so much about this?' Tara asked, looking at me. And I just couldn't.

'My aunt. She's involved in it,' I said.

'I don't know, Ronan.'

'Look, Tara, I know things are really shit. But you need help. The hospital have already called social services. But at least this way you know a bit about the people who want to help. So it's not all one-sided.'

She stopped and nodded before burying herself in my chest. I hugged her back.

'Do you want me to phone my aunt?' I asked.

She nodded into me.

I rang Aunt Sarah and told her the situation. At the end of the call she said she was on her way.

When we got back to Tara's, there was a car outside. Tara ran inside, calling Annie's name, and I followed slowly.

Inside the house there was a woman in the living room with Annie. They were watching some Disney movie and there was a bag of Annie's things beside them.

I left Tara alone. It wasn't my business. So I sat on her garden wall and waited for Aunt Sarah.

Tara came out a few minutes later and put her hand on my back.

'Ronan, thank you so much for tonight. She actually seems really nice, this woman.'

'What's happening?' I asked.

'She's phoned Dad, and we're going to stay with him until Mum's better. Together. The hospital said that Mum will be fine, that the cut is superficial.'

'Are you OK?'

She breathed in and looked back at Annie who was loitering at the door. 'I have to be.'

'You should talk about it, you know. Tell Jules even.'

'I can't. I've been such a dick to her, why would she ever listen to anything I said?' She looked down at the ground, twisting her foot on a weed.

'I have a feeling she'd understand.' I said it gently and she looked up at me, her brown eyes sad.

'Mum was right what she said last time you were here.

You're not like other guys.' She gave a tiny shrug and stretched up to kiss my cheek. 'Thanks, Ronan.'

'Tara!' Annie called from the doorway.

'Coming,' she replied, not taking her eyes off mine. 'Give me a second.'

'Fine!' Annie slammed the door and I laughed.

'I'd better go, I guess,' Tara said but didn't move towards the house.

'Oh yeah, sure. I'll just wait outside for my aunt to get here.'

She nodded. 'Can I ask you something?' I noticed her playing with the weeds again with her foot.

'Of course. What is it?'

She took a deep breath before she said, 'Are you in love with her? Jules, I mean?'

There was no hesitation. 'Yes.'

She gave me another sad smile and walked towards the house, closing the door behind her. As I waited on the little brick wall for Aunt Sarah to pick me up, I thought about the wall I'd sat on outside Daniel's party, with Jules, the feeling of fucking ecstasy when I found out she was BASIC. How all my thoughts began with Jules, ended with Jules and how I'd made a huge mistake.

75

Juliet

After I watched them walk out of the door, I turned back to Michael, who was staring at me.

'They're gone, so can we actually have *our* date now?' Michael said.

'What's that supposed to mean?' I asked, confused.

Francis looked at Michael as if he was scared of what he might say.

'All you've done the whole night is stare at Ronan and Tara. None of us could talk to you.'

'Michael.'

'And what about *your* actual date?' Michael pointed at Harry, who was staring at me too.

'Harry, I . . .'

'It's OK. I had a really nice time,' Harry mumbled.

'Bullshit,' Michael said.

'Michael –' Francis cut in, looking increasingly worried.

'No, you didn't. Don't lie. None of us had a nice time. Francis was trying to talk to you about chess, Harry was trying to get your attention but all you could do was stare at Ronan and Tara, as if it was going to make him magically appear at your side.' I'd never seen Michael so pissed off at me.

My face was bright red, and I could feel pressure behind my eyes. Was it that obvious?

'Harry, I'm sorry.'

'I didn't realize you were still into him,' Harry said quietly. Guilt pooled in my stomach.

'I'm not . . .' I stopped there. I couldn't lie any more. 'I'm sorry.'

'So, I'm guessing I won't see you at the match tomorrow then?' Harry looked right at me and I could feel my eyes ready to overflow.

'I still want to come,' I said pathetically.

'I don't think it's a good idea,' Harry said. Then he stood up. 'Would you mind moving so I can get out please?'

I picked up my crutches and moved out of the way. Harry didn't even look at me when he walked past.

'Let's get out of here,' Michael said after Harry had left. He stormed towards the door, then held it open for me and Francis. Because even pissed-off Michael can't be rude.

We drove home in silence, dropping off Francis first. Then we pulled up outside my house.

'It's like you haven't even noticed that anybody else exists this last while, J. Like you've taken some kind of Tara pill, obsessed with a guy who just isn't interested, only care about yourself and you're not listening to a word anybody else has to say about their lives.'

I couldn't stop the tears this time. They pooled in my eyes. Not because what he said was unfair. Because it was true.

'Did you ever think that this date was a big deal for me? I was so excited about introducing Francis to my *best friend* and my best friend couldn't have been less interested.'

He was right. About everything. I thought all I could think about was Ronan, when really, all I could think about was myself.

I pressed my shirt sleeve into my face.

'I'm sorry.' My voice was quiet, through the tears. I wondered how many times you could say sorry before it lost all meaning.

Michael got out of the car and opened my door for me so I could get out.

'Michael . . .' I started.

'No.' Michael put his hand up and turned his face away from me. 'I'm angry right now and I need to deal with this anger in a healthy way. I shall be in contact when it has subsided. *If* it subsides.'

'OK,' I said. Because there was nothing else to say.

I tried to crutch my way to the door in a way that made it look easy instead of the awkward, painful mess it was.

I opened the door and Mum was on the other side, as if she'd been looking out. 'Jules, what's wrong?'

And I burst into tears. Properly this time.

Mum hugged me and we went into the living room where I sat on the sofa, and she just stared at me until the heaving sobs calmed down.

'What happened?'

'Nothing,' I mumbled.

'Jules. You can tell me anything; maybe I can help.'

'You can't help this, OK?' It sounded harsher than I'd wanted.

Now Dad had appeared as well. 'Hey, kid. What's up?' he said, before he realized. 'Oh. What happened?' He whispered something to Mum. She shrugged.

'Shall I make some hot chocolate?' She put her hand on my leg.

And it just happened. The anger. I don't know if it got mixed up with everything else, but I didn't mean it. Well, I didn't mean it the way it came out anyway.

'I don't need hot chocolate. I'm not a fucking baby,' I said through gritted teeth.

'Jules,' Dad stepped in, sounding surprised.

'You treat me like I'm eight years old. I'm eighteen. I'm an *adult* and sometimes shit things happen and you just have to deal with them yourself, and that's the way it is.'

'We're just trying to help.' Mum sounded sad.

'You've helped enough. I've already ruined your life. Please, God – stop helping me and live your own lives.'

'Jules, what are you talking about?'

Mum and Dad looked genuinely confused.

'Art college, Mum. You were supposed to go to art college but instead you stayed at home to look after your stupid crippled daughter and you had no time left.'

'Jules, no.' Mum was shaking her head as if to make her point. 'No, that wasn't it at all.'

Dad sat down in the chair opposite us as Mum explained.

'Dad and I decided that we'd put it off. It wasn't anything to do with time. I could have made it work if I'd wanted to.

I wanted to be here, for you.' She was hunched down beside my chair now, her hand on my leg. 'Art college would have meant me being away too much. And I didn't want that, not when you were in so much pain.'

'I would have been fine. You didn't have to do that. You didn't have to give up your life because of me.'

'Jules, look at me.'

I looked up and she cupped her hands round my soaking, hot face. '*You* are my life. I didn't give up anything. You really don't have any idea what I see, do you?'

I looked at a blurred version of Mum's face.

'I see a kid who has had so much more to deal with than the average kid. I remember being a teenager and it's bloody hard, never mind having to deal with arthritis as well. I'm so proud to see you get up every goddamn morning and go into that school, despite the crutches, despite the pain. And I know you say you're fine, Jules, and you are, of course you are, you're dealing with it. But I just wish I could do something to help you. But I can't, Jules. I can't do anything except take you to appointments and be there when you get home from school.'

A tear slid down Mum's cheek and she swiped it away.

'Art college would have taken that away. Me being here, Jules, it's not much, but it's all I can do. Does that make any sense?'

My face crumpled again, and I hugged her, the smell of her trademark Chanel Nº5 calming me.

And it did make sense, I suppose. It maybe even made sense why they treated me like I was a still a child.

'I didn't mean to swear at you.'

'It's OK. You must have learned that word from your father,' Mum said, forcing out a laugh. 'We'll try and remember that you're not a little girl any more.'

'Quick, Melanie, cancel the clown we ordered for next year's birthday,' Dad said in a stage whisper.

I narrowed my eyes at him and then laughed.

'You can tell us what happened tonight, you know. We're not *that* old that we don't remember teenage stuff.' Dad was trying to get it out of me.

But this was something I had to deal with myself. All of it.

'No, it'll be OK. But thanks.'

And I'd felt better for a minute, after getting that out. But as soon as I'd made it to my room, it all hit home again. That my life was a complete and utter mess.

76

Ronan

Aunt Sarah looked just like Mum except with dark hair instead of dyed blonde and she had more flesh than bones. She rolled down the window and pulled over to the kerb.

'Hey, stranger,' she said. 'Get in.'

Part of me wanted to walk away, just say that actually, I didn't need any help. I was fine. Mum and I were *fine*. But another part wanted to get into her car and tell her everything. How hard it was to keep pretending everything was OK. How the image of his body twisted over and over in my mind until I felt sick all over again. How I couldn't sleep, and instead I'd lie awake, leaning against the wall and waiting for the three knocks then two knocks that he used to do when we were kids. And sometimes, I still thought I heard them.

'Hey,' I finally said, getting into the car.

'Ronan. It's been so long since I've seen you. You've lost weight.'

'Nah, I'm grand.' I waved off her concern but didn't move my hand when she squeezed it in hers. She hadn't turned the engine off and we just sat there for a moment, in the warmth of the car, words too hard to say.

'So, tell me about your friend. What happened?'

'Her mum's ill. Mentally, I think; makes her do some crazy shit and Tara, that's my friend, looks after her. She has a little sister, too, so I guess things are pretty tough at home.'

Aunt Sarah nodded and looked at me. I knew she was waiting for me to talk about Mum. Use this opportune moment to spill my guts all over her BMW.

'Did you pass on the details? For Family First?'

'Yeah, I did, thanks.'

'And Ronan, you know they'd help you too.'

'I'm fine.'

'I know you think you're fine. But the way she is, the way you're living, it's not OK. And I'm here to help. You can still come and live with me, and I'll get your mum some proper help. You need to be allowed to grieve.'

I moved my hand away from hers and shoved it into my pocket, squeezing the pawn until it hurt my palm, the little ridges digging into my skin.

'I don't want to.'

'You don't want help? Or you don't want to grieve?'

'I just want to get through this year, so I can leave this place. And forget. And maybe if I did that, then I could forget I even had a brother, and it wouldn't fucking hurt so much.'

I hadn't cried since that day. The day Aunt Sarah and I went to the morgue. The day they pulled out his body with a number on the shelf. A number. No name. He'd been reduced to a number. But that wasn't what made me cry.

What made me cry was the fact he didn't look like Ciaran. Dark circles, grey skin, rainbow bruises up his arms. How could someone go from being so fucking great to this? This shadow of the person he'd been. It didn't matter how fucking smart he was then, how many prizes he won or how good he was at chess, or how easily he got girls. All that mattered was that he wasn't there any more. And it was because of Alex and Sasha. *They'd* given him drugs. *They* started all of it and just acted like they'd done nothing at all. And then they didn't even bother coming to the funeral. It was Mum's fault too, piling on all that pressure. The way she kept going on and on and on at him about Cambridge, about chess, about whatever the next thing was.

And I just stood on the sidelines and watched it happen.

'I should have done something.' I didn't mean it to come out, and it barely did, through tears that had clogged my throat, but the look on Aunt Sarah's face, I won't forget it. It was pain. And sadness, and she couldn't do anything except hug me.

'Ronan, this is not your fault. None of this is your fault.'

'I could have told the police; I could have stopped him. I could have done *something*. Alex gave him weed and Mum . . .'

'Ronan, look at me.' Aunt Sarah put her hands on my shoulders and wiped tears from her own eyes. 'Ciaran made some terrible choices. We *all* make bad choices but this one, it cost him his life in the end. There was *nothing* you could do. This is not your fault.' I looked away, taking off my glasses to wipe my eyes. I could hear her words, but they weren't going in. I couldn't let them be true.

'Do you still have the video?' she asked gently.

I nodded and thought of the video that I'd never watched. The one that the videographer took like it was a fucking wedding. But I knew Mum would need it. That she couldn't bring herself to go, but one day, she'd need to see it.

'Do you want to send it to me, and I'll show her?'

I shook my head.

It was something I needed to do myself. Or at least be there when it was happening.

Aunt Sarah wanted to come into the house. To see Mum and talk it all through. But I convinced her that we should wait. At least until the tournament was over. I didn't know how she was going to react, and right now I needed every bit of headspace I could get.

I made a promise I would phone her. As soon as the tournament was over, then we'd do it. Together.

77

Juliet

The message from Harry came about an hour later.

> **HARRY:** Hey, Jules, I was just thinking we should leave dating for now. It's pretty obvious you're into someone else. Happy to stay friends or whatever. See you at school.

And that made me cry all over again.

There weren't even any texts from Michael, commentating on the date. Because why would there be? What kind of friend was I? A pretty shit one.

What Michael had said played over and over in my head like a heartbreaking song on repeat. I'd only been thinking about myself. Selfish. And I couldn't just use my disease as an excuse. Yeah, it took up a lot of headspace, and I was used to the pain reminding me about it constantly, but that didn't mean that other people didn't have important stuff going on too. Or just stuff I should ask about.

Right then I swore I would be a better friend. If Michael ever decided to talk to me again.

I looked up my 'English Revision' and stared at the beautiful people. I don't even know why I was doing it. To kick myself when I was down? All their beautiful kneecaps laughing at my stupid swollen ones.

No Chess Life messages either. Not that I expected any, but still.

The next morning it was like karma had actually caught up with me and took the form of pain. A lot of pain. It was either that, or my period was on its way. The pain always got worse on the run-up to that for some reason. And even though it showed up once a month, I never kept track of when it was, so it was always a surprise after a week of barely being able to walk.

My head was spinning, and I could barely open my eyes. I reached for the glass of water and painkillers beside my bed, wincing as I pulled myself up to take them.

Despite the total brain blur, yesterday's memories hit me like a slap in the face. Harry had dumped me, Michael had dumped me, Ronan was with Tara. And the worst thing? Two out of three of those things were my fault.

But I couldn't just sit here and feel sorry for myself. Not any more.

I picked up my phone.

> **ME**: Hey. Everything you said yesterday was right. I've been a selfish bitch and have been way too focused on Ronan/ Tara/ me. I'm so sorry. I'm going to be a better friend, I promise. If you'll have me back? 🌀

MICHAEL: Still pretty pissed tbh . . .

ME: How can I fix it?

MICHAEL: You can promise that the next time I introduce you to my boyfriend you'll actually make an effort and pretend like you're interested?

ME: I AM interested

MICHAEL: Could have fooled me

ME: I know. ☹ Can we try again? Another date?

MICHAEL: Not sure Harry would fancy it . . .

ME: No, definitely not. I meant just me

MICHAEL: Maybe . . .

ME: I promise to do better with Francis. And you. I know I've been a shit friend. Let me make it up to you 🙏

MICHAEL: . . . I came out to my parents last night

ME: What??? Can you FaceTime?

Michael's face appeared on my phone. He gave me a smile.

'Yeah, I finally did it. I wanted to be able to invite Francis to my house at some point and I was so pissed off with you, I think my nerves disappeared a bit.'

'Oh my God, Michael, this is huge! How did it go?'

'Yeah, I mean my mum was super happy, well, not as happy as she was when I told her I wanted to do Law next year, but happy I told her. She even cried!'

'Judge Crawley can cry?' I was shocked.

'Apparently so.'

'And your dad?'

'Well, turns out he's not as emotionless as a sandwich. He hugged me and even *he* looked like he was going to cry. So yeah, total relief as well as the discovery that I have emotionally unstable parents. Jules, are *you* crying?'

'No.' I wiped away tears with the sleeve of my hoody. 'Maybe. I'm just so happy for you. Can we please be friends again?'

'You're on probation.' Michael smiled properly this time and then he hung up.

78

Ronan

When I woke up the next morning it was as if my head was clear for the first time in forever. I knew what I wanted to do. I needed Jules to know everything.

The tournament was tomorrow, and I wanted her to be there, but at the same time I wanted it to be her choice.

I was sick of doing everything wrong. Thinking I was helping Ciaran by ignoring what was happening, the same with Mum. Giving Tara the details of that charity made me see how much someone else could help, just by knowing. It was like I could see the weight fall off her shoulders.

The message that Mum sent, the one that made me break up with Jules – she needed to know about it. Needed to know that it was something bigger than me that made me want to let go of the best thing in my life.

I opened Chess Life.

ALONELYPAWN: Hi, Jules. I have something
    I want to tell you. And I get it if you
    don't want to listen, I wouldn't blame
    you. But I'm just going to go for it,

leave it here and hopefully you'll
understand why I couldn't tell you
before.

I have a secret. The kind of secret that
eats away at you from the inside,
spreading its darkness like cancer. I
wanted to tell you. Every day we spoke
online I hoped the words would just
come out. But they didn't. They
couldn't. I was terrified you'd think I
was some terrible person, and maybe you
will, but I want you to know that THIS
is the reason I ended things. It had
nothing to do with you, or Tara, and
I'm sorry if I made you feel like it
was. The last thing in the world I'd
ever want to do is hurt you.

For the last few months I've been living
in a shadow.

The brother I told you about? He died.
And as if his death wasn't bad enough,
it was my fault.

It started with weed. Stupid shit like
that. But then things got worse. Harder,
darker drugs. Coke, speed and finally
heroin.

I've been blaming other people. My old
friends, Alex and Sasha, for giving him
weed and smoking it with him, my mum

for piling on loads of pressure about
university and chess. But most of all,
I blame myself.

I should have done more to stop him. I
saw the signs but I buried them and
made excuses for him.

I miss him more than words can say. My
mum misses him so much that she pretends
that he's still alive, tidying his
room, doing his washing, waiting for
him to walk through the door. She didn't
even go to his funeral.

That message I got when I was at your
house? The one that made me leave? It
was from my mum, telling me that Ciaran
was coming home for dinner. How fucked
up is that? We sat there all night,
waiting for him. And I'm such a coward
that I couldn't say anything then
either. Couldn't tell her that he wasn't
coming because he died seven months
ago, because I couldn't bear to see the
look on her face.

I can't do this alone. Not any more.
That's why I'm telling you. It's my
'excuse' for being a terrible nearly-
boyfriend. I can see I should have told
you then, when you were so open with me
about your disease. I should have been

open with you too. I just didn't want
to make things worse.
Seeing you with Harry hurt more than any
physical pain I've ever had. I hated
that we couldn't be together. Seeing
you every day and not being able to
touch you was like torture.
I should have fought harder for you. I
should have told you the truth, stood up
for you and told everybody that you were
the one I wanted. Because you were.
You are.
You are the funniest, most frustrating,
most beautiful person I've ever met and
I'm begging you to give me one more
chance.
No more secrets.
I love you,
Ronan

Signing off was like someone standing on my chest and giving one final push on my heart before getting off. A release I hadn't felt in a very long time.

There was a crash downstairs.

'Mum?' I called.

Silence.

I walked downstairs quietly, looking through the open door to the living room. Nope, she wasn't in there. Then I heard another crash.

'Damn it!'

I walked into the kitchen to find a pile of clothes all over the floor, a broken cup bleeding coffee on to my ... Ciaran's hoody.

'Mum, what are you doing?'

'What does it look like I'm doing, Ronan? The washing. I don't know how your brother manages to create so much of it. He should just put his clothes away after he's worn them, not dump them in the washing basket.' She shook her head and let out a small laugh at the wet hoody in her hands. She picked up more clothes and put them in the basket.

I swept bits of china from around her feet. The big bits. But there were so many tiny slivers of porcelain drowning in coffee.

The basket was overflowing. It looked like his entire wardrobe.

'Mum,' I said. She looked at me. Her make-up was different. Still flawless, but less. I hadn't noticed how much she'd aged. She always used to joke about how people thought she was in her thirties. But now, she looked her age. She looked more than her age.

'Let me help.'

'Thanks, Ronan, but I'm OK. You know, I've had years of being a single mum to two boys. I'm past the point of needing help.'

I just watched her walk towards the washing machine, her shoes crunching the broken cup into hundreds of microscopic pieces.

I told myself things would get better, over and over in my head as I cleaned up the mess Mum had made. Aunt Sarah was going to help, Juliet knew, things had to get better, because they really couldn't get any fucking worse.

I turned on Chess Life to check if she'd replied. But she hadn't read my message.

I sent her another one.

```
ALONELYPAWN: I would love you to be
    at the tournament tomorrow. It's at
    11 a.m. in Ellis Hall. I understand if
    you don't want to come, but if you do,
    it would mean the whole world.
*YOU HAVE RESIGNED THE GAME*
```

I slept that afternoon. Better than I'd slept in months. It was as if there was some space now. Not much, but a tiny bit, where I could finally relax, and breathe.

79

Juliet

After Michael hung up, I felt a bit better. I don't know what I'd do without Michael, and I was embarrassed that it took a fight like that to make me realize how much I'd been taking him for granted. I was going to try and focus on other people, not just think about me and my feelings. And definitely not Ronan.

I walked over to his hoody that was still sitting on my desk and put it on the floor, out of sight, behind my bin.

There was a knock at the door.

'Jules?' It was Mum. She was almost whispering.

'Yeah?'

'Tara's here to see you. Do you want me to send her up?'

My heart thudded. And not in a good way. What was *she* doing here?

'What? She's here? Like in the house?' I was whispering too, just in case.

Mum nodded.

'Fine,' I said. Because I didn't know what else to say. It would have been childish to say I didn't want to talk to her, even if I didn't. I guess part of me was intrigued about what she had to say.

Mum went back downstairs and then I heard slow, gentle footsteps getting closer. I sat at my desk, pulled out a notebook and started doodling on it.

'Jules?'

I turned round and there was Tara, wearing jeans and a hoody, her hair scraped back from her face. No make-up. I could tell she'd been crying. I turned back to my desk and my drawing.

'What do you want?' I asked, trying to sound nonchalant. I'd had enough time to practise this exchange in my head to know what it should sound like.

'To say sorry.'

I snorted. I couldn't help it. It wasn't as easy as that, after completely destroying someone's self-confidence by chipping away at them and then exploding with something like 'Crutch Girl' in front of a crowd of people.

'Sorry for what?'

'Can you turn round, please?' she asked.

I spun myself round on the chair.

'What is it, Tara? Back to call me something else? Or is Crutch Girl all you can come up with?' I said. All the anger had come flooding back now she was here. All the hurt. From that, from the little comments, from the way she took Ronan.

She winced. Was she crying?

'Jules, I didn't mean it. I really didn't mean it.' She wiped her cheek with her sleeve.

'You said it in front of *everyone*, Tara. What kind of friend does that? What kind of *person* does that?'

She walked over to my bed and sat down, squeezing her

sleeves into her eyes. She pulled them away. Tears threatened to spill out of my eyes. No, she wasn't going to make me cry, not again.

'Jules, you have everything. You have this perfect family, you're totally hot, and everybody likes you. It wasn't fair. The Crutch Girl thing . . .' She winced when she said it. 'That was the only thing I had over you, because in every other way you're better than me.'

'Tara, you're supposed to be my friend. You don't need to have anything *over* me. Whatever that even means.'

She wiped a tear that had escaped. 'I know.'

'Then why? I really don't get it, Tara. I'm sorry, but your life, it's a million miles away from mine, in a good way, I honestly don't believe how you could want anything of mine.'

'Didn't Ronan tell you?'

She looked at me like I should know exactly what she was talking about.

'Tell me what?' We'd barely spoken in days, and even before that it was just stupid banter.

'About my mum.'

'No, what? Why would Ronan tell me anything about your mum?'

'He knew.' She said it so quietly I could barely hear it.

'Knew what?' It was like she was speaking in code.

'Jules, my mum's sick. Like *really* sick. She has this personality disorder and ends up in psychiatric hospital all the time. I look after her. And Annie.'

I couldn't believe what I was hearing. 'Jesus, Tara, why didn't you tell me?' Then, when I thought about it, it all made sense.

Why we never went to her house. Days Tara had off school. Guilt swam in my stomach. I'd never asked.

'How could I tell you? You have this perfect life with these perfect parents, it's like something from a sitcom. Seriously, Jules, you're so lucky.'

That's what she thought? I could barely get my head around it.

'I should have asked more, about your family.' I picked at a fingernail as the realization of how little I knew about Tara's home life hit me. As well as that, it made me think about how awful I'd been to my own parents.

Tara shook her head. 'I would have just lied.'

'So, what now? Can you get help?' I asked.

She nodded. 'Ronan helped. He gave me this number, for this charity. I don't know, his aunt seemed to know something about it. It helps kids with parents who are going through shit. So embarrassing, right?' She forced out a laugh.

'No. Not at all.'

She twisted her hands together. 'We're living with Dad at the minute, across town. With him and his new girlfriend. I might be moving to St Anne's.'

'You're moving school?'

'Yeah, maybe. It's just closer to Dad's and this time it looks like Mum might be in hospital for a while.'

'I'm glad she's getting help. And I'm glad you're getting help too,' I said. And meant it. I got up and walked over to the bed to sit beside her.

'Yeah, thanks.' Tara's tears had started again.

I hugged her. And that made her cry even more. I let her

lean on my shoulder even though it was painful, because as much as she'd hurt me, here she was, spilling her guts like she never had before. I hoped it made her feel better.

'I'll miss you, you know,' I said, when she'd pulled away from the hug. 'If you move schools.'

And I would miss her. Yeah, she'd hurt me, but all the good stuff over all our years as friends didn't just get erased. But at the same time, maybe a break would be good for us.

She wiped her nose with her sleeve. 'I'll miss you too, Jules. I'd better go.'

Before she left, she turned in the doorway.

'I hope you end up with Ronan. He really likes you. Not me.'

'Thanks, Tara,' I said. She looked so sad then, but I let her go with a half-smile, not really knowing how I felt about it all.

I didn't open Chess Life for the rest of the day. In fact, I didn't even look at my phone. I watched movies with Mum and Dad and tried to put everyone and everything out of my head.

I dreamed about Ronan that night. One of those dreams that wakes you up at five a.m. with a stupid smile on your face and then crushes you with disappointment when you realize that it wasn't real. That he wasn't right beside you, in your bed, his heartbeat in time with yours.

I turned on my phone to look at his Insta, just so I could see his face.

Then I saw the little pawn flashing.

80

Ronan

The day of the tournament. I felt different. Before, it felt like everything was riding on today, and it kind of still was. I had to win, had to finish what he started. But after telling Jules, it felt like it was out there in the open and I could breathe.

I hoped she'd turn up. To see her walk through that door would mean everything.

I'd been up all night. I wasn't tired. For once it wasn't even the insomnia. I was buzzing. Halfway through the night I switched from Coke to coffee and now I knew what people meant by 'too much caffeine'. I had a shower and got dressed again, pushing the pawn into my pocket beside my competitor's ticket. I walked into the hall to see Ciaran's door wide open and no sign of Mum. Then I heard her, the hairdryer on in her room. It stopped.

'Ronan?' she called.

I'd barely spoken to Mum all weekend. Aunt Sarah had come round last night after I saw her at Tara's on Friday. She left with a promise that she'd be back soon and to call her immediately if I needed her. This time I meant it when I said I would.

I thought about pretending I hadn't heard, but Mum could see me standing there.

'Yeah.'

'You ready?'

She knew?

'Em, yeah. Almost ... I just wanted to go over a couple of moves first.' I pushed her bedroom door further open. She was putting on lipstick.

'Why do you need to do that, silly? It's Ciaran's day today. Is he up yet?' She looked at me, expecting an answer.

'Mum.'

'Do I look OK? Do you think this is too much?' She stood up and turned round. She was wearing a dark green dress and a cream jacket. She looked like she was going to a wedding.

'Mum, I don't think ...' I squeezed the door handle until my palm hurt.

'You don't think what? You think it's too much? Should I tone it down a bit? Should I ask Ciaran?'

'Ask Ciaran?' I said it to myself, to nobody. But she heard.

'Yeah, your brother – the one competing in the tournament today. Honestly, Ronan, sometimes I think your ears are painted on.' She went back to brushing her hair. I was scared she'd completely lost her mind.

'Mum.'

She turned on the hairdryer.

'Mum.' I said it louder. She kept drying her hair.

'*Mum!*' I shouted it this time and she turned it off, looking at me.

I was going to say it. It was there, on the tip of my tongue, ready to fall out of my mouth at any second. She was just staring at me, waiting for whatever I was going to say.

And I was going to say it. I really was.

'You look really nice.'

She smiled at me, and I had to turn away. But before I left the room I turned back and said, 'I'm going to leave early so I can get good seats.'

I thought I was braver than that. But when she was there, just looking at me with happiness all over her face I just couldn't destroy it.

I twisted the pawn in my pocket. A pawn. Weakest piece on the board; couldn't move backwards.

Wouldn't move backwards.

Not yet.

'Great, Ronan. Thanks.' She turned back to the mirror and turned on the hairdryer. 'Oh, and don't forget to take some money from my purse for a taxi.'

I rifled through her purse and took a twenty. Then I left her to it, walked down the stairs and straight out of the door, the ticket and pawn in my pocket.

> **ME:** She thinks Ciaran is playing in a tournament today. Don't let her come. Please. After the tournament, we can talk to her.

AUNT SARAH: I'm on my way x

I didn't phone for a taxi. It was a long walk to Ellis Hall, but I needed it.

81

Juliet

OK, I was awake.

Reading Ronan's message was like a bucket of cold water. Everything he said, about his brother, the way he felt, how he'd been hiding it all this time? I felt numb.

Then came the pain, that actual physical ache that comes from somebody else's hurt. Like when Mum used to cry at movies, I would cry too, or when Gran died, and Dad lost his job and looked so sad behind his 'it'll-be-fine' smile.

Except this time, the pain was worse. Because it was mixed with guilt.

Thinking about myself and all my own stupid problems all the time when everyone else had shit going on too. I wiped a tear from my eye, hard. No, I wouldn't cry. This wasn't my sadness, and I wasn't about to make it about me. He needed me today. And I was going to be there.

> **ME:** Do you and Francis fancy going to a chess tournament today?

MICHAEL: Why are you awake so early? And yes. Why?

ME: Ronan's playing

MICHAEL: You're back on? When did that happen?

ME: I'll explain on the way . . .

MICHAEL: What time am I picking you up?

ME: Half ten?

MICHAEL: See you then. Put some effort into your outfit. I'm going back to sleep

ME: Good night xx

I turned on my light and psyched myself up to get out of bed. Eventually I managed, swallowed some painkillers, crutched my way to my wardrobe and pulled it open. Today, I had to look amazing. It was weird. Right then I wasn't thinking about my swollen knees or my not-totally-straight elbow.

I was thinking about how much I wanted Ronan to see me and think 'wow'.

My heart hurt when I looked at all the amazing clothes that Mum had bought and I'd never worn. Tags still on. I made a promise to myself to be nicer to Mum, and Dad too. Just be a better daughter in general. They were doing the best they could.

My eyes fell on a dress. One that Mum had bought months ago. A black skater dress that would look incredible with my glitter Converse. A couple of months ago I would have looked right past it, probably thinking some mean thoughts about Mum – how she knew I didn't wear dresses so why would she even buy it? Maybe she knew me better than I knew myself.

I put it on my bed.

Sitting down at my dressing table, I opened the huge box of make-up in front of me. Barely used.

For the next hour and a half, I watched YouTube tutorials on make-up. Loads of them.

By the end, after loads of mistakes, I loved what I saw in the mirror.

Ronan kept filling my mind. I picked up my phone and stared at his message again, the words making me ache all over again. Should I write back? After something like that? No. I put the phone down. I needed to talk to him in person.

My stomach flipped, thinking about seeing him.

At breakfast Mum and Dad didn't even ask what was happening, even though it was nine a.m. and I was wearing a full face of make-up with my pyjamas.

'I'm going to a chess tournament today,' I said when I caught Dad giving Mum a quizzical look.

'Oh really? Are you playing? Can I come?' Dad asked.

I saw Mum shoot him a look.

'No, not me. I'm just going to watch,' I said, and ate the pancakes Mum had put down in front of me.

They didn't ask any more questions. And just as I was going upstairs to get changed, Mum said, 'You look really lovely, Jules.'

'Thanks.' And this time it didn't feel like she was only saying it because she had to. But because she actually meant it.

I put on the dress and the trainers. I even managed a tiny spin in the mirror. OK, it wasn't a proper spin, more a slow and controlled turnaround, but still. I put on my cropped denim jacket and heard Michael's music outside.

I went downstairs to an open door and Michael standing there, staring at me.

'Juliet, you look unbelievably beautiful. Seriously. And you know I don't use the B-word lightly.'

I smiled at him in thanks as I walked out of the door, yelling, 'Bye, Mum. Bye, Dad,' behind me.

'Oh . . .' Michael stopped halfway down the driveway. 'Tara sent me this really weird message this morning, saying sorry for being a dick. It was quite disturbing actually. What does she want?'

I thought about telling him everything. She hadn't asked me not to say anything to anyone. But I decided against it. It wasn't my business to tell, and Michael would find out sooner or later through the grapevine anyway. I hoped it wouldn't be a huge thing. That everyone wouldn't be talking about Tara and what was going on at home.

'Aw, I dunno, maybe she had an epiphany? Realized the error of her ways. She apologized to me yesterday too, for the Crutch Girl thing.'

Michael waited until we were in the car to reply.

'What? Really?' I wondered if he knew there was something I wasn't telling him.

'Yeah, and it was like she really meant it too.'

'So was it like Cady at the end of *Mean Girls*, and the Spring Fling apology? That totally awesome speech that you know makes me cry every time. Or was it more of a Regina apology, yelling at you for all your wrongdoings but secretly we know she's remorseful deep down, before you push her in front of a bus?'

I burst out laughing. 'It was definitely more of a Cady apology.'

'Wow.' Michael still hadn't started the car. 'I didn't think she had it in her. Do you think she's sick or something?'

'I don't know. But whatever it was, it felt real.' I looked at Michael, who still looked unconvinced. 'Oh, and Cady didn't push Regina.'

'I know. Just thought it would be a better ending.' He started the engine. 'But I do love a good villain-to-not-as-much-of-a-villain story.'

'Me too. Can we go now? I'm getting kind of desperate to see Ronan.'

'Say no more.' Michael sped away from the kerb.

He pulled up outside Francis's house five minutes later, getting out to open the back door for him.

'Hey, Francis,' I called, half-waving into the back seat. The strength of his aftershave almost made me choke.

'Hey, Jules. So Cinderella is going to the ball then? Or chess tournament?' he said.

Michael looked over at me. 'Yeah, I told him everything. Obv.'

'You look amazing,' Francis said, leaning through the middle of the seats to look at my outfit.

'Aw, thanks.' I smiled. And resisted the desire to play down the compliment.

'And he doesn't know you're coming?' Francis asked, like he was totally invested, which made me smile.

'No!' Michael answered for me. 'It's the most romantic thing I've ever heard in my whole life.' Michael fanned his face. 'Ellis Hall, here we come!'

Twenty minutes later Michael pulled up on to the pavement, right outside the door. 'I don't think you can park here,' I said, suddenly nervous.

'J, this is an *emergency*. I can park wherever the hell I want. Now get those crutches and go and get your man.' My smile made my jaw ache.

'Here.' Francis handed me my crutches.

'Go, go, go!' Michael yelled. I started walking carefully on the cobblestones. They'd catch up, no problem.

The reception area was empty when we went in. It was silent except for Michael yelling 'She's here!' to no one in particular.

'Can I help you?'

A woman in a suit came towards us. 'The tournament has already started.'

'Yes, I'm just here to see someone who's competing. Ronan Cole,' I said.

'You can't go in – *nobody* is allowed in while the game is in play.'

'Can I see if he's on the list anyway? He might have already been knocked out.' I was almost begging. She couldn't turn us away *now*.

She pursed her lips and looked at her clipboard. She ran her hand down a huge list.

'Sorry, there's no Ronan Cole here,' the woman said and something in my stomach dropped.

'Wait. He has to be here. Ronan Cole. Would you mind checking again, please?' I smiled at her, hoping it would thaw her expression. It didn't.

'I'm sorry, there's only a Ciaran Cole here. No Ronan.'

His brother.

Michael was beside us now. 'Nah, not having that, Brenda.' He had his hands on his hips. Then he turned and walked towards a pair of double doors, looking through the little window.

'He's in there, Jules!' Michael called.

The woman looked at Michael. She was so mad.

'Step away from the door,' she angry-whispered.

Michael was beside me again. He tapped my arm and waved me towards the door.

'I'm telling you; you're not allowed in there. Don't make me phone security.'

'Phone away, Brenda, because we're going in.' Michael half picked me up and ran towards the door, with Francis close behind us. We stopped, looked in. There were a few tables of people still playing, some with their backs to us. I couldn't see Ronan.

Michael pushed the door open.

'My name's Linda,' I heard from behind me.

82

Ronan

Something was going on behind me, but I couldn't turn round. I noticed my opponent glance at the doors. And that must have distracted her because her next move led her right into checkmate.

Click.

I had to keep my head in the game. I was so close now.

She stood up to shake my hand and squeezed it much harder than her smile suggested. I waited for the next person to sit down. The final. I could hear people shuffling in their seats, someone talking behind me and a 'shush' from the person with the microphone.

Focus. I needed to focus.

Another girl sat down in front of me. She didn't smile. She was tiny. And so angry-looking, like she was just waiting for me to say something so she could yell 'shut up'. But I didn't say anything. Neither did she.

The hall was silent again, except for some shifting in seats to my right. Probably her family or friends. I wasn't about to get distracted now. Not this close to the finish line.

She knew what she was doing. Confident moves that made

me think. She snorted at the move I made but I refused to react. I had to win. For Ciaran.

Then it hit me.

Why?

Ciaran wasn't there. He'd never be here again.

I played on autopilot as much as I could. So tired. I rubbed my eyes under my glasses and caught her smirking at me. That pissed me off. I focused on a pawn. I moved it up the board. I could tell she was confused. Annoyed.

'I told you that you had to leave. You are not allowed in here.'

'Shh, you're disturbing the game. It's the fucking final, Brenda.'

'It's *Linda*.'

I knew one of those voices. Michael. What was he doing here? I turned to my right and there he was, trying to ignore a woman in a suit who looked like she was going to explode. And Michael's boyfriend? The angry woman gave up and stormed back towards the door, her heels clicking on the floor.

And there, behind her.

My whole world.

I blinked. Convinced I was seeing things. It was really her. Jules. Then she waved, this tiny wave that rolled right through me and woke me up, raising the hairs on my neck and churning my stomach. She smiled and I nearly got up right then, ditched the tournament and followed every single instinct I had to go and kiss her. But I was nearly there. And I was ready now.

I pushed the pawn up the board. My opponent couldn't work out what I was doing, and I enjoyed how much it irritated her. Sixth rank, seventh rank, eighth rank. I'd made it. Promoted. Like he'd said. One day maybe I'd promote myself too, just like a pawn. And they waited to see what I wanted to promote to. The pawn that had made its way up the entire board. But it didn't matter.

Click.

'I resign.'

I stood up, shook her hand, gave the pawn in my pocket one last squeeze before walking over to where Jules was sitting.

'Did you just quit the match?' Michael's mouth was wide open.

'Yeah. For some reason it didn't seem to matter any more.' I saw Jules looking up at me, her eyes a misty grey sea, sparkling with tears.

'You came,' I said. Behind me people were cheering for the winner, but I just heard silence.

'How could I not?' she said. Her cheeks flashed pink.

Michael nudged her.

I held out my hand and pulled her up. Michael picked up the crutches and handed them to her. She pushed her arms through and looked up at me.

It was impossible not to kiss her.

83

Juliet

He kissed me.

I was just about to say something when his mouth was on mine, his hand behind my head, pulling me gently towards him. He slipped an arm round my waist, and I felt my body relax into his, my heart beating hard against his chest. I felt him take my weight and one of my crutches slipped from my arm. It didn't matter. I knew I wouldn't fall when he held me. I trusted him with my whole heart. My beautiful safety net.

And it wasn't like that teen-movie kiss, when they get together at the end after an hour and a half of, Will they? Won't they? It wasn't fireworks and butterflies and a missing piece.

It was so much better.

84

Ronan

I'd never wanted to kiss someone so much in my life. And it was like she felt the same because we just melted into each other. I'd never seen her look so beautiful. The little dress and the denim jacket, the way some of her hair was caught in a button and black eyeliner was smudged beneath her eyes. She was perfect.

And she was here. I pulled her closer. I needed her to know I was there, that we could deal with our shit together.

I wished we were somewhere else, without all these people watching. I wanted to be alone, to get to know her, everything about her. Every thought, every pain.

I needed her to know that she was so far from being 'basic' it hurt.

85

Juliet

'I think this is the most romantic thing I've ever seen,' I heard Michael say, way too close to someone who was in a kissing situation. He tapped me on the shoulder.

I pulled away from Ronan.

'Everyone's gone and I'm starting to feel a bit like a voyeur,' Michael said.

Francis laughed and kissed Michael. 'Don't want you feeling left out.'

'Hey, Michael, and Francis, is it?' Ronan asked, nodding at them both.

'The one and only,' Michael said.

We walked out of the big double doors and on to the street.

Francis sat in the front of Michael's car this time, and I sat in the back with Ronan.

I leaned into him. Not because I needed to, but because I wanted to feel the heat of his body on mine, the thud of his heart against my back, beating almost as quickly as mine.

'OK, where am I going then?' Michael asked into the back seat.

Ronan looked at me.

'There's something I need to talk to you about. Can we go to Maggie's?' His eyes were huge and scared behind his glasses.

I squeezed his hand. 'Of course.'

'Maggie's, please, chauffeur,' I called.

'Your wish is my command.'

86

Ronan

We sat in the same booth that we'd sat in that day we'd cut school.

Strawberry milkshake for me and the salted caramel disgustingly sweet thing, plus a side of waffles, for her.

'I'm so glad you came,' I said. 'I mean, I wasn't sure, after you read everything, whether you'd still want to . . . Whether you'd still want me.'

I looked down at my milkshake and felt her take my hand. I looked up at her.

'Ronan, of course I still want you.'

'You don't think I'm an awful person?'

I had to ask. I needed to know. I mean, I knew she wasn't going to say 'yes, I do think you're awful'. Not to my face, but I thought I'd be able to tell from her reaction. Her body language.

'Are you serious? How could I think that?' she asked. And she looked so sincere that there was a lump in my throat.

'Because I should have done something. I could have stopped it.' There was pressure behind my eyes. I forced it away.

'None of this was your fault, Ronan. None of it.'

'I should have told the police. Or Mum. I should have told my mum earlier.'

'You were only sixteen! You don't think your mum knew? Deep down on some level she must have known something was wrong.'

She squeezed my hand harder, and I tried desperately not to cry.

'But why didn't *she* do anything?' My voice came out shaky.

She looked like she was thinking about what to say. 'Maybe she couldn't either. I can't pretend to know anything about this because I'm not a psychologist or anything. But one thing I do know? Because it's absolutely obvious? This wasn't your fault.'

Jules got up and slid into the seat beside me, leaning her head on my shoulder and sliding her fingers through mine.

'I hate that this happened to you and your family. That you have to live with all this pain, but I'm here. Whenever you want to talk, whatever you need.'

I couldn't stop them then. Tears that slid under my glasses. I pushed my fingers into the corners of my eyes, and Jules took off my glasses, wiping them on her sleeve before handing them back to me.

'Sorry,' I said.

'For what?' She looked confused.

'For getting so upset on what should be our first proper date.'

'Ronan, I don't just want chess games and milkshakes, and taking the piss out of each other. I want all of you.'

And then there really was space. Space in my chest and my head. So I asked her.

'I need to talk to my mum. About Ciaran. Will you come with me? Being with you, it makes me braver.'

I didn't know what she was going to say. It was a big ask. But she didn't even hesitate.

'Of course I will,' she said.

Then she kissed me, our hands still tangled together, my heart crashing against my ribs.

87

Juliet

In the taxi Ronan inhaled and looked at me through his glasses. I loved his glasses. A magnifying glass into his soul. And his soul was scared. I hadn't said anything the whole way there, just held his hand. Nothing I could have said would make him feel better about his brother or his mum. I just hoped that he knew I meant it. That I would be there for him. He'd told me what he needed to do. Show his mum the video of Ciaran's funeral. My heart ached for him.

'You OK?' I asked.

'I will be, I think.'

'It's really brave, you know, what you're doing.' I thought about all the times people had called me brave, for all the blood tests, for the needles in my knees, for doing my own injections. But this? This was real courage.

'I just hope it works,' he said, as the taxi pulled up outside his house.

Ronan's house was just like mine. Four-bedroomed, double-garaged, detached. But there was something different. And it was probably because I knew about Ciaran but there was a sadness that fell like a curtain, dimming the porch light and casting a shadow over the lives inside.

A grey car sat outside and withered summer plants ran up the driveway.

Ronan took my hand and helped me out of the car, waiting until I'd adjusted my crutches before walking towards his house.

A woman came to the door before he had a chance to open it. She had Ronan's cheekbones and blue eyes tinged with red. She was pretty. My heart hurt for her.

She smiled.

'Mum, this is Jules.' He stepped aside so she could see me. And she didn't look down at the crutches; she looked into my eyes, the same way he did.

'Nice to meet you, Jules. Are you coming in?' She smiled at me, wide and welcoming. But I noticed that her hand was shaking as she tucked her blonde hair behind her ear. 'Oh, Ronan, Aunt Sarah is here if you want to go and say hello.'

We walked into the living room where there was another woman sitting on the sofa, dark-haired, pretty, like a more-alive version of Ronan's mum. She stood up when we walked in, her smile making me feel immediately more comfortable.

'Ronan,' the woman said and came towards us. She put her arms round him.

'This is Jules.' Ronan pulled out of the hug. She turned and smiled at me. 'Lovely to meet you, Jules.' I smiled back, starting to feel a bit out of place. But I shoved that feeling away. I was here for Ronan.

'Mum, can we talk a minute?' Ronan said softly.

'Of course, love.' The words she was saying were normal but there was a shake to her tone.

Ronan looked at me.

'Do you want me to stay?' I asked.

Normally this sort of thing would have made me feel awkward. Barging into someone's personal life like this was something I just didn't do. But I could see how much he needed me.

He didn't say anything, just nodded. His mum and aunt didn't say anything either, just sat on the sofa opposite us. His mum looked like she was in a daze, while his aunt put an arm round her.

And I sat there, with my heart in my throat for Ronan.

88

Ronan

For a minute nobody said anything. Then Aunt Sarah began. 'Ronan, I've had a chat with your mum. About Ciaran, about everything.'

I looked at Mum, who was clearly finding it difficult to look at me. She was looking at her hands, picking at her red nails. Chipped. Her eyes were swollen and red. Then she exhaled with a noise that sounded like all the life was leaving her body, before huge sobs took over.

'Mum?' My voice sounded small, like I was much younger. Seeing Mum like that, it hurt. I felt Jules take my hand and squeeze it.

Mum didn't answer me, just took a deep breath.

'But there's something you want to do, isn't there?' Aunt Sarah said, giving Mum the words that she couldn't seem to get out herself.

Mum nodded. 'I need to see it.' Her voice shook. 'The video.'

'Are you sure?' As much as I wanted her to accept what had happened so we could both start dealing with it, I knew how much it was going to hurt her. My own voice was shaking now. I let myself think of Jules's hand on mine.

'I'm sure,' Mum said, and I saw Aunt Sarah squeeze her shoulder.

'I'm here,' she whispered.

I took out my phone and found the video. My hand trembled.

I handed her my phone.

All she needed to do was press play.

She looked at it, unsure, tears streaming down her face. Her fingers were hovering over the screen, knowing that after this, there was no more pretending. She made a noise. A mix of a breath and a word.

Then she pressed play.

They'd made it black and white, and played The Smiths over it, Ciaran's favourite band. It was beautiful.

My eyes flooded beneath my glasses.

She watched the whole thing. Sitting there, her dress and face both stained with tears, with her hand over her mouth and her heart breaking all over again.

It hurt to watch her. It hurt to listen to that song, the one Ciaran played on repeat almost constantly. It felt like I was doing it all over again. It just hurt so fucking much.

'I had it recorded. I knew you couldn't be there, not that day, but I thought some day you might want to see it.' I tried to speak through the tears, pushing my words out so they didn't crack. 'I'm sorry I didn't do more to make you go.' Jules slid closer to me, so our legs were touching. Like she was letting me know she was still there.

I looked up at Aunt Sarah, who was crying too. Then back to Mum.

'Ronan,' she said again. The video finished. She put down the phone with a shaking hand and looked at me.

She stood up and came towards me. I let her hug me like I was a kid again, allowed myself to cry into her shoulder and to think about how fucking unfair life could be.

89

Juliet

He'd done it. And I was so proud of him. I held back my own tears and moved out of the way when his mum came over to hug him.

When she finally let go, she excused herself, leaving us in the living room with his aunt, who turned to me.

'I'm so glad Ronan has a friend like you,' she said.

All I could do was attempt a smile back because I didn't trust myself to speak without crying.

She followed Ronan's mum out of the door.

'Are you OK?' I asked, turning to Ronan who was staring at the paused video himself.

'I will be, hopefully,' he said and shrugged. I put my hand on his leg.

'Want to go upstairs?' he asked.

'Sure.'

His room. A boy's room. It was all navy and checks and movie posters on the walls. Weirdly tidy. I sat down on the bed next to him.

'Do you think your mum might be able to get some help now?' I let myself lean into him again.

'I hope so. I mean, that was the first step, I guess, but now Aunt Sarah knows what's really going on, it might help.' He was fishing in his pocket for something. He pulled out the pawn.

'The pawn was Ciaran's favourite piece.'

'What? The pawn? Really? What am I missing?'

He let me hold it. I turned it over in my fingers, trying to find something special about it.

'Remember when I told you that it's the only piece that can be promoted to something better? Well, Ciaran used to call me a pawn. He said he hoped I'd be better some day.'

'Ronan . . .'

'No, it's OK. I mean, all this stuff with Mum and Ciaran; it's been really hard to deal with. But things sort of feel better now, with you. As if I'm finally getting my promotion.'

I leaned my head on his shoulder and breathed him in.

I held the pawn in my palm towards him and he put his palm on top of mine, squeezing it between us.

'If it's any consolation, I don't think you ever needed a promotion. You've always been pretty great to me.'

Then he looked right at me with those blue eyes, still shining with tears.

'Thanks, BASIC.' And he gave a sad smile. 'Do you think it'll ever stop hurting?'

And what could I say? No? I didn't know. I'd never gone through something so awful. But what I did know was that I deeply missed my old life, the one I had before my diagnosis. I grieved for the life I could have had, and the pain was still there, but it hurt less now as I'd learned to live with it. But what Ronan went through? It was so much worse.

'I don't know if the pain will ever go away completely,' I said gently. He looked a bit shocked when I said it. 'But it'll get easier for you to live with.' I opened my hand and looked at the pawn in the centre of my hand. 'But from what you said, it feels like he is such a big part of you, I can't see how you'll ever truly lose him.'

Ronan took the pawn from my hand and squeezed it. 'You might be right. Destined to have his voice in my ear, calling me a pawn for all eternity.' He managed a laugh.

'If you're a pawn, what does that make me?'

He looked at me and tilted my chin towards his with his other hand.

'A queen.'

And then he kissed me. After a moment, I pulled away from him, just far enough so my mouth wasn't on his any more.

'Can I ask you a favour?' I said.

'Anything.'

'Call me Juliet?' Michael was right – maybe I did deserve my name.

And maybe the idea of my own movie-style love story wasn't totally ridiculous after all.

90

Ronan

Two months later

Yeah, things weren't perfect, but they were better.

I was worried about how things would go this Christmas. The first one without Ciaran. Mum was trying. After some more talks with Aunt Sarah and a few (thousand) backwards steps, she agreed to get some help. To go and talk to someone.

She still hadn't touched his room but apparently the psychologist had said it was OK and it would be something she'd do in her own time. When she was ready.

She still hadn't visited his grave either. But neither had I. For me, he wasn't there, in this hole in the ground, he was part of me, like Juliet had said. In the way I spoke, in my chess games. Maybe it was the same for Mum.

'Aunt Sarah will be here for dinner. Will you be back?'

'Yeah, I should be. Just going to drop off this present at Juliet's.'

'Oh, tell her I say hello and why don't you invite her round here on Boxing Day? Sarah's going to cook. I'm sure she has plans with her family tomorrow.'

Mum's smile was thin and tired. I returned it.

'I'll ask her, Mum. Thanks.'

'Ronan?' Mum looked like she hadn't decided what she was going to say.

'Yeah?'

'I love you, you know.'

'I know.' I smiled. I thought about hugging her, but we didn't really do that, so it would have been weird. 'See you later.'

I walked to Juliet's. It was cold but I needed time to psych myself up to give her the present. My wrapping was messy; the little box that I'd bought rattled as I walked. I flicked between being completely and utterly embarrassed, and excited to see her face when she opened it.

By the time I got to her house my ears were throbbing from the cold, and at the same time I was hot under the stupid jumper she wanted me to wear.

I stood outside, behind the hedge, and took out my phone.

```
*YOU HAVE INVITED PRETTYBASIC TO PLAY A
  GAME*
*PRETTYBASIC HAS ACCEPTED*
ALONELYPAWN: Winner gets to decide on the
  movie we watch?
PRETTYBASIC: Deal.
ALONELYPAWN: e4, there's a surprise.
PRETTYBASIC: Luring you in.
```

ALONELYPAWN: I was a Grandmaster at seven
  you know . . .
PRETTYBASIC: You already told me that lie.
ALONELYPAWN: My fingers are cold.
PRETTYBASIC: Where are you?
ALONELYPAWN: Outside your house.
PRETTYBASIC: What the hell? Ring the
  doorbell.
ALONELYPAWN: Taking your pawn first.
PRETTYBASIC: Feel better now?
ALONELYPAWN: Yes, all warm and
  tingly . . .

Juliet's front door opened. Her dad was standing at the door, smiling. The smell of something baking hit me in the face, as well as heat. There was a soft glow from fairy lights that decorated every door frame in the house.

Jeffrey abandoned chewing a bauble on the biggest Christmas tree I'd ever seen and ran over to me. I bent down to stroke him.

'Ronan, what are you doing out here? It's freezing! Come on in! That's a . . . nice jumper.'

He looked at my chest.

'Thanks,' I said and pretended I didn't notice the WTF look on his face.

'Oh, I meant to ask you.' Juliet's dad had his hand on my shoulder, leading me in and closing the door behind him. 'Have you ever used the Albin counter-gambit?'

Before I could answer, I heard her.

'Dad, really?' Juliet's voice came from the top of the stairs. 'Hold on, I'm coming to save you.'

She slid her crutches down the stairs, held on to the bannister and started walking towards us, one step at a time.

'Why don't I come to you?'

I looked at her dad, as if to ask for permission to go up. Not that he'd cared about the million times we'd been up there before.

'Go ahead.'

I had to stop myself from running up the stairs with her crutches. But that was the thing with her – any extra time apart just felt like a waste.

She'd gone back into her room and was sitting in the bed when I got there. She wore this fluffy white jumper with snowflakes on it over a little red skirt and stripy socks.

'Sexiest elf ever,' I said, sitting down beside her.

'Is that a Slipknot Christmas jumper?' she asked, screwing up her face.

'Yeah, you said to dress festively.'

'Lucky that you're hot enough to pull it off.'

My phone buzzed in my pocket.

'Aren't you going to check that?' she asked with a smile.

'I'm kind of busy right now.' I pulled her face gently towards mine and kissed her. She tasted like chocolate. She put her hands on my ears to warm them, then pulled away.

'I have a present for you,' she said with a look that held a secret.

'Me first,' I said.

91

Juliet

I thought it would feel weird having a proper boyfriend, but it just felt like we'd been together forever. All the Chess Life banter just kind of transferred to real life. I'm not saying we stopped playing chess. We didn't. (And I beat him once even though he tells people I cheated.)

Now, instead of Michael picking up Tara he picks up Ronan, and on Fridays, Francis meets us at Maggie's, and we hang out there for a while. Turns out Francis and Ronan are both into death metal so while they talk about that, me and Michael show each other funny TikToks (and take the piss out of Ronan and Francis).

It was great that Francis was at St Anne's because he could tell us how Tara was getting on. He said she kind of just slipped into the background but seemed to have a couple of new friends. He said he'd keep an eye on her and let us know if he thought she was struggling. I still talked to her. Online mostly. She'd ask about Ronan, and I'd ask about how things were at home. Turns out her dad has really stepped up and has sorted out some help for her mum as well as acting like a 'proper dad'. Though apparently that meant not being allowed to hang out at Westing Park whenever she wanted. Despite the fact she said this was 'totally unfair', I got the impression she actually liked having some rules. I was careful not to go on too much about Ronan (even though it was hard).

Oh, and Harry invited us all to one of his football matches. Turns out he's not just good but insanely good and is being scouted by one of the English teams and I'll probably see him on television one day. I still feel shit about how I treated him, but the invitation to watch his match seemed to be confirmation that he'd accepted one of my million apologies.

When I woke up on Christmas Eve morning, I felt like a kid again. Except this time the excitement wasn't for Santa. I couldn't wait to see Ronan. Even Mum and Dad had commented on how happy I seemed.

I'd spent all afternoon getting ready. Thinking about the present that I'd wrapped for Ronan; when I'd give it to him; what I'd say. What would he say? And it wasn't like it was before, when I was terrified of saying the wrong thing. There was something about Ronan once I really got to know him, that made me feel like I could say anything.

But I still wanted it to be perfect.

Over the last couple of months, he'd told me all about his friends at St Anne's and we even talked about meeting up with them at some stage so he could clear the air.

We also spent a lot of time together, alone. Not doing that, yet. But I felt safe with him. Like we were the only two people in the world. And I guess, that was the next step. One I decided I was ready to take.

He looked so hot in his Christmas jumper. Which sounds like an oxymoron, but seriously. It was Christmas Eve and there he was, black ripped jeans, black and gold jumper and the smile that still made me melt.

He said he had a present for me. But I'd rehearsed what I was going to do with mine, so he'd just have to wait.

'Wait! No, not yet!' I closed my eyes and refused to look at the box he was trying to hand me.

'What? Why?' He laughed.

'*Mine* first.' I leaned across the bed and grabbed my phone, while he stood there with a confused look on his face.

'My present's on your phone?' he asked.

'Why don't you check?' I said.

He took out his phone and sat down on the bed beside me.

```
PRETTYBASIC: I've been thinking a lot
   about being ready.
ALONELYPAWN: Ready for what?
PRETTYBASIC: To take your knight.
PRETTYBASIC: Sorry, that was too easy.
   You're getting sloppy.
ALONELYPAWN: Ready to lose again?
PRETTYBASIC: HA.HA. NO. Ready for, you
   know . . .
ALONELYPAWN: I don't know. And I don't
   know why we're talking on this when
   you're RIGHT BESIDE ME.
```

```
PRETTYBASIC: Because I'm too embarrassed
   to say it.
ALONELYPAWN: Say what?
PRETTYBASIC: Nope. Can't do it. Just open
   your present.
```

I threw it on to his knee. The tiny, wrapped gift with a bow on the top.

'What the hell?' He laughed and held it up, shaking it.

'Just open it.' I covered my eyes.

I heard the paper being torn away, and then Ronan pulled my hands away from my face.

'I knew what you meant when you said you were ready, but this Christmas condom really confirms it.'

'You're such a dick! Why didn't you say anything?' I elbowed him.

'I wanted you to say it.'

'Say what?'

'That you want to have sex with me.' God, his smile was so hot.

'I'm ready to have sex with you,' I said, then covered my face again.

He pulled my hands away gently.

He leaned over and kissed me. Slowly, the tip of his tongue exploring my lips.

I moved back on my bed, so I was lying down, my head on the pillow. Ronan followed me, balancing himself over me on his elbows.

Then he took out his phone and mine buzzed on my bedside table.

ALONELYPAWN HAS RESIGNED THE GAME

He pecked me on the lips and sat up on the bed. 'My turn,' he said. I pulled myself up beside him.

He handed me a box wrapped in gold paper. I opened it. Inside was a wooden box with a heart carved into the lid.

I shook it. 'Exciting,' I said.

'It's just something really small. Stupid, actually.'

I opened it without replying to him. Because I knew it wouldn't be stupid.

There she was, the queen, nestled in silver tissue paper. Wooden, painted white with a crown made of golden metal.

'It's the queen, because, you know, you're like . . .'

'Ronan.' I put my hand on his leg and looked at the eyes that couldn't keep still. 'I love it.' I took her out of the box, feeling her weight and holding her to my chest, trying to force back the pressure behind my eyes. I was *not* going to cry. 'I love *you*.'

Ronan smiled, moving closer towards me so our faces were almost touching.

'I love you too,' he said.

And then he kissed me.

I thought the kisses might lose their shine after a while. Like, it just became so habitual that all the feelings got diluted.

And maybe they did, with other people. But with Ronan, every kiss felt new, like it was the first one, surprising my body all over again.

So yeah, what I'm trying to say is, I was totally right.

Christmas teen movies are the worst.

Ridiculously cheesy, unrealistic portrayals of love.

Real life is so much better.

Acknowledgements

This book would not exist without Ruth Knowles, book-wizard and editor extraordinaire. I don't think I'll ever be able to thank you enough for seeing something in my WriteNow application.

To Sara Jafari, it was an absolute joy to work with you. Your insights have been invaluable. To Shreeta Shah, Laura Dean and Leena Lane, you are incredible at what you do. To Janelle and Ben for creating the most perfect cover art. To everyone at Penguin who has worked behind the scenes in any way on this book and on the Writenow programme: thank you, thank you, thank you!

To my agent, Lauren Gardner, thank you for taking a chance on my #PitMad tweet and for being so enthusiastic about this book.

To the NI SCBWI writing group. You mean so much more to me than cats, craic, critique and too much wine. I feel honoured to know you all. A special thanks to Emma and Lauren for the emoji education.

To the #VWG, my online-turned-actual friends, thank you for everything. You are all freakishly talented. It makes me feel inferior and uncomfortable. Stop it.

To Fíona Scarlett. You have the best notebooks. You're a class person and an even better friend. To the endlessly supportive Julia Kelly. Your friendship means the absolute world. To Wiz Wharton, your friendship and early feedback on this book mean everything.

To Catherine Johnson. On the Curtis Brown Writing for Children course in 2017 you told me I could write. I haven't stopped since. I will be forever grateful.

To Dr Michelle McHenry. Like Jules, the phrase 'I'm fine' comes out of my mouth at an exhausting rate. Thank you for seeing the pain through these words and for the quality of life that I owe to your help.

To Bill and Colette, your unwavering interest and enthusiasm for the publication of this book always makes me smile. I hope you like it.

To my mum and dad who could not be better parents. For not making a big deal of my arthritis but always being there when I need help. There aren't enough thanks in the world for everything you do/have done. PS I'm sorry for all the stress when I had brain surgery. I hope that publishing a book makes up for it and cements my place as favourite child. (Adam has not published a book, just saying.)

To Chris, my husband and best friend. Thank you for always being my first reader. For making me hot-water bottles, getting my chargers from upstairs, my painkillers from downstairs, and the million other things you do to make my life easier. I love you.

To Lyla and Rory. You could not be more perfect to me if you tried. Love from your biggest fan.

To my extended family, to my friends, old and new, I am touched by your support and interest in this book.

To everyone who reads this book. Thanks a million, I truly hope you like it.